T0023198

WEDDING STATION

Books by David Downing

The John Russell series
Zoo Station
Silesian Station
Stettin Station
Potsdam Station
Lehrter Station
Masaryk Station
Wedding Station

The Jack McColl series
Jack of Spies
One Man's Flag
Lenin's Roller Coaster
The Dark Clouds Shining

Other titles
The Red Eagles
Diary of a Dead Man on Leave

WEDDING STATION

DAVID DOWNING

Copyright © 2021 by David Downing

Soho Press, Inc.
227 W 17th Street
New York, NY 10011

Library of Congress Cataloging-in-Publication Data
Names: Downing, David, 1946– author.
Title: Wedding station / David Downing.
Description: New York, NY : Soho Crime, [2021]
Series: The John Russell series ; 7

ISBN 978-1-64129-347-1
eISBN 978-1-64129-108-8

Subjects: LCSH: 1. Russell, John (Fictitious character)—Fiction.
2. World War, 1939-1945—Fiction. 3. Berlin (Germany)—Fiction
4. GSAFD: Historical fiction. 5. Mystery fiction.
PR6054.O868 W44 2021 | DDC 823'.914—dc23 2020019809

Printed in the United States of America

10 9 8 7 6 5 4 3 2 1

For Sacha and Jill

On 30 January 1933 Adolf Hitler was appointed Chancellor of Germany. Wishing to further consolidate his power, he arranged for new elections to be held in early March, but on 27 February, in the midst of an increasingly violent campaign, someone set fire to the Reichstag parliament building.

A Degenerate Cuckoo

As the packed Stadtbahn train emerged from beneath the roof of Friedrichstrasse Station and rumbled onto the iron bridge across the Spree, John Russell saw the fire. First as dancing reflections on the rippling water, then as flames licking skyward above the bend in the river.

And then it was gone, masked by the bulk of the Moabit tax office. For a moment Russell wondered—or merely hoped—that he was drunk enough to be seeing things, but as the train pulled past the adjoining electricity station he knew that was not the case. The building that housed the German parliament really was ablaze.

Other passengers had seen it now. There were gasps, low whistles, even one doubtful cheer. Russell's new companion, whose enthusiastic kiss on the Clärchens Ballhaus dance floor had seemed so promising half an hour earlier, and whose body was currently pressed against his own, could only come up with a nervous giggle. In the silence that followed, his cup of desire, fairly brimming five minutes before, drained sadly away.

Their train took the long bridge over the Humboldt Hafen and into the Stadtbahn platforms that hung over the throat of Lehrter Station. The fire was now hidden by the latter's roof, but everyone in the carriage seemed to be talking, if only to themselves. There was excitement in some voices, consternation in others. And fear, Russell, thought. Fear above all.

"Ours is the next stop," the girl told him.

Her name, he remembered, was Henni.

"And my parents are away," she reminded him with a smile.

After descending the stairs at Bellevue, they walked arm in arm down the affluent-looking Flensburger Strasse, stopping halfway down, at her instigation, for a kiss and a squeeze. She was quite lovely, Russell thought. Old enough to be free, young enough not to know or care what the fire behind them would mean before the night was out. All hell was going to break out, as the arsonists had no doubt intended.

It occurred to Russell, with only the slightest flicker of shame, that Henni's bed, apart from its most obvious attraction, would be one of the safer places he could spend this particular night. He didn't think the SA stormtroopers would be prioritising foreign ex-communists on their list of prospective victims, but there was always the chance of putting himself in the wrong place at the wrong time. He currently lived in Wedding, a much poorer part of the city, and his apartment was only a stone's throw away from streets famed as communist strongholds. In Wedding the local brownshirts would be out in force, out for blood.

But the giggle had told him too much about her. About himself for being with her.

And he was a journalist. Working, for almost three weeks now, on the crime desk of a daily newspaper. And if he wasn't much mistaken, the orange sky behind him craved his professional attention.

"I'm really sorry," he said, when they reached the steps leading up to her house, "but I have to go to work."

Her expression suggested he must be mad. Or joking?

"I'm a reporter," he explained. "The fire we saw. It's something my editor will expect me to cover."

"Well then, that's that," she said, looking more confused than angry.

"You're a great dancer," he told her.

She shook her head and started up the steps.

He walked back down to Bellevue Station, and then eastward along the side of the River Spree. On reaching the Lutherbrücke he could see the Reichstag in the distance, still spurting flames like a torch held up to the sky. A Nazi one, he assumed. They did love their torches, and who else would this spasm of pyromania serve? The communists would be blamed, the dogs let loose.

He entered the forested Tiergarten. There were still patches of snow on the ground from Saturday's fall, and it felt decidedly chilly among the dark trees. He thought of Henni, who might already be warm in bed, and allowed himself a rueful smile.

There were other people about, and Russell judged it wiser to take the smaller paths than the better-lit roads. Every now and then a flicker of flame would show through the trees, and he would adjust his course accordingly. He sensed rather than saw others moving in a similar direction, all drawn by the fire and silenced by what it might mean.

He was still in the trees when he made out the cordon of men on the open ground ahead. Brownshirts mostly, with a smattering of regular police, confronting a motley crowd of the curious, some clearly out for a night on the town, others still on their way home from work. Many of the park's unofficial residents—most of them homeless and unemployed—were also on hand, enjoying the free entertainment. Some were holding their palms up to the burning building three hundred metres away, making the most of the complimentary warmth.

Russell approached the brightest-looking stormtrooper

he could see—"spoilt for choice" was not the phrase—and pulled out his press card.

The man barely glanced at it. "I can't let anyone through," he said, with surprising civility. "Follow the perimeter round to Budapester Strasse—that's where the command post is."

Russell thanked him—you never knew when an SA friend might prove handy—and followed the instruction, taking the chance to weigh up his fellow spectators as he walked. Most of them looked like they were attending a fireworks display, faces reflecting the glow, mouths hanging half open, uttering ooohs and aaahs when something noisily cracked in the blazing Reichstag building.

There didn't seem many fire engines on hand, but three more came racing up Budapester Strasse as he approached the SA command post. They were followed by three black Mercedes saloons, each of them flying the Nazi flag. Germany's new Chancellor stepped out of the first, the Nazi propaganda chief out of the second. The third was either just for show, or President Hindenburg had fallen asleep.

Hitler and Goebbels strode through the checkpoint and on towards the Reichstag, presumably keen to inspect the job their hired hand had done. Hitler looked in a rage, either feigned or real, neither of which was unusual. Goebbels limped along in his wake looking faintly amused, which also seemed par for the course. Göring was now visible in the distance, wagging a fat finger in some unfortunate's face. "The gang's all here," Russell murmured to himself. And he did mean gang.

Several of the men around the command post were journalists Russell recognised, and none were receiving permission to breach the cordon. He talked to those he knew, and then retraced his steps around the perimeter, listening in on unguarded conversations and asking the occasional question. There were few who didn't have their suspicions, but none who had any evidence. Back among the journalists, he heard that one communist had already been arrested, and that others were likely to follow. All 300,000 members of the German Communist Party, if Hitler had his wish.

What now? Russell wondered, lighting up a Da Capo cigarette. They were an indulgence, but he couldn't bring himself to smoke one of the cheaper brands the SA manufactured as a profitable sideline for their rank and file. He would cut down his intake instead, save the money that way.

It was gone eleven. The early editions should have been printed by now, but if this wasn't a night for "holding the presses" he didn't know which would be. He had nothing much to report—and doubtless the paper's political team were already on top of the story—but he might as well make his way down to Kochstrasse and see if there was anything he could do.

The office was a ten-minute walk away. As he cut across Potsdamer Platz Russell noticed that Haus Vaterland and its seven themed restaurants were all still brightly lit and crowded. And why shouldn't they be? The news would seep out across Germany overnight, before erupting across front pages and airwaves. Most of the diners across the way had no idea their world had taken another big turn for the worse in the hour or two since they'd sat down.

Leipziger Strasse was quieter, all the stores having closed some time before. Russell turned left down Mauerstrasse, whose only occupants were a couple in evening dress, the woman throwing up in the gutter while the man held her handbag. At the corner of Kochstrasse the Café Friedrichshof was open but poorly attended, most of its usual press clientele out seeking or writing last minute copy. Russell walked on another hundred metres to the building that housed the *Morgenspiegel* and a dozen other newspapers and magazines. Once inside he cocked an ear for the printer machines in the basement, but as he'd suspected they were still biding their time.

His boss, editor Theodor Hiedler, was large without being fat, with a good head of wavy dark hair for his age and a face that looked forgetful fronting a mind that was anything but. He was currently talking into one of his telephones, looking annoyed but doing his best not to lose his temper. One of the owners, Russell guessed. They would not want their editor taking them out on a limb.

The large open newsroom was as crowded as Russell had ever seen it, despite the hour. There were still a lot of faces he couldn't put a name to, but none of the hostile glances he'd encountered during his first few days at the paper, when many had wrongly assumed that his appointment in place of a Jew was part of some Aryanisation process. The Jew in question had simply seen the writing on the Nazi wall, and quit as a prelude to leaving the country.

"And what have *you* got for me?" Hiedler shouted in greeting.

"Next to nothing," Russell replied, making his way to the editor's desk. He had already discovered that anything less than complete frankness drove Hiedler to distraction. "One arrest so far. A communist, needless to say, allegedly caught with a lighted match in his hand. A fire-fighter I talked to said at least a dozen fires had been started almost simultaneously. More than one pair of hands could manage, was his opinion."

Hiedler smiled at that. "Did you get the Red's name?"

"No, they hadn't given it out when I left."

"I expect they soon will."

Half an hour later they did. The messenger was a Prussian Interior Ministry lackey, the message on a single sheet of Ministry paper strewn with typing errors. The man already arrested was a young Dutch communist named Marinus van der Lubbe; others involved in this Soviet-inspired plot against the German people would soon be joining him behind bars. The German people would be expecting a vigorous response from their government, and harsh new measures would be announced over the next twenty-four hours.

The lackey had barely left when Johannes Oertel arrived with fresh information. Russell had known the wiry political reporter for several years, and knew why Hiedler had such faith in him.

According to Oertel, van Lubbe was well known in communist circles as a loner with a screw loose. Which made him someone who might want to set such a fire, but probably not with such efficacy. Van Lubbe was apparently more than half-blind following eye injuries sustained in his youth, and probably incapable of setting so many fires in such a short time. There was no doubt he'd been inside the Reichstag, but had he been alone? Several sources had told Oertel that Göring had been on the scene with almost indecent haste, and that the tunnel connecting his Air Ministry to the Reichstag could have been used by a team of SA arsonists.

Hiedler kneaded his chin between thumb and forefinger, then shook his head. "We'll stick to the official version," he said, to murmurs of dismay. "We'll point out any inconsistencies, but we won't offer any alternative narratives. No speculation, just the known facts. I want to be still publishing a week from now." His gaze went round the assembled reporters. "I know," he said with a sigh. "Believe me, I know."

Not long after, as he laid himself out on one of the camping beds supplied for overnighters on the fourth floor, Russell could still see the look in his editor's eyes. He could also hear and feel the presses in the basement far below as they pounded out copies of the official version. Sensible caution or the latest in a line of surrenders? Probably both.

It was still dark and very early when he woke, but he knew he wouldn't get back to sleep. After pulling his outer clothes

back on and visiting the toilet he climbed the stairs to the
roof. The city was still there, and quieter than he expected.
Seeing a cigarette flare in the gloom, he walked across to
find Johannes Oertel leaning against a balustrade.

"You could almost believe you were somewhere else,"
Russell observed.

"The calm before the you-know-what," Oertel replied.

The two of them stood there, smoking their cigarettes
and staring out across the barely visible city, finding nothing
else to say.

Back on the third floor Hiedler was already at his desk.
"You carry on with the missing scientist," he told Russell,
referring to the story he was already working.

This seemed small beer after the events of the previous
evening, and Russell said as much.

"Not to the scientist's wife," was Hiedler's response.

Russell nodded, and went back to his desk on the other
side of the newsroom. It was still too early for interviews, so
he grabbed his coat and hat, and took the short walk across
the street to the Jädickes Konditorei, Kochstrasse's other
great magnet for newspapermen. Their coffee wasn't quite
as good as the Café Friedrichshof's, but the pastries more
than made up for it.

The place was already almost full, the conversation predictably focused. "They'll take out the communists first,"
one man said to a colleague who feared for the Jews. "And
no one'll lift a finger." He lifted five of his own: "the socialists, the unions, big business, the churches, the army. They
all hate the communists worse than the Nazis, and they don't
seem to realise that once the communists are gone there'll
be no one left to take the Nazis on. With more than words,
on the streets, where it matters."

"Maybe the Generals will step in," someone suggested.

"Only if the Nazis threaten them with the SA, and Hitler
won't be that stupid. No, the Army'll wait and see, and so

will business. They'll wait and see which Hitler comes out on top, the nationalist or the socialist. If it's the socialist . . ."

"It won't be . . ."

The discussion went on. This was what the seasoned professional journalists lived for, Russell thought. Exciting times. Only this was the sort of excitement that might well prove fatal to some of them. He wondered if his predecessor on the crime desk had already left Germany. An extraordinary number of the country's writers and artists were known or rumoured to have done so in the month since Hitler's accession.

He drained his second cup of coffee and looked at his watch. It was only just gone seven. His son, Paul, would still be bed, and he felt a sudden need to see him, to make sure he was all right. There was no real reason he shouldn't be, but still. He could telephone the boy—his ex-wife's new partner, needless to say, already had one installed at their home—but for reasons he couldn't explain he actually needed to *see* him.

The quickest way was by U-Bahn, so he strolled down to Potsdamer Platz, where a street cleaner was scrubbing what looked like a large splash of blood from the sidewalk. One passing woman looked and quickly turned her face away, a couple stopped, stared and bravely asked the cleaner to satisfy their curiosity. "Well it ain't paint," he told them.

Down on the U-Bahn platform Russell watched two Ruhleben trains go through before his own arrived. Alighting fifteen minutes later at Fehrbelliner Platz, he climbed the stairs to the surface and started down Brandenburgische Strasse. Wilmersdorf was one of Berlin's more affluent districts, and there was no sign of overnight trouble, no pools of blood staining these tree-lined streets. If it wasn't for the smoke still smudging the sky behind him, he might have been thinking he'd had a bad dream.

Wilhelmsaue, the street that Ilse and Paul now lived on,

was prettier than most. The maid answered the door, and as usual Russell wondered how Ilse squared the communist principles she still proclaimed with having a servant. One day he'd ask her.

He was not invited in—he was, after all, only ever here to collect and return his five-year-old boy.

Ilse came to the door, the surprise in her eyes a welcome change from the usual annoyance. "What are you doing here?"

He asked if she'd heard about the Reichstag.

"Yes, but . . ."

"I know I'm being foolish, but I just felt like seeing Paul."

"No," she said. "I don't think it's foolish. You can walk him to school if you like."

As if on cue, Paul came rushing down the staircase. "Papa!"

It was only a five-minute walk to the junior school that his son had been attending for the last six months. Paul had been told about the fire, but seemed unconvinced of its significance—it was only a building, wasn't it? And no one had been killed, had they?

Russell agreed, and changed the subject to what they would do the next day. A couple of hours with his son after school on Wednesdays, and an overnight stay each Saturday, were what he and Ilse had compromised on when they separated.

"Could we go to Siggi's?" Paul asked. The konditorei on Brandenburgische Strasse was one of their regular treats.

"We could," Russell accepted.

Paul had already moved on. "When can we go to see Hertha?"

"Soon," Russell promised. "If your mother agrees." The boy had been begging to see his first football match for weeks, and the fact that no one in his family thought him old enough had not left much of an impression.

They were at the school gate, and Russell was pleased to see several other boys happily greeting his son. Paul had changed schools when Ilse moved in with Matthias, and Russell was glad the boy had landed on his emotional feet, at least in this regard.

The missing scientist had lived and worked in Dahlem, which was five stops farther on the same U-Bahn line. On the train Russell's thoughts drifted back to Ilse, and how they were going to sort out their future. She had told him she wanted to marry Matthias, which was fair enough in itself. But she couldn't without a divorce, which would probably mean Russell losing his right to live and work in Germany. Ilse didn't want Paul to lose his father, so she and Matthias were prepared to wait, but not forever. As far as Russell could see, a painless resolution of the issue was unlikely.

Then again, there was always the chance the Nazis would throw him out anyway.

It now seemed somewhat ironic that he and Ilse had been thinking of leaving Germany before their marriage collapsed and she met Matthias.

The train reached Dahlem-Dorf, where the inbound platform was packed with Borse traders and high-ranking government bureaucrats. On the streets outside it felt slightly less chilly, thanks to a pale-looking sun. The Kaiser Wilhelm Institute, where Professor Richard Wackerhagen had worked until his disappearance, was a ten-minute walk away.

Russell spent most of the morning there, interviewing any colleague, porter, cleaner or canteen worker who would speak to him. He interviewed the distraught Frau Wackerhagen for a second time, but she had nothing new to suggest. Neither did the neighbours. The man had simply vanished, and for no apparent reason. He had no politics to speak off, no obvious enemies at the Institute. His work seemed academic to the point of parody, and there wasn't the slightest whiff of illicit romance.

In mid-afternoon Russell walked back to the station. The sun was still shining, the suburban streets as placid and smug as those Women's Institute meetings his American mother had bravely hosted in Guildford before the war. He wondered how things had gone today in working class districts like Neukölln, Friedrichshain and Wedding. He would soon find out.

First, though, he had to write and submit his copy. Five hundred words when three would do: "It's a mystery!"

Back at the office on Kochstrasse, the latest news was that President Hindenburg had signed a decree at his Chancellor's request. The details arrived soon after Russell, and were enough to sober the most inebriated journalist. Reading through the liberties stripped away, Russell looked in vain for any chink of light. From this day on the German people would do without freedom of speech or association, would lose their hitherto unfettered press and any rights to privacy by post or phone.

"It's the end of any judicial oversight," as a clearly shaken Hiedler put it. "Now they can do whatever they want."

"They still have to win Sunday's election," Russell suggested hopefully.

Hiedler gave him a withering look. "With most of the communists in jail how can they not?"

Russell shrugged his acceptance and went to write his five hundred words. They came surprisingly easy, mostly, he supposed, because they didn't matter. After handing the copy in, he could think of no reason not to go home. He decided to walk the three miles—after nine years in Germany he still hadn't switched to kilometres—and get some much-needed exercise. He opted for the straightest route rather than the longer and quieter way he usually preferred. The more people there were around him the safer he'd feel.

The brownshirts were certainly out in force. Lorries full of stormtroopers on Unter den Linden, a squad on foot outside the entrance to Friedrichstrasse Station. More lorries went by as he waited to cross Invaliden Strasse, and he risked eye contact for a glimpse of the triumphant faces. This was their moment—as Hiedler had said, now they were free to do what they wanted. They could beat up, arrest, even kill, anyone whose face they didn't like; they could steal whatever took their fancy, be that an item of jewellery or someone's wife or daughter.

With the Ringbahn bridge just up ahead, he turned up Reinickindorfer Strasse, and then worked his way through the side streets that crossed and ran either side of the Panke. This large stream with its sylvan banks was one of Wedding's few scenic treasures, and on more than one occasion in the last few months Russell had found himself enjoying the view from a bridge parapet. He might have lost his wife, his son and his political faith, he might have been all but unemployed in a country in thrall to barbarism, but moonlight still rippled in water and sunlit trees were always a joy to behold.

Not this evening, though. Looking down from the bridge on Schönwalder Strasse he saw two bodies—two *corpses*—lying in the shallow water. Any blood had long been washed away, but bullet holes were visible in one man's neck and the other's shirt.

Russell was shocked, although he didn't know why. Not by the violent deaths—he'd seen enough of them in the trenches. Not by the casual disposal, or even the realisation that there were no authorities left who could be relied on to take the corpses away. For who in their right mind would walk into the police fortress on Müllerstrasse and report the dumping of these two murdered men? They couldn't be brought back to life, so why take the risk of bringing oneself to the police's attention? Russell certainly had no intention of doing so, and after a last guilty glance strode briskly away from the stream and its human debris.

Gerichtstrasse, when he reached it, looked almost shockingly normal. Admittedly, the Nazi flags were more numerous than ever, but that was to be expected. The one hanging over the entrance to his own building had been replaced by a larger version only a few days before, Frau Löffner apparently deeming it prudent to be one step ahead of her fellow *Portierfrauen.*

Aware of how well-informed the woman usually was about the local situation, Russell was happy to find her lurking in the hallway. And she did have news to share. Hitler's lads—her usual sobriquet for the brown-shirted Stormtroopers—had been overactive the previous night in the nearby streets to the north. "So much noise—I don't know how we got any sleep."

She stifled a yawn, as if in proof. "And this morning they were here! There must have been ten of them charging up the stairs! Herr Habicht wouldn't answer his door so they broke it down, and the owners will be furious. I mean, I liked Herr Habicht, I did, but why give them the excuse? Anyway, they took them away . . ."

"Them?"

"Oh. They arrested Herr Klausener as well, but he went like a lamb. He looked more shocked than upset. Which didn't make any more sense than Herr Habicht refusing to answer his door. I mean, how did the two of them expect the Nazis to react after something like that?"

"You mean the Fire?"

"Of course the Fire."

"You think the communists did it?" Russell asked. Frau Löffner was many things, but stupid wasn't one of them.

"The government says so."

"Governments have been known to lie."

She looked doubtful. "Not on something as big as this. Not when the lie will probably come out."

"Maybe." Russell wondered if the *Portierfrau* had unwittingly put a finger on what was new about the Nazis—that they actually didn't care if the lie came out. Shame to them was a foreign concept. Probably invented by Jews.

"There's a letter for you," Frau Löffner was saying. She ducked back inside her door and returned with it. "It came yesterday. I should have taken it up, but my knees . . ."

It was an official letter, which didn't bode well. Seeing her look of expectation, he put it in his pocket. "I don't suppose the boiler's been repaired," he asked.

"They said they would come yesterday," she told him. "But of course they didn't. I begged them but they don't care. Now they're saying Friday, and they sound like they mean it. We'll see. But now that we have these new people in charge maybe others will find they need to shape up."

Russell let that go, marvelling anew at the high expectations so many working-class people seemed to have of Hitler and his cronies.

He wished her a good evening and climbed the stairs. Herr Habicht's broken door had been nailed shut, presumably to protect his Marxist library, but Herr Klausener's was gaping open, revealing an unmade bed and a bed stand crowded with photos of his children. Russell hadn't known either man well—communists and ex-communists were rarely friends—but both had seemed decent enough. Over the next few days they would all find out how well or badly the arrested communists were being treated.

His own door was still in one piece. After letting himself into the two-room apartment, he closed the door behind him and tore the envelope open. A man named Mechnig "required" Russell's presence at his office on the Bendlerstrasse at 11:15 A.M. on March 1. Which was tomorrow. According to the letterhead Herr Mechnig worked for the Resident Foreign Nationals section of the Prussian Interior Ministry, and it was Russell's right to residence that he wanted to "discuss."

It had to be better than a visit from "Hitler's lads," was Russell's first thought on waking with the interview in prospect. Not that the one precluded the other.

The room was frigid, his breath alarmingly visible, and climbing out from under the mountain of blankets took some resolution. After pulling on the rest of yesterday's clothes—he was still wearing most of them—he went to the window. The inner surface was iced over, the sky outside depressingly clear. The people on the opposite sidewalk all seemed to be wearing most of their wardrobes, which suggested a temperature well below freezing.

He turned his attention to the morning ahead, and the interview at its heart. He needed to look presentable, which was easier said than done. But first a bath.

For most of his years in Berlin he had enjoyed the bourgeois luxury of a tub at home, but since the split from Ilse and his enforced relocation to an area he could actually afford, he'd had to make do with the Public Baths. In truth, it wasn't much of a hardship—the baths were deep, the water hot, and the building itself only fifty yards away.

Sometimes, though, you had to wait, and today seemed particularly busy, as if cleanliness had suddenly come back into fashion. Or maybe half of Wedding had official interviews to attend. While Russell waited he read through a soggy copy of the *Berliner Morgen-Zeitung* that someone had left on a bench. The new Reichstag Fire Decree was spelt out in detail, and was every bit as draconian as he and his *Morgenspiegel* colleagues had feared.

The bath was hot and heavenly, and he only reluctantly clambered out when the banging on his cubicle door grew desperate. Back across the street, he stopped to call the office and let Hiedler's secretary know that an official appointment would make him late. The building might have a dodgy boiler, paint peeling from every damp wall and unreliable electrics, but it did, unlike most apartment blocks in Wedding, boast a communal telephone. That and the rent were the two major reasons he'd chosen it.

Up in his room, he rummaged through his meagre wardrobe for something smart enough, but the best he could find was his usual work outfit. The suit was just about passable, the shoes a little bit less so, but looked better with some spit rubbed in. The frayed shirt collar and holed socks wouldn't have passed inspection by his mother, but he assumed Herr Mechnig would be satisfied with taking a general impression.

His coat at least was relatively new, and he might not need to remove it.

What else did he require? All the official documents he had, which wasn't many. His passport, his press card, his copies of the marriage certificate and Paul's birth certificate, all went in the old leather briefcase Ilse's brother Thomas had given him several birthdays ago. What more? Some pieces of his work, carefully selected.

Papers gathered and outfit donned, he studied himself in the mirror. He needed a haircut, he realised, but otherwise it could be worse.

He stopped to check both rooms before he left. The copy of *Mein Kampf* was artfully placed on the bed stand, the bookmark—a photo of its author—inserted close to the back, suggesting a literary pleasure almost accomplished. In reality, he and Ilse had read the book together several years earlier on the "know your enemy" principle, underlining the most ludicrous passages. On the day Hitler became Chancellor Russell had thought it wise to spend half an hour rubbing out all their additions.

He had got rid of all his political—mostly Marxist—tracts,

but had hung on to several novels that now gave him reason to worry. The authors concerned were still in the shops,
but probably not for much longer. He wrapped the suspect
books in a piece of brown paper, tied the parcel together
with string, and then, in a fit of paranoia, took the whole
thing apart to check that his name was on none of the fly-
leaves. Satisfied that it wasn't, he tied the package together
again.

One last look around. There seemed nothing left to
incriminate him, an ideal state of affairs in Hitler's brave
new world. On his way downstairs he jokingly wondered,
not for the first time, if the notion of joining Hitler's Party
was as ludicrous as it sounded. As a foreigner they'd probably turn him down anyway, and the application would look
good on his record.

After dumping the books in one of the large rubbish bins
outside the Baths, he decided on a tram into the city centre.
The U-Bahn would be warmer but smellier, and he seemed
to be developing an aversion to travelling underground if it
wasn't completely necessary. Which was more superstition
than sense, but he suspected a sizable chunk of the German
population was finding weirder and weirder ways of coping
with life in a never-ending crisis.

For once the No.16 tram had a few seats to spare, and
he was happily settling into one when a heavily pregnant
woman loomed suggestively in front of him. By the time
he'd given up his place all the others were taken, which
didn't seem much of an omen where the rest of the day was
concerned.

The tram rattled south past the smoke-hazed Stettin Station yards, hissing and sizzling on the ice-coated overhead
wires. After crossing the Spree on the Ebertsbrücke—no
floating bodies there—it occurred to Russell that visiting
the British Embassy beforehand might strengthen his hand
for the meeting with Herr Mechnig. There could be new

official advice for people in his position. Perhaps even free legal help.

Alighting at the stop before the tunnel, he walked west along Unter den Linden to the junction with Wilhelmstrasse. A new "brown store" had opened on the southern side, and two SA men had their noses almost touching the window as they scanned the treasure trove of leather accessories that lay within.

The large embassy building was just beyond the Adlon Hotel, its single Union Jack looking somewhat outnumbered by the swastikas festooning Germany's Whitehall. The receptionist, a young German girl who spoke perfect English, listened to his pitch, gave him a sympathetic look, and picked up her internal phone to summon assistance. A few minutes later a young man bounded down the stairs to offer a vigorous handshake. His name was Dick Quigley, and he was probably younger than Russell. He was definitely better-dressed. With his Oxford bags, dazzling shirt and perfectly symmetrical bow-tie he looked like he'd just been called away from a stately home lawn party.

He took Russell up to his office at the back of the building, a small room that boasted a glimpse of the nearby Tiergarten. The two frames on his desk contained photographs of a youngish woman and an older couple. Girlfriend and parents probably. The former looked a bit like Henni. Russell had written the latter a brief apology, only to realise he hadn't taken note of her house number.

Quigley sat down behind his desk and clapped both hands against the sides of his head. "Brainbox not really in gear yet," he said cheerily. "Bit of a celebration last night."

The last few days hadn't offered much cause for celebration in Russell's world, and his curiosity must have shown in his face.

"Oh, you haven't heard," Quigley exclaimed. "We won the Fifth Test. In Australia. Cricket," he added, as if he'd suddenly realised that he was talking to someone from outer space.

Russell hadn't thought about cricket since his school days. "Ah," he said, in lieu of any other response.

"We won the Ashes. You know what they are?"

"Of course," Russell said, not at all sure.

"Well anyway, it's been a pretty controversial series. The Aussies objected to our tactics—short bowling and the like. All perfectly within the laws of course. And it kept Bradman quiet. Sorry," he said, raising both hands, "I'm getting a bit carried away."

Russell smiled. "Just a bit."

Quigley beamed back. "But living here—I mean, it's hard to imagine the Nazis playing cricket, isn't it? And I think that should tell us something about who and what they are."

Russell had a brief, disturbing mental image of a gloved and padded Hitler squatting behind a set of stumps. "You may be right," he said, pointedly checking his watch.

Quigley took the hint. "So what can I do for you?"

Russell explained his family situation. "I guess what I want to know is if anything's changed since Hitler took over."

"Not as far as I know," Quigley answered. "But it's early days."

"So my right to stay on account of my German wife still holds?"

"Until they say otherwise."

"And if we get divorced? Will having a German son allow me to stay?"

"I doubt it, but I don't honestly know. You'd have to ask them."

Russell nodded. "I may have to, but I think that might open a can of worms."

"It might. There are no guarantees, I'm afraid. When push comes to shove, any government can throw out anyone it wants to. They mostly don't because their own citizens abroad often end up carrying the can." Quigley's shrug would have made a Frenchman proud. "The only thing we can do is let you know when the rules change. Give me your address and I'll put you on our alert list."

Which was better than nothing, Russell thought, as he made his way outside. He had hoped he'd have time for a coffee at Café Kranzler, but his watch insisted he didn't.

The Foreign Ministry was only just down the street, but it took him a while to find Herr Mechnig's department. The man himself was busy, of course, and Russell was kept waiting half an hour in the company of several extravagantly moustachioed Bulgars. Resigned to being seen after they were, he was pleasantly surprised to be shown in ahead of them. They didn't look upset, so were probably waiting for someone else.

Herr Mechnig, a balding man in his thirties with a very pale face and eyes, gestured his guest into the upright seat across the desk. It was unusually hot in the room and Russell, deciding he'd rather look scruffy than covered in sweat, took off his coat and hung it on the back of the chair.

Herr Mechnig took a fresh form from a pile on his right, and took out his pen. After offering Russell a brief cold glance he began: "Name?"

"John Russell."

The pen started moving. "No middle names?"

"No. My parents were lazy," Russell added, hoping to break the ice.

Mechnig sniffed and drew a dash in the requisite space.

His birth date, address, occupation and marital status were all written in. "And I have a son," Russell volunteered. "A German son. Paul. He'll soon be six."

Mechnig put down his pen. "Did you fight in the war?" he asked.

"I did."

"For England, I presume."

"That's who called me up."

Mechnig sniffed again. "You didn't think it was your patriotic duty to volunteer?"

"I did not."

"Because of your communist beliefs?"

"I wasn't a communist then."

"So when did you become one?"

Russell took a moment before replying. "After the war, and all the suffering it caused on both sides, I found inspiration, like many others, in the Russian Revolution and its idea of a better society."

"And how long did you entertain the illusion that Bolshevism might lead to such a desirable outcome."

"About six years, I suppose."

"You left the Party, the KPD, in 1927."

"Officially, yes. But I had not been an active member for several years. My son was born in 1927, and my wife and I were determined to have a normal family life."

"And do you have one?"

The bastard knew, Russell realised. "We did," he said, "but we're having some problems at the moment."

"You are living apart."

"Temporarily. I'm sure this is only a bad patch. Lots of marriages have them."

"She's living with another man, I believe."

"He's a family friend," Russell said, trying to sound indignant.

Mechnig looked faintly amused. "You do understand that your permission to reside in Germany rests on your remaining married?"

"Surely having a German son must count for something?"

"Regrettably not. The rules are the rules, and while we are sometimes prepared to be flexible, that does not usually happen when the person concerned has a political history like yours. In my experience, once a communist, always a communist."

"I respectfully disagree," Russell said. "Mussolini was a member of the Italian Communist Party for several years, but no one holds that against him now."

That at least interrupted Mechnig's flow, and Russell decided to go on the attack. "I'm a crime reporter," he said, "and most crimes—murder, theft, fraud, you name it—are not political. So my politics, if I still had any, would not be relevant to my current position. Until quite recently, as I'm sure you know, I was a freelance journalist, and I'd like to show you the last pieces I wrote, for both the German and British papers." He reached into the leather briefcase. "It was a series of articles about the current famine in Ukraine, which Stalin and the Russian Party deliberately allowed to take place. I don't think anyone could read them and think I'm still a communist."

Mechnig took the copies and started leafing through them. It was pure luck on Russell's part that these were the last things he'd written, because he really had been outraged by the Soviet government's actions, and it showed. After their publication, those old comrades he was still in contact with had all stopped speaking to him, mostly, he suspected, because they knew he was right.

Mechnig handed the articles back. "An impressive critique." He allowed himself the luxury of one tight little smile. "Very well, Herr Russell," he said. "I see no compelling reason to revoke your present status. For the moment. But you must repair your marriage, and we will of course be monitoring your journalistic work. We National Socialists are welcoming people, but we will not be taken advantage of, nor let the attainment of our national destiny be put at risk by a few degenerate cuckoos in our German nest. They will be sent back to where they came from."

It sounded like a closing speech, and it was. A flick of the eyes towards the door, and Russell knew he'd been dismissed. He took the risk of offering his hand, and was rewarded with a fleeting clammy grip. "Thank you," he said, with all the false sincerity he could muster.

It could have been a lot worse, he thought, as he walked down Wilhelmstrasse's canyon of government buildings. He seemed to be safe for the moment, though he wasn't looking forward to telling Ilse she must wait for any divorce. For once he had the Nazis on his side, he noted ruefully—the moves towards greater equality in marriage over the last decade was likely to be swiftly reversed by the new government. If he wanted to be obdurate, he probably could, but falling out with his son's mother and prospective stepfather was not something he wished to countenance.

Realising he hadn't yet eaten, he stopped at the Jädickes Konditorei for a hurried coffee and cake before reporting in across the street. He was barely through the door before Hiedler's beckoning finger attracted his attention. "Your mystery is solved," the editor announced as Russell reached his desk. "Or at least the body's been found. In the Grunewald."

"In what state?" Russell asked, wishing he felt more surprised.

"I don't know. It's at the Alex."

"I'm on my way."

The Berlin police HQ was on Alexanderstrasse, a block south of the city's unofficial centre, Alexanderplatz. Russell took the U-Bahn from Hausvogelplatz and was outside the multi-domed four-storey monolith in less than fifteen minutes. The reception area inside was fuller than he'd ever seen it, mostly, as far he could tell, with people seeking information about arrested relatives and friends. The corridors beyond weren't much emptier, with police and SA bustling around and shouting out orders, and roped or handcuffed prisoners lining a lot of the walls.

Expecting the morgue to be piled high with corpses, Russell was surprised to find it no busier than usual. The thought crossed his mind that many of the post-Fire victims were, like the ones he'd seen in the Panke, still waiting to be recovered.

The Professor had already been placed in a drawer. The attendant allowed Russell a brief unrevealing look and closed it up again. "A heart attack," he said. "No sign of external injuries," he added, responding to Russell's sceptical look.

So what had he doing in the Grunewald, and why had the body not been found until now?

Up on the second floor, the Kriminalinspektor in charge of the case, whom Russell had already met on several occasions, had answers to both his questions. "One of the people we talked to said the Professor liked a long walk when he had something to think through, and it seems"— the Kriminalinspektor pointedly pushed his office door shut—"that the Professor was most unhappy that some of his Jewish colleagues were being pressured to resign their posts at the Institute. Which *could* explain what he was doing in the Grunewald."

"It could," Russell granted. "But how come no one found him for five days? I know the Grunewald's big, but most of the time you can hardly move for walkers and people on bicycles."

"Ah, well, we think we can explain that too. He probably had the heart attack on Saturday afternoon—he'd been working at the Institute that morning—and Saturday evening was when we had all the snow. It's been cold ever since, and some of the snow is still on the ground. We think his body was covered, and only became visible again when the layer on top of him melted."

"Sounds feasible," Russell assented.

"It's the only explanation that does. There was no sign of

violence and he wasn't robbed. Case closed, thank God. I've got a dozen others to deal with."

"The place does seem rather busy," Russell observed. "How are relations with the SA?"

The Kriminalinspektor gave him a look. "As well as can be expected."

Once Russell had got back to the office and written his copy it was time to pick up his son from school. He had made this early departure from work on Wednesdays a condition of accepting the job, and much to his relief Hiedler had proved understanding, or desperate enough to agree the stipulation. Walking down the stairs Russell wondered how many people like himself were going to derive real benefits from the Nazi campaign against the Jews. All those jobs coming free, all those apartments going for a song.

He reached Paul's school just in time, a lone male amidst the crowd of women waiting at the gate.

"Are we going to Siggi's?" were the first words out of Paul's mouth.

"We are." The cake shop was only a few minutes' walk away, and had an outside terrace where they could take turns identifying passing automobiles. It also sold some of the best strudel in Berlin.

With the temperature down below forty, they were the only customers willing to sit outside, and his son's hot chocolate gave off a satisfying plume of steam. Paul managed to get most of the cream-filled *bienenstich* into his mouth, and Russell's poppy seed strudel was delicious as ever.

They spotted cars for a while—"A Fafnir! A Duesenberg Model J!"—the latter wearing an oh-so-elegant midnight blue livery. In its wake one of the new economy Hanomags rattled past, looking rather out of its league in upmarket Wilmersdorf.

Paul, though, had other things on his mind. "Matthias

says boys don't usually start going to football matches until they're at least ten."

"Well he's probably right about *most* boys," Russell said diplomatically. "But I went when I was eight, and I think you're going to go a lot earlier than that."

"So when?" Paul asked.

"In the next few weeks, I promise. I don't know who Hertha are playing at home, but I'll find out."

Paul rode his luck. "And can we go to the cartoon cinema on Saturday? And Luna Park?"

"One of them at least." Russell checked his watch. "Time to get you home."

Unusually, it was Ilse who answered the door. "How are things in Wedding?" she asked, once Paul had kissed his father goodbye and bounded up the stairs.

"As you'd expect," Russell said, knowing where this was going.

"I have to admit I'm worried about Paul staying with you this Saturday," she said. "With the election on Sunday . . ."

Russell bristled inside, but could see she had a point.

"It's only this Saturday," she persisted. "Things are bound to calm down once they've won the election."

"I hope so," he concurred. The last time he'd looked, moving to a district less prone to stormtrooper violence had been beyond his means, but now that he had a regular job he should probably try again. And he could also find other work to supplement his income—only the other day he'd been told by a friend that many of Berlin's private English tutors had decided that Hitler's accession was reason enough to make their way home. Another collateral benefit, Russell thought. The Nazis really were a gift that kept on giving. "I'll take him out on Saturday and bring him back here," he told Ilse.

"Good," she said, forcing a smile. "And you take care of yourself," she added, softening the dismissal.

On the tram ride back to Wedding he mulled over the situation. He couldn't imagine life without his son, but the years of timetabled meetings that his and Ilse's separation entailed seemed somehow chilling. The arrangement had all the spontaneity of a couple meeting for sex at a certain time each day, whether or not they were in the mood.

As for sex . . . Chance would be a fine thing, he thought, picturing Henni's face on the dance floor. If he could recognise the house, he supposed he could leave her a note. But he knew he wouldn't.

The Moustache Lounge

Russell set off early for work, and decided to walk despite the heavily overcast sky. After consuming a *Bauernfrüh-stück* of ham, onions and diced potatoes at a cheap eating place he liked just behind the Lazarus Hospital, he continued on down Friedrichstrasse to the Kranzler Café for coffee and a lengthy perusal of the newspaper rack. It had been decided that the soon-to-be elected Reichstag would have its first session in the Garrison Church at Potsdam. The Nazis would announce their four-year plan, and Frederick the Great would doubtless be applauding in his crypt below-stairs, but it was not anticipated that many communist or socialist deputies would attend. This was hardly surprising, given the numbers already locked up. It was certainly a sure-fire way to win an election, Russell thought, arresting your opponents ahead of the vote.

Some communists had escaped the SA and police, one at least reaching Sweden, where the local papers had brazenly chosen to interview him. Göring was apoplectic—the Swedes, he said, were determined to pick a quarrel with Germany's new government. What other reason could they have for talking to a communist?

The Nazi *Beobachter* was more concerned about "pacifist excesses," offering a long list of those it considered guilty. Those whose names Russell recognised—the physicist

Albert Einstein, the novelists Erich Remarque and Thomas Mann, the *Tageblatt* drama critic Alfred Kerr—had already left the country, as, it seemed, had a staggering percentage of Germany's scientists, poets, film-makers, dramatists and visual artists. What sort of government delighted in sending a country's best minds into exile, Russell wondered. This sort, he supposed, watching the arrival of several black-shirted *Schutzstaffel* officers, and the waiter's desperate eagerness to find them a table.

Despair was always the easy option, one of Russell's comrades in the trenches had been fond of saying. But Russell had never believed it. In his experience, despair was more than a little debilitating.

It was drizzling outside when he emerged, but not enough to make waiting for a tram worthwhile. Reaching the newsroom ten minutes later, he found one of Hiedler's famously terse notes sitting on his desk: "Dead line boy at Moustache Lounge."

A line boy was a male prostitute in his late teens. There were, a fellow journalist had once explained to him, about a dozen varieties of male prostitute in Berlin, from muscular working class *Bubes* through early teen Doll Boys to the self-explanatory Kitty Receivers, who were also known as Bottom Men. It was a whole other world to Russell.

The Moustache Lounge was at 2 Gormannstrasse, one of many homosexual clubs or *Dielen* in the streets around Oranienburger Tor and Rosenthaler Platz. Or at least, there had been a lot of them—over the last few years the authorities had introduced curfews and other restrictive measures, and some were expecting the Nazis to go even further. Others thought the stormtroopers and their famously homosexual leader Ernst Röhm would ensure the clubs stayed open.

Russell took the U-Bahn to Weinmeisterstrasse. The Moustache was a short walk round the corner, and currently guarded by a small cordon of bored-looking uniformed Kripo. He brandished his press card more in hope than expectation, and the nearest man simply gestured him through the half-open entrance. The lobby wasn't much wider than a passage, but the room beyond was deep and broad enough for at least fifty tables. A bar took up most of the wall on the left, flights of stairs to the cellar and upper floors the one on the right. At the far end of the room a miniscule stage was swathed in plastic flowers.

At the bar a couple of plainclothes detectives were conducting interviews with staff. Russell waved his card again, hoping for a similarly helpful response, and was pleasantly surprised to get one. "Upstairs," he was told.

"Who's in charge?" Russell asked.

"Glassl," the man said. "Kriminalinspektor Glassl," he added.

Russell made his way up to the next floor, knowing why everyone was being so helpful. Walter Glassl was well-known for his love of the public eye, and giving the press a warm welcome would be a crucial part of his underlings' remit.

As Russell reached the first landing light flashed in one of the rooms down the corridor. He walked down to the open doorway, and rather wished he hadn't. The room boasted a large bed, a couple of upright chairs and walls bearing numerous drawers and photographs of males doing sundry things with their cocks. Things that the boy on the bed would never do again. His had been sliced off—none too cleanly and before he died, if the twisted face and copious blood were any guide.

There were four other males in the room: the police photographer, Kriminalinspektor Glassl and two crime reporters Russell knew from the missing professor briefings. Benno Eglhofer was from the *Tageblatt*, Franz Puttkammer from the *Volks-Zeitung*.

"Which paper?" Glassl asked him.

"The *Morgenspiegel.*"

"Rothstein's replacement? Well, see you spell my name right. That's Glassl with two *s*'s."

A uniformed Kripo appeared in the doorway. "The Morgue wagon's here," he told Glassl.

"About time. Well, tell the idle bastards to come and get him."

The two men who came with the stretcher looked like they'd been working all night, which was probably close to the truth—Russell presumed that over the last few days they and their wagon had been much in demand.

"Roll it up in the sheet," Glassl barked, as the two men reached for the naked body. "We don't want anyone having nightmares."

It occurred to Russell that something was missing. "Have they found the cock?" he asked Eglhofer as all of them followed the laden stretcher downstairs.

"If they have, they're keeping it under wraps."

"Maybe Glassl's got it in his pocket," Puttkammer suggested, his eyes on the street-bound stretcher.

The Kriminalinspektor came back from consulting his men. "Right, gentlemen," he began. "The boy's name was Fredo Ratzel, and we think he was seventeen. We think he was killed last night, and not found until this morning because someone left a DON'T DISTURB sign on the door."

"Any sign of a motive?" Puttkammer asked.

Glassl shrugged. "It's more likely that one of their games got out of hand. Drugs probably."

Some game, Russell thought.

"Do you have any suspects?" Eglhofer asked.

"You can say I do, yes," Glassl said smugly. "We have a witness who saw Ratzel arrive with another boy named Timo Baur. They live together apparently, down in Rote Insel. And Baur's disappeared, which looks suspicious. So . . ."

"So this witness knew both boys?"

Glassl looked uncomfortable. "He said he'd met them once before, a year or so ago."

"And you think he's a reliable witness?" Russell asked. "I mean," he said, looking round the room—"given the context."

"The man is an SA Sturmhauptführer," Glassl said, before hastily adding that such information was naturally off the record.

"Of course." Russell didn't want to antagonise such a press-friendly detective.

"Have you found the victim's member?" Eglhofer asked.

Glassl looked pained at the thought. "No, not yet."

"Do you know where the victim lived?" Puttkammer asked.

"Not yet, but we soon will. Find his room and we might find Timo Baur, or at least get a lead on his whereabouts." Glassl held up both hands. "All right, gentlemen. I should have more for you this evening. If not, then tomorrow morning. Thank you."

They watched him head for the exit. "What's this place specialise in?" Russell asked, knowing that most of Berlin's *Dielen* liked to distinguish themselves by promoting their own sexual menu.

Puttkammer grimaced. "The clue's in the name. Men over forty who're in love with their own facial hair. They spend the evening stroking their moustaches and drinking; they watch a man on stage pretending he's Marlene Dietrich, and when the *Bubes* and the line boys turn up around midnight they all get to fuck a tight young arse." He shook his head. "What an advert for the Republic, eh?" He looked at his watch. "I must be off. See you boys at the next atrocity."

Russell and Eglhofer followed slowly in his wake, only to find that the drizzle had turned to rain. As they watched from the awning, Russell thought about what they'd been told. "What do you think of Glassl's theory?" he asked the other man.

"Theory's too generous," was the response. "He may be right about the friend—a lot of these children *are* almost feral. But most of the action in dumps like this takes place in the toilets or the alleys out back." He smiled. "You should see the toilets in there—they're fancier than the Adlon's, but they're not exactly discreet. For that, you need a room, and I counted the ones upstairs. There are only four, and they'll cost a damn sight more than those two boys could ever afford. If both of them were there, they won't have been alone." He pulled a thin cigarette case out of his inside pocket and offered Russell a Sulima. "Maybe we'll find out more from Glassl this evening, but I won't be holding my breath." He snapped the lighter shut. "Anyway, I have a stabbing in Schöneberg to look at. I'll see you this evening."

A stabbing, Russell thought, as the other man strode away. With arrests running into thousands, and deaths into the hundreds, a stabbing seemed almost trivial. But not to the victim, as Hiedler would doubtless say. Maintaining a sense of proportion was likely to prove something of a challenge in Hitler's world.

He thought about ringing the office to see if anything new had come in, but realised he wasn't as ready as Eglhofer to let Fredo Ratzel go. Dying in such a brutal manner surely warranted more than a quick dismissal.

A dingy café next to the U-Bahn station provided somewhere to sit and try to make sense of his notes. What did he know? A young male prostitute had been sadistically murdered, for reasons unknown, at an establishment that catered to moustachioed homosexuals. Russell supposed the gruesome details were newsworthy, in the worst sense of that word, but he doubted whether Hiedler would let him be brutally explicit. Some sort of euphemism—"cut off in his prime"—came to mind. Whoever and whatever he had been, the young man deserved better than that.

But what else was there? A missing boyfriend probably

on the run, Glassl scouring Berlin. With the Stormtroopers busily manhunting 300,000 communists, a single teenage fugitive seemed like an infinitesimal footnote. Eglhofer's point about the room costing money was well-made, but conflating that with an SA witness seemed like asking for trouble. A decision for Hiedler, that one.

He could always try to find out more about the victim. But not now—mid-morning didn't seem the sort of time to seek out Ratzel's fellow line boys. He would come back this evening.

Six o'clock was not late enough. The rain had long since stopped when Russell returned, but the evening was dank and dark, the lights on Gormannstrasse fighting what felt like a losing battle. There were only about twenty men in the Moustache Lounge, most of whom gave his clean-shaven face a thoroughly disapproving look. The tiny stage was lit but empty.

Russell perched himself on a barstool and ordered a Palsenhofer from the barman who'd been there that morning.

"You're Press," the man said with a marked lack of approval.

"Uh-huh. Is it usually this quiet?" Russell asked, surveying the sea of mostly empty tables. "Or has last night's misfortune put your customers off?"

The barman shook his head. "It'll get busy in a couple of hours." He smiled to himself. "Why, are you looking for action?"

"I'm looking to buy information."

The other man looked wary, but not opposed in principle. "So what would you pay to know?"

"Nothing controversial. Where can I find the local line boys at this time of night?"

"You don't look the type."

Russell gave him a look.

"Five marks."

"Two. I can always ask at the bar a few doors down."

"Done," the barman agreed, holding out a palm.

"So where?" Russell asked, once the money had changed hands.

"At the bar a few doors down," the man said triumphantly.

Russell laughed, took a last swig of his lager, and walked to the bar in question. It was not much bigger than his bedroom in Wedding, and the décor made the Moustache Lounge seem classy. The photos on the walls of bronzed young men in shorts staring moodily into the distance were more artistic than pornographic. None of those pictured had moustaches or beards, and neither did any of the bar's youthful patrons. There were six of them in all, five playing cards at a table, one reading a book by the stove. They all looked well under twenty, and were uniformly clad in the sort of thick woollen sweaters that conjured up thoughts of the Navy.

The way the twelve eyes looked him up and down made Russell more than a little uncomfortable, and he was reminded of things Ilse had sometimes said about the way men looked at her.

"I'm a journalist," he said. "John Russell. If I buy a round, will you answer some questions?"

"Which paper?" a blond boy asked.

"The *Morgenspiegel*."

"That's not a bad paper," another boy said. "Why not?"

No one demurred, and Russell ordered drinks at the tiny bar, thinking how sad it was that war, inflation and depression had made it impossible for apparently intelligent youths like these to feed themselves in any other way. Prostitution had always been around, always been acceptable to some, but had never seemed so widespread or so shockingly ordinary.

He passed out the drinks, and asked if they'd heard about the boy who'd been killed at the Lounge.

"Of course," a blond young man at the table said. He looked older than the others, and seemed like the spokesman. "But we don't know who killed him."

"But you knew him?"

"Everyone knew Fredo," the youth replied, apparently studying his hand of cards.

"What can you tell me about him?"

The young man sighed and carefully placed his cards face down on the table. "None of us knew him well—he wasn't one of our group—but we ran into him quite often, at the Lounge and other places. He was a strange one. He read a lot—always had a book in his pocket—but he spent the rest of his time body-building."

"What sort of books?" Russell asked, purely out of curiosity.

"Anything. Thomas Mann. Tom Shark."

"Did he have any . . . I don't know what you'd call them . . . special services he offered?"

They all laughed at that. "He didn't need to," one of the younger-looking boys said. "He was a Breslauer."

"He came from Breslau?" Russell asked, not understanding the significance.

That had them almost hysterical.

"No," the blond youth explained when the laughter died down. "A Breslauer is someone with a really big cock. They're much in demand, as you can imagine."

"Ah," Russell said. They obviously didn't know Ratzel's had been cut off, and he saw no reason to spoil their day. "Did Fredo have a steady boyfriend?" he asked, hoping it wasn't a stupid question.

The way they shook their heads in unison was almost eerie.

"The police think he did. A boy named Timo."

The blond boy scoffed. "The police are idiots. He shared a room with Timo, but they were just old friends. I think they came here from Stettin together."

Russell was acutely aware he was out of his depth. "The police think Timo might have killed him."

No one would believe that. "Timo? He wouldn't hurt a fly," another boy chipped in. He had dark floppy hair and was wearing a green sweater that almost came up to his ears.

"Well, no one seems to know where he is. I don't suppose you lot have any idea?"

If they did, they weren't saying. Several looked pointedly at their cards, as if willing Russell to end the interrogation.

"Did he and Fredo hang out anywhere in particular?" Russell asked.

"The new Karls-Lounge," the blond boy volunteered. "It's on Linienstrasse, close to the Blue Stocking. You must know that—the place where crippled soldiers go for crippled hookers. Up near Oranienburger Tor."

Russell remembered the first time he'd heard about the Blue Stocking—he and some friends had been drunkenly listing "wonders of the post-war world," and someone had brought up the club in question. He found himself hoping that his current companions, with their fresh eager faces and youthful cynicism, had something better to look forward to.

It would have been nice to blame a much-interrupted night on the Nazis, but no one hammered on Frau Löffner's door, and the noise of stormtrooper depredations elsewhere in the district jerked Russell awake on only two occasions. His bed was more to blame than Hitler's minions, its broken springs stabbing up through the mostly hollow mattress like that devilish machine in one of Kafka's stories.

He felt better after the Baths, and set off through the pleasantly milder weather to catch a No.3 tram to the Alex.

Kriminalinspektor Glassl had put off yesterday evening's briefing until this morning, and Russell was expecting to hear a tale of failure dressed up as steady progress. Given the feverish state of the city, and the demands which that and Sunday's election had placed on the Kripo, finding a single boy in hiding felt like a near-impossible task.

As expected, Glassl was long on optimism, short on results, and the half-dozen crime reporters were sent back to their offices with little new to say. The police had found Ratzel's "lair," and confirmed that he shared it with his fellow pervert Timo Baur. They had also discovered a photograph of several boys at Luna Park, one of whom the *Portierfrau* had identified as Baur. The picture had been enlarged— the wonders of police technology!—and passed around. It had shown what was probably a human figure, but nothing more distinctive than that. Copies had been promised for the evening editions.

No one had asked after the missing member, and Glassl himself hadn't mentioned it.

At the *Morgenspiegel* office, Russell reported Glassl's lack of progress and his own conversation with the line boys the previous evening. Hiedler told him to visit the "new Karls-Lounge" later that day; in the meantime he should get himself down to Grunewald. A Nazi election canvasser had been attacked on a doorstep, and hurt seriously enough to end up in the new Martin Luther Hospital.

"I thought they canvassed in packs," Russell commented.

"They probably didn't think they needed to in Grunewald," Hiedler suggested.

The attack on young Fritz Gerwien took up the rest of Russell's day. Gathered round the injured hero's hospital bed at the local Party's invitation, he and a dozen other crime reporters were treated to a scenic tour of the man's injuries, which amounted to little more than a collection of multi-coloured bruises. They were then told that the assailant, Ralf Ordenewitz, had been taken into custody, and would soon be put on show at the local Kripo station, only to find when they got there that the SA had taken the prisoner away. The local SA leader then denied, admitted and re-denied this, all in the space of two hours, before eventually admitting that Ordenewitz had been moved to a nearby barracks to free up his cell for their Kripo colleagues. Once there, however, he had foolishly tried to escape through an upstairs window, and fallen to his death. Given the circumstances, the journalists were "advised" that any reporting should await the SA's internal investigation, which would of course begin immediately. Ordenewitz's body would be released to his family, but only after the investigators had finished their work. In the meantime, both body and family were out of bounds to everyone else.

"One does wonder whether the SA are stupid enough to think that bruises heal on a corpse," Eglhofer mused on their taxi ride back to Kochstrasse.

In the *Morgenspiegel* editorial room, Hiedler just shook his head and suggested that Russell get back to his line boys.

Reasoning that it was still a trifle early in the day to find them up and about, Russell treated himself to an early dinner of bratwurst and spätzle at the local Wertheim's restaurant and caught up with the news. None of it was good, which wasn't in itself unusual, but he found it hard to remember a time when it had seemed so irretrievably awful.

The Catholic bishops had apparently written to Hindenburg, asking him to make sure that the election was free and fair, and the President had duly passed the message on to Hitler, who had doubtless shared a chuckle with his cronies while consigning it to his wastebasket. Meanwhile journalists were being arrested for reporting the widespread suspicion that the Reichstag Fire had been started by the Nazis. The communist leader Ernst Thalmann had also been taken into custody, and anything that might help his party win seats in Sunday's election—posters, meetings, pamphlets—had been summarily banned.

While Russell had been out in Grunewald that afternoon the streets in the centre had apparently been gummed up by marching Nazis, with Göring taking the salute from the Interior Ministry balcony. According to a colleague who'd witnessed this, Göring had been wearing a pink-edged brown cloak over his uniform, like "a fat Napoleon with no sense of style."

How, Russell wondered—not for the first time—had a sophisticated country like Germany—the land of Beethoven, Heine and Goethe—ended up with such a sinister bunch of clowns at its helm?

The boss clown was off to Königsberg in East Prussia to give a major speech on the eve of Sunday's vote. Königsberg's loss would not be Berlin's gain, however—loudspeakers were being hung from lampposts along twenty-four of the capital's major thoroughfares, and patriotic citizens urged to place their wirelesses in open windows so the neighbours wouldn't miss a word. The bastard would probably be audible on the moon.

Russell supposed that Franklin Roosevelt's inauguration might qualify as good news, but the new President's notion that "the only thing we have to fear is fear itself" sounded limp enough for a Christmas cracker motto. He should try living here, Russell thought.

An hour or so later he was walking past the entrance to the notorious Blue Stocking, scanning both sides of Linienstrasse for the relocated Karl's Lounge, when he noticed the pair of vehicles parked with little precision a hundred yards ahead. One was an open lorry, the other a car. There were a couple of brownshirts out on the sidewalk, which probably meant more inside, and the car, a black Opel, suggested someone of rank. Russell couldn't read the sign above the door from where he was, but he instinctively knew it was Karl's.

A small crowd of onlookers had gathered on the oppo-site pavement, but Russell decided not to join them—the SA had a nasty habit of collecting witnesses just for the hell of it. Some thirty yards farther on, the inset doorway of an aban-doned shop offered sufficient concealment and a grandstand view, and he settled down to wait.

It wasn't long before the stormtroopers came out in pairs, each with a line boy sandwiched between them, and half-lifted, half-threw their prey onto the back of the lorry. A couple of the boys were clearly frightened, but most looked defiantly contemptuous. With seven on board, their captors climbed up after them, and corralled the boys into a space at the front. "Have a good feel," Russell heard one man sneer. "It'll be your last."

A few seconds later an officer emerged. Over the last few weeks Russell had thought it prudent to memorise at least some of the many new uniforms, and this was a Standartenführer. Which in itself was rather surprising—men of such rank weren't usually observed leading raids on obscure Berlin *Dielen*. As the man climbed into the Opel the nearest streetlight caught a high-browed and almost baby-like visage.

The car sped off towards Oranienburger Tor, the lorry hurrying behind it, like a dog afraid of losing its master.

As the sound of the motors faded the watching crowd dispersed. Russell walked across the street and in through the unattended doorway. Karl's Lounge was about twice the size of his bedroom, not much better-decorated, and in some disarray. Chairs and table had been knocked over, and the shards from more than one beer glass now carpeted the wooden floor. Some grim-faced patrons were putting the place back together, while other seemed frozen in shock, tears running down their otherwise inanimate faces. Most were a similar age to the line boys Russell had talked to the day before.

It took a while for anyone to notice him, and when they did the response—"what the fuck do you want?"—was not the most welcoming. It took several minutes of arguing that their arrested friends needed all the publicity they could get if they weren't just to vanish down some Nazi oubliette, to convince most of those present that he was on their side. Which was gilding the lily a little, but at least it got them to talk.

The SA had only been interested in Timo Baur, and those naïve or dim enough to admit knowing him had been taken away for questioning. Those left behind knew him just as well, but no one had seen him since the killing. He might still be in Berlin, he might have gone back to Stettin. And why were the SA so keen to find him? Everyone knew he hadn't killed Fredo Ratzel, so why did the SA insist that he had?

When it came to who really had killed Fredo, his comrades were at a loss. One of the moustachioed crew might have been responsible, but they were such a pathetic bunch that it didn't seem likely. And Fredo had other, less innocent regulars.

"Like SA men?" Russell asked.

"Maybe a few," was the answer he got, and only reluctantly.

"Tell me about Fredo," Russell said, moving back to safer ground.

They all had something to say about Fredo. He had never known his father, who had conceived him on leave, then died at Verdun. His mother had married again, a sailor who was always away, but still managed to give her three daughters. Fredo was forever sending money home to Stettin.

His love of reading was mentioned again, along with the revelation that he wanted to be a writer. His favourite meal was *Königsberger klopse* and *kartoffelbrei*—East Prussian meatballs with mashed potatoes—and he often trespassed on roofs to look at the stars. He was inclined to be tetchy first thing in the morning and inordinately proud of his *Breslauer* cock.

Russell wrote all the memories down in his notebook, feeling sad and slightly guilty that none would appear in print. He told them he would let them know if he heard any news of their friends, and leaving them his card, asked them to let him know if Timo ever surfaced. The looks on their faces told him that was unlikely. These young men trusted no one but one another, and who could blame them?

It had been a deeply depressing day, and as he passed the Main Telegraph Office the sight of a bar on the opposite side of the street convinced him he needed a drink. Or two. The place was full of postal workers, and decidedly devoid of women, which seemed about par for the way his life was going. Russell bought a beer, leaned himself against a spare length of bar, and gazed at his fellow Berliners with something less than human kindness.

One glass proved enough. Outside the bar he paused for a moment, deciding between home and the office. He doubted Hiedler was still at the latter, but chose to hope he would be, rather than face his rooms on Gerichtstrasse. A young couple embracing on the Ebertsbrücke reminded him that normal life continued, a lorry-load of stormtrooper thugs rumbling across Markgrafenstrasse that it only did so under duress. All the lights were burning in the newspaper buildings on Kochstrasse, but for how much longer?

Hiedler had gone home, and Russell agonised over whether or not to raise his suspicions with the night editor. He hadn't had many dealings with Rainer Kempka, and these days it paid to think twice before venturing onto thin ice, but what was the point of the job if he couldn't even tell a colleague the truth? He walked across to the editor's desk and went through everything he'd seen, heard and deduced.

"We don't have enough to start making accusations," Kempka decided, with what looked like some reluctance. "But keep digging. Get a name for the Standartenführer, and take things up with Hiedler on Monday, once the election's out of the way. I'll leave him a note."

Russell went down to the paper's photographic library on the first floor. Half an hour later, he had a name to go with the face and uniform: Standartenführer Oswald Steimle. A trip to the archives next door provided more information: Steimle was thirty-two, from Munich, and a card-carrying member of the National Socialist Party since 1923. He had joined the SA the following year, and over the ensuing nine years had risen steadily through the ranks. If he was married, it wasn't mentioned.

Which was all very interesting, Russell thought, but where did it get him? He had his suspicions, but seeking confirmation would be dangerous, and probably pointless.

Heading back up the stairs he ran into a breathless Johannes Oertel. "You live in Wedding, don't you?" Oertel asked.

"For my sins."

"Well, if you're going back there tonight, be careful. The SA have emptied every building on the streets around Kosliner Strasse, and they're probably finding communists in every other cupboard. They've left hundreds of families standing outside, just trying to keep their children warm. Most of the locals are savvy enough not to protest, and by the time I left there still hadn't been any serious violence, but I'd be surprised if that's still the case. Most of the brown-shirts have been drinking to steady their nerves, and it won't take much to set them off."

"Right, thanks," Russell said, but Oertel was already half-way across the vast room. Another night upstairs, he told himself. He might as well move in, and spend his Wedding rent on wine, women and song.

It felt early to grab a bed, but they might be in short supply later on, and the thought of going out again was not appealing. So he took himself upstairs and lay there with the light on, idly thumbing through an abandoned book about German explorers, and filling the room with cigarette smoke.

He found himself thinking about the man who'd attacked the Nazi canvasser. The late Ralf Ordenewitz. Russell and his fellow journalists had been given no proof that the man had attacked the young Nazi, but assuming he had, he hadn't used anything more than his fists. And no one had offered any reason for the attack—other than saying that the man must have hated Nazis. Well, Russell hated them too, but he didn't start throwing punches the moment he met one. Ordenewitz must have been provoked.

And now he was dead. "Trying to escape"—they couldn't even be bothered to think up a less clichéd story. His SA abductors had killed him, either for sport or in some righteous rage over their badly bruised comrade. And they would escape scot-free. They would get away with silencing witnesses and secluding the corpse, with telling people like him to fuck off.

Could he and his colleagues have done any more? In retrospect Russell had to admit that they could. Ordenewitz's neighbours might have seen something, and they hadn't been placed out of bounds. They should have been questioned, if only to show some form of resistance.

Which was easy to say, Russell thought, lying in bed twelve hours after the fact. He knew the only difference made would have been to himself and his prospects of staying in Germany—the neighbours would either have sworn they'd seen nothing or found themselves in trouble, and Ordenewitz would still be dead.

So why bother? Because even the limited freedom of a bourgeois press would not survive a supine press corps.

Then again, it was probably only a matter of weeks. The office beneath him was still full of men and women who wanted to tell the truth as they saw it, but Russell couldn't help thinking they were all on borrowed time. Truth had lost the battle, as Sunday's election would prove, and the lie would be enshrined in law at the point of a gun.

As on the morning after the Fire, Russell took a cup of canteen coffee up to the roof, but this time there was no one there to share the view. Overnight rain had left puddles in the street below, and lowering clouds still filled the sky, dulling the icy chill of recent mornings. The city looked at peace, and when the low murmur of urban life was interrupted it was car horns rather than gunfire that did the interrupting.

An intricate mask, Russell thought. A scene in a book he'd read as a youth came back to him, as it often had in the trenches. The author had imagined another world, one in which blood came out of the body as smoke, in which wars came to a natural end when the thickness of smoke in the air meant that soldiers could no longer find their enemies.

If that was the way the world worked, how much smoke would hang over Berlin this morning?

On the street below the doors of the Jädickes Konditorei were in constant motion, and the bakery within was doing its best to keep the mask in place, wafting heavenly smells out into the morning air. And why not, Russell thought. Who was it said that there weren't any problems in life that a German pastry wouldn't solve?

The man had been exaggerating, but not by much. After eating two and downing a much better coffee, Russell felt almost ready to face the world. The morning newspapers provided the "almost"—the Nazi-supporters were already tasting victory, and the more liberal papers sounded shriller than usual, as if they couldn't quite believe their own desperation.

There were a lot of events planned for the day, as the warring parties made their final pitch ahead of tomorrow's election, and everyone seemed to be expecting trouble. The police and their new SA "auxiliaries" would certainly be out in force, with all that that implied for public safety. The notion of an innocent bystander had apparently passed them by—you were either in range of a truncheon or you weren't.

Ilse, he reluctantly realised, would be loath to let Paul out at all on a day like this. The thought of giving up any of the much-reduced hours he spent with his son was unwelcome, but on this occasion it probably did make sense to play it safe.

Once back in the office, he phoned to make sure he had read her correctly. He had.

"But he wants to see you," she said, "so why don't you come to lunch at Thomas and Hanna's tomorrow? I've already asked Thomas and he'd love to see you."

"Ah," Russell said, wondering how to respond.

"Matthias and I will be there," she said, knowing the reason for his hesitation. "It's about time, don't you think?"

"It probably is," he conceded. Dealing with the fact that another family had risen from the ashes of his own. One he could still be a part of, if he so chose. Rather than someone who just hovered at their door. "I'd love to," he said. "What time?"

"Around one," Ilse told him, sounding pleased.

"Tell Paul we'll do the things we planned next week."

"I think he's already counting on that."

They said their goodbyes, and he hung up the phone, his feelings decidedly mixed. It felt like a line had finally been drawn under something already long gone, a line that would let him move on, as she already had.

"Kempka wants you," one of his colleagues told him, interrupting his reverie.

"You're on half-shift, right?" Hiedler's deputy asked him.

"More if you need me," Russell said.

"They won't sanction the overtime. And this should only take you a couple of hours. What we know—what we've been told—is this. A train from Danzig was stopped in the Polish Corridor, whereupon a gang of Poles—presumably Poles—climbed on board and stole anything they could carry from the passengers in First Class—money, watches, jewellery, a few furs. The train should be arriving at Stettin Station in around twenty minutes, and they've set aside a room for the press to interview victims and crew."

"Do we know how it was stopped?" Russell asked.

Kempka shook his head. "Ask them."

"And who has set aside this room?"

"Another good question."

Russell was beginning to like Hiedler's deputy. He grabbed his coat from his desk, took the stairs two at a time, and hurried down Kochstrasse to the U-Bahn Station. Luck was with him—a northbound train came in as he reached the platform and he arrived at the DRG Stettin Station just as the Danzig express steamed in. Around a dozen of his fellow hacks were already crowding the waiting room assigned for the briefing, and it wasn't long before a couple of passengers and two members of the on-board crew were ushered in to answer their questions. Despite or because of their official escort, all of them looked like they'd rather be somewhere else, and the stories that slowly emerged seemed less and less credible with each new question.

What had stopped the train? Nobody knew. A signal perhaps.

How did you know you were in the Polish Corridor? The Polish police had said so.

In Polish? No, they both spoke German.

So how did you know they were Polish? They were wearing Polish uniforms.

And did the gang of thieves speak Polish? No, they spoke German as well.

"As do most Poles who live in the Corridor," one official insisted with a notable lack of accuracy. "It was German land until 1918," he added, as though that settled the matter.

The briefing was ended, the witnesses hustled out, leaving most of the assembled pressmen shaking their heads in disbelief. Even the ones from the Nazi rags looked embarrassed, if only at the levels of incompetence on display.

"Why even bother?" one man asked Russell as they emerged back onto the platform. "The election's already won."

"Just pray they don't get better at it," another man said.

It occurred to Russell that the Nazis were already thinking ahead. Once all their domestic scapegoats were locked up they'd badly need some foreign ones. He took the story back to Kempka, and asked his advice on what to write.

"Nothing," the editor told him. "If they want us to print fiction as fact, they'll need a more convincing tale."

Which Russell supposed made sense. Telling the truth and exposing the lie would be to invite arrest. And probably doom the paper.

He signed off and left the building, freshly aware that his new job looked likely to prove short in either weeks or integrity. He told himself not to let it be both, and treated himself to a rueful smile.

What was he going to do with the rest of his day? He'd grown used to Saturday afternoons with his son, and the prospect of one without the boy left him feeling strangely bereft. A grown-up film, he decided, but first he needed to change his clothes.

The tram carried him up Markgrafenstrasse, crossing Leipziger Strasse and Unter den Linden. Strings of loudspeakers were being connected and checked on both these streets for Hitler's speech that evening, and on the corner of the former a stormtrooper was standing guard over an open crate of torches. Who was going to steal them? Rival medievalists?

He took the usual route home after leaving the tram on Müllerstrasse, and was relieved to see that someone had taken the corpses out of the Panke. His own street seemed unusually quiet for a Saturday, more like a Sunday in fact. Maybe the city was holding its breath ahead of tomorrow's result, or perhaps it was only him.

He managed to evade Frau Löffner on the way in, but not on the way out. "So how bad was it last night?" he asked her.

"They didn't come here," she said. "They surrounded the streets around Kosliner Strasse, and they went through every house. Every room and cupboard, I should think. People round here don't have much—you know that—and they just chucked stuff out of windows. Children's toys even." She paused, and visibly reined herself in. "Maybe they just got carried away, and went a bit too far. And there's good news too. Herr Klausener is back. He has a few bruises, and he seems very quiet, but you'd expect that. He'll get over it."

"Any news of Herr Habicht?"

"Not a word. But the way he fought them . . . well, I don't think he'll be back for a while."

If ever, Russell thought.

"Will your son be staying tonight?" she asked.

"No, his mother thinks it wiser to keep him at home."

"Very sensible."

"But I'll be seeing him tomorrow."

"Of course you don't have a vote, being a foreigner."

"I don't. But who will you be supporting?" Russell asked with a grin, doubting he'd get a straight answer.

"That would be telling. I just want an end to all this violence. Everyone does."

Which was fair enough, Russell thought, as he waited for a No.5 tram outside the Ringbahn station. Provided you could live with whichever side won. The ride through Charlottenburg seemed to take forever, though he wasn't in any real hurry. Getting off where the tram crossed the Ku'damm, he walked along the southern side to where the Ufa Theatre Pavilion and Marmorhaus faced each other across the boulevard. One was showing yet another Frederick the Great panegyric, the other a drama based on a poem by Ibsen. It was hard to work out which would be more depressing.

He walked on to the Gloria-Palast on Auguste-Viktoria-Platz, which was offering a thriller, *Salon Dora Green.* The poster outside featured a stern Paul Hartmann and a rakish-hatted Mady Christians above silhouetted men confronting each other. It looked run-of-the-mill at best, but Russell vaguely remembered a kind review. And the next showing was only ten minutes away. What the hell, he thought, and joined the queue.

The film was no better or worse than expected, and couldn't be accused of confronting its audience with anything real. Which, judging from the expressions on his fellow leavers, was exactly what they wanted.

Darkness had fallen outside, and the brightly lit Ku'damm looked like it always had, full of glamour and promise. The Romanisches Café was only a short walk away and Russell had a sudden urge to visit it again. The café had long been famous for its literary patrons. Writers like Brecht, Döblin, Kastner and Remarque had been regulars; the artist George Grosz had sat there and sketched them, and anyone else who took his fancy.

It wasn't as packed as it used to be, but most of the thousand tables were occupied. Russell grabbed one going empty close to the street, ordered a beer and meat dumplings, and surveyed the scene around him. It might be his imagination, but everything seemed subtly subdued, the conversations less energetic, conducted in something closer to whispers than ordinary speech, the gazes aimed at passers-by more anxious than interested.

His Patzenhofer arrived, and he sat there sipping and smoking a cigarette, remembering when he and Ilse had come here for a weekly treat, when Paul was still a baby, happily gurgling at anyone leaning over his pram. Good memories, he thought, and wondered if he'd have felt the same before his talk with Ilse that morning.

The mood was shattered by a squeal from the nearest loudspeaker, and with barely any preamble the new Chancellor launched himself into the usual peroration. Lock up the Reds and other traitors, send home the parasite foreigners, make the Fatherland strong again. And so on and so on, round and round, lie after lie feeding on well-chosen grains of truth.

Russell watched the faces around him, a few truly enthralled, most tight-lipped with vacant eyes, their minds apparently somewhere else. But this was the Ku'damm—across most of Germany the numbers would be reversed. An astonishing number of people actually believed this shit.

The SA were much in evidence now, patrolling the pavement, watching the faces, hoping that someone would laugh or curse when they shouldn't. Russell let his face assume the mask of grim reverence that the occasion required, and when the dumplings arrived a few minutes later found himself wondering whether he should wait for Hitler to finish before tucking in. Seeing that others were eating while ostentatiously listening, he allowed himself to do the same.

What had things come to? It was farcical. And also terrifying.

The voice soared and dipped, grated and pleaded, promising heaven, threatening hell. And finally it was silent, subsumed in the Leuthen chorale and the ringing of Königsberg church bells. The faces around him seemed to crack back open, the mouths unpursed, the eyes alive.

"Germany awake!" Russell muttered, but only to himself.

Sunday started foggy, but soon cleared. Russell treated himself, not to mention his family, to another bath across the road, and then spent the usual age searching through his wardrobe for something that looked half-decent. He would buy some new clothes when he got paid, if the new mattress left anything over. And Paul's birthday was coming up soon—he wanted to buy the boy something memorable.

Feeling hungry, and not wanting to wolf down his lunch, he stopped for a snack on Gerichtstrasse before heading across to the No.28 tram stop. Why was he feeling so nervous? He'd known all these people—all but Matthias—for almost ten years.

Passing the voting station on Nettelbeckplatz he noticed the several stormtroopers standing outside, but as far as he could see they weren't escorting voters in to help them with their choice. If they believed intimidating looks were enough, they were certainly mistaken—half of those coming back out had "fuck you" written all over their faces.

Not that it would matter. The result was a foregone conclusion, the defiance of places like Wedding not much more than a gesture. Hitler would probably get his Reichstag majority, and if by some chance he didn't, he'd keep jailing opposition deputies until he did.

The tram took him south to Schöneberg.

Ilse's brother Thomas lived on the edge of the so-called Bavarian Quarter, a relatively affluent district of ten or more streets that radiated out from Bayerischer Platz. The area was known for its high population of Jewish professionals, and as far as Russell could see the Nazis were letting them be for the moment—as yet there was none of the vicious graffiti that the SA had painted all over the Jewish working-class districts. As usual, class trumped everything else.

He rang the doorbell, and the man who was still his brother-in-law came down to let him in. Russell had liked Thomas since their first meeting, now almost a decade ago. Their different political allegiances—his to the KPD and Thomas's to the Social Democrats—had often led to arguments, but these had never really impinged on their mutual affection and trust, and once Russell had left the Party the friendship had only deepened.

Thomas worked for the family printing and publishing firm, and was set to become its director when his and Ilse's father retired that summer. Three years older than Russell, he had a lovely wife named Hanna and two delightful children, ten-year-old Joachim and seven-year-old Charlotte. The family was the happiest Russell had known—they all seemed at ease with themselves and so pleased to be living with one another. Their only problems, as Russell himself had observed, were the country and times that they lived in.

Thomas loathed everything about the Nazis, and despaired at the left's failure to fight them effectively. Not, as he ruefully acknowledged, that he had any answer himself. Now that the rule of law was a thing of the past, the only three options open to a man with socialist sympathies were keeping quiet, emigration and underground resistance. The first might be hard on the soul, but the others were a damn sight harder, particularly for a man with a wife and young children.

Russell had worried that his break-up with Ilse would compromise their friendship, but the worst that had happened was a form of compartmentalisation—the friendship had simply continued without its original family context. And now even that might be repaired. Thomas was the sanest person Russell knew, and the two of them shared more than most: a dry sense of humour, a love of discussion, a reluctantly burgeoning cynicism. Thomas always seemed so *grounded* to Russell, who often felt emotionally dimmer. And there was always the fact that they'd both been at Ypres, on opposite sides, unknowingly firing guns at each other across that dreadful blanket of unrecovered corpses. The war had left similar scars on them both, and they knew it.

Upstairs, the four-room apartment seemed full of milling children. Ilse's new partner, Matthias, greeted Russell with a broad smile and a firm handshake, and said, with what felt like sincerity, how glad he was to see him there. Ilse gave Russell a kiss on both cheeks, and a whiff of the perfume she had always favoured, before Paul burst between the two of them and grabbed his father's hand. "Come, please, I want to show you something."

The something was a Märklin model railway set. "It's Joachim's but he says I can borrow it," Paul said, picking up the locomotive with commendable care for a five-year-old.

"Have it, more likely," Thomas said quietly in Russell's ear. "It hasn't been out of its box in years."

Russell swallowed the thought that Matthias, not himself, would be helping Paul set it up.

"A drink," Thomas suggested, and the two of them went to join the other adults in the kitchen. Hanna was still at the stove, Ilse pouring aperitifs for the five of them. "Have you voted yet?" she asked her brother.

"For what it's worth," he affirmed.

"We did it on the way." She sighed, and raised her glass. "Well, here's to the upset of upsets."

After they'd clinked their glasses in sombre solidarity, Hanna announced that lunch was ready and that Thomas should round up the children. A few minutes later the eight of them were squeezed around a dining table made for six.

The pork schnitzel and warm potato salad was delicious—Hanna had always been a splendid cook, and how neither she nor Thomas ever put on weight was something of a mystery. Between courses Ilse and Thomas compared notes about their children's schools, and Joachim surprised everyone by suddenly announcing that several of his course books had been taken away by the teachers. Who hadn't told them why.

"They're not wasting any time," Thomas commented, as Hanna brought in an enormous *kirschtorte*.

The cake absorbed them for several minutes.

"So how's life on the crime desk?" Thomas asked Russell. "What stories have you been working on?"

Fredo's murder didn't seem appropriate for lunch time or children, and neither did the snow-shrouded scientist. He told them about the fictional Polish train robbers, and the ludicrous Nazi attempts to sell the story as fact.

"I read it," Matthias confessed, naming one of the Nazi-supporting papers. "And I thought at the time, this sounds a bit strange."

"Why would they do that?" Joachim asked, as if he couldn't believe it.

"They think getting their way is more important than truth," his father told him. "And because it works. Most people believe what they see in print."

"It must be very different being a reporter," Ilse said to Russell. "Different to doing your own research and writing things at home."

"And taking instructions from others," Thomas added with a grin. "Not something you're used to."

"Very true," Russell admitted. "But I like going out and talking to people. What I don't like . . . well, the way things are, it feels like I've arrived at a party just as it's breaking up. All the liberal editors feel like they're walking on eggshells, or waiting for the boom to drop—sorry, I'm mixing my metaphors. It's just—it's like my editor said the other day—most of our conversations these days are grounded in disbelief. How can this or that be happening? And yet it is.

A small group of utterly disgusting people have somehow managed to seize control of this country. I hardly meet anyone with a good word to say about them, but they're going to win this election, and God knows how bad it'll get. Our free press is already full of lies, and the next step will be to empty it of truth." Russell scanned the ring of gloomy faces. "Sorry, but you did ask."

Thomas laughed.

"I have to disagree with you on one point," Matthias said. "You said you hardly meet anyone who supports them, but I meet a lot. And I say with the greatest respect, that people like you and Thomas here . . ."

"Are not typical," Thomas interjected.

"You're not," Matthias said. "And you tend to discount those you think are wrong. Who you *know* are wrong. And I agree with you—they *are* wrong, at least about the Nazis. But when they say the republic has failed them, they're right, no matter how wrong they might be about the reasons. They see the effects, not the causes. And they believe there's a chance that Hitler will put the economy right, give them new jobs, that he'll help the little man. And that's what they care about. The things that upset us—the attacks on the Jews and the communists, the violence and the contempt for legality, the restrictions on the press—none of those things matter that much to people who feel they don't have a future unless things really change."

"But the Nazis don't have a magic wand," Russell objected.

"You know that. All of us around this table do. But most people don't."

"So how about some good news?" Hanna suggested.

"We want a dog," Charlotte said brightly.

"A big dog," her brother added.

"I'm not sure that counts as news," Thomas said. "Or good, for that matter."

"When we move, perhaps," Hanna told them.

"I didn't know you were moving," Russell said, wondering why Thomas hadn't told him.

"We're not, but we're thinking about it. Hanna wants a garden to grow vegetables. And I shall probably need one to bury the local *Blockleiter*, if our new one is any guide. He introduced himself yesterday, and gave me a complimentary flag."

Russell asked where they were thinking of moving to.

"Grunewald, most likely. Somewhere not far from the Ringbahn."

"We'll be moving that way too," Ilse added unexpectedly. "Matthias's father won't last much longer, I'm afraid, and when the time comes we'll be moving into his house to help take care of his mother." She smiled at her partner, and Russell found himself doubly struck, first by how happy she looked, and then by how unexpectedly pleased he felt to see her that way. She and Matthias seemed right for each other, in a way that he and Ilse never had.

The party broke up around five. Ilse's new family headed down the street to their car, Matthias carrying the train set box for Paul.

"Okay?" Thomas asked Russell, as they watched the car recede.

"More than okay," he replied.

Red Lili

Heading into work the next morning there was no escaping the election result. There seemed more swastikas than ever hanging from buildings, poles, lampposts, even the occasional tree. Several cars were sporting pennants on either side of their bonnets, and one enthusiastic tram crew had a flag billowing out on the roof of their vehicle. Russell knew that back in Wedding, and in the other working class districts, the mood would be mostly sombre, but riding his tram into the centre, most of the faces he saw on the pavements exuded an air of quiet satisfaction. This was the day, they seemed to say, when Germany finally turned a corner and got back on track. When the economy started growing again, when the jobs would start flooding back. An end to the long despair, an end to the country's humiliation. Hitler and his Nazis had won, and they would make Germany strong again.

Russell read through the details in a café on Alexanderplatz as he waited for the latest briefing from Glassl. The Nazis had won 43 percent of the vote, and with their Nationalist allies had a comfortable working majority in the new Reichstag. Over seventeen million Germans had voted for a party that prided itself on its use of violence for political ends, trumpeted its commitment to overturning the European peace settlement, and promised to remove the Jews from public life.

The only consolation was that twenty-two million people had voted for other parties. Seven million had voted for the socialist SPD, a staggering 4.8 million for the communist KPD, most of whose candidates had been under arrest or on the run. Of those Germans who'd chosen to vote, almost a third had opted for the parties of the left.

Not that it would matter, at least in the short run. The number voting against the Nazis might say something about German decency, but Hitler had his victory, and with all of the communists and many of the socialists effectively banned from taking their seats, he would have the two-thirds majority he needed to set aside any legal constraints. "Four years is all Hitler's asked for," as one young man had loudly told his wife or girlfriend on the inbound tram. "Four years without all the nay-sayers getting in the way," he had added rather ominously.

He wasn't the only one with nay-sayers on his mind. Kriminalinspektor Glassl still hadn't found Timo Baur, and neither had his colleagues in Stettin. The election had left him with too few officers to mount a successful manhunt, Glassl claimed, and Baur's fellow perverts had obstructed his city-wide search at every step. Some of them had been taken into custody, and would soon be facing charges of some sort. As for the fugitive, he was no doubt skulking in some Jewish cellar in Neukölln, waiting for his pervert friends to tell him that the coast was clear. In the meantime, the boy's picture—the one so blurry it could have been Josef Goebbels—was now on display in every Berlin and Stettin police station. Timo Baur *would* be caught.

Russell made his way to the *Morgenspiegel*, where an unmistakable pall hung over the newsroom. The election result, while politically disappointing to anyone on the left—or indeed anyone with brains or a shred of morality—had specific implications for Berlin's more liberal press. All those who worked for the *Morgenspiegel* knew that the owner and editor would now face the starkest of choices—abandon the paper's liberal principles and take a sharp turn to the right or find themselves closed down.

Hiedler, at least, seemed in a combative mood. After beckoning Russell into his inner sanctum, and pointedly telling him to close the door, the editor asked about the Ratzel case. "Kempka left me a note," he explained. "About an SA raid."

Russell went through his suspicions again, that the deployment of a high-ranking officer like Steimle on such a routine matter suggested the possibility—no more than that—of an even more senior officer's involvement in Ratzel's gruesome death.

"Perhaps it was Ernst Röhm," Hiedler said flippantly, with a glance at the door to make sure it was closed.

The SA leader certainly fitted the bill, Russell thought. A lover of violence and one of Glassl's "perverts."

"A good last story to run," Hiedler rhapsodised. "And it would be the last," he said, bringing himself back down to earth. "It might be worth it," he added, not even convincing himself. "Plus, there might be an obvious reason why the Kripo can't find Baur."

"The SA have him in one of their barracks."

"Or have killed him already."

Russell sighed. Here they were, in the newsroom of an old-established newspaper, casually assuming that the current forces of law and order had kidnapped and probably murdered a young man who was yet to be accused, let alone convicted, of an actual crime. It was astonishing how swiftly behaviour once considered beyond the pale had come to be the norm, and how seamlessly people had adjusted their expectations to the new political realities. "If the SA got to him first, that's the end of it," Russell conceded. "But if they haven't, and Baur knows they're after him, he might come to us as a last resort. If we print his name, and any accusations he has, that might be some protection." He looked at Hiedler. "I know Röhm would be a step too far, but I assume we'd take the risk of naming anyone who isn't that elevated, or so close to Hitler. Stressing, of course, that the man concerned must be a rotten apple in the wholesome SA barrel, one whom the SA would want to get rid of."

"You left your number with Ratzel's friends," Hiedler guessed.

"I did. And I'll visit them again in a couple of days."

"Good. In the meantime here's another story. One that I hope has no political ramifications." He handed Russell a single sheet of paper. "Three burglaries over the last fortnight, in Dahlem, Grunewald and now Schmargendorf. They were each investigated by a different division, so the common factor has only just come to light. The thief leaves a calling card—a playing card, in fact—and it's always the queen of hearts."

"Expensive, buying a whole pack of cards for each burglary," Russell commented.

Hiedler gave him a look. "Whoever it is has been reading too many English—what do you call them?—penny dreadfuls?"

"That's the Americans. I've forgotten what we call them."

"Whatever."

"What's he stealing?"

"Oh, the usual. Jewellery, cash, a painting from the house last night. The only thing unusual is the calling card, so make the most of that. A nice juicy mystery to take the people's minds off their new masters."

In Schmargendorf Russell found most of Berlin's crime reporters gathered round the Kriminalinspektor who'd just been given the case. His name was Handschuh, and he seemed less keen than Glassl to offer up information in exchange for self-publicity. The only titbit he offered the waiting hacks was the latest means of entry, which echoed that of the previous two: a diamond-tipped cutter and suction cup had been used to quietly remove a circular section of glass. The playing card had been left on the living room mantelpiece, and yes it was the queen of hearts, and yes it was the same make of cards as on previous occasions. The police would be visiting all shops where such cards were sold, and enquire after anyone buying in bulk.

Russell was underwhelmed, and sensed that most of his colleagues felt the same way. But this was the job, and off they went in shared taxis to interview victims, neighbours and other possible witnesses, all the while hoping in vain that a more intriguing story would turn up to claim their attention. Once back at the office, Russell searched through the archives for anything similar in days gone by, and found precisely nothing. He pumped up the story as best he could, laying out the relevant facts before letting his imagination off the leash. Did the queen of hearts represent the thief's lover, sat waiting at home with her growing pile of spoils? Or did she symbolise a great, unrequited love? Was he giving her Berlin by flooding the city with her likeness? Or could the thief be a woman? A special kind of woman of the night? A bored young princess perhaps, sheathed in black, tiptoeing through those very same mansions she had graced with her beauty only weeks or hours before?

More fiction than fact, Russell thought. But what the hell.

"I like your story," Hiedler told him later. "There are no Nazis in it."

By the time he'd eaten and caught the tram home it was almost ten o'clock, and until he encountered Frau Löffner an early night seemed in prospect.

"I'm glad you're back," she told him. "Herr Dickel is here."

"Who is he?" Russell asked, suspecting that he wouldn't like the answer.

"The new *Blockleiter*. He's talking to everyone in the block."

"They're not wasting any time, are they?" Russell observed. The Nazi *Blockleiter*, or block leaders, had appeared a few years earlier, as Party members given the job of drumming up votes in their local neighbourhood, and Hitler's new government had recently announced plans to expand and regularise the role, with a representative on every block.

"This one's jumping the gun," Frau Löffner was saying, in a disapproving tone. "He says he's just getting to know his charges, for when he takes up the job officially. Like we're all children in need of his guidance," she added in a whisper. "He's with Frau Allofs at the moment, and she won't take long. He's seen everyone else, so you'll be next."

Russell climbed the stairs, wondering how he should play it. There'd been a *Blockleiter* at his last address, but as a foreigner without a vote he'd rarely been bothered. Things would be different now. Loyalty and obedience to the new regime would certainly be monitored, and not by holding secret ballots.

He scurried round his rooms, checking for anything remotely seditious. Should he pose as the foreigner above the fray, a sympathetic neutral? Should he just play the Englishman, polite but stand-offish? Neither seemed right—the Nazis hated neutrals, and they didn't like being patronised. They loved foreign supporters, but anyone investigating his own past would find such a conversion hard to swallow. He was still in search of alternatives when the promised visitor arrived.

"Herbert Dickel," the man introduced himself. He was about Russell's age, tall, with a classic Nordic face and short blond hair parted down the middle. His brown outfit looked crisper and cleaner than the average stormtrooper's.

"Frau Löffner told me to expect you," Russell said with a welcoming smile. "Please come in. Have a seat."

"Thank you, but I'd rather stand," Dickel announced, his eyes sliding this way and that.

A sheet of paper in the German's right hand bore a list in Frau Löffner's recognisable scrawl, and Russell thought he could see question marks alongside some of the names. He decided he'd rather not have one next to his own.

"You are John Russell," Dickel said, consulting the list. "Born 1899, in Southampton, England."

"I was actually born at sea," Russell said helpfully, "the day before we docked at Southampton. My parents were returning from America," he added. "My mother is American."

"Ah. But she and your father live in England."

"No. My father died in 1925, and she returned home the next year."

Dickel blinked and changed the subject. "And you are a journalist. With the *Berliner Morgenspiegel*." A brief frown of disapproval here, though whether for pressmen in general, or his newspaper in particular, Russell couldn't tell.

"I'm a crime reporter," Russell volunteered. "Nothing to do with politics," he added, and instantly wished he hadn't.

"If there's one thing I've learned from the last few years, Herr Russell, it's that everything is political. Everything." Dickel was slowly circling the room now, staring at drawing and cupboards as though willing them to open. And then he stopped, his eyes drawn through the open bedroom door, as Russell had intended, to the bookmarked copy of *Mein Kampf* lying on the bedside stand. "Are you an admirer of our leader?" the *Blockleiter* asked.

"I think he has many interesting things to say," Russell offered, taking care not to sound too effusive. "Many insights," he added. "Germany is fortunate to have him."

"Indeed," Dickel said, as if that was beyond dispute. "I am assuming you have permission to live in Germany."

"I had an interview with Herr Mechnig at the Interior Ministry last week. The Resident Foreign Nationals section on Bendlerstrasse."

"That is good. But do you have papers you can show me?"

Russell gathered what he had together—his passport, his press card, his tax status.

"There is nothing here concerning your right to reside," Dickel told him.

"Ah. When I came here nine years ago things were different. I was given a temporary permit that needed renewal every six months. Or maybe every year, I really don't remember. But when I married a German national, that gave me the right to permanent residence. And the same for her in England."

"Do you have the marriage certificate?"

"I do."

Show me."

Russell dug it out of his officialdom drawer.

"And where is Ilse?" Dickel asked as he perused it.

"We're separated at the moment. She's staying with friends."

Dickel raised an eyebrow. "The people on Bendlerstrasse are aware of this?"

"They are. Herr Mechnig assured me that I only lose my right of residence if I divorce. I also have a German son," he added, thinking that if Dickel was a father that might induce some sympathy.

Dickel chewed on a thumbnail and stared at his list. "I have him here," he said with a faintly disapproving tone.

"Good," Russell said, wondering what he could say to ingratiate himself. "Tell me if I'm talking out of turn," he began, "but how do you see the *Blockleiter*'s role? As a crime reporter I'm interested in how neighbourhoods might be

organised more efficiently to combat the criminal ele-
ment."

Dickel looked surprised. "An interesting idea. I see myself
as making sure that everyone is on the same page, reading
the same book, so to speak, and that could apply to fighting
crime as easily as cleaning up our rotten politics. We have to
go forward together, united. There is a time for dissent—
after all, if our party had not given such a resounding no to
the traitor's republic, we would not now be leading a national
revival. But that time is now past. We will not leave anyone
behind, but neither will we let them hold us back. A common
purpose, yes? The people together will prove irresistible. Do
you not agree?"

Russell assured him he did, thinking how timely a spontaneous stiff-armed salute would have been, if only he could
have kept a straight face.

Dickel nodded, and at last made a move towards the
door. "Any problems with neighbours, come to me," he
said, turning in the open doorway. "I live at 37, apartment
4. And any suspicious activity, come to me."

Russell half-expected a line about the enemy never sleeping, but the man just gave him a wafer-thin smile and set off
down the stairs. Russell followed discreetly, waiting on the
first-floor landing for the sound of the front door closing,
then continued on down. "So what do you think?" he asked
the lurking Frau Löffner.

She grimaced. "He's very pleased with himself."

"He is, isn't he." And a bit of a fool, Russell thought.
Which didn't mean he wouldn't be trouble.

As far as the crime desk was concerned, Tuesday proved
relatively uneventful. The Queen of Hearts burglar had
presumably taken the night off; either that or his latest
victims were still unaware of their victimhood. Timo Baur
had not been apprehended, at least not by anyone who

wanted publicity. The only editor brave enough to both run and ridicule the Danzig train story had been arrested the previous evening and returned to his wife that morning, covered in blood and bruises. The paper's owners had announced his resignation in a statement as curt as it was craven.

Gathered in a café near the Alex, Russell and several other colleagues drew up new rules of guidance for Berlin's crime reporters. In the event of a crime being reported, a journalist should: find out whether (a) the SA was directly responsible, (b) the SA was linked to the crime in any way whatsoever, and (c) the SA gave a toss that the crime had been committed at all. And if no was the answer in all three cases, then the story should be fearlessly pursued.

There was lots of laughter, most of it bitter.

It turned into a day of expected announcements. Formal notice was given of a new Propaganda Ministry led by Hitler's "wizard with words," the oh-so-clever Doctor Goebbels. It seemed highly unlikely that the newly hung loudspeakers would ever come down.

The introduction of the promised Enabling Act was also said to be imminent, its approval by the new Reichstag more or less guaranteed. The bill would give legal cover to what was already happening—with all the levers of physical power at their disposal the Nazis could already do whatever they wanted with virtual impunity. The one thing that might hold them back was foreign disapproval, and in this regard too the day brought a straw in a wind. The government had held back a telegraphic dispatch by an American foreign correspondent, quoting in justification the International Telegraphic Convention of 1875. This stated that any government could "refuse to transmit any messages that might be injurious to the country." From now on the world would know less about what was going on in Germany, and that would certainly suit the Nazis. The cynic in Russell guessed it would please other governments too, because turning a blind eye would then be much easier.

He went back to Karl's that evening more in hope than expectation. There were fewer of the line boys there than before, and while they were all still looking their muscular best, the overall mood seemed deflated. Russell's round perked them up a bit, and they showed no reluctance to talk. Some of those arrested by the SA had been released, albeit in most cases bloodied and bruised. Others were still in custody, or at least they hoped so. And there had been a major falling-out among those not arrested, some of whom had moved their base of operations to another *Diele* down the street, one that stormtroopers patronised. "They know they'll get more beatings," as one boy put it contemptuously, "but they'll be on the winning side."

And to top things off, the New Karl's Lounge was being closed down. A nervous-looking owner had popped in earlier to give the barman his notice, and warn him that the SA intended to take possession early the following week. He had no idea what their plans for the premises were.

If there was any news of Timo, no one was letting on.

"They can't find him here or in Stettin," Russell told them. "Is there anywhere else he talked about?"

There wasn't.

It was over, Russell thought, as he made his way to the U-Bahn station. Timo Baur was dead, and his body would probably never be found. His SA murderers might think themselves untouchable, but why take the slightest risk if you didn't have to?

A sudden awareness of running feet behind him spun Russell around. It was one of the line boys, the thin one with red hair who had never uttered a word during Russell's visits to Karl's. "You nearly gave me a heart attack," he said, as the young man stopped beside him, breathing heavily.

"I just want to talk. Somewhere private," the line boy added, looking around. The pavements weren't busy, but neither were they empty. "I know somewhere," he said. "It's only a minute away."

"Okay," Russell agreed. It didn't feel like a scam, and he wanted to hear what the boy had to say.

The somewhere turned out to be an overgrown patch beside the local fire station. The only illumination came from a nearby streetlight, but Russell could see enough discarded sheaths and cigarette ends to know what the patch was often used for. He offered his companion one of his own cigarettes and hoped there were no Kripo hiding in the bushes.

The boy wasted no time being coy. His name was Adolf Jetzinger, "but everyone calls me Jet, because these days Adolf puts some punters off. Timo and me, we're partners. I mean, real partners, you understand?"

"You love each other," Russell guessed.

"Yeah, we do."

"Have you seen him?"

"Not since Fredo was killed. But he left a note where I sleep."

"And where's that?"

The alarm was instant: "Why do you need to know that?"

"I don't," Russell responded with equal alacrity. "Tell me what he said in the note."

"That's he's okay, and staying away from his own place and Karl's until the police find out who killed Fredo."

"He may have a long wait."

"That's what I think. But if he came to you, and told his story, could you keep him safe?"

"I would try," Russell said, resisting the temptation to simply say yes. "And if it didn't look like I could, I'd buy you both tickets to somewhere else."

As Jet considered this offer, Russell wondered why

he had made it. If Timo had a dynamite story to tell, it wouldn't be one the paper could print. So what was the point? The point was knowing, he realised. He wanted to know who had done that to Ratzel. There was something about these lost boys, something that made him ashamed.

"Okay," Jet was saying. "I know the places he likes to go. He must be sleeping in one of the parks, but he can't stay hidden all day—he'll need money for food, and that means punters."

"So you've been looking?"

"I went to Luna Park last night, after I got the message. We both love the place, and the punters pay well. I didn't see him, but I did get seen—the guards there like beating us up, so I don't want to go there again on my own. If you come with me tomorrow I'll be safer, and if we find Timo you can talk to him."

"What if the guards come after us both?" Russell asked.

"They won't. You look too . . . normal."

"You could look normal too," Russell said.

"I could try," Jet said, with the hint of a smile.

"But not tomorrow," Russell said, reluctant to sacrifice his precious hours with Paul.

"Thursday would be better for me," Jet said, without any explanation.

"Nine o'clock outside Halensee Station."

A slight hesitation. "Okay."

As Russell sat with his coffee on Wednesday morning, the sound of the band grew slowly louder. His newspaper had already informed him that the schools were closed that day "in honour of the patriotic cause," and here was the children's new occupation: marching up Unter den Linden in Nazi uniforms, learning nothing. Except, perhaps, what fools the adults in power were. Would Paul's be one of these earnest faces in seven or eight years' time? The prospect was appalling.

At the office the only fresh crime news—a small epidemic of SA assaults on American visitors—was news the paper was now forbidden to print, since it might prove "injurious to the country." The lack of any other reported criminal activity was more surprising—either the Nazis had succeeded in abolishing crimes or they were the only ones left committing them.

Hiedler sent him down to the archives to seek out new "Crimes of Old Berlin," an occasional series the *Morgenspiegel* ran when contemporary news was in short supply, and Russell waited in vain for some juicy new story to call him back up. Visiting the newsroom after his canteen lunch he learned that three political stories were vying for prominence. The Italian Ambassador had dropped in on Hitler to deliver the Duce's congratulations on the Nazis' electoral success, and Karl Liebknecht House, the old communist headquarters, had been formally occupied by the brownshirts. The SA leader in Berlin—the most appropriately named Count Helldorf—had vowed that for every stormtrooper killed in Berlin-Brandenburg three communists would be executed. Which was, Russell thought, a creative interpretation of the existing legal framework. The third story concerned Göring's new campaign against the "cult of nudism." Russell supposed the bloated bastard should be thanked, because the thought of Fat Hermann shedding his toga was enough to make anyone shudder.

After all this, his two hours with Paul were an unalloyed relief. What bliss, he thought, as his son chattered happily on about the toys he most wanted and the cars going by, to be so unaware of the darkness that threatened their world. Russell's thoughts strayed back to his own childhood, to Guildford before the war, years that had then seemed steeped in innocence, at least to a boy growing up.

The politics then had been almost as fierce, what with mass strikes, the struggles for pensions and sick pay, Irish Home Rule and the suffragettes, but at the time it had all passed him by. He'd been playing football, or riding his bicycle along the Wey, or suddenly having the girl across the street slip into his thoughts. And then the war had come, and even far from the fighting everything seemed changed. Another three years and he'd been in the trenches himself, watching bodies blown open in showers of blood and tissue.

He prayed that his son would be spared such horrors, but remembering the morning's parade, found himself fearing the worst. He warned himself not to let the future cloud the present—even the Nazis would shrink from conscripting five-year-olds.

Back on Wilhelmsaue, Russell got a surprise—it was Matthias, not Ilse or the maid, who came to the door. "Do you have a few minutes?" Ilse's new partner asked him. "There's something I'd like to talk to you about."

"Of course," Russell said, feeling reluctant but knowing he couldn't refuse. Matthias probably wanted some sort of date for the prospective divorce, and Russell could see his point. He would just have to make Matthias see his. Herr Mechnig could not have been clearer.

Paul had vanished, and there was no sign of Ilse as Matthias led Russell through to a large room full of books, polished wood and leather-covered furniture. The books were mostly on science or nature, not the sort that Russell—or Ilse in the old days—would have had on their shelves. There was a wide window behind the capacious desk, but by this hour the only things visible were the lights from distant houses.

They both sat down, Russell in the solitary armchair, Matthias in the middle of the sofa. "I have a friend," the latter began, confuting the former's expectations. "Wilhelm Zollitsch. We were in the war together, officers in the same regiment. He comes from a more aristocratic background than I do, but that didn't seem to matter at the time—one of war's few saving graces, I always thought. We both came through it, I in large part because of him—when a shell threw me up in the air and I broke both legs coming down, it was him that carried me out of the fire-zone. By the time my legs had healed the war was over.

"And we remained friends, despite living on opposite sides of the country. Not close friends—a letter or two each year—but there were, there are, things we both remember that no one else could share. You understand?"

"I do," Russell said simply, thinking that he and Ilse could say the same of their comrades' marriage.

"Wilhelm stayed on in the army after the war." Matthias paused to look round his opulent study, as if to confirm that his decision not to pursue a military career had been the right one. "He's a colonel now. When he was posted to the General Staff in 1929, he and his family moved to Zossen, and we started seeing each other again. Ever since then we've met up every few months for a drink or a meal. We did so on Monday.

"He's several years older than I am, and he and his wife, Dagmar, had a daughter, Lili, just before the war. Wilhelm's wife died in the flu epidemic when Lili was still a small child, and the girl was brought up by nannies and governesses. Her relationship with her father has been, well, difficult is the word he uses. She's always been headstrong, and he says he used to find it enchanting, but that as she grew older the enchantment turned to exasperation, and lately even to anger. They still share the same house, but they hardly talk to each other anymore, and he's been worried about what she gets up to. You know what Berlin has to offer the young—or did until recently—and I think he imagined her getting pregnant or dying of a heroin overdose. But when the bad news came, it was something

else entirely—she'd fallen in love with a young communist
and joined the Party. And now she's disappeared. And he
needs help to find her."

Which is where I come in, Russell thought.

"I said I'd talk to you because you might still have contacts who would know where to start looking."

"Among the communists?"

"And the police."

The idea of seeking out communists while the Nazis were
doing the same did not appeal to Russell. It would endear
him to neither, and involve visiting parts of Berlin where
the chances of his being arrested or killed were alarmingly
high. The doubts must have shown on his face.

"My friend is a rich man," Matthias said almost apologetically, as if worried that this might not endear his friend
to Russell. "And I'm sure he will pay whatever is necessary
for any news of Lili. Good or bad."

"Why not approach the Nazis directly?" Russell wanted
to know.

"Because that would mean revealing that his daughter is
a communist. And there's no love lost between the SA and
the regular Army. It might make things worse."

Perhaps it would, Russell mused. The thought of earn-
ing a large sum of money was certainly alluring, as Matthias
must have known it would be. Russell swallowed the pang of
resentment—the man was just trying to help his friend. "But
what about the girl?" he asked. "If she's really committed she
won't want to come home. And she won't take kindly to some
stranger seeking her out. Nor will her comrades."

"I think Willi probably knows all that. He doesn't want
her to come rushing home—well, he probably does, but he
knows that's not very realistic. He just wants to know she's
safe."

Russell grimaced.

"Just alive would be something," Matthias insisted. "Go

and see him. He lives in Grunewald now, so it'll only take a few hours of your time."

Russell sighed. "I'll go and see him, but I can't promise anything. Most of the comrades I knew—who Ilse and I knew when we were still in the Party—she must have told you this: after we left they wanted nothing to do with us. I stayed on just-about-friendly terms with a few, but I haven't seen any for quite a while. And I've no idea where I'd find any one of them now. If they've any sense they'll be in Sweden or France, and if they're not . . ." Russell shrugged. "It's not as though I can visit Karl Liebknecht House and ask to look at the membership list."

"I understand that," Matthias said. "But . . ."

"I'll see him," Russell repeated. For the money, for a girl who might well be in over her head, for her distressed and probably undeserving father. And, as Russell admitted to himself, to have Matthias in his debt, and more patient than he might otherwise be when it came to Ilse's divorce.

They were all good reasons, Russell thought as he made his way back to Wedding. But were they good enough? He told himself he could still say no.

Back at Gerichtstrasse, Frau Löffner had taken a telephone message from his friend Ulrich Beyschlag, inviting him round to dinner that Friday. Ulrich and his wife, Olga, were also ex-communists, but almost aggressively so, and unlikely to be of any help. He hadn't seen them for weeks, but then he hadn't seen any other friends either.

He hadn't wanted to. It was partly his own situation post-Ilse, feeling sorry for himself, resenting the transparent efforts friends made to pair him with suitable women. It was partly the times. All conversations either started or ended with the Nazis, how dreadful they were, how helpless everyone felt, how wonderful it would be if they could all wake up from this nightmare. But they wouldn't. Things were not going to get better for what looked like a

very long time, and that half of the population that hated
everything the Nazis stood for and did would just have to
wait it out. To make sure they survived, their humanity not
too tarnished.

It occurred to Russell that who you knew was going to be
even more important than usual. A grateful Army colonel
might be very useful.

Having taken down Russell's number at work, Matthias rang
him next morning. Zollitsch would like to meet him as soon
as possible, either at his home in Grunewald or at some
other place of Russell's choosing. As he was meeting Jet in
nearby Halensee at nine, Russell suggested the colonel's
home at seven. Matthias passed on the address, and said he
would let his friend know when Russell was coming.

After an early supper of smoked pork chops and mash,
Russell took the tram out to Grunewald. The colonel's
small villa was two streets away from the Blau-Weiss Tennis
Club, and close to the edge of the forest. A large and beautiful cedar rose high above the building, and a gleaming
burgundy Horch stood in front of the open garage, as if
expecting an urgent summons.

It all felt a long way from Wedding or Neukölln, or
wherever the daughter had landed in search of something
different.

A middle-aged housekeeper answered the door, and
escorted him through to a room at the rear, where the colonel was waiting. He almost leapt to his feet, offered a hand,
and solemnly thanked Russell for coming. "A schnapps," he
suggested. "I already have one," he added with a smile.

Russell accepted. Zollitsch was probably approaching
fifty, well-built with thinning hair above a friendly face. At
first sight, at least, he was not what Russell had expected.
There was nothing of the stick-up-the-arse Prussian ste-
reotype about him, nothing that cried out "disciplinarian

father." He wasn't in uniform, and the room wasn't full of military souvenirs, battle maps and portraits of dead generals. The only painting on the wall was of a lovely but rather sad-looking woman in her twenties. The dead wife, Russell assumed.

"Lili looks a lot like her," Zollitsch said, reading his mind. "But that's where the resemblance ends," he added wryly.

Russell could already see why Matthias liked the man—there was self-awareness at work, allied no doubt to a sharp intelligence. Zollitsch would hold one of those unsung General Staff jobs that made everything run smoothly, and be extremely good at it. "Matthias says you want me to find your daughter," Russell said.

The colonel nodded. "I appreciate that may not be easy, and may even prove dangerous. But if you are willing to look for her, I will pay for your time and any expenses, and throw in a substantial bonus if and when you bring me news of where she is."

The figures he quoted seemed over-generous, and Russell's face must have shown as much.

"I can afford it," Zollitsch said. "One thing about life in the military—there are limited opportunities to spend your pay. But I should tell you that you won't be alone in looking for her. I have already hired a man named Höschle, a retired policeman whom another friend recommended. He knows the city and has many contacts at the Alex, which should give him an advantage. But he has never moved in communist circles, and knows no one who could help him there. According to Matthias, you do."

"I did," Russell said, wanting to be clear. "Anyone still in 'communist circles' is either in hiding or on the run. The best I can say is that I have some idea where to look."

"Understood," Zollitsch said.

"Then the first thing I'll need is a photograph."

Zollitsch reached for the album beside him and passed it

across. "The last picture in there was taken on her birthday, January fourteenth."

She was standing in the snow, a thick scarf wrapped around her neck and long blond tresses. Her face was like her mother's, with large expressive eyes, a small straight nose, and a mouth that doubtless looked more generous when she wasn't pursing her lips so hard. There was a picture on the opposite page of her in a running costume, breaking the finishing tape on what looked like a sports day race.

"She's always been very athletic," her father said, following Russell's gaze.

His expression was revealing—this was a man who loved his daughter but had no idea who she was. A poor father, Russell thought, but not because he didn't care. Because he didn't know how to be better.

"And I've failed her," Zollitsch said, as if he could hear Russell's thoughts. "I do realise that. But my feelings are neither here or there. It's Lili you need to know about, and I wish I could tell you more. But, to be brutally honest, I know next to nothing about the life she has lived these last few months."

"Do you know anything about the boy she's fallen in love with?"

"His first name is Ewald, and his father used to be a mayor. She didn't mean to tell me either—we were arguing, shouting almost, and I think she said that about the father to show me that the boy came from a respectable family."

"She didn't say where the father was a mayor?"

"No."

"Well, if it was one of the Berlin districts, he shouldn't be hard to track down. There aren't that many, and finding a mayor with a son named Ewald shouldn't be too difficult. Though if he was a communist mayor he's probably under arrest, and if he wasn't he may not know where his son is. I'm sorry," Russell said, "I'm just thinking out loud."

"It's somewhere to start," Zollitsch said.

"Okay."

"And Höschle wants to meet you, to coordinate your search. Here's his telephone number—his block number, I believe." Zollitsch passed across a slip of paper.

"Can I call him from here?"

"Why not? The telephone's in the hall."

It took the best part of ten minutes for Höschle's grumbling *Portierfrau* to fetch him, only a few seconds to arrange a meeting the following day. The man sounded less than enthusiastic, but then people in his line of work weren't known for their *joie de vivre*.

Back in the living room, Russell felt obliged to give the colonel a warning. "Your daughter and this young man may have been arrested by the regular police, but if they are in custody, it's much more likely that they're being held by people who have no time for the usual legal channels. Since the Fire thousands of communists have been detained in unauthorised barracks and camps. Perhaps a thousand in Berlin alone." And hundreds of those would already be dead, Russell thought but didn't say.

Zollitsch's eyes narrowed, and for a moment the father became the soldier. "I do read the papers. I know what's happening in places like Neukölln. And no, I don't approve. And not just because my daughter might be a victim. Understand me—I hate communism, always have, but the Nazis are no better. God knows, they may even be worse. I'm a democrat, one of those soldiers who stayed with the army in 1918 because we didn't want the Freikorps and their right wing friends to take it over completely. I believe in elections, and anyone's right to stand in them. Including the communists. I think their views are mistaken, but holding them shouldn't be a crime."

Russell agreed, but that world was gone. He wrote down

his *Morgenspiegel* number while Zollitsch filled out a cheque, and told the colonel to call him if anything useful came to mind, or if Lili got in touch. "One last thing," he added, as Zollitsch took him to the door: "I can't force her to come home if she doesn't want to."

"I understand. I just want to know where she is, and whether or not she needs my help."

And that was that. Russell walked slowly back to the tram stop on Hohenzollerndamm, where he took out the cheque to make sure of the figure, and barely resisted the shameful impulse to pump the air with a fist.

A tram soon arrived, and he was outside the Halensee Station with plenty of time to spare. Which was all to the good—even though night had fallen, Jet would be nervous of waiting alone in such a public place.

Assuming he came at all. Nine o'clock came and went with no sign of the boy, and the temperature was dropping sharply. Russell was close to giving up when Jet emerged from the station, nervously glancing this way and that but at least looking less like a line boy than he had two days before. With shorter hair, drabber clothes and eyes devoid of make-up, he looked almost normal. "If Timo sees me like this, he'll run a mile," was his response to Russell's smile.

They crossed the Ku'damm and walked down Bornimer Strasse to the nearest Luna Park entrance, where Russell bought the tickets. He and Paul usually had to queue on their Saturday visits, his son's excitement mounting as he listened to the sounds coming over the wall, but freezing Thursday evenings were clearly less popular. Once inside Russell could see that the restaurants and taverns were doing decent business, but many of the stalls had no customers, their tenants moodily staring out at the night. The uniformed stewards were present in their usual numbers, but none seemed unduly interested in Jet.

The two of them walked slowly past the artificial basin, where the water slide had deposited its happily screaming patrons in the old pre-war park, Jet hungrily scanning the open spaces for any sign of Timo. The mountain railway was apparently the latter's favourite ride, and they waited by its exit gate to watch the latest set of riders come out. There were only a few of them, and all in mixed couples.

Next they tried Timo's favourite bratwurst stall, where Russell brought them both rolls, and the holder admitted he hadn't seen their quarry for at least a week.

Which didn't sound hopeful. They continued on round the park, skirting the end of the Halensee, where the new water slide wasn't working, and tried their luck on one of the shooting ranges. After an hour they were back at the Mountain Railway, and after watching another train arrive without Timo, Russell was ready to call it a day.

"He loves the fireworks," Jet insisted, but it turned out that these had been cancelled as well. "Only at weekends," a steward told Russell, with the air of someone who knew his job would soon be gone.

"We can come back on Saturday," Jet said as they left.

"Sunday," Russell told him, wondering if his son would want to come on Saturday. He rather hoped not. The place was becoming depressing, and he didn't want Paul involved in his work life, knowingly or not.

The Alex seemed slightly less frenetic on Friday morning, the SA presence less numerous. While an optimist might have assumed that things were returning to normal, Russell thought it more likely that the brownshirts now had locations enough of their own for holding and questioning those they considered enemies.

Kriminalinspektor Glassl was surprised but not displeased to see him. "We've found the queer's cock," he announced. "Floating in the Humboldt Hafen, tied up in a bag. At least,

we're assuming it's his. It's still pretty big, even after a week
in the water."

"No distinguishing marks, I suppose?"

"None."

A pity, Russell thought. He'd been thinking that a revealing tattoo might be the reason the cock had been taken
away. "And no sign of Timo Baur?" he asked.

"Not as yet."

"I'm sure you'll find him eventually," Russell said,
before turning to the real reason for his visit. "Off the
record, can you tell me anything about these detention
centres that the SA are setting up? I have a personal interest," he added quickly, as Glassl's expression hardened. "A
friend of a friend has a daughter who's foolishly fallen in
love with a communist—she's not oneself of course—and
now she's disappeared. The father is desperate to find out
if she's been arrested.

Glassl shook his head. "I can't help you there. If people
play with fire . . ." He shrugged. "The accounting that's now
going on . . . well, when the laws are out-dated, illegal meth-
ods can sometimes seem appropriate. But it won't last for
long. Once something's been cleaned, it's clean. And that's
that." He shrugged again. "In the meantime . . ." The look
and straightened back encouraged Russell to consider the
subject closed.

He took the hint and was on his way downstairs when
he ran into the Kriminalinspektor in charge of the Queen
of Hearts case. And much to Russell's surprise, Handschuh
gave him the broadest of smiles. "I loved your bored princess," the detective told him.

There was something trustingly old-school about
Handschuh, and after making sure there were no fresh
developments in the Queen of Hearts case, Russell risked
raising the matter of the SA detention centres.

Handschuh's quick look over his shoulder offered a

classic example of what Thomas had told Russell was now called *"der Deutsche Blick,"* the German glance. These days it paid to be sure that no one was listening.

"Come to my office," the detective said.

They walked up the two flights in silence, and Handschuh made sure to close the office door behind them.

"What do you want to know?" he asked, taking the seat behind his desk and gesturing Russell into the other.

"Off the record—whatever you can tell me about these places." Looking around, Russell decided that Handschuh's office was the neatest he'd come across in all his visits to the Alex.

"Too much and too little. They've been springing up all over the city, not just in the areas you'd expect. The obvious places are SA barracks and storm bars, but they're also in abandoned factories, old communist offices, unoccupied houses, even a couple of disused churches. There's no registration process, and the first we know of one is when some neighbour or passer-by tells the local Kripo that they've heard something." The detective grimaced. "Screams, more often than not. An officer gets sent to the building in question, and is told to mind his own business. If he's one of the good ones, he reports it to his superiors, and they to theirs. All the way up to Göring, for all I know. But nothing ever gets done."

They sat in silence for several moments. "So finding out who the SA are holding . . ."

"Like looking for a needle in a haystack. If the SA are keeping records—a big 'if' I would say—then they won't be showing them around. Not to us, and certainly not to the press."

"Right."

"They do release people. Usually much the worse for wear, but they do get out. Some have even come here to complain." Handschuh smiled, presumably at the naiveté. "So I guess you could talk to them, ask if they've run into the girl you're looking for. But it's still a needle in a haystack. There are dozens of these places."

Russell had a mental picture of Nazi Berlin as painted by Hieronymus Bosch: a grid of peaceful tree-lined streets, and in the lacunae between them, people screaming their heads off, shackled to wheels of fire.

"I don't suppose you know where she was arrested?" Handschuh was asking. "Because that would narrow the search."

"I'm not even sure she has been. It just seems likely."

"You've got your work cut out."

"I think we all have," Russell said sombrely. "But thanks for your help."

"You're welcome."

On reaching the office he noticed that Hiedler looked more depressed than usual, and soon found out why. "Yesterday it was the foreign correspondents all being lectured and threatened," the editor exclaimed. "And today it's our turn. I've just had the *Tageblatt* editor on the phone: the bastards are shutting him down for four days."

"Why?"

"Specifically? Because he published an editorial this morning suggesting that the government's commitment to legality is pure pretence, and that all these "unauthorised arrests" that Göring and Co. are so keen to lament must be officially sanctioned. And generally, because shutting one editor up will scare the pants off the others."

"The *Tagenblatt* is farther to the left than the *Morgenspiegel*."

"You think the Nazis are that discerning?"

"Maybe not."

"You bet not. They're giving us a choice: either die in the open or die inside."

Or both, Russell thought. This was becoming a gem of a week. "So which sword are we falling on today?"

Hiedler laughed. "The Jewish one, I guess. You heard what happened yesterday in Essen?"

"I did." The Nazis had successfully picketed all the Jewish-owned stores in the city centre.

"Well, they're at it here today. The Tietz store in Neukölln and the Kaufhaus des Westens. We've got people at both, but they won't see anything new—lots of BUY GERMAN signs, a crowd of idiots letting off steam, the police doing nothing. And how do we report it? A few weeks ago we'd have quoted the official line, and then balanced things up by quoting a doubter, imaginary or otherwise. But now even the suggestion that there might be another valid point of view is considered seditious. Our only remaining option is to criticise individuals for going too far and making the government and country look bad. And in doing that, we implicitly accept the idea that there's such a thing as an acceptable racial boycott. Which there fucking isn't!"

Russell didn't know whether to laugh or howl.

"All right," Hiedler said, once he'd taken a moment to calm down. "Let's pretend we're still living in a civilised country. Have you got any updates for me?"

"None," Russell told him. The recovered cock was unprintable, and probably best left unmentioned. "Is there anything new for me?"

"Take your pick," Hiedler said, handing across two notes, which Russell took back to his desk.

The Charlottenburg Kripo had arrested a stagehand at the Ku'damm theatre after a spate of backstage robberies—there wasn't much to the story but some of the people involved were famous.

A bank manager in Friedrichshain had absconded with most of his customer's cash, and the police had watchers at all the main stations. He had probably taken off from

Tempelhof yesterday, Russell thought. If the man was Jewish they could lead with the story; if his customers were, it probably wouldn't get printed.

Russell spent the day filling both stories out, and after handing the copy in headed up Friedrichstrasse for his meeting with Höschle. The buffet under the Stadtbahn station was crowded, but the ex-policeman was seated as promised, deep in a corner and reading the *Abendpost.* About fifty-five, he was wearing a well-worn suit and heavy-looking boots. His head was probably bald under the homburg, the grey moustache verging on over-flamboyance. The eyes looked sleepy for six in the evening.

"I've nothing much to tell you," was Höschle's opening offer. "I've been speaking to contacts at the Alex and some of the district stations, but so far I've found no trace of the girl. I assume you'll look for the boyfriend's father, and talk to him if you can."

"I will. What about the unofficial detention centres? Have you got any contacts in the SA?"

"A few," Höschle said, sounding evasive. "It's true that there are people being held in those places . . ."

"Most of those arrested I would say."

"Oh I doubt that. And sooner or later they'll all have to be brought back into the system."

"Maybe," Russell agreed, not wanting to antagonise the man.

"So you have my number. If you'll give me yours?"

Russell wrote down the Gerichtstrasse number, and reached for his hat.

Höschle wasn't done. "What did you think of Zollitsch?" he asked.

"I thought he seemed a decent man."

"He seems to think this is all his fault, and maybe he's right. If I had a daughter act the way his has, I think I'd wash my hands of her."

"Do you have children?" Russell asked.

"Yes," Höschle said in a tone that deterred further questions.

Russell wondered what they had done. "I'll be in touch," he said, getting up. It had been a full day, and as he made his way to the U-Bahn entrance he found himself regretting his acceptance of the Beyschlags' invitation to dinner.

He and Ilse had met the couple in 1925, after a move across the city had led to their joining a new local branch of the KPD. They were all roughly the same age, and Ulrich, like Russell, had served through the final year of the war, though of course on the other side. Now he was an administrator at the new St. Joseph Hospital in Tempelhof, which was only a ten-minute walk from the couple's small apartment near Viktoria Park.

Olga, whom Russell had always thought the brighter of the two, taught English at a secondary school a similar distance away. It was she who let Russell in. "It's only us," was the first thing she said. "A friend from work was coming, but her father's been taken ill."

"I'm sorry to hear that," Russell said, feeling secretly relieved. "About the father, I mean. Just the three of us is fine by me."

"Good," Ulrich said emerging from the bedroom, "but first you have to say hello to the dragon." A giggle could be heard from behind him.

Russell spent several minutes with four-year-old Lucie, enjoying her ingenious descriptions of the characters' motives in her newest picture book. When he re-emerged, Ulrich was setting the table and Olga busy stirring something in the kitchen. On the way over Russell had taken the conscious decision to go easy on the politics, but it turned out his hosts had other ideas, and were indeed relishing the presence of someone they could bounce their ideas off.

"I think it will pass," Ulrich said. "But something needed

to change. The country needed . . . oh I don't know . . . it needs to rally itself. As a nation we've lost all our confidence, and people without it struggle to be kind. Maybe Hitler's our best hope of getting it back. Once he's done so . . ."

"We can thank him and tell him goodbye," Olga interjected from the kitchen.

"Yes, but don't say that too loudly," Ulrich joked. "Did you hear what happened in Moscow on Wednesday?" he asked Russell.

"No."

"It only got reported in the socialist papers, and there's only a few of them still publishing. The shop on Dudenstrasse where I get mine has them hidden beneath the counter, along with the nude magazines. Anyway, Moscow has finally caught up with everyone else. They're calling for a working alliance of communists and socialists—common self-defence forces, joint demonstrations and strikes, etc etc. Can you believe it?"

"We have a saying in England about closing the stable door after the horse has bolted."

Olga laughed. "I like that."

"It feels like speaking ill of the dead," Ulrich went on. "But the KPD is finished. In more ways than one. People won't trust them again. Or the SPD, who've been just as sectarian. Like it or not, we've got the Nazis for years, so the only question worth asking is how we push them in a better direction? They are human beings. Most of them, anyway."

"Do you know about the SA detention centres?" Russell asked.

"Everyone does," Ulrich said. "They're a stain on . . . on whatever Germany likes to think it is. But I don't see what we can do about them. The bastards have won, and we have to live with their victory. Or Olga and I do. You could go back to England."

"Not with my son."

"No, of course not. I wasn't thinking."

"I have to live with their victory too. But maybe you're right and things will get better now that they feel secure."

"We can only hope," Ulrich said with smile.

Russell could see that making the best of things was a sensible way to go, especially when you did the sort of work that they did. Hospital administration was as politically neutral a job as one could hope for. Unless he was ordered to line up handicapped children for enforced sterilisation—one of the Nazis' more outlandish ideas—Ulrich was unlikely to be faced with any great moral dilemmas. And neither was Olga with her English-teaching—learning other languages wasn't politically charged. As long as they kept their heads down, these two could bring up a family and lead what most people thought was a normal life. Unlike himself, Russell thought. Anyone wanting a quiet life in Hitler's Germany could hardly have a worse job than his.

Olga was announcing it was time to eat, and carrying plates of dumplings and spätzle to the table. Once seated they toasted "a better future" with the Riesling Russell had brought, and spent the next ten minutes enjoying the food. Their conversation, when it resumed, did not return to politics. They talked about the past, about people they'd known, about their work and their children. Olga asked Russell how things were with Ilse, and seemed really pleased that they were better. The three of them discussed the latest films, plays and books, and Ulrich insisted on their listening to his latest jazz recordings, "while we still can."

It was all very enjoyable, and Russell was glad that he'd come, but there was something slightly out of kilter, something missing or unspoken, which he couldn't quite put his finger on. At one point Olga mentioned that she wasn't sleeping well, and rejected Ulrich's suggestion that their daughter's troubled nights were the cause. "I think it's the anxiety," she said. "Not knowing how bad things are going to get."

Ulrich squeezed her hand. "It'll settle down," he told her.

The look she shared with Russell suggested otherwise. When he was leaving a little while later, a question occurred to him: "I don't suppose you've run into any old comrades during the last couple of weeks? The ones who stayed in."

"Funny you should say that," Ulrich said. "I was in Neukölln last week, doing some shopping, and I was heading back down Bergstrasse towards the U-Bahn when I saw Bruno Aretin on the other side of the street. He was going in the opposite direction, and I think he saw me at the same time because he speeded up a little. I thought at the time he looked like a hunted man—you know, collar up, head down."

"You never mentioned it," Olga said accusingly.

"No, I didn't. I felt guilty, as though I was somehow letting him down."

As Russell passed Herr Klausener's door on his way up to bed, he noticed the ribbon of light underneath it, and had what was probably a foolish idea. "Nothing ventured," he murmured to himself, rapping his knuckles on the polished wood.

He could almost hear the hesitation inside, before the door cracked open and two timid eyes peeked out. "Herr Russell," Klausener said, clearly relieved to see it was him.

"Could I talk to you for a minute? Inside would be better."

The relief went out of the eyes. "I suppose so, but . . ."

"Thank you," Russell said, moving a foot across the threshold.

Klausener reluctantly let him into the room. "I was about to turn in," he said.

The man did look tired, and several years older than he had last week. "This won't take a minute," Russell said, his eyes taking in the two empty bookshelves. "I just have one question for you."

"Yes?"

"Where did the SA take you?"

Klausener looked startled. "W-why do you want to know that?"

"I have a friend who hasn't been released," Russell lied. "From farther up the street. He was arrested the same night you were."

"You won't get him out."

"Probably not. But his wife will at least know where he is."

Klausener just stared at him, a tear running down one cheek.

"I won't tell her who told me," Russell promised.

Klausener closed his eyes. "It was the old factory on Badstrasse, the one where they use to make safes. Behind the police station."

"I know it. Thank you. That's all I wanted to know."

"I'm going back to Hamburg," Klausener volunteered, as he showed Russell out. "I have relatives there," he added, as if they might make all the difference.

After the door closed behind him, Russell paused on the landing outside. The urge to continue on up the stairs was strong, but the need to see for himself proved stronger. He walked back down, and out into the night.

The streets were mostly empty, just a few people heading home after working a late shift or having a drink. Wedding went to work early, even on a Saturday, and most of its residents would be in bed by now. There were no distant sounds of trouble, but Russell knew he was running a risk just by being out alone. The SA hated everyone but each other, and at this time of night they'd mostly be drunk, and looking for someone to grind in the dust. An English journalist would be manna from heaven.

His destination was less than a mile away. As he neared

the end of Uferstrasse he could see the police station up
ahead, the factory looming behind it. The station was in
darkness, but there were many dimly lit windows in the
building beyond. He stopped for a moment and almost
turned back, but forced himself onward, albeit ready to
run at a moment's notice. He could hear the Panke softly
rippling in its gully on the other side of the street, and wondered if the stream would offer the best escape route. Was
that what the two men who'd died had thought?

He decided he would walk past the factory and on to
the busy Osloer Strasse, whose lights he could see in the
distance. He wasn't sure what to expect, but the yard full of
lorries bearing swastika flags was certainly no surprise.

And then, as if on cue, the scream he'd imagined cut
through the night air. Slightly muted by walls and shuttered
windows, but leaving no room for doubt.

Russell stood there, frozen to the spot.

A second scream followed about fifteen seconds later,
and a third after that, longer and even more anguished.

Russell didn't know what to do. The thought crossed his
mind that he'd never been more frightened. Not for himself,
and not even physically. It was nothing like the piss-running-
down-your-legs fear he'd experienced in the trenches.

Maybe frightened wasn't even the word. He was standing
outside a building in which a man was screaming his heart
out, and there was nothing he could do about it. It was just
the way Handschuh had said. If he banged on a door the
best he could possibly hope for was a short and sweet "fuck
off"; the much more likely outcome involved being dragged
inside and given ample reason to scream himself.

There was no one he could appeal to with any chance of
success. Not in this building, not *anywhere*. Not at the police
station, not at the courts, not among his fellow citizens,
who were all as frightened as he was by the probable price
of even the slightest defiance. Not at his newspaper office,

where crimes of the state were already unreportable. There was no father one could run to, no mother who would set things right. Perhaps, he thought, it was as basic as that.

The "rule of law" had always seemed an abstract concept, one that he believed in, and had more or less taken for granted. Its absence was anything but abstract. It was screams in the night, with no hope of rescue.

A door to the yard suddenly opened, spilling yellow light and a couple of laughing brownshirts. As they climbed into one of the cabs, Russell headed back the way he had come, keeping to the shadows of the trees that lined the Panke, forcing himself to walk when all he wanted to do was run.

The Ungrieving Widow

After a night of broken sleep Russell woke later than usual. An overcast sky would have suited his mood, and the sunlight slanting in through the window seemed almost insulting. After staring at the ceiling for several minutes he managed to convince himself that getting out of bed would be better than the alternative.

What he would do with the day was another matter. It was his first Saturday off work, which should have meant more time with Paul, but Ilse was still wary of letting their son sleep in Wedding, and had suggested that his father spent most of Sunday with him instead. Somewhere that wasn't a stormtrooper playground.

Which might make perfect sense, but still didn't feel right. Russell told himself that the situation wouldn't last for ever, that, in Ulrich Beyschlag's words, things would "settle down" eventually. Lying awake in the early hours he had hit on the idea of spending Saturday night with Paul at a hotel, either here in town or out by the Havelsee, where they could hire themselves a boat after breakfast. With Zollitsch's advance, he could probably afford it. But not next weekend, he reminded himself, because that was the Saturday set aside for Paul's sixth-birthday celebrations.

As he crossed the street to the public baths, Russell reminded himself that Matthias's friend Colonel Zollitsch would be expecting some return on his investment. Since he had to go birthday shopping in the city centre, he might as well drop in at the office and check through the archives for Ewald's mayor father. He was doubtful that this line of enquiry would lead anywhere useful, but it had to be pursued.

Submerged in the steaming water, he thought about Ulrich's sighting of their old comrade Bruno Aretin. Where were people like him going to hide? The KPD had more than 300,000 card-carrying members at the last count, and surely no more than one in five could have fled abroad or been taken away. The leaders would mostly be gone, the young and the single in pre-arranged safe houses guarding the Party's material assets, its presses, weapons and records. But what of the ordinary members? Most would have partners and children, a lot would have older relations in their care; they couldn't just head for the hills. So where were they? Hunkered down at home, hoping to be ignored? Staying with courageous friends or family? They'd all be on the SA lists, but were the brownshirts intent on sweeping the board? Arresting or driving out all the leaders and prominent activists might be enough to render the KPD impotent, but would it sate the brutes? He doubted it.

Back across the road, Frau Löffner had more reason to be positive. As she happily recounted, Hitler had let it be known the previous evening that the "disturbances" would have to end, before people started comparing the Nazi revolution with the communist one in 1918. "It was all on the wireless," she said. "People are to stop molesting individuals. Particularly foreigners, because that puts us in a bad light, but us Germans as well. The government is in charge now, and it will decide who gets molested, not some oik on the street."

Russell doubted whether Hitler had put it quite that way, but if the Nazi leader really was trying to rein in his troops,

that had to be good news. Not least because Ilse would have
less reason to keep Paul confined in Berlin's more middle-
class districts.

His optimism lasted about twenty minutes. Reading the
papers over breakfast at the café beside Wedding Station, he
found that Hitler's new initiative was rather more qualified
than Frau Löffner had made out, and that an almost simul-
taneous speech by Göring offered a very different message.
The police were not a "defence squad" for Jewish stores;
they were not there to protect "rogues and vagabonds, swin-
dlers, profiteers and traitors." The nation was "aroused,"
accounts were being "settled."

But not today. Later that morning, when he visited two
of the largest Jewish-owned department stores downtown,
there were no SA pickets insisting that "Germans buy from
Germans." Both toy departments carried a number of excit-
ing-looking accessories for his son's new model train set, but
Russell decided to find out what Paul already had before
making his choice, and come back during the week—the
two stores were only a short walk from the *Morgenspiegel*
office. He also popped in to one of the bookstores on Leipziger Strasse, and noticing a copy of Erich Kastner's *Emil
and the Detectives* wondered whether Paul was old enough to
appreciate it.

"Buy it while you can," the shopkeeper told him, "because
I don't think there's any doubt that Herr Kastner will be on
the black list they've promised us."

Russell bought the book, and leafed through it over
lunch in the Wertheim restaurant. Two questions suggested
themselves: what point would there be in banning a book
that most German children already knew by heart, and
where would he hide the damn thing from Herr Dickel?

His next port of call was the *Morgenspiegel*'s archive room.
Berlin had twenty district mayors at any one time, and after
two hours of poring over indexes and articles he had the

names of forty-three men who'd held the post in the last seven years. Wives were sometimes named, children rarely even mentioned, and Russell was resigning himself to a grand tour of the city's record offices when the picture he needed leapt out of a musty page. "Treptow's Social Democrat mayor Artur Lutz," the caption read, "with his sons Ewald and Fritz." The paper was from June 1925 and the elder son Ewald looked around twelve, which seemed about right.

A further search through the picture library turned up several more pictures of Mayor Artur, including one of him outside his home at 23 Graetzstrasse.

There was no direct connection between Kochstrasse and Treptow, but a walk and two tram rides brought Russell within a block of the Lutz address. It was an area with many industrial premises—the Schade family printing works were not far away—but Graetzstrasse, tree-lined and purely residential, was noticeably more middle class than most of the district. Walking up the street in search of No.23, Russell noticed a couple of posters in support of the Centre Party and an unusual paucity of swastikas. This was not Hitler territory yet, but his lads had been to visit. Planks were nailed across the porch of No.23, and the splintered door behind had clearly been kicked in. The ground floor curtains weren't drawn, and with no one nearby on the street Russell took a quick look through the window. Everything inside seemed defaced or broken.

After closing the gate behind him, Russell noticed an old couple emerging from one of the houses opposite. He walked towards them, wondering how direct he should be. "Excuse me," he said. "I'm from the Housing Authority and I'm here to interview the owner of No.23. But I think someone's made a mistake. It looks unoccupied."

"It is," the man said, trying to pull the woman away.

She resisted. "The old mayor lived there, but he was

arrested right after the Fire," she said. "We watched them drag him out. But we didn't know him," she added, belatedly aware that silence might have been safer.

This time the man succeeded in moving her on.

"Thank you," Russell shouted after them. He should have asked about the son, he realised, but chasing after the couple seemed unwise, and there was no one else to casually approach. Not that it mattered. The son would not be coming back.

The Landwehrkanal was at the end of the road, and Russell decided a long walk back to the centre would do him good. On a Saturday afternoon the paths and cobbled quays were busy with walkers and anglers, the chugging barges almost as numerous as they were in the week, and the early spring sunshine found rainbows in the oil-slicked waters. Spirits boosted, he left the canal on the southern side of the Tiergarten, intent on walking through the trees and catching a homebound tram at the Brandenburg Gate. Now that the forest's population of homeless and unemployed had been moved on by the authorities, the sun-dappled glades felt wonderfully peaceful, and when the burnt-out Reichstag suddenly loomed into view, Russell felt like he'd been coshed from behind.

At the end of an avenue of trees, the scorched and hollowed dome rose up against the pure blue sky, a monstrous reminder of promises broken, faiths betrayed, opportunities lost. All the dreams of a better world that had sprung from the war and the revolution, scattered on this fetid wind.

The Zoo was Paul's first choice on Sunday morning, and he clearly wasn't alone in that—the queue at the Budapester Strasse entrance stretched back along the Aquarium's outer wall. Once inside, they went to the usual favourites, the monkey houses first, the elephants second, then on to

the café for drinks and, in Russell's case, a short but welcome rest. The camels and walrus then had to be revisited,
before they spent some time inside the aquarium, where
Paul impressed his father with his reading of the information boards.

It was a good zoo, and Russell was ready to admit that
his belief in London's superiority was probably childhood
nostalgia. His mother had often taken him there when the
family went up for the day, his father disappearing "on business."

A proper lunch followed in the adjacent Tiergarten, and
then they took a Stadtbahn train to Westkreuz, the nearest point on the Ringbahn. Paul had just turned four when
he first suggested taking the train round the city, and the
pair of them had been doing it every few weeks ever since.
Today as they passed through Wedding Station and across
the Gerichtstrasse bridge, Paul pointed out Russell's apartment building and asked when he'd been staying there
again. "Soon," Russell said, pleased that Paul still wanted to.
He told himself that he worried too much about losing his
place in the boy's affections.

It was around five when they got off at Schmargendorf,
only two stations short of the complete circuit. It wasn't a
long walk to Wilhelmsaue, but Paul was clearly tired, so they
took a tram part of the way. Once Ilse had answered the
door, and Paul had hurried off for a much-needed pee, Russell asked her to ask Matthias what the boy needed for his
train set. He would ring for the answer tomorrow.

She gave him a smile, and thanked him for agreeing to
look for Lili Zollitsch.

It was time he made a start, he thought, walking back
towards the tram stop. But in a couple of hours he was due
to meet Jet for their second look round Luna Park, so Lili
would have to wait another twenty-four hours, always assuming he'd think up a way of tracking her down.

He tried his best over supper and a couple of beers at a café on the Ku'damm, but walking the streets of Wedding and Neukölln in hope of seeing a face he recognised felt more like desperation than a plan. He suspected that Lili would prove as elusive as Timo Baur.

Jet clearly hadn't found the latter—his face as he came out of Halensee Station was a picture of misery. Nor, he reported, had there been any further message from his missing boyfriend. But as they walked down to the Luna Park entrance he passed on some news that Russell found hopeful—the SA had been back to Fredo and Timo's room in Rote Insel, and all but torn the place apart. They must have been looking for something, but Jet had no idea what it might be. Whatever it was, it looked as though they'd either killed Timo before he could point them in the right direction or—and this was the hopeful bit—Timo was still at large.

When he offered the latter likelihood to Jet, the hope in the eyes was almost painful. "You think so?"

That was as good as their evening got. The park was more crowded than it had been on Thursday, but as far as Russell could see, innocent fun seemed thin on the ground. Everything felt slightly hysterical, up to and including the ooohs and aaahs that went with the very short firework display. Jet ran into a couple of acquaintances, neither of whom had seen Timo, and who both eyed Russell with a blend of dislike and suspicion. Timo himself was conspicuous by his absence, and Russell saw the hope he'd engendered earlier slowly drain away.

As they prepared to part, Jet said he'd come back on his own next time. It was nothing personal, but Russell must have seen how the boys had looked at him. If he found Timo he'd be in touch.

"How?" Russell asked. "Can you leave me a message at Karl's?"

"It's closed."

"Then how can I get hold of you?"

"You can't," Jet said definitively. "I don't know where I'll be," he added to soften the blow. "But I suppose if I knew where you live I could come to you."

It sounded more like a last resort than an expectation, but Russell wrote out his address on a page torn from his notebook.

"Not so posh," was Jet's verdict on Wedding.

The Monday morning papers, consumed along with coffee and rolls at Kranzler's, offered predictable fare. There were the usual attacks on random Jews in which riding whips featured prominently, the usual claims that such attacks were purely a press invention. There was also the obligatory ludicrous statement, in this case Göring's claim that if he deigned to speak at the current disarmament talks in Geneva then "the last word would be spoken."

Being both vicious and pompous was usually hard to pull off, but Göring did it with ease. You could find a hundred bad things to say about Goebbels, but the little shit was never pompous.

At the *Morgenspiegel* office, Hiedler was busy with his political team, so Russell seized the chance to ring Ilse. She had the information he wanted—the important elements that their son's model train set lacked were signals and a signal cabin. Joachim had owned one of the latter, but his infant sister had sat on the miniature building, and it had never been replaced.

There was also a card game one of Paul's friends had that she knew he would like. She didn't know its name, but it involved turning over pairs of cards and matching them. The cards had country maps and pictures of their capitals, so it was also educational.

By the time they were finished, Hiedler was too, so Russell

reported in. He recounted the trips to Luna Park with Jet, and his feeling that the story was probably dead.

Hiedler didn't disagree. "Your rogue princess had the weekend off," he told Russell, "but your bank manager has been caught. The Stettin police found him queuing for the Swedish ferry, holding a suitcase full of Reichsmarks. He's being brought back to Berlin—quote—as soon as he's fit to travel—unquote."

"Jewish then."

"How did you guess?" Hiedler asked drily. "In the meantime, another theatrical story." He passed the brief across. "Or cinematic, I suppose I should say. Have you heard of Greta Sonnermann?"

"Vaguely. Wavy blond hair, slightly chubby face?"

"She'll open up to you. According to her, she's being followed and generally harassed. But apparently not by the state," Hiedler added with a smile. "The studio has scheduled a press conference for noon. On the set of the film she's currently making."

"Sounds like advertising."

"It probably is. If so, a nice day for you."

The train to Neu Babelsberg took about half an hour, and a bus was waiting at the station to ferry arriving pressmen to the studio complex. There were plenty of hacks on hand, including Eglhofer from the still-suspended *Tageblatt*. "There's a buffet after," he told Russell, as if that explained his presence.

The food was worth waiting for, which was more than could be said for the press conference. The performances were even less convincing than the bizarre medieval banquet setting.

Greta Sonnermann, in costume dress, made a series of unsubstantiated accusations against an unknown male. She'd been watched from her garden at night, her Mercedes limousine trailed by a grubby-looking Hanomag. Letters had been received, and copies of these were passed out as she spoke. They read like fan mail to Russell, though "one day you will be mine" could be construed as a threat.

As Greta fought back the tears her producer took up the reins, lambasting the notably absent local police for their failure to take any action.

This dereliction of duty became more understandable during the question and answer session, in which the producer conceded that he'd only informed the local authorities a few hours earlier. Asked to describe her unwelcome shadow, Greta said she'd never seen him up close, but had gained a long-distance impression of swarthy skin and a hooked nose. Asked to describe her own feelings, she said they were hard to put in words, and raised a tear-stained face to the crowd like some tragic warrior queen.

She looked much better a quarter-hour later, falling on the excellent buffet with a ferocity that must have worried the film's continuity girl. "She must have gone hungry as a child," Eglhofer said, which wasn't as flip as it sounded—in Greta's teenage years many Germans had.

"Maybe," Russell agreed, as a younger woman on the far side of the set caught his eye. Slim and dark-haired with a lovely face, she seemed to sense his look, and for several seconds they stared at each other. A line of people came between them, and when he saw her again, the woman was talking to a handsome young man in a knight's costume. She, he realised, was dressed as a serving wench.

On the drive back to the station, he overheard one colleague ask another about Greta's performance. "I've never seen her act better," was the unflattering reply.

On his way home to Wedding after handing in the story, Russell turned his mind back to Lili Zollitsch. Now that the mayor clue had proved a dead end, how he should go about finding her? Where was he going to look? What story was he going to tell? Getting his pitch wrong might prove dangerous for her, and almost certainly would for himself.

Neukölln and Wedding were the likeliest areas, and the latter was on his doorstep. There was no shortage of cafés and bars in the streets north of the station, where red-daubed hammers and sickles had once embellished every large expanse of brickwork. The SA had taken over all the best-known communist hang-outs, more to show who had won than because they liked the décor, though publicly burning portraits of Lenin and Stalin had given them joy for a while. But you'd never needed a Party card to gain entry—all sorts of people who saw themselves as left of centre had drunk in such places, and were now presumably drinking at one of the myriad places the stormtroopers hadn't colonised.

He tried three of them that evening, nursing a Patzen-hofer in each, and pretending to read the evening paper as he shamelessly eavesdropped on conversations. And the one thing that stood out from these was a marked reluctance on everyone's part to express a political view. Which was all to the good from Russell's perspective. The Nazis never got tired of expressing theirs.

It was in the third bar that he decided to stick a toe in the water. Two men at the bar—both workers in their forties, he guessed—were talking to the much younger barman about the Great Inflation ten years before. There was nothing overtly leftist about what they were saying, but Russell found the conversation's tone and analytic content familiar from his own years in the Party.

He decided to take the risk. Approaching the bar for a second glass, he asked the threesome if he might ask a question.

"Depends what it is," one man replied sensibly.

Russell took the photograph of Lili from his inside pocket. "Have any of you seen this girl?" he enquired, watching the faces for any hint of recognition.

"She's a looker," one of the customers noted.

"A bit young for you," the other replied. "But no," he told Russell. "Who is she?"

"She's disappeared, and her father wants her found."

"A friend of yours? Or are you one of those new private detectives the Americans have?"

"A friend of a friend."

"More to the point," the barman said slowly. "Why are you looking in here? She doesn't look like a Wedding girl. Or a drinker come to that."

In for a penny, Russell thought. "Her father thinks she's run off with a communist lad."

"There aren't any communists here."

"I'm sure there aren't. Look, I used to have friends in the Party myself, and I don't want to speak out of turn. But I'm looking for someone who's seen her, and"—a touch of invention—"the father thinks the boy might live in Wedding. So I've been trying all the cafés and bars I can find that aren't full of brownshirts."

The three men looked pained, as if they were imagining the worst, either for her or themselves.

Russell pushed his luck: "Is there anyone you know I can talk to, someone who might have a better idea of where I can look?"

The two customers shook their heads, but the barman had a suggestion. "Try Arno," he said. "Thirteen Kosliner Strasse. The Nazis know all about him, but they haven't arrested him. He's almost ninety, so maybe they think he's ga-ga. He isn't, but knowing Arno he may well have fooled them into thinking he is."

"Either that or they've left him there like a tethered goat," one of the others suggested.

"Something interesting from our man at the Charlotten-burg nick," was Hiedler's greeting next morning.

"They've arrested Greta Sonnermann for overacting?"

"Not yet. And this story could be important."

Russell glanced through Hiedler's sheet of notes. A man named Konrad Mommsen had been knocked down by a vehicle on the Charlottenburg Ufer. The driver hadn't stopped, and Mommsen had died in the ambulance *en route* to the Robert Koch Hospital. His papers had identi-fied him as a thirty-eight-year-old genealogist.

"See what I mean?" Hiedler asked as Russell put the sheet down.

"Not really."

"You're slow on the uptake this morning. Which job will have got more important now that the Nazis are in power?"

"Ah."

"Ah indeed. We know they hate Jews, and beating up the ones they meet in the street won't satisfy them for long. They'll want restrictive laws, and for those they'll need a precise definition of what makes a Jew a Jew. There must be millions of Germans who have *some* Jewish blood, so that can't be the definition—Hitler would probably find half his Party have the dreaded virus. So will it be one parent, or just the mother? Or a certain number of the grandparents? They'll have to decide, and then use state records to rule on indi-vidual cases. And once that happens, a lot of people will start wondering whether or not they meet the new criteria. And since they won't want to put their heads above the parapet by checking their ancestry in the public record offices . . ."

". . . they'll go to a professional genealogist. Are there that many of them?"

"I looked through our classifieds and there's more than twenty advertise with us, including our victim. And I'll lay odds if you look in the archives, you'll find there was only a handful a year ago."

"So checking one's racial purity has become a growth industry. How depressing."

"Indeed. But maybe we can use this hit-and-run—if that's what it was—to shine a little light."

"You think he might have been murdered to cover up some dreadful stain in someone's ancestry."

Hiedler shrugged. "It's possible. Why don't you go and find out." He passed another note across. "Mommsen's office address. It was in his classified ad." As Russell got up to leave, the editor added a caveat. "Just don't come back and say it was an SA lorry."

Konrad Mommsen's office was in one of the small blocks built behind the glamorous properties lining the Ku'damm. A *hinterhaus*, the Germans called it. Access was sometimes from the rear, but usually, as in this case, by way of a lengthy passage. There was a cabaret club on one side that had clearly seen better days, and a gallery on the other that apparently still thought modern art had a future in Hitler's Germany.

Three flights of stairs took him up to Mommsen's office, the dead man's name neatly inked on the door's frosted glass. Ringing the bell, rapping the pane and rattling the handle all failed to evoke a response, and he was searching his pockets for something to pick the lock when a female voice behind him made him jump.

"He's not here," she said from the next doorway down, clearly amused that she'd given him a shock. She looked about fourteen to Russell, with blond hair twirled in those Brunhilde plaits that Germans seemed to love so much.

Russell refrained from divulging that Mommsen would never be back. "I don't suppose you know where he lives," he asked, more in hope than expectation.

"On Lietzenburger Strasse," she said. "Number fifty-one. It's only a five-minute walk away. We went out for a while before he got married," she added, seeing his look of surprise. "But he was much too old for me."

Russell thanked her and left before she could ask his age. He knew that the street in question ran parallel to the Ku'damm, and continuing down the narrow passage brought him straight to it. The police car a hundred yards down was outside No.51.

He flashed his press card at the uniformed Kripo by the open door, and brazenly walked straight past him. There were no sign of other journalists, as there would have been had the tip-off come from the Alex. This might be his first scoop.

The blonde hadn't given him an apartment number, but the open door on the first landing was suggestive. Two men were talking just inside it, and Russell stopped to listen.

"I thought she was English at first, but now I think she's American," one said.

"She doesn't seem that cut up," the other responded, suggesting this was Mommsen's flat.

"Maybe. People react in all sorts of ways. If you'd done this as many times as I have . . ."

"Doesn't she speak any German?"

"She thinks she does, but her accent's terrible—she seems to understand my questions but I can't make head or tail of her answers. We'll have to wait for the interpreter."

"That could be hours."

Rarely in life, Russell thought, did something get laid on one's plate in such a munificent manner.

He put his head round the door. "Press," he said, holding up his card.

"That's all we need," the older man said. He was probably in his fifties, stoutly built with a craggy face and stubble-cut grey hair.

"I couldn't help overhearing," Russell said. "About the woman not speaking German. I'm English, but I've lived here the last ten years."

The older detective raised an eyebrow. "Out of choice?"

Russell smiled. "More or less. And if you need an interpreter right this minute . . ."

The two detectives looked at each other.

"I won't report anything she says," Russell promised. "Or not without your permission."

"Why not?" the older one wearily agreed.

Russell offered a hand and introduced himself.

"Kriminalinspektor Kuzorra," the older one said. "And he's Kriminalassistent Bloch," he added, with a nod towards his bespectacled partner.

They trooped into the living room, where a woman of around thirty was sitting on the sofa and smoking a Turkish cigarette. She had auburn hair in ringlets, a face that was probably pretty when she smiled, and a body that was gently straining at the polka dot dress that encased it. She certainly didn't look happy, but she didn't seem grief-stricken either.

"Tell Frau Mommsen that you will be translating my questions and her answers," Kuzorra instructed Russell.

He did so, and once she had signalled her acquiescence in a strong American accent, Kuzorra began. He first made sure that she understood what had happened, that her husband had been hit by a car while crossing a street, and had subsequently died on the way to hospital.

She said she did, almost dismissively, as if her thoughts were past that point.

Kuzorra asked how long they'd been married.

"A year," she said. "Almost to the day." They had met in New York, fallen in love—"if that's what you call it"—and got married, all in less than two weeks. They had honeymooned at Niagara Falls, and he had brought her home to Germany on the *Europa*—the memory dragged up a fleeting smile. "And then . . ." She waved her hands. "Well, let's be nice about it. We both realised we'd made a mistake, but I was the only one stuck in a foreign country. Not knowing anyone, not speaking the lingo."

Kuzorra asked if she knew what her husband was doing on Charlottenburg Ufer.

The answer was no. Not that she knew where that was. "Probably visiting one of his women," she suggested, with only a tinge of bitterness. Maybe getting himself killed had been atonement enough.

Kuzorra thanked her, repeated his condolences, and warned that she might be questioned again. As the three of them got up to go, she asked Russell if she could speak to him alone.

"Of course," he told her, "but I need to speak to the detectives before they leave. I'll be back in a few minutes."

He caught them up on the sidewalk. "So, help me with my job," he told Kuzorra. "Was it an accident?"

The detective leaned his bulky frame against the side of the Horch 400. "It looks very like it. It's a dark stretch of road, and if the driver saw Mommsen at all he must have seen him too late. We have a witness who heard the collision, and who confirms how dark it was. Too dark for him to tell us much about the car. Not big, not small. Probably black. He said the engine had a 'throaty' roar when the driver accelerated, which he did after hitting Mommsen."

"Panic?" Russell wondered out loud.

"Or an impressively instant decision in favour of self-preservation. With that description . . . well, unless our man drives into a garage and asks for the blood to be wiped off his bonnet I doubt we'll ever know." Kuzorra pushed himself off the car. "But thanks for your help with the grieving widow."

Russell went back up to the apartment. She was still on the sofa, lighting a fresh Sulima from the stub of the last one. Her face looked harder than it had, as if she had told herself to get a grip.

"I need help," she said simply. "Not speaking German, it'll be a nightmare sorting things out."

"Your embassy will know what to do," Russell suggested, resisting the temptation to divulge his own part-American ancestry. He didn't know that much about her, and already suspected he wouldn't want to.

She waved a hand dismissively. "They'll be too busy—I went there last week and there was a line of Jews a mile along. And I doubt they would send someone over. I need someone to go through Konrad's papers, someone like you who can read them and then tell me what's there. I'll pay you, of course, though you may have to wait for the money. I only have a few pfennigs in my purse."

"Did your husband make a will?"

"I don't know, and I don't suppose I'd recognise a German one if I came across it. But you would."

"True."

"And I don't even know how it works here. In the States if you die without one, everything goes to the next of kin, the wife or husband if there is one. Is it the same over here?"

"I'm not sure," Russell admitted. "I think so, but I'm not certain."

"Of course there may not be anything to inherit," she said resentfully, reaching forward to tap the ash from the end of her cigarette. "The apartment's rented . . . which reminds me—I'll have to get hold of the people he rented his office from. I need to find out what he had in the bank, but will they tell me if I take my passport and wedding certificate? If you came with me, we could find out where I stand."

"I can do that," Russell assented, mentally balancing helping her out with the access it afforded him to her husband's finances.

"And then there's life insurance. I don't suppose he had any, but I'd like to be sure." She puffed on the cigarette. "And there might be another problem. I don't mean to speak ill of the dead, but my husband wasn't what you'd call an honest man. If he had any money it may be . . . tainted is the word, I suppose. Hot money, as we say in the States."

"You think he committed actual crimes?"

"I couldn't tell you which, but . . . you know, don't you, when someone is crooked?"

"I think you need legal advice," Russell told her. "I'm sure I can find you someone who speak English . . ."

"That would be wonderful. But first I want you to look through my husband's papers, and see what's there. Will you do that for me?"

"Of course," Russell said, thinking that this really was his lucky day. If there was anything newsworthy about the man's death he seemed certain to be the first to find out.

"With discretion," she added, echoing, perhaps unconsciously, the promise in her husband's advertisement.

He nodded. "Are his personal papers here or at the office?"

"At the office, I assume. There may be some in that," she said, gesturing towards a walnut bureau. "But he hardly ever used it."

"You have a key to the office?

"Oh, no, the police took that. They said I'd get it back later today."

Russell wondered what Kuzorra would be looking for. He was certainly smart enough to duplicate Hiedler's insight, that in the current political climate genealogy might not be the safest profession. "I'll come back this afternoon," He promised.

"Thank you."

A thought occurred to Russell as he got up to leave. "Frau Mommsen, does your husband have an appointment book?"

"Yes, he does. He always brought it home on weekends. And please, call me Donna."

• • •

Russell took the U-Bahn from Uhlandstrasse back to the office. Hiedler had just left for a working lunch with the own-ers, so he took himself down to Wertheim's for a bowl of the roast beef stew before walking up to the toy department and purchasing their one remaining signal box. After deposit-ing this in his office locker and checking that no spectacular crimes had been committed in his absence, he decided that enough time had passed for Kuzorra to be back at the Alex.

The detective's office took some finding, but then the Alex was known for its Kafka-like accessibility.

"You again," Kuzorra said, affably enough, when Rus-sell put his head round the door. "Are you here as a hack or a widow's helper?"

"Both," Russell said, sitting down without being asked. "She hasn't got a penny to spend, and I wondered if there was any cash in the deceased's effects. Just to tide her over."

"There was sixty marks or so in his wallet. But the Char-lottenburg Kripo still have the effects. I can call them and ask them to take the money over. I don't think she'd want the clothes back. They're pretty bloody."

"Thank you," Russell said, pleasantly surprised by Kuzor-ra's amenability. Most of the Alex detectives he'd met thought being obstructive was a matter of principle. "Frau Mommsen said you'd send the office key back this after-noon. She wants me to find out where the bank account is. That sort of thing."

"I think I saw a bank book."

"Did you find anything that would interest a hack?" Rus-sell asked with a smile.

"Not yet. We've taken the work folders, which include the family trees he drew up for each of his clients, and if we come to the conclusion that someone deliberately ran the man over then—and only then—someone will have to go through them."

"And if it was an accident?"

"I don't know. Either the folders will go back to the clients, or they'll just be destroyed."

"And if it was murder, and your reader discovers that someone high up in an anti-Semitic Party turns out to be half-Jewish?"

Kuzorra smiled. "A question for my superiors, I should think. But, given where we are, I find it difficult to imagine such information being released. Officially, at least."

Russell nodded. "So I might get an anonymous tip-off?"

"I wouldn't bet against it. This place is so crowded these days, and no one locks their doors."

"And in the meantime I'm free to look through his office?"

"It's her office now. Go next door and tell Bloch I said to give you the key."

"And you'll ring the Charlottenburg Kripo about the money?"

"Didn't I say so?"

After stopping off at the apartment to tell Donna Mommsen he had the key, Russell went back to her husband's office. It was larger than he'd imagined, but short on furniture, with only a couple of upright chairs facing each other across the desk and a tall wooden cabinet stood against one wall. The view from the window was mostly of brick, though craning one's neck revealed a thin strip of sky.

No attempt had been made to personalise the space. There were no ornaments or framed photographs; the only thing on the wall was a calendar still showing January. It didn't look as if Mommsen had spent much time here, but then why would he have done? What would he have used it for, other than meetings with clients? Most of his actual work would have been in state and district record offices.

The shallow drawers of the wooden cabinet were empty, having presumably held the client folders now at the Alex, but the contents of the desk drawers looked much as Mommsen would have left them. His passport was in the top one on the left, and this gave Russell his first sight of the dead man's face. He had certainly been handsome in a Siegfried sort of way, but was there something in the eyes you wouldn't trust? Maybe. Or was Russell just seeing what he expected to see? There were several stamps inside the passport, including those recording Mommsen's US arrival and departure some twelve months before.

Russell slipped it into his pocket, and opened the drawer below. Here was the financial stuff: a cheque book, a neatly clipped pile of statements and a three-month-old letter from the bank informing Mommsen that he was overdrawn. According to the latest statement he wasn't anymore, but neither was he doing much better. Since covering the overdraft in January he had made few deposits or withdrawals, and the account held a paltry forty-three marks. It looked as though the business had been doing rather badly.

Or was it? The appointments book, which Russell found in the other top drawer, told a very different story. Mommsen had seen seven new clients in February, and another six in the first two weeks of March. He supposed it was possible that they'd all said no, but it didn't seem likely, and in March at least Mommsen had paid nothing into the bank. Russell copied out these recent clients' names and addresses, thinking he would probably find at least one who'd be willing to talk.

Mommsen might have insisted on cash as a way of avoiding tax. That would explain the sixty marks in his wallet, but not why there wasn't much more. If the genealogist wasn't spending a fortune on mistresses, drugs or gambling

there had to be another account. But Russell could find no
evidence of one. No cheque book, no pass book, no unexplained number scrawled on a piece of paper.

There might be an honest explanation for these financial peculiarities, but Russell's instincts told him that the
man was worth looking into, that his death might be part of
a bigger story. He leaned back in the chair for a moment,
wondering if this was one of those hunches that detectives
and journalists often got in the movies.

There was no insurance policy either, and it looked as
though Mommsen was three months in arrears with the office
rent. He opened the final drawer still hoping to find a will,
but all it yielded was a Thomas Cook brochure. Inside a June
tour to Venice was circled in ink. Mommsen might have been
waiting to surprise the wife, but Russell thought an adulter-
ous dalliance more likely, and decided not to mention it.

Back at the apartment, he was impressed by how well she
took the financial news. Looking at the latest bank statement she reached the same conclusion as Russell: "The
bastard must have put his money somewhere else."

But where? Russell could only suggest they start at the
bank—he would take her there next morning. He was letting her know that the local Kripo would soon be around
with the cash from her husband's wallet when an officer
knocked on the door and handed it over.

Grieving or not, it seemed almost cruel to leave her so
alone, and he half-expected pleas to stay and keep her
company. None were forthcoming. She would be all right
for the night, he thought; in fact, she would probably be
fine full stop, whether or not any money turned up. Donna
Mommsen seemed like a survivor, and one who wouldn't
make the same mistake twice.

On the trip back across town he considered how he was going
to frame the story. He could just lay out the facts—a badly lit

road, a driver who didn't stop, the pretty American wife left all alone—and leave a few hints that there might be more to it. The idea that some people might feel the need to falsify their ancestry was almost a satire on the Nazi obsession with race, but he had to be careful, and perhaps it might be better to simply point out what Mommsen's work entailed, and leave readers to connect up the dots on their own.

Of course, if Kuzorra's witness was right and it really had been an accident, then he wouldn't be writing a follow-up. No crime would have been committed, and any inconvenient bloodlines that Mommsen had discovered would remain his clients' secrets. At least until some other genealogist went looking. Either on his own behalf, or that of the state.

Hiedler was gone by the time he got back to the office, and Kempka was all for holding fire until the police ruled out foul play. Russell wrote the piece accordingly and wearily travelled home—he felt like he'd spent most of the day criss-crossing the city. The thought of spending the evening alone in his flat was more than usually appealing, but the guilty sense of letting Zollitsch and his daughter down drove him back out.

His first port of call was 13 Kosliner Strasse, where Arno Knoden lived. The octogenarian wasn't at home, according to the friendly *Portierfrau*. And no, he hadn't been arrested yet. He always played skat with friends on a Tuesday night, and when he came back at midnight he wouldn't be too coherent. If Herr Russell wanted a conversation then tomorrow would be better.

Russell continued on his way, hoping he'd be as active when he reached that age. He spent time in another three bars, and brought out the picture of Lili in two. Her looks were admired and her probable fate lamented, but no one confessed to having seen her.

It was in the third bar that Russell picked up an

abandoned copy of one of the evening papers, and chanced across a story in one of the inside pages. A district records office in Wilmersdorf had gone up in flames the previous night, and most of the papers inside were now ash. Arson was strongly suspected, and several Jewish youths had been taken into custody by the local police.

A coincidence? Or support for his hunch that something was awry? Russell imagined a possible sequence—Mommsen discovers that X has a Jewish grandfather, and tells X in which office the records are kept. X then kills Mommsen and burns down the office, thereby eliminating both sources of the threat to his future.

It was an attractive theory, if rather far-fetched. He would find someone who'd worked at the office in question and ask whether Mommsen had done any recent research there.

Russell was up early on Wednesday, hoping to be at the bank with Frau Mommsen soon after it opened. Passing through the downstairs hallway he caught the date on the wooden block calendar Frau Löffner used to remind her tenants when their rent was due—Fridays were ringed in white paint. Today was a Tuesday, March the 15th, which Russell remembered from school as the Ides of March. Whatever they might be. Something to "beware" rang a distant bell.

Outside the sun was shining, lifting the curse off Berlin's intrinsic greyness. The tram ride took longer than he hoped, but he was at the Ku'damm by eight, and knocking on Frau Mommsen's door five minutes later. The bank was only a short walk away on Fasanenstrasse, but she insisted on their taking a taxi, and finding one took forever. She also expected Russell to pay—"I assume you'll get it back on expenses."

Russell hoped so—after rent, eating out and paying off

the debts he'd incurred as a struggling freelance, there wasn't much left of his new *Morgenspiegel* salary.

The bank manager was as helpful as he could be, which wasn't very much. After regretfully explaining that the account could not be accessed until probate was settled, he outlined how she should start that process. As Russell had thought, the first thing to do was find a lawyer, and once they'd left the bank he promised to start looking that day.

"Thank God for the sixty marks he had in his coat," was Donna Mommsen's response. "That should keep me alive for a few weeks."

Russell thought about Mommsen's apparent lack of earnings, and where any other cash might be. "Have you searched the flat?" he asked her. "There might be more stashed away."

Her eyes lit up. "I'll do that when I get back."

Russell's next stop was the Alex, where bad news awaited.

"It was an accident," Kuzorra told him. "We have two more witnesses," he added, shoving a sheet of paper across his desk. "The woman was out walking her dog, and the man was standing on the other side of the canal, right across from where it happened. Both respectable citizens, as far as Bloch could tell." The detective smiled. "Sorry to disappoint you."

There was nothing in the detective's voice or manner to suggest that Kuzorra was covering anything up. "So this is a coincidence?" Russell said, passing across the newspaper page that featured the office fire.

"I think it must be," Kuzorra said, scratching his scalp. "If Mommsen was murdered, then it would be worth pursuing. But now we know he wasn't, and I"—he gestured towards the stack of files on his desk—"have too many other cases."

"So this one's closed. And the client folders won't be looked at."

"Ah. As it happens, they have been. Bloch must have mis-understood me, because he took them home last night and read them through. And, I'm pleased to say, found abso-lutely nothing. None of Mommsen's clients had the wrong sort of blood in their veins."

"That is disappointing," Russell said wryly. After thanking Kuzorra for his time, he made his way out of the Alex, and over to the mobile canteen on the far side of the square. As he perched on a convenient wrought iron bench enjoying his bratwurst roll two things occurred to him. The fact that Mommsen's death had been an accident didn't make him an innocent. And if most of the genealogist's money was missing, then maybe some of his files were too.

Kuzorra might be done with the case, but Russell wasn't done with the story. At the *Morgenspiegel* there was nothing in need of his urgent attention, so he took the U-Bahn to Hauptstrasse, and walked the rest of the way to Fregestrasse. The torched record office had occupied three rooms on the ground floor of a three-storey building, and luckily for those living above, the fire had been spotted before it took serious hold. Ignoring the *Feuerwehr* KEEP OUT signs, Russell took a look through each of the shattered windows. Walls and ceilings were blackened, floors ankle-deep in ash.

Inside the building it was a different story. The down-stairs hall still smelt of burning, but the three rooms across from the record office were functioning as normal, judging by the clatter of typewriters. A secretary in the front room confirmed that the *Feuerwehr* had arrived quickly enough to contain the fire, probably because the local station was only two blocks away.

Ten minutes later, Russell was given more bad news by the local fire chief: the blaze had probably not been started deliberately. "I won't say we've ruled out foul play completely," the man conceded, "but we haven't found any evidence of it. And what facts we have point the other way.

All three men who work in the office are smokers, and it looks like the fire got started only minutes after the last one left. Which strongly suggests a cigarette left burning. I mean, if you wanted to destroy the records, why set a fire at that time of day, when there's so many people walking past who could raise the alarm? Doesn't make sense, does it?"

The fire chief was probably right. Russell walked back to the building in question, and interviewed the proprietors of the shops on either side. The newsagent on the right was surly and unhelpful, the delicatessen owner on the left hard to stop talking. He only knew the registrar, archivist and clerk by sight, but the female secretary was an old and frequent customer. Frau Scheringer was a widow, her husband having died in the war. She came in most days after work to buy the makings of her supper. She lived upstairs, on the second floor.

When Russell arrived at her door, she carefully examined his press card before inviting him in, and then wondered out loud if she should be speaking to a journalist. Her little Schnauzer, "Bertie," had no such doubts, yapping away at the visitor's ankles until Frau Scheringer reluctantly shut the dog in her bedroom.

She hadn't heard about Konrad Mommsen's death, but recognised the newspaper picture that Russell showed her. The genealogist had been a fairly regular visitor at her record office, and, she assumed, at most of the others across the city. He couldn't have done his job any other way.

She couldn't tell Russell who Mommsen had been researching on recent visits. The request slips were normally kept on file for six months, but all those currently held would have perished in the fire. And even if they hadn't been, such information was confidential. The archivist or clerk might remember a name, but they were bound by the same regulations. And no, she didn't have their addresses to hand, but one lived in Dahlem, the other in Kreuzberg.

Russell took down the names and wondered if either would take a bribe. He decided probably not, given that blame for the fire was still to be apportioned.

He was decidedly circumspect when writing his copy, first pointing out the coincidence of the genealogist's death and a fire at one of the places he worked, before using the fact that both had been accidents to prove that truth was occasionally more inventive than fiction.

After handing it in, he had time to check the news desk before setting off for his Wednesday appointment with Paul. There had been further government statements demanding more discipline and decrying "individual actions," including one from Göring himself. Perhaps the Nazis were feeling more secure now that all the elections were over—they had triumphed again in local and state ones the previous Sunday. Or perhaps they worried they were going too far for their Conservative allies and backers. That morning the latter's favourite paper, the *Deutsche Allgemeine Zeitung*, had gently taken the Nazis to task for "the blurring of the borders of authority."

The picketing and trashing of Jewish stores seemed to have stopped, or at least grown less widespread, which had to be something. All the people who put such "excessive zeal" down to "teething troubles" would be congratulating themselves on being proven right—Hitler really was listening, and would soon have all his less respectable supporters back in their box.

On a sunny winter afternoon all Paul wanted to do was collect his football from home and take it to the nearby Volkspark for a kickabout. Russell thought his son was growing more coordinated, and the practice he claimed he was doing to improve his left foot seemed to be paying off. Watching him race away across the grass to collect a misplaced shot, Russell realised that tickets to Hertha's next home game would make an excellent birthday present.

On the walk home they talked about school. Russell asked Paul if the books were being changed, and when his son said yes, asked what reason had been given.

"Because the old ones weren't German enough," Paul told him, in a tone that suggested the answer should have been self-explanatory.

At the door Paul asked if they could go to the Funkturm on Sunday—a school friend had been the previous week and thought it fantastic. The elevators were lightning fast and zoomed you up to an observation platform, from which you could see the whole city. "And the restaurant has Coca-Cola."

Back in Wedding, where American sodas were decidedly thin on the ground, Russell didn't think his liver could cope with another evening trawling the bars. After a decent supper he would walk up to Kosliner Strasse and see if the octogenarian comrade was home, but nothing more than that.

The pork knuckle, which he vaguely remembered shying away from during his first few months in Germany, tasted even better than usual. So did the applecake and cream, which suggested not eating since breakfast might have sharpened his taste buds. The coffee was less to write home about, but then the Wedding Station café wasn't exactly Kranzler's.

Kosliner Strasse proved outwardly quiet—either the SA were rampaging somewhere else or the appeals for greater street discipline were having an effect. The *Portierfrau* at No.31 was stood in her doorway, causing Russell to wonder again why she and her colleagues never brought out a chair and made themselves more comfortable. "He's in," she said with a deadpan face.

The man who opened the apartment door was certainly

old, but the skin hanging off his cheeks and the shuffling bow-legged gait left less of an impression than the sharpness of the pale blue eyes. "John Russell, I presume," he said in a slightly croaky voice. "I've been expecting you. Come in."

Of course you have, Russell thought. "Thank you," he said. The room he entered was remarkably bare—Russell assumed that like every other leftist Knoden had deemed it safer to jettison his books, but the number of other personal items seemed pitiably small.

"The older I get, the more I realise how little I really need," the old man replied to the unspoken question.

There were two seats, both of them heavily worn. Russell suspected that Knoden had a lot of visitors, and that some of the more recent ones had come to report on himself.

"You are remembered," Knoden said, once they were both sat down. "The 'English comrade.' Some were sorry to lose you, others . . . you know how it is. Some comrades think that anyone who quits will always be a traitor."

"And you don't?" Russell asked.

"A direct question, and I will try to give you an honest answer. Since the revolution in Russia those of us on the left have had two masters: the old idea of a fairer, less brutal world—socialism, in short—and the duty to support the only government on earth that is trying to make it happen." The old man smiled to himself. "I know many believe the Soviets have become a lost cause, but I haven't given up on them. Maybe I'm just too old to start again, or maybe hope has made me blind, but I can't bring myself to write them off." He paused, and looked straight at Russell. "But I've had enough doubts not to condemn those like yourself who think differently. In my head, at least. Out in the world we sometimes need to make choices."

"We do," Russell acknowledged. "And I'm still hoping for that fairer world. It's just that these days it's hard to see a way from here to there."

Knoden smiled at that. "This girl you're looking for. Can I see her picture?"

Russell passed it across.

The old man gazed at Lili for several seconds, then handed the picture back. "How old is she?"

"Nineteen."

"Old enough to know her own mind, I would say."

"Maybe. I've never met her. And if I find her and she tells me to get lost, then that's what I'll do. I'm not trying to rescue her from the Party—if she's still out there, then fine. But if the SA have her, then rescue seems like a good idea, and if I can find out where she is her father can start pulling strings."

"Would that we all had such powerful fathers."

"We don't. But you wouldn't leave her in the SA's clutches because you can't save all the others?"

"You are right, of course. And I will ask around," Knoden said. "I can't promise anything, but come back on Friday around this time."

"Thank you," Russell said. "For that and for seeing me."

The old man's grunt was part-amusement. "I'm afraid the two of us meeting here is riskier for you than it is for me. These days one of the bastards is always lurking about, pestering Frau Nortz about anyone who comes to see me."

"The *Portierfrau*? Can she be trusted?"

"Her husband was killed on this street in 1918. A good comrade."

Arriving back home ten minutes later Russell found his own *Portierfrau* taking out some rubbish, and clearly the worse for schnapps. "Have you heard?" Frau Löffner whispered loudly. "His Eminence has declared that we're now living in a 'Third Reich.' Damned if I remember the first two, but don't you English say 'third time lucky'?"

"We do," Russell affirmed, mentally adding that in this particular case it hardly seemed appropriate.

The Safe Factory

Russell got off the Ku'damm-bound tram where it crossed the Landwehrkanal and walked down Charlottenburger Ufer to where the accident had happened. The police sign calling for witnesses presumably marked the spot, but there were no obvious marks on the road, and Konrad Mommsen's blood had long been washed away. The canal was wider here than it was downtown, but the man leaning on the balustrade would have had as clear a view as the darkness allowed.

Russell had noted down the addresses of the two new witnesses in Kuzorra's office, but assumed the man would be out at work by nine in the morning. He was hoping to find the woman—one Frau Hilberg—in the apartment block across the road.

After crossing the fatal stretch of tarmac with more than his usual caution, he walked up to the second floor flat and rapped on the knocker. Frau Hilberg answered the door. An overweight middle-aged woman with a wonderfully cheerful face, she seemed thrilled to meet a member of the fourth estate. "Come in, come in," she urged, before insisting on making him coffee. It seemed kinder to accept than refuse, and while she was in the kitchen he took a look through the window that overlooked the road and canal. The site of the accident was no more than twenty yards away.

Once they were seated she happily went over what she'd witnessed. The sounds had come first: the squealing brakes and a loud thump, a few seconds' silence giving way to an engine noisily revving. By then she'd been at the window, looking down at a spread-eagled body, and catching a glimpse of receding taillights.

Had she seen anyone else?

"There was a man on the other side of the canal. I saw him toss his cigarette into the water. And by then people were out in the road, seeing if they could help. Our *Block-leiter* lit the torch he carries on marches so they could see what they were doing. People were shaking their heads, but I heard later that he only died on the way to hospital."

"Did you see anyone else on this side of the canal? Before everyone rushed out, I mean."

She thought about that. "There *was* someone, much farther up on the other side of the road, the way the car was going."

"Someone walking?"

"Yes."

"In which direction?"

"This way, I think. Though if he heard the accident he could just have turned around when I saw him. You wouldn't believe how loud that thump was."

"I can imagine," Russell said sympathetically, though Frau Hilberg seemed more excited than upset. She was certainly a convincing witness, and the squeal of brakes she'd heard seemed proof enough that Mommsen's death had been an accident. But what had the genealogist been doing out here? Meeting the man who'd been walking away? The man who might have seen the number of the car. The man who, as far as Russell knew, had ignored the police appeal for witnesses to come forward.

Which wasn't, he admitted, in itself suspicious. What sane man would voluntarily enter a police station in times like these?

He thanked Frau Hilberg for her coffee and time, and was heading down the stairs when she offered one more piece of information. "That man on the other side of the road. I think he was wearing a uniform."

Continuing south on a tram through Charlottenburg, Russell counted the uniformed men on the sidewalks. He stopped when he reached twenty, against fifty-three in civilian clothes.

He got off at the usual stop just south of the Ku'damm, and walked down Lietzenburger Strasse to No.51. He needed to pass on the details of the lawyer he'd found, an allegedly bright young man in Schöneberg whom one of his work colleagues had recently used.

Donna Mommsen smiled when she saw who it was at her door, and seemed in much better spirits. A cynic might have concluded that the death of her husband had brought her back to life.

As far as Russell could tell, Konrad Mommsen's mourners were few and far between. According to Kuzorra there were no known relatives, though "maybe some will come out of the woodwork when they find out he's dead." The detective had also told Russell that the genealogist's life was mostly a blank, that the first trace they could find of his existence was less than three years old. It wasn't just other men's pasts that Mommsen had magicked away.

His widow was grateful for the lawyer's name and number, and promised to call him later that morning. In the meantime, she had a question. "What if more money turns up? I mean, can I just take it and spend it?"

It didn't sound like a hypothetical query. "Why, have you found some?" Russell asked.

She only hesitated for a couple of seconds. "Yes, I searched the flat like you suggested, and there was a wad of notes in one of his shoes."

"How much?" Russell asked. "I mean, if it was a million marks the police may well find out."

"No, nothing like that. Just another four hundred."

"That much, you can always say he gave it to you. To buy yourself a new dress. Something like that."

"Do you think I should open my own bank account?"

"That sounds like a very good idea."

"I thought the same bank Konrad used. The man there seemed nice."

"He did."

"One last favour—will you come with me? And to the funeral people. That's two, I know. But I'll pay you for your time."

Russell sighed inwardly. "I have Saturday morning off this week. How does ten o'clock sound?"

"Thank you, yes."

"And I don't expect to be paid." He wasn't sure he liked Donna Mommsen all that much, but he did feel sorry for her.

When he got to the office, a studio press release was waiting on his desk. It featured a gushing thank you to the Babelsberg police from Greta Sonnermann, along with a brand new still from her current film. The accompanying note from an absent Hiedler told him that a man had been arrested the previous night after scattering rose petals in the actress's swimming pool.

The slew of question marks and exclamation points that concluded the missive made Russell smile. After dialling the appropriate Babelsberg number he asked for the arresting officer in the Sonnermann case. "I just need to check some details and make sure I get his name right."

The man was another Glassl, on the line in seconds, carefully spelling his name and rank. The arrest had been made by an unnamed uniformed cop whom Kriminalinspektor

Widmann—with two n's—had wisely stationed in the shrub-
bery close by the pool.

"I see you haven't released a photograph of the man you
arrested," Russell said. "Could you provide a description for
my readers?"

The Kriminalinspektor was only too pleased to. "He's a
big man. Fat you might say. Fair hair, a stupid expression.
Straight off an East Prussian farm, if that's not too fanciful."

"Not at all. I can visualise him perfectly. Thank you."

Russell hung up. So no swarthy skin or hooked nose,
he thought. But Greta's description would be what people
remembered. Mud stuck, as his old countrymen were prone
to say, but lies clung even tighter. So much so that these days
it felt like scraping them off was a full-time occupation.

He typed out the story, stressing the discrepancy between
Greta's description and the man arrested. It wouldn't win
him many friends in the film industry, but he supposed he
could live with that.

Before clocking off, Russell took the chance to call Colonel Zollitsch and report on his progress. Or the lack
thereof. As he'd assumed, Lili had not been in touch
with her father, and the only hope Russell could offer
was Arno Knoden's promise to put out the word. He
didn't mention Knoden's name, because he wasn't sure
such knowledge would be safe with Zollitsch. The phrase
"never trust an officer" had a long pedigree.

The colonel's emotionless tone did nothing to confirm
or allay this suspicion. Russell sometimes thought that those
Britons who cherished their stiff upper lip should all come
out to Germany and see how it was done.

Once the call was over he went for his coat and hat. He
had two yearnings, he realised, as he clattered down the stairs
towards the street. One was for peace and quiet, the other
for Chinese food. He would walk along the Landwehrkanal

until he reached the zoo, then head up the Ku'damm to the restaurant he and Ilse had frequently patronised. He hadn't been to the Green Dragon since their final visit more than a year before, the one at which they'd agreed to part.

A five-minute walk brought him to the old basin near Anhalter Station, and from there he followed the dark canal westward. He couldn't seem to get the Mommsens out of his mind. Whether or not Konrad's death had been an accident, the man had been up to something, and blackmail seemed the likeliest option. The cash that Donna had found might be unrelated to his work—the horses, perhaps, or cards—but surely she would have picked up some sign of such interests. She wasn't a stupid woman.

An empty bench appeared between bridges, and Russell sat down for a smoke. As a train passed noisily over the girders behind him, a coal barge chugged by in midstream. An oldish man was at the tiller, his dog asleep on the cabin roof. He had probably passed this spot a thousand times, under the Kaiser, under Weimar and now under the Nazis. Some things stayed the same.

Russell turned his thoughts back to Mommsen. Say the genealogist had found that one of his clients had a compromised ancestry—now there was a phrase for the times! What use could he make of such information? An honest man would tell the client he had bad news for him or her, but stress that it would travel no farther. As Mommsen's advertising had claimed—discretion was guaranteed. A dishonest man—which even his widow said he was—would have put a further price on that discretion, and taken another large payment for destroying his own research.

Russell unthinkingly tossed his cigarette stub into the oily canal, and was pleasantly surprised not to see flames. Walking on towards the Viktoriabrücke he realised that truly wiping the ancestral slate clean would have required more than that. The official records would still be out there, and Mommsen might have made another deal to pilfer or destroy them. Burning down offices didn't seem like a very efficient method, particularly since the client could only be truly reassured if the records were in his own hands. Russell had no idea how easy it would be to steal such papers, but the offices were hardly bastions of security, and some of the people who worked in them were bound to be corruptible. Where there was a will . . .

He walked under the Potsdamer Strasse bridge as another barge passed in the other direction, filling the air with petrol fumes. If Mommsen was stealing personal records and selling them to their subjects, then all would be happy, Russell thought. The clients would have a load off their minds, Mommsen and any helper would rake in the cash. A victimless crime, if you weren't a Nazi. A betrayal of the *volk* if you were.

But where was the cash and where were the records that Mommsen would surely have kept, if only as copies, for his own protection? Donna Mommsen might have found more of the former, but Russell didn't think so—she wasn't that good an actress. And if she'd found the latter, which would of course be in German, how would she know what they were?

And then there were the clients. Had they read the news of their genealogist's death with relief or apprehension? The man who knew their secret was gone, but had he left any records behind? Russell wondered if anyone had asked Kuzorra that question.

He stopped in his tracks as another thought occurred to him. Maybe some of the clients hadn't chosen to employ Mommsen. Maybe the genealogist had used his hours in record offices to seek out families that challenged Nazi racial taboos, and then taken his findings to them.

He would probably never know, Russell thought. And the families concerned would continue to worry that things that had happened before they were born would suddenly come to light, and turn their lives upside-down. Because as long as the clowns in power trumpeted their racist rubbish, and as long as ordinary people refused to see that rubbish for what it was, anyone less than the Nazi conception of pure was anyone else's prey.

As Russell kicked a stray pebble into the water, an animal roared in the zoo ahead. It probably wanted a transfer to some other country.

Still, he thought, it wasn't all gloom. The social and political context was worsening by the day, but he had to admit to enjoying his work. He admired his editor and got on well enough with most of his colleagues; getting out and meeting people was usually much more intriguing than working at home. He was under no illusions about how long the job would last—the Nazis were going to clamp down on any signs of dissent, starting with the Jewish-owned papers and continuing with any that dared express a liberal opinion. The constant government complaints that the opposition press made up news rather than simply report it were just the beginning—once the existence of facts was denied then everything was a lie. Everything but power and the will to use it.

Russell liked fiction as much as the next man, but he couldn't imagine agreeing to lie for a living. Better to side-step the issue, work where lies weren't necessary, writing on sports or transport or countries far enough away that they weren't on Hitler's map. He had thought the crime desk might prove a safe haven but most of the stories he'd covered so far had political hazards running right through them, like the letters in a stick of seaside rock. Which shouldn't have come as a shock when the forces of law and order were the people committing the crimes.

He crossed Viktoria Platz and walked west along the Ku'damm's northern sidewalk. As he approached the Green

Dragon restaurant he remembered standing outside it on the night he and Ilse parted, feeling a poignant blend of sadness and relief. He didn't think either of them had ever regretted the decision, and he hoped she would say the same of their years together. He certainly would.

The man on the door recognised him, but had the sense not to ask after Ilse. Perhaps she'd been here with Matthias, he thought. And why not? Why had he been boycotting the place?

The interior hadn't changed, save for the small Nazi flag by the till. Maybe Göring ate here—he seemed to eat everywhere else.

The menu was also the same, and he ordered his usual favourites. The place was almost empty, but it was still early by Ku'damm standards, and would probably soon fill up. He and Ilse had used to eat dinner quite late, often after nine.

Eight years they had been together, and the first five had been almost perfect. Or so he had thought at the time. When marriages collapsed, they often seemed to fall backwards, crushing those better days in their past. He thought they'd shared the blame, but perhaps he was kidding himself. He had certainly not been a good provider, but then he hadn't anticipated two married communists finding this failing important. Paul, of course, had changed everything, an emotional fact he'd been far too slow to recognise. Maybe he'd learned stuff that would help him next time, as one married friend had suggested. Of course she was still with her husband.

His dishes arrived, and were every bit as good as he remembered. He'd like to bring someone here, he thought, as a smiling young couple sat down a few feet away. Maybe he was ready for another go—the prospect at least seemed possible, which was more than it had done a year ago. Over those months Olga Beyschlag had served up three quite lovely teachers, and he had passed on them all, emotionally if not sexually. There had also been several Hennis whom he hadn't left at the door.

Back out on the Ku'damm feeling suitably replete, he slowly ambled back towards the Memorial Church. The mood on the street seemed strange, but then he hadn't been here in the evening for quite a while, and perhaps it was his expectations that were out of kilter. A lot of the old clubs and cabarets seemed to have closed, taking their wild and often annoying spontaneity with them, leaving . . . what? Well-dressed people were smiling, laughing, on their way to dinner or some entertainment, but there was something forced about it all, as if this was the time they were supposed to have fun, and they were damn well going to have it. There were flags and uniforms everywhere, which maybe jaundiced his view, but it felt like the country he loved had fallen under a spell, and was almost sleep-marching into the future.

Russell and his brother-in-law had lunch together every few weeks, and after scheduling a Friday morning meeting with a magazine proprietor in Mitte, Thomas had booked a table for two at the Haussmann Restaurant on Jägerstrasse. He was already there when Russell arrived, chatting with the wine waiter.

"The usual Moselle?"

"Suits me," Russell replied, sitting down. "So how's everyone?" he asked, once the waiter had gone to collect the bottle.

"My father's not too well, but I don't think it's anything serious. The children are fine. Hanna's talking about going back to work, mostly, I suspect, because the Nazis are so keen on women staying at home. If we manage to move, I think she'll decide she'd rather be out in the garden."

Russell noticed a man at a nearby table turn to see who was talking, a frown on his face. Needless to say, an enamel swastika was pinned to his lapel. Russell caught his eye and held it, until the man looked away. "An unhappy eavesdropper," he told Thomas quietly. His brother-in-law had never been good at self-censorship.

Thomas just grunted.

"How are things at work?"

"Good enough, I suppose. The meeting this morning—we just signed another printing contract. But"—he remembered to lower his voice—"I do worry about the future. With Jews making up a third of the workforce . . ." He spread his hands in a gesture of helplessness. "It's never been an issue up till now; relations have always been fine, and my father thinks I'm worrying unduly. But the poison seeps in, doesn't it?"

"Usually."

"I knew I could rely on you to counter my pessimism. But seriously, I can't see what more I can do to pre-empt any trouble, short of inviting Hitler around for a lecture on Christian forgiveness."

"He and his Party may take matters out of your hands," Russell suggested.

Thomas didn't think so. "They'll go after the professional Jews—the lawyers and doctors, the university professors. And Jews in the public eye—musicians and film stars, other celebrities. As long as working class Jews keep their heads down they'll be all right. They're vital to the economy, and Hitler's staked his reputation on getting things moving again. He may be a racist bastard, but he knows which side his bread is buttered."

The waiter arrived to take their order. As usual Thomas wanted the Rhenish speciality of blood sausage, onions and apple mashed potatoes, and for once Russell felt like having the same. Their eavesdropper was leaving, but a look in their direction suggested he might have something to say. A few seconds later he was looming over their table, exhaling wafts of beer breath all over Thomas. "You, sir," he hissed, "should learn some respect for our leader."

The look Thomas gave him would have flattered a cock-roach. "He may be your leader, but he certainly isn't mine."

The man strained for a cutting retort, but could only come up with a threat. "You and your kind will soon find out who are the masters in Germany," he forced through gritted teeth before striding away.

"My kind," Thomas murmured. He raised his glass. "To our kind."

Russell raised his and both of them drank. "As for *their* kind . . . we had a great story the other day. It seems the SA visited Lion Feuchtwanger's villa in Grunewald—Feuchtwanger's abroad, by the way—and they took away his latest manuscript. The day after that they went back to steal his car. You can just imagine the conversation down at the *Sturm* bar—'Helmut, we forgot to take the car!'"

"I was wondering who they'd get to read them the manu-script," Thomas said drily. "How are things going at work?"

"Interesting, most of the time. Frustrating too." Rus-sell went through the Konrad Mommsen story, and all the unanswered questions it had left him with.

Thomas agreed that murder and arson would have been an improvement on two unrelated accidents. "At least for the journalist."

Their food arrived, halting conversation for the next ten minutes. Once desserts had been eaten and coffee ordered Russell took a deep breath and introduced the subject of Ilse and Matthias. "Your sister hasn't said so in so many words, but I imagine she wants a divorce."

"You think she'd tell me?"

Russell gave him a look. "You or Hanna, and Hanna would tell you."

Thomas's shrug conceded that this was true. "Ilse's torn.

She doesn't want Paul to lose his father, but she does want a child with Matthias."

"And she wants that child to be legitimate."

"Of course."

Russell sighed. "Can you see a way through this? Because I can't."

"I'm afraid I can't."

Russell smiled. "I had this fantasy the other day, that the three of us could all travel to Switzerland. Ilse and I would get divorced, and she and Matthias would get married. The German authorities would never know."

"But everyone here would still think the children were bastards."

"That was the flaw," Russell admitted.

"One of them, at least. You'd be better off getting divorced and burning down the records office a few days later."

"Probably. Of course I am doing this job for Matthias's old army friend . . ."

"Ilse told me. Well he'll be in your debt, but finding the girl sounds like a nightmare. The sort of places she'll be hiding are not ones I'd want to visit, even if Hitler does get his thugs to stop stamping on faces they don't like the look of."

"So far I've only been looking in Wedding, and I don't think I've been in any danger. But then I haven't found any trace of her either." He told Thomas about meeting Arno Knoden, and the mixed feelings he'd had about the man.

Thomas was sympathetic. "I was never a communist, as you know very well, but I can't help admiring people like that, even when I disagree with them."

"I wish we could say the same of our friends on the right."

Thomas shook his head. "Their day has come. Let's pray it's a short one."

A complaint had arrived at the office during Russell's absence. The production company behind Greta

Sonnermann's new film considered his exaggeration of "a minor discrepancy" between the actress's description of her persecutor and the man's actual appearance was "cruel and misleading." No allowance "whatsoever" had been made for Fraulein Sonnermann's "understandably acute distress."

"The scriptwriters have been working overtime," was Russell's observation.

"I doubt they'll be paid for it," Hiedler replied. "I'm told the company's going bust, which is why they set up the whole charade. And the young fool the police arrested is paying the price. All he actually did was trespass on her property, and scatter the roses in her swimming pool. They were artificial, by the way—he got them from the props department, where he works. Or used to. And the reason he did what he did? After all her trouble with "swarthy face," he thought she needed cheering up."

"Unbelievable."

"If only. The studio have decided to be generous—dismissal is apparently punishment enough. And Greta comes out of the whole sordid business almost literally showered in roses. When you write this up, please be sure to mention that she's turning forty this year."

"Punishment enough?" Russell asked.

"No, but it'll have to do."

It was a pleasant evening, warmer than it had been despite the cloudless sky, and Russell decided to walk home. He was crossing the Unter den Linden when he saw the two cleaners, one ferociously scrubbing the sidewalk, the other squeezing a sponge full of reddish water into a galvanised bucket.

The man at the newsstand opposite was happy to say what had happened. A car containing a Nazi bigwig had driven by, and one young spectator had been spotted with his arms by his sides and a smile on his face. Half a dozen stormtroopers had waded in and carried him off, apparently deaf to his shouts that he was American.

"I thought Hitler and Göring were trying to stop such incidents," Russell said cautiously.

"Ah, some of them just can't help themselves," was the worldly response.

Russell walked on, thinking that until things "settled down" flinging an arm at the sky like a clockwork soldier seemed like a small price to pay for personal safety.

Arno Knoden, he knew, would not agree.

When Russell arrived at the old communist's block later that evening, Frau Nortz nodded him on up the stairs with something approaching a smile. Knoden was quick to answer his door, and quick to tell his visitor that he had done what he had promised. "I have asked around, and I do have news. There is a girl, a recent recruit, who has blond hair and is roughly the age you mentioned. The man who told me this doesn't know her name. He has seen her only once, last Monday he thinks, while engaged in Party business. In Neukölln."

Several thoughts occurred to Russell. This was better news for the colonel, in that it offered at least some hope. But finding her hadn't got much easier. Neukölln covered a sizable area of the city's south-east, with scores of industrial premises and warrens of working-class tenements, all honeycombed with alleyways, railway tracks and towpaths. The district's SA had a vicious reputation, which was something given the competition. But they didn't have Lili Zollitsch, or hadn't as recently as Monday.

There was one obvious question. "Did the comrade say what Party business he was engaged in?"

"He did not, and I didn't ask him." Knoden raised a gnarled hand to ward off further questions. "You must understand. More than half of the Neukölln Party activists have been arrested, leaving those still at large with a vital job to do. The fight with the Nazis is over, and we have lost. So now we fight for survival, and a future. The Party has assets—you will know what they are—which must be put beyond the Nazis' reach, and those comrades still at liberty will be using every hour at their disposal to do so." The old man's blue eyes seemed to bore into Russell's. "And even those who've been taken still have a part in the struggle, because every minute the brutes spend flogging our men or abusing our women is a minute they won't be out on the streets.

"They will come for me eventually, because they know where I am and they'll run out of others to torture. I believe I am ready. No one likes pain, but there are worse things. Like knowing that the struggle I lived for has ended in such a defeat, and that I won't live to see the tide turn. I was born in 1848," he said unexpectedly. "You know what that means?"

"That you're as old as the *Communist Manifesto*."

"Exactly. I met Engels several times. I've been in meetings with Lenin and Stalin; I was Liebknecht's friend. I spent several weeks on Trotsky's train during the civil war." He smiled. "Though that's not something to brag about these days," he noted mischievously.

"With any luck my heart will give out," he said, as much to himself as Russell. "But I'm glad this girl's still alive. I hope you find her and I hope she tells you that she's far too busy saving our future to cosset her colonel father. And then you can tell him how proud he should be of her."

"I may do that," Russell said. "And thank you." As he got up to leave someone could be heard shouting outside, but the view from Knoden's window was unenlightening. Russell said goodbye and hurried down the stairs, hearing more raised voices as he did so.

Frau Nortz was on her way back in as he reached the

front door. "They've closed off the street again," she told him as they passed.

An amplified voice was now ordering all residents to exit their homes, leave the doors open, and assemble on the sidewalk outside. Away to both left and right lines of torch-bearing stormtroopers were blocking off both ends of the two-hundred-metre-long Kosliner Strasse. Open lorries were parked in front of the cordons, their headlights flooding the street between them with yellow light, and casting the shadows of advancing brownshirts along the tenement walls.

Russell's first instinct was to dive into one of the many dark passages and hope to find a back way out. But one or all might be cul-de-sacs, and the brownshirts were carrying rifles. Joining the tenants emerging from Knoden's block seemed like the lesser evil.

Soon they were all on the sidewalk, as were their neighbours to left and right. SA men were entering the buildings in groups of three or more, and presumably searching each home for people on their wanted list. And they were being thorough. It was almost half an hour before they began to re-emerge, mostly empty-handed, at least as far as Russell could see, though God only knew what they'd pocketed. One group came out carrying an elderly woman, whom they lowered none too carefully onto the sidewalk, and when one man was brave enough to protest, he was clubbed by the nearest stormtrooper, and left unmoving where he fell.

At least no one had been thrown from a window. Not yet anyway.

The residents had mostly been quiet while they waited, either bored because they thought they were safe, or apprehensive because they knew they were not. Russell was thinking he belonged in the former category until he realised he'd come out without his papers. These were still in his winter coat, which the day's warm weather had persuaded him to leave at home. His press card, which he did have in his pocket, might prove a two-edged sword.

The SA were now concentrating on the residents gathered outside each block, first forming queues, then checking each person's papers against their lists. Knoden was one of the first to be questioned in his group, and to Russell's relief and surprise was given leave to go back to his room. Only one man ahead of him was escorted down to a lorry, his mask of defiance betrayed by visibly shaking limbs.

Five men from other blocks had been led away by the time Russell's turn came. When he started explaining that he didn't live on Kosliner Strasse the young stormtrooper told him to shut up. "I'll ask the questions. Show me your papers."

When Russell explained that he'd left them at home, he was told that that was a crime in itself. "I have a press card," he told the man, pulling it out of his pocket. "And I'm English," he added, knowing that might make things worse.

"This says nothing about your being English," the stormtrooper said after examining the card, "or who you write for. Perhaps you write for a Red paper."

"I write for the *Morgenspiegel.*"

"It doesn't say so." He called a subordinate over. "This one," he said.

"Your leader has given orders that foreigners are not to be molested," Russell interjected, as the subordinate grabbed hold of his arm.

"If you really are one, I'm sure you won't be," his interrogator said with a grin, before jerking his head in the direction of the lorry.

Conscious of the club in his escort's other hand, Russell allowed himself to be led down the street, and lifted with more than necessary vigour onto the back of the vehicle. Five and a half pairs of eyes looked him over with dull curiosity; the half outstanding was a mess of fresh blood.

He'd been in worse situations, but not for a very long time.

The lorry's engine burst into life, and as it pulled slowly away Russell could hear the sadistic cheers of the watching stormtroopers. He already had a least favourite destination in mind, and his heart duly sank when the driver turned right onto Uferstrasse. And no matter how much he mentally urged the man to swing left or right, the driver just kept moving straight ahead, all the way to the doors of the derelict factory that Russell had walked past the previous week.

The moon was out tonight, and the site was bathed in a ghostly glow. He and the other six men were hustled into the nearest building with clubs and rifle butts—nothing too painful, more like a warm-up than the actual game. After passing down a corridor whose chequered plate floor drummed beneath their feet and traversing a darkened workshop the size of a concert hall they finally came to a much smaller room where benches lined three of the walls. Ordered to sit, they looked, Russell thought, like footballers waiting for their kit to arrive.

Some hope. Nobody was speaking, as if all of them knew the time for talk was over. The stormtroopers standing guard looked bored, and were probably hoping someone would give them an excuse to swing their rifles. Like cats, Russell thought—after the capture there had to be games. At least cats had beauty to recommend them.

A Sturmführer appeared in the doorway, list in hand. "Pöhner," he said, sounding like a doctor's receptionist. A dark-haired young man sitting opposite struggled to his feet, inhibited, as far as Russell could see, more by sheer reluctance than any physical failing. He went through the door without looking back.

Russell felt the fear rising in his own throat. He swallowed and looked down at his hands, which were clenched around his knees. At least they weren't shaking, at least he hadn't pissed himself. Time enough, probably. But this wasn't the trenches, and he wasn't about to walk across an open field under a sky full of plummeting shells. You couldn't explain to a shell, couldn't argue with the way it was heading. The SA—or so some people said—were actually human beings.

He wouldn't mention the war, though. They might not appreciate his fighting for the enemy.

But he had to keep his head above the fear. Had to be sure he didn't provoke them. No jokes, no smart-aleck remarks. It was resentment against people like himself that had led a lot of these men to join the Nazis in the first place, and stoking it would only make them angrier. Most of them weren't very bright, and unsurprisingly didn't much like being told so, whether directly or not. He would talk to them as equals and agree with their aims. He would share their contempt for the Versailles Treaty, which wouldn't be that difficult.

He was feeling slightly better when a scream of pain cut through the silence, and had them all gulping for air. It came from the direction in which the young man had been taken, and sounded alarmingly close. Another followed a few seconds later, longer and more piercing, until it abruptly cut out. The six of them there in the room were staring at their feet, all thinking the same thing—how can I avoid it?

Over the next half hour the second and third men apparently did, but neither they nor the first man came back.

Russell was fourth. The Sturmführer escorted him down a long corridor, and into a well-lit room that had probably once housed machines of some sort. The walls were bare brick, the floor bare wood with a few rusted fittings. Something that looked like a vaulting horse without the pommels stood on one side, a washing tub complete with mangle on the other. It could have been a macabre stage set, if not for the obvious freshness of the blood.

If the set designer's aim had been to terrify, then Russell could testify to his success.

A door led through to another room where a stool and chair sat either side of a metal table. The SA Sturmbannführer in the chair had ginger-blond hair and a pale complexion, with greenish eyes behind spectacles that gave him an almost owlish look. A cap, cigarettes and a rawhide whip lay on one side of the table, a pile of documents on the other.

Russell was pushed roughly down onto the stool.

"Name?" the Sturmbannführer asked. His voice had a chronic smoker's hoarseness.

"John Russell."

"The journalist," the Sturmbannführer said, lifting Russell's press card from the top of his pile. "You have an English name."

"I am English," Russell said, swallowing an impulse to sarcasm.

"Speak some."

Russell's mind went blank for a moment. "Three blind mice, see how they run . . ."

"That could be French or Hindustani, couldn't it, Hermann?"

"It could, Sturmbannführer," a voice right behind Russell said.

Oh good, a double act, Russell thought. The disdain must have shown in his face, because a slight nod from the Sturmbannführer resulted in something very hard being rammed into the small of Russell's back.

After wheezing for a while Russell managed to convey that his papers and passport were in his rooms on 51 Gerichtstrasse.

"And why would an Englishman choose to live in Wedding?" the Sturmbannführer asked with a rhetorical tone.

"Because he's an English Red?" Hermann suggested. "Or he's really a Russian?"

"Is either of Hermann's guesses correct?" the Sturmbannführer asked Russell.

"I'm living in Wedding because the rent is cheap, and since I separated from my wife it's all I can afford." He didn't want to mention Paul, didn't want his presence in the room.

"She took all the money, eh?"

"Something like that." Russell thought of bringing up the leadership's new policy of not mistreating foreigners, but that might prove a large red rag to these particular bulls.

He was still weighing pros and cons when the Sturmbannführer brought the matter up himself. "When our leader is bending over backwards to protect foreign guests to our country, the least we expect is that those guests obey our laws."

"I am sorry I left my papers at home. I shall not let it happen again."

The Sturmbannführer kneaded his stubbly chin and then sighed, looking like someone resigned to a course of action he wouldn't have willingly chosen. "Hermann, send someone over to 51 Gerichtstrasse. And put our foreign guest in one of the cells. I may want to see him again."

Trying not to show how relieved he felt, Russell allowed Hermann to prod him down a new corridor and into what several units of shelving suggested had once been a storeroom. There was nowhere to sit, and he was still lowering himself to the floor when the door clanged shut and the light went out. "Hey!" he shouted reflexively, not that anyone would hear. Or care.

The room had no windows, but as his eyes adapted the light seeping under the door allowed him to make out the shelves on the opposite wall. He remembered in France how clear moonlit nights had felt safer, even though the opposite was usually true. Human beings didn't function too well in total darkness.

Sitting there alone in the gloom was certainly an

improvement on the Sturmbannführer's stool, but his back throbbed and he couldn't seem to stop shaking inside. Think, he told himself. Distract yourself with logic.

The good news was that being a foreigner must have worked in his favour, or they wouldn't have sent someone out for his papers. And when they confirmed he was who he said, they might well let him go.

But probably not before he told them what he'd been doing on Berlin's most famous communist street. Their initial suspicion would be that he was one, but if Herr Mechnig of the Resident Foreign Nationals section of the Prussian Interior Ministry had known that he wasn't, and that he had in fact long left the Party, then any SA investigator consulting the same official records would surely discover the same. And since everyone knew that the communists hated ex-comrades worse than anyone else, the Nazis would know he knew nothing of the Party's current organisation, personnel or plans.

A loud wail of obvious pain cut through these semi-optimistic thoughts. Shouting followed, and a high-pitched screech. And then, as if in answer, a woman's piercing scream rose and hung in the air like a blade twisting in flesh.

Russell's blood ran cold, leaving him shivering from head to toe, and fighting the impulse to cover his ears. Over the next half hour, the harrowing cries kept recurring. Several times he thought they had stopped, and each time the silence was broken he felt another layer of his sanity stripped away. And when, at long last, the screaming really did seem to be over, he found himself wondering if death was the reason, and whether it had been a release.

It was almost two in the morning when someone approached the storeroom door, and his heart took off like a galloping horse.

He was already up on his feet when the key turned in the lock.

"This way," the stormtrooper told him, gesturing with his handgun.

They seemed to be walking deeper into the factory, but at least they were heading away from the mangle and vaulting horse. A corridor led to an outside door, and for a few wonderful seconds Russell thought they might be about to release him. But no. A quick walk across a yard, and they were back in another part of the complex. The administrative offices, it looked like, which might be good news.

This time the man behind the desk was a Standarten-führer, the SA equivalent of a colonel. And he had a name, printed in gold on a black office deskplate: Felix Wipperman. He didn't look blessed with any more human kindness than the Sturmbannführer, but looks could deceive, and despite the name there wasn't a whip on display. Russell had always found it harder to identify class in Germany than he had in England, but if his first interrogator had seemed authentically proletarian then this one bore a much more petit bourgeois stamp. It was probably just prejudice on his part, but was there something venal in the man's eyes? There was also a striking resemblance to Göring, especially where girth was concerned.

The Standartenführer didn't waste any time. "What were you doing on Kosliner Strasse?"

It was the question Russell had expected, but he still wasn't sure what his answer should be. Should he say he'd been there on a story, talking to someone he couldn't name, because journalists never revealed their sources? He decided not. Why would anyone here give a flying fuck about journalistic ethics?

The truth would be better. They already knew about Knoden, so saying he'd been to see the old man wouldn't hurt him. And explaining the reason for his visit might, he suddenly realised, both get him off the hook and help find Lili. If the girl was in SA custody then Wipperman had a much better chance of finding her than he did, and Russell couldn't imagine Zollitsch refusing to pay what would be a ransom in all but name.

But what if she wasn't in SA custody? Would he be naming her just to save himself? He couldn't see how he'd be putting her at greater risk, but Wipperman was waiting for an answer and he had no time to think it through.

"I was visiting Arno Knoden," Russell said, his mind still racing through possibilities.

"A known Red."

"In the past. He's eighty-five years old. He's not involved in politics anymore."

"So he'd like us to believe. And in the unlikely event he's telling the truth, why would you be interested in him?

Russell's mind was made up. They were scouring the city for communists anyway, and he wouldn't say anything that would actually lead them to Lili. "I'm looking for a young woman," he said eventually. "A girl really. She's not a communist but she seems to have run off with a young man who is. Her father's a colonel in the regular army, and he's asked me to look for her."

The Standartenführer looked interested for the first time. "Why did he come to you? Why not look for her himself?"

"Because, a long time ago, I was in the KPD," Russell admitted, sure that Wipperman already knew as much. "So he thought I'd have a better chance of getting their people to talk than he would." Russell shrugged, and played what he hoped was his trump card. "And he's not just relying on me—he's also offered a big reward."

Wipperman tried not to look like he cared. "How big?"

"Five hundred marks."

The eyes widened. "What is the young woman's name?"

"Lili Zollitsch," Russell said, "but I doubt that she's using it. She's only nineteen," he added. "And rather too trusting, according to her father." He hoped that Wipperman would ask the other custodians of private hells like this one if they had a pretty young blonde in custody. If she'd been caught in the last few days then her father would find out where she was, and if she hadn't then no harm would be done.

Russell reminded himself to exculpate Arno Knoden. "Anyway, I went to see the old Red because I thought he might still have some useful contacts. But he doesn't. I think he's probably a little gaga. He seems to have lost interest in just about everything, including politics."

The Standartenführer waved this away. "Do you have a photograph of the girl?" he asked.

"No," Russell told him, thankful that he'd left the one Zollitsch had given him at the office. "I was shown one, of course, but the colonel refused to let it out of his sight. She's nineteen years old. Slim with long blond hair and blue eyes. A lovely face, her father says, but then fathers always think that."

"I will make enquiries," Wipperman said. "And if I hear of a girl like that I shall contact you, because I suspect the colonel would be somewhat shocked by what he found in one of our makeshift establishments," he continued, his tone reminding Russell of someone warning a guest how untidy they might find the house. "Not to mention the state his daughter might be in," Wipperman added blithely. "I make no apology—these Red bitches fight like cats—but he should be prepared for the worst."

Shouldn't they all, Russell thought. He was beginning to congratulate himself for turning the tables when the Standartenführer fired a last warning shot.

"You tell a convincing story, but then lying for a living is what journalists do. And if I find you've lied to me, you'll be back here, and it won't be for a civilised chit-chat. You do understand me, Herr Russell?"

"I do."

"Then you are free to go."

A few minutes later Russell was walking out through the factory gates. No one was screaming behind him, but he could still hear those from hours before, and a surge of his own undigested terror had him retching through the wire fence that bordered the Panke.

Once that was done, he just crouched by the fence, fingers hooked on the wire, until the frenzied barking of a distant dog brought him back to the world. The room on Gerichtstrasse had never been a sanctuary, and now seemed less one than ever, but it was the only home he had. Forcing himself into motion, he started down Uferstrasse, hoping that Lili was still at large, and that he wouldn't need to rely on Zollitsch having five hundred marks to buy back his daughter.

It was past three in the morning when he let himself into his flat. Some things had been moved, and one drawer was open, but the man or men sent to fetch his papers had not taken the opportunity to ransack the place, and nothing seemed to be missing. For reasons best known to themselves, the SA had been on their best behaviour, or perhaps they just knew they could always come back.

While utterly exhausted, Russell knew that sleep was unlikely. After boiling water for tea on his small electric hob, he took the resultant brew to his threadbare armchair and sat in the dark trying and failing to let his mind go blank.

Moving into the bedroom he found *Mein Kampf* leering up at him, and narrowly resisted the temptation to fling it out of the window. The thought of Herr Dickel coming across a Nazi bible lying in the gutter might have been funny six hours before but didn't seem so now. Not when Russell had printed his name on the inside cover.

After reminding himself that he'd slept through worse in the trenches, he got into bed and hopefully closed his eyes.

Four hours later he was still awake, and sunlight was filtering in between the curtains. He was not due in to work that day, but the night editor might have left a message asking him to update one or more of his stories for the Sunday edition. Once a quick trip downstairs to Frau Löffner's notice board had shown him there was none, he walked across to the public baths and found himself standing right behind Herr Dickel in the queue for cubicles. A silent prayer that the man would not turn round went unanswered, and Russell was treated to a long exposition of the *Blockleiter*'s thoughts on "socialist traitors" and what should be done to them.

When Dickel's turn for a cubicle came, Russell found himself hoping the man would drown.

His own allotted minutes in the steaming water felt far too short, but he suspected several hours would not have been enough. Back across the street, Frau Löffner was waiting in the hallway, looking more worried than usual. "An SA man called round last night," she complained. "At one in the morning! I don't know why he had to wake me up—he had your key. He said you had sent him to collect something, so I just let him go up and get it. I hope I did the right thing. He seemed like a regular type, and one doesn't like to argue with those people."

Russell assured her she had done nothing wrong, and apologised for her being disturbed. "I was picked up in one of their sweeps," he explained. "And they needed to verify who I was. Once they did that, they let me go."

"Of course," she said, as if such things should be expected. She was obviously in the mood for a chat, and was eager to know if Russell thought the Nazi leaders sincere in their calls for an end to the violence. "Even Göring is saying it now," she said, sounding more surprised than pleased.

"I hope so," he said.

Climbing the stairs ten minutes later he realised he had to get out of the house. And out of Wedding. He couldn't leave Berlin because missing his son's sixth birthday party was out of the question.

After packing the boy's presents into a holdall and making doubly sure his papers were in his pocket, he hurried out of the building and headed for the nearest tram stop. He had no particular destination in mind, but had always felt more at ease in the centre than anywhere else. The first to arrive was a No.91, and after taking it as far as the Brandenburg Gate, he walked down Unter den Linden to Kranzler's Café. If any spot in Berlin felt like a home away from home, this was his, but not, it turned out, on this particular morning. He bought his usual coffee, and spread his usual paper, but the former tasted too sweet and the latter failed to hold his attention. He found himself nervously watching the street, where a gang of city workers were preparing for another parade. The swastikas on Unter den Linden seemed more numerous than ever, and Russell had a vision of them all coalescing into one enormous flag, and covering the city like a giant shroud.

He told himself to get a grip. The sun was shining, he was free, and a birthday party beckoned.

The crowds out shopping on Friedrichstrasse and Leipziger Strasse didn't seem worn down by worries, and the pickets all seemed gone from their normal posts outside the Jewish-owned stores. At the office they were surprised to see him, particularly as there was nothing new that merited his attention. He retreated to the canteen and took another stab at reading the morning papers before eating a desultory lunch.

Paul's party was due to begin at two, and finding himself too early, Russell spent half an hour on a bench in the Volkspark, where he and his son had played football only three days before. His circumstances hadn't changed since then, but he knew the night in the factory had shifted something inside his mind. What it was, and whether it was permanent, he couldn't yet tell.

But this was his son's day, he told himself as he walked to the house on Wilhelmsaue. There were eight other children invited, Paul's two cousins and six of his friends from school. Thomas's son Joachim began by pointedly sticking with the adults, but eventually found it impossible to resist a leadership role in organizing the games.

Russell put on a cheerful mask, and his son was much too wrapped up in all the excitement to notice. After the birthday tea, which ended with cream being worn like haphazard make-up on most of the faces, Paul opened the family presents, and Russell was pleased to observe that the envelope containing the Hertha tickets evoked the broadest smile.

Both Ilse and Thomas had noticed he wasn't his usual self, and after all the guests had left, and Matthias had asked Paul if the two of them could set up the model railway, Russell told his wife and brother-in-law what had happened. Ilse's spotless modern kitchen seemed worlds away from the Uferstrasse factory, and as he told the story Russell had the sense of straddling two wildly separate Germanys, one in the light and one in the dark. Only they weren't separate. The same people lived and shopped and held birthday parties in both of them.

"I was scared," he avowed. "I still am, although I've no real reason to be. They must have let me go because I'm a foreigner—I can't see any other reason why the sadist should have sent me on to his superior. And the superior just wanted to show me who was boss. I think he'd have let me go with or without the reward for finding Lili."

"The others are probably still there," Thomas said quietly. "And part of you is still there with them. Scared."

"Maybe."

"Couldn't you put the story in your paper?" Ilse asked. "No," she said, answering herself, "I know you couldn't."

"The paper would be punished, and I'd be deported. If I was lucky." Russell hesitated, but only for a moment—he knew he had no choice. "Look, Ilse, the way things are, I can't have Paul staying over at my place in Wedding. I'm just imagining the SA kicking my door in at three in the morning and him being there."

"Of course," she said. "I was hoping you . . ."

"Had the sense to see it. I do. It feels bad, and I don't know how to tell him. If I say it's not safe there, he may worry about me."

"He will. He does, I think. And we must do all we can to reassure him. But better he worries than ends up where you did last night."

"Exactly. But I want him to know that it's temporary. That I love him, and want to have him with me as much as I can."

"Just tell him that," Thomas said. "In those words."

"I will. OK."

"Everyone thinks things will have to calm down eventually," Ilse said. "It could just be wishful thinking, I know, but . . ."

"It will calm down," Thomas insisted. "And I'll tell you why. Up until now the SA have only been a problem for the left, but they're starting to become a problem for those on the right as well. The more people like Röhm go on about the SA becoming the new regular army, the more the Army will feel threatened, and the Generals will fight to preserve their role. The same goes for the business leaders. They backed the stormtroopers in their fight with the left, but now the left is beaten they no longer need them. Business likes order, and the stormtroopers are still stirring things up. When Hitler's conservative allies insist on his reining them in, what objection can he raise? If all the physical threats to his regime are gone, why does he still need a private army?"

"I hope you're right," Ilse said, "because at the moment we're at their mercy."

"We are," Thomas conceded. "I guess the moral of the story is: don't hang around in places that used to be communist strongholds."

Russell gave him a wry smile. "Which is exactly what I have to do if I'm ever going to find Lili Zollitsch."

Thomas sighed. "Look, why don't you sleep at our place tonight?"

Russell was tempted, but knew he shouldn't. He remembered his father shouting at him because he refused to get back on his bicycle after he'd fallen off. A hot summer day on the Weyside towpath; he must have been about Paul's age.

"Thanks, but no," he told his friend. "If I can't live a normal life, I'd be better off leaving. And Berlin is my home. Tomorrow Paul and I will go to the Funkturm, and see the city laid out in all its glory."

Family could be a wonderful thing, Russell thought as he walked towards the U-Bahn station. His first one had been just him and his parents, both of whom came from small families themselves. The nearest relatives were too far away to visit in a day, and on the few occasions they met up for Christmas it was like staying with strangers. His German family had started with Ilse, but soon expanded to take in her brother's, and now seemed set to include Matthias. Russell doubted whether he and Ilse's new partner would ever be bosom buddies, but the man was good to Paul, and, Russell had to admit, hard to dislike.

They weren't all on the same political page, which in less fraught times might have been a problem, but given what was happening to their country, their city, their lives, any previous differences seemed to be almost irrelevant. Might bringing his family together and making its members stronger be another unlooked-for consequence of Nazi rule?

Or was he whistling in the dark? His family wasn't in Wedding, and he had no desire to hurry back there. The lights of the Ku'damm seemed a much better bet, and it was only after eating a good dinner, sitting through a dreadful Hungarian film at the Marmorhaus, and spending two hours in a bar, that he caught the last tram back to Wedding.

Gerichtstrasse was reassuringly silent and empty, all but the hall light out at No.51. There was no Frau Löffner, no message for him on the board, no sign that his room had been entered again.

"A one-off," he said out loud, hoping to convince himself. Perhaps Thomas had been right about being more careful where he went. Perhaps he'd just been unlucky with his timing. But with his particular past, his current job and his foreign ancestry, he knew he had to be a damn sight more careful than most of his fellow Berliners.

He took himself to bed, hoping exhaustion would put him to sleep, and found himself recalling something a chaplain had told him at Ypres, that when waking hours are full of nightmares, sleeping hours will not be.

His and Paul's Sunday excursion to the Funkturm was a triumph over the conditions. Berlin hadn't seen significant rain for a fortnight, but on this particular day it appeared with depressing frequency, and the view from the tower's observation platform was severely curtailed. The one moment of excitement was when a plane on its way into Tempelhof suddenly dropped out of the low-hanging clouds only a few hundred feet above their heads.

The restaurant was well-stocked with the American elixir Paul craved, and Russell, having recently read how much caffeine the drink contained, felt obliged to refuse the boy a third bottle. Sleepless nights before school were not to be recommended.

With the weather prohibiting any outdoor activity, they

walked to Witzleben station and took their oft-repeated journey on the Ringbahn, which this time featured views shrunken and blurred by mist and rain. After talking about the day before's party Paul surprised him by asking if he felt any better today. Russell felt pleased that his six-year-old son was aware of the people around him, sad that his troubles had left any mark on the birthday. "I just had a headache," he told Paul. "It's gone today."

If Books Could Kill

The Monday morning rush hour was a damp affair, drizzle turning to rain and back again, Leipziger Strasse a sea of umbrellas as Russell's tram rumbled across it, the brilliant sparks from the catenary wires reflecting in the shopfront windows. A momentous week was in prospect. Tomorrow in Potsdam Hindenburg and Hitler would co-star in a ceremonial opening of the new Reichstag, and two days after that those elected deputies still at liberty were due to vote on an Enabling Bill designed to short-circuit what was left of German democracy. You could say one thing about Hitler—he didn't sit still.

In the meantime, like most of the country's male inhabitants, Russell had a job to do. There were three new stories waiting on his desk: two matrimonial disputes that had ended in hospitalisation, and a fight in a Neukölln bar that had proved even more conclusive. The latter looked less likely to interest his readers, and leaving it till last might give him some free daylight hours in Neukölln to plan his search for Lili.

Needless to say, the two domestic imbroglios had occurred at opposite ends of the city. The first had happened late the previous evening out near the stockyards in Friedrichshain, a few hours after he and Paul had rattled through the area on their train. The unlikely victim was a burly stormtrooper, who according to the local Kripo had been knocked right over by his enraged wife, cracking his skull on their iron stove in the process. He was unconscious in the State Hospital, the wife under arrest. Her motive for the alleged assault, as told to Russell by the neighbour she'd fetched in its aftermath, was her husband never being home. "There's a fucking parade every other day," she'd reportedly said. "And after the parade, they drink."

According to the neighbour, others had seen the Stormtrooper need three attempts to guide his bulk through the block's front door, and when his wife claimed he had simply fallen down drunk most were inclined to believe her. One exception was the local *Blockleiter*, who had insisted that service to the fatherland must always take precedence over husbandly duties, and then compounded the insult by advising the childless wife to fill up her days raising a family. "Are *you* going to give me one?" had been the reported response.

The second violent confrontation had taken place out in Spandau. Two trains and a bus later, Russell found himself outside the new and already decaying block of flats in which a husband had beaten his wife to a pulp for the sin of refusing to give up her job. Or at least, that was the way the already-present Eglhofer told the story. "He's a National Socialist, and he expected her to be a National Socialist wife. Her getting promoted was the last straw."

After interviewing what neighbours they could find— all of them women, most of them thinking the man had a point—Russell and Eglhofer went to the local hospital, where the woman in question was still unconscious, but just about holding her own.

As they stood on the Spandau Station platform waiting for a train back into the city, Eglhofer suggested that any woman with a brain was going to have her work cut out in Hitler's new Reich.

"Those with a brain will know to keep quiet," Russell replied.

"Of course. But add women to all the others who'll be keeping quiet—the Jews, the liberals, anyone who isn't fully signed up to all their idiocies—and think how much brain-power this country will lose. Our economy, our culture—we'll end up so far behind everyone else. It's a road to economic oblivion, hung with flags."

Hitler failing on such a grand scale was almost reason to be cheerful, Russell thought, until you remembered the millions who were still unemployed. After parting company with Eglhofer he took the U-Bahn out to Neukölln, and stopped for lunch at a workmen's café just north of the Ringbahn railway bridge. Once ensconced in a window seat he was ideally placed to watch the flow of pedestrian traffic on the adjacent sidewalk. It was too much to hope that Lili would stroll past, but if he was lucky, either that day or another, an old Party friend like Bruno Aretin might do so. If he was luckier still the comrade in question wouldn't just tell him to please get lost, and should he be blessed beyond reason the man or woman concerned might trust him enough to suggest where the girl might be found.

It was the sort of bet that bookies laughed at behind their hands, but what other options did he have? And people were always saying what a small world it was when they ran into someone they knew.

But his hour in the window went unrewarded, save for the plate of sausage and spätzel he consumed with an eye on the street. Neukölln did seem less cluttered with swastika banners than most of Berlin, but it was only a matter of time before Goebbels had his way. Tomorrow's political circus in Potsdam was getting the full treatment, and new loudspeakers were being hung above the sidewalk opposite. Or maybe just repaired—he suspected wire-cutters might be a popular tool in this particular district.

The bar in which last night's fight had occurred was just off Bergstrasse, about a hundred metres north of the café. The fight itself hadn't ended in a knifing, as the original report had claimed, but in what most of the witnesses thought was a heart attack. Both men involved had been fall-down drunk, and no one seemed sure that a punch had been landed. The only certainty was that one of the two men had collapsed and died before the ambulance arrived. A tragedy, but not a crime.

And not much of a story, Russell thought selfishly. Wondering how he might make it more interesting his thoughts turned to Prohibition, and whether the Nazis would bring it in. He doubted it. Hitler might be a teetotaller, but most of his brownshirts were anything but. And it hadn't been much of a success in America.

With time on his hands, Russell went back to the café for coffee and another hour's vigil, but no familiar faces passed by. On the U-Bahn back into town he bought and skimmed through an early evening edition, in which starstruck expectations of the morrow's jamboree shared print space with announcements of new restrictions on Jewish doctors, lawyers and orchestra conductors. How did that work, he wondered. If the orchestra was fully Aryan, how did the Jewish conductor insinuate his Jewishness into the music?

Back at the office, Hiedler and two of his political reporters were studying the just-released text of the prospective Enabling Act. It was what they'd all expected, a thoroughgoing shutdown of the democratic process. The bill was for four years, and in that time any law Hitler chose to introduce became the law of the land. The Reichstag would continue to sit, but would not be involved in legislative work. What it would do, other than collect its Nazi and Conservative members' salaries, was not clear.

"They've still got to get it passed," one of the reporters said hopefully, inviting pitying looks from his colleagues.

Russell wrote up his morning stories and was pleased when Hiedler agreed that the bar fight in Neukölln was not worth reporting. He was getting ready to leave for home when a man in an SA uniform appeared in the doorway across the newsroom, and one of the copy boys pointed the visitor in his direction. "Shit" was the word that came to mind.

The four leaves on the uniform said the man was a Sturmhauptführer—a captain in the regular army—and the lack of an escort hopefully meant he hadn't come to make an arrest. An emissary from Standartenführer Wipperman, Russell guessed correctly. Had Lili been found?

A young blond woman had been located in the Pankow detention centre, the Sturmhauptführer told him, after clicking his heels and announcing his name was Buchrucker. If Russell would care to accompany him, they could drive there now and see if it was Lili Zollitsch.

"Who does she say she is?" Russell asked.

"She has refused to give her name," Buchrucker admitted. "Despite persistent questioning."

Russell knew what that meant. "Then of course I shall come," he told the Sturmhauptführer. He doubted it was Lili—Pankow was a long way from Neukölln—but he could hardly say no without inviting some "persistent questioning" from Wipperman.

Having waved off Hiedler's mute query with a smile and a cheery wave, he followed the clicking boots down to the street. The Horch in front was blocking the sidewalk, but the swastikas flanking the bonnet inhibited any vocal complaints. Buchrucker gestured him into the back, and then took the seat beside the young driver, which suited Russell just fine. With the evening rush hour in full swing their progress was slow, and he had plenty of time to study the faces of those who noticed the flag-bedecked car. The looks were mostly admiring, although sometimes the admiration was a trifle wary. It was hard to imagine Hitler without his army of thugs, but even without them he probably had enough popular backing to keep him in power for years.

Once across the Spree, the traffic began to thin, and the driver was able to go a little faster. It was raining again, and as they motored north on Schönhauser Allée an occasional rumble of distant thunder could be heard above the rhythmic thump of the windscreen wipers. Every now and then the Sturmhauptführer would wind down his window a couple of inches to flick the ash from his cigarette, usually showering Russell in the process.

The detention centre turned out to be another abandoned factory, which according to the prominent sign-boards had recently hosted a company making weighing machines. Another victim of the Depression, Russell assumed. Many of its dismissed workers would have joined the Nazi ranks, and some were probably back here now doing very different work. Wall Street had a lot to answer for.

The usual trucks were parked outside, the usual bored-looking brownshirts standing guard at the entrance, and as Buchrucker led him inside Russell had a sudden moment of panic. Had it all been a trick to put him once more at their mercy?

He told himself that he was being ridiculous, that the SA was not known for subtle wheezes. A kick in the head was about as devious as Stormtroopers got.

Unreasonably buoyed by this thought, he waited while Buchrucker instructed a subordinate, then followed him down an echoing corridor and into a large empty room. "She will be brought to us here," the Sturmhauptführer told him.

Ten minutes went by, and Buchrucker was showing definite signs of irritation when the twin doors finally swung open, and two brownshirts appeared either side of someone in oversize trousers and a wrongly buttoned shirt. The threesome were halfway across the floor before Russell could be sure of the prisoner's gender.

Her face and bare feet were badly bruised, and whatever abuse the clothing concealed had almost bent her body in half. When the two men hoisted the woman straight for inspection, dangling her between them like a human scarecrow, it looked like she wanted to scream, but no longer had the energy.

Her face looked wet, Russell noticed, as if it had just been washed. One eye was virtually closed, the other seemed merely vacant. The lips were cut and chapped, the nostrils brown with dried blood.

It wasn't Lili Zollitsch.

"Is this her?" the Sturmhauptführer asked.

Russell hesitated, his mind desperately seeking some way to get her away from there. He couldn't think of one. If he said yes, Zollitsch would receive a thousand-mark bill for a girl he didn't know. Which he would probably refuse to pay, condemning the girl to re-arrest and Russell to God knew what. "No," he said, wishing he didn't have to.

Buchrucker gave the brownshirts a dismissive flick of the wrist. "Standartenführer Wipperman will be disappointed," he said, sounding so himself.

The woman and her jailers were disappearing through the doors. "Whoever she is, she deserves better than this," Russell said, surprised and slightly alarmed by his own audacity.

"That is not your business," Buchrucker told him. Almost sadly, Russell thought, but he was probably imagining it. Or maybe the man had a daughter of his own, and had briefly imagined what she would look like broken.

Back outside the Sturmhauptführer offered Russell a lift back to Wedding, and the scene of his own brief incarceration. Thinking an outright refusal might be considered judgemental, Russell settled for a ride to the nearby

Ringbahn station, claiming an appointment elsewhere. Half an hour later he was sitting on the elevated platform at Wedding Station, watching night fall across the city, reluctant to face the thought-spinning silence of his room on Gerichtstrasse. An image of the battered young woman hung in his mind, an image he suspected would only fade away when a different one of Lili took its place.

Tuesday had been declared a public holiday in honour of the Potsdam ceremonials, but journalists were unfortunately exempt. The traditional criminal fraternity had declined to take the day off, as Russell discovered on arriving at work. Four lorries stacked with cases of liquor had been driven away from a Treptow warehouse in the early hours of the morning. "Take Ernst," Hiedler told Russell, meaning their apprentice photographer. The paper's experienced snappers were all on their way to Potsdam.

The weather was better that day. The two of them took a tram down Köpenicker Strasse, and walked to the riverside site. Several uniformed Kripo were combing the warehouse for clues, the detective in charge holed up in the manager's office. It was Glassl, so Russell began by asking if Ernst could take his photograph. After mumbling something about only being a public servant, the detective reluctantly agreed that his picture in the paper might help the investigation.

Not that he had any doubts when it came to the thieves' identity. The communists were desperate, had nothing to lose. And who else had the organisation—not to mention the vehicles—to mount such a daring operation?

Russell could think of one other organisation, but suggesting it seemed almost cruel, so he settled for innocently asking whether Glassl had any idea why the KPD had put so much an effort into stealing booze when its whole existence was under threat.

"Like I said—desperation," the detective insisted. "Cornered animals, they hardly know what they're doing."

But do it with remarkable efficiency, Russell thought.

"And to sell it, of course," Glassl added. "To buy guns, most likely."

When Russell asked the detective if he had any actual evidence to back up this theory, Glassl just smiled and said: "Not yet. But someone will talk, and that will be that. You'll see."

Russell waited while Ernst took a photograph of the half-empty warehouse, having artfully positioned a broken bottle in mid-floor. "You'll go far," he told the boy.

"Mr. Hiedler says a picture's worth a thousand words," Ernst said.

"Some are," Russell told him.

They got back to the city centre just as events in Potsdam were getting underway. It looked like the loudspeakers had multiplied by ten over the last few weeks, and with every window-perched wireless offering up the same, escape was almost impossible.

"It's like we're there," Ernst said wonderingly as they walked towards the office. Crowds were coalescing around the loudspeakers, and just up ahead a stormtrooper was telling a woman who tried to walk past him that she should stop and listen like everyone else. Russell took the hint and sat himself down on a convenient step.

The commentator was painting a verbal picture of the Potsdam Garrison Church, and providing a potted history of the building and its skeletal resident Frederick the Great. Hindenburg popped up next, with a short speech extolling the glories of the past and how they might bind the nation together. Hitler responded, his voice sounding humbler than usual, the same old lies tripping off his tongue.

The military parade that followed was gushingly described, but the real business was over, and the crowds were allowed to disperse, at least for a while. A huge torch-lit march was scheduled for that evening, and people were advised not to leave it too late to claim their vantage points.

Russell was determined to be home by then. The first time he'd seen such a march he'd been reluctantly impressed—there was something about them that appealed to most human hearts. Maybe it was age-old memories of fire as the only source of light when the sun was gone, maybe just the child's excitement lurking within the adult. Whatever it was, it worked. And knowing it did, the Nazis had mixed the magic with bombast and cruelty until it all became one. The rapture they made was riddled with poison, and these days Russell found watching the upturned faces almost unbearable.

He wondered if Glassl was right for once, and the communists really had stolen the booze. If so, they had imbued the idea of drowning one's sorrows with more than the usual poignancy.

The woman in the Pankow factory crossed his mind, as she had throughout the day. Such shafts of anguish served no purpose, and certainly didn't help her, but he welcomed them nevertheless. If you didn't feel grief or shame in Hitler's new world you were probably less than human.

It was almost dark when Russell approached the entrance to his block on Gerichtstrasse, and the shadowy figure who suddenly blocked his path gave him quite a shock.

It was Adolf Jetzinger. "Can we talk?" the young man asked. "I'm going to the station, so could you walk that way with me?"

"Okay." It seemed a better idea than taking Jet upstairs, and giving Frau Löffner heaven knew what ideas. His visitor was clearly not intent on advertising his sexual proclivities, but in Wedding he still looked a duck out of water. As far as Russell was aware there had never been a homosexual *Diele* in the area—generally speaking, the Reds were no more tolerant of such behaviour than the Nazis were. "There's a café under the station," he suggested as they turned onto Hummel Strasse.

"No, I can't stop," Jet told him. "I only came to give you something." After scanning the street ahead and glancing back over his shoulder, he dug inside the rear of his belt and pulled out a dog-eared book. "It's Fredo's journal," he explained, handing it over.

Russell wedged it inside his own trousers. "Where did you find it?" he asked, wondering if this was what the SA had been looking for.

"I didn't. Timo had it, and he found me. A couple of days ago."

They turned onto Ravene Strasse. "Where is he? Can I talk to him?"

"No. He doesn't want to see you. Or anyone else," Jet added in mitigation. "But he wants you to have the journal."

"Does he know who killed Fredo?" Russell asked.

"No. He wasn't there. He thinks it must have been a john, but he doesn't know which. Or why Fredo was killed. He found the journal in their room, and he knew it was risky to take it with him, but he couldn't destroy it—Fredo was so proud of his writing. So I told him you should have it. Maybe show it to a publisher or something. I don't know."

"I'd still like to talk to Timo."

"He won't. And we're leaving tonight. Leaving Berlin."

They had reached Reinickendorfer Strasse, a hundred yards down from the station, and Russell accepted defeat.

"And thank you," Jet added.

"I haven't done anything yet."

"You cared, I think. And that's something."

Russell couldn't help smiling at that. "Do you need money?"

Jet grinned. "Always."

Russell handed over most of what he had on him. "I'll take it off the publisher's advance," he told Jet.

They were outside the fire station, across the street from the stairs to the Ringbahn platform. "Goodbye then," Jet said, offering a hand to shake.

Russell stood there watching as the young man threaded his way through the traffic and jauntily skipped up the steps. "Good luck," he murmured, as an eastbound train rumbled over his head. The news that Jet and Timo were together again had provided an unexpectedly pleasant end to his day. A love affair that might last, unlike Hitler and Hindenburg's.

And he also had Fredo's journal tucked inside his belt. Back in his apartment he went straight to the final entries, hoping for some clues to the killer. What he found were pieces describing Fredo's recent visits to art galleries, and lengthy explanations as to why he liked or disliked particular paintings. His ideas were less than original, the writing often turgid.

Russell started again at the beginning, where Fredo wrote about his childhood with an endearing innocence but not much insight. His writing was also so small that reading it almost required a magnifying glass. And there were a lot of pages.

Another day, Russell thought disappointedly, closing the journal and reaching for Kastner's *Three Comrades*. If the papers were right, and Kastner was soon to be banned, he needed to get it finished.

There was a telegram from Frau Mommsen on his desk when Russell reached work on Wednesday morning. Her telephone had been disconnected on account of unpaid bills, and she needed to see him as soon as possible. Could he ring her neighbour—the number was in brackets—and say when he was coming?

After seeing Paul that evening was the answer, and he apprised the neighbour accordingly.

A second message informed him that Kriminalinspektor Glassl was seeing the press at ten o'clock, which only gave him half an hour to reach the Alex. A taxi seemed in order for once, and duly deposited him outside the main entrance with five minutes to spare.

Glassl had progress to report. The four lorries had been found, in woodland outside the city limits. They had been stolen from four different SA groups, three of which, he pointedly revealed, had reported the theft ahead of the robbery. The communists were the obvious suspects, and Glassl had further "proof" of their guilt. A number of similar lorries had been seen at the Potsdam yards—where the Reds had always been strong—late in the previous evening. In Glassl's opinion the cases of stolen liquor were now on their way to hundreds of bars across the nation.

Russell wrote it all down, unsure what to think. If the witness reports were true, then the theory certainly fitted them. If they were fabrications, and the SA were responsible, would the men involved have been stupid enough to use their own lorries? Or subtle enough to report only some of them stolen before committing the robbery?

Not that he cared very much. No one had been hurt, the owners were doubtless insured, and quite a few Germans were getting their booze on the cheap.

What did seem increasingly serious was the declining credibility of official pronouncements. Looking around at his fellow journalists' faces, he could see that few believed a word they were hearing. These days no one trusted the authorities to tell the truth, unless of course it was in their interests to do so. Each piece of evidence, true or invented, was equally suspect. Everything came down to opinion, which usually meant prejudice.

Russell's instincts told him the brownshirts had done it.

With the Reds as ready-made scapegoats, and next to no chance of punishment should the truth accidentally come out, a gang of brownshirts had stolen the liquor and sold it on to their comrades' wretched *Sturm* bars.

None of which he could say, or even suggest, in his report.

Back at the office, he found that he also had updates to write—both of Monday's domestic victims had died in hospital overnight. Their two assailants had now been charged with murder, but Russell suspected only one would be punished. Writing up the piece, he did his best to paint her in a sympathetic light, but doubted it would make any difference.

At three he left for Paul's school, arriving there in time to watch the children stream out, each with a small Nazi flag in one hand. "What's this?" he asked when his son appeared.

Paul gave him a look. "Our flag," he said, as if he couldn't believe that his father didn't know.

Russell wondered whether to point out that it was actually the ruling party's flag, but decided that explaining the distinction to a six-year-old might prove difficult. In the event that Paul chose to put his teacher right, it might even be dangerous. Better to leave well alone.

"Can we go to the park?" his son asked, and Russell readily agreed. After the last few days, kicking a ball around felt like a refreshingly innocent pastime. He didn't play himself these days—the last time he had with any regularity had been in the KPD youth section's five-a-side league. He had of course played in the war—there hadn't been much else to do in the weeks spent out of the line. Nothing you could do for hours, at least.

After dropping off the swastika and picking up the ball, they walked down to the Volkspark, where boys around Paul's age had already started a game. Russell was more than happy to let his son join in—several days of rain had muddied up the ground and he still hadn't gotten round to buying the new suit he'd promised himself. Or the new mattress.

His son was getting quite good, he thought, watching the boy weight a pass to perfection. And when Paul eventually scored a goal, it was a proper shot with the instep, not a child's toe punt.

Walking back to house, he learned that the flag they'd brought home from school was a sample of worse to come. That morning the boys in Paul's class had been marched up and down in the playground. "It was funny," Paul said, "we kept banging into each other." He didn't know what the girls had been doing.

Six-year-olds drilling? Russell wondered if any of the parents would complain. And if they did what the official response would be.

Ilse answered the door. "Are you . . . I don't know what the word is. Okay? After, you know . . ."

"More or less," Russell said. He wouldn't mention the subsequent trip out to Pankow. Why spoil her evening for no purpose?

There was something about her face that triggered a memory, and he suddenly knew what it was—this was the way she had looked in the first few weeks of carrying Paul. An emotional pang came as no surprise, but the absence of hurt was a pleasant one. He knew that he shouldn't say anything. If he was right, she would tell him in her own good time.

As he walked away from the house he wondered how long it would be before he had to agree the divorce. Before his son growing up would be something he witnessed in letters and annual visits.

Live in the present, he told himself. Even this one.

At least it was a lovely evening, sunny and mild, with more than a hint of spring. It was only a mile or so to Donna Mommsen's flat, and he thought he might as well walk.

He wondered what she wanted this time, what fresh problem had arisen in her dealings with foreign official-dom. He told himself to be nice—losing her husband might not have broken her heart, but the woman's situation was still far from enviable. And good Samaritans surely got their reward, if not in life then after death. The eastern ones certainly did—after banking all that good karma they got to come back as something better.

Frau Mommsen was leaning expectantly out of the window when he reached Lietzenburger Strasse, and she wasted no time after letting him in to the flat. "I found these," she said, holding a notebook in one hand, a small steel key in the other.

"Where?" Russell asked.

"Under the floorboards over there." She gestured towards one corner of the room. "I was lying in bed and I suddenly had this memory of coming in here and finding Konrad on his knees. Months ago, this was. He said a carpet tack had come loose, and I had no reason not to believe him. He looked shifty, but then he often did, usually for no reason I could fathom. Anyway, I pulled away the carpet, and jiggled away at the boards, and one came up. And there they were."

Russell skimmed through the notebook.

"It must be a code," she said. "Konrad once told me he did that sort of thing in the war. He said he wanted to fight, but they told him his brain was worth more to the Father-land than his body was."

"It's a code all right." There were lines and lines of figures, interspersed with dots, broken up into separate sections. One for each of Mommsen's clients, perhaps.

"I've been trying to work out what it means for . . . hours," she said, shaking her head.

The momentary hesitation was revealing, Russell thought. He guessed that she'd found her treasure trove days ago and had done her best to work out what it was without involving anyone else. It was only after accepting defeat in this endeavour that she'd turned to him.

He was still wondering why Mommsen would have bothered to put whatever it was in code. If the Nazis had found the notebook they would have extracted the key under torture, so what was the point? Maybe the man had enjoyed the process. "Your husband," he asked Donna Mommsen, "was he a trifle obsessive? Did he like to get all his ducks in a row, get everything organised absolutely perfect? Or was he a bit slipshod, inclined to do things on the spur of the moment?"

She grimaced. "The only spontaneous thing he ever did was marry me," she said, sounding almost surprised at the realisation. "Why do you ask?"

"I can't understand why he encoded the stuff before he squirreled it away. It's like hiding it twice." He shrugged. "And where there's no logical reason, there's often a psychological one."

"I see what you mean. And yes, he would do something like that."

"Well, I don't suppose it matters," Russell said. Whatever his reasons, Mommsen had taken them to the grave.

"And what about the key?" she asked.

It was small for a door. "My guess would be a safety deposit box."

"What's that?" she wanted to know.

"It's a lockable metal box you rent at a bank. It's fireproof, and people use them to store documents and valuables, and things they want to keep secret. The boxes are kept in a back room, and only the renter has a key."

"So it might contain money?"

"It might."

"Could we go and see?"

"First we'd have to find it. It's probably at the bank where your husband kept his account . . ."

"The manager didn't mention it."

"He might not know about it. But in any case, it'll be in your husband's name, and I doubt they'll give you access until probate has been settled."

"I see. Well, I suppose that's not a terrible hardship." She shook her curls. "But what's this all about? Hiding things under floorboards and notebooks in code. Do you think he was he a spy?"

Russell shook his head. If he told her what he suspected, she would realise that any money in the safety deposit box was illicit, and that the notebook would probably prove as much. If she wanted to inherit the former, she'd be wise to burn the latter. And he didn't want that.

"I don't think so," he replied. "Look, let me try and make sense of it. With help, if I need it—I'm sure I can find someone who knows about this stuff. Someone we can trust," he added, seeing the look on her face. "And then we'll know what your husband was doing, and where any money came from."

"All right," Frau Mommsen said doubtfully. She didn't want to let the book out of her sight, but couldn't see any alternative.

"If it turns out the notebook's worth money, I'll be happy with ten percent," Russell offered, in the hope of convincing her that she wouldn't lose out.

"All right," she said again, with slightly more conviction. "You can ring me when you know something," she told him. A neighbour had helped her locate the telephone company, and she expected to be reconnected the following morning. The lawyer Russell had found her had also been to see her, with the news that probate would probably take six weeks. "I can't wait to get back to the States," she concluded with feeling.

Walking down Ku'damm five minutes later, the notebook tucked in his inside coat pocket, Russell wondered what

he'd done to deserve two such dubious sources of reading matter in less than twenty-four hours. This second one
would be dangerous to hold onto if anyone other than he
and Donna Mommsen were aware of its existence. Legally
speaking he should take it to Kuzorra, but would the detective want to waste time on a crime where the criminal was
already dead? Handing the notebook in would also scup-
per her chances of keeping any ill-gotten gains, and his of
pursuing what might prove a wonderful story. No, he told
himself. Or at least not yet. First he would find out what was
between the covers.

As his tram reached Wedding he pondered the wisdom of
keeping the notebook up in his rooms. What if the SA conducted one of their street searches on Gerichtstrasse? There
might be nothing in the book—though putting whatever it
was in code suggested otherwise—but even having it in his
possession was probably a criminal offence. It was evidence
in a police investigation, albeit one that seemed over. Come
to think of it, so was Fredo's journal.

A hiding place was needed, at least for the moment.
Inspecting his sparsely furnished apartment, Russell
couldn't come up with anything brilliant, and settled for
aping Mommsen. A floorboard in the bedroom was loose
enough to prise up, and the space beneath looked custom-
made for his two illicit works of literature. He would leave
it open for a sudden deposit whenever he was at home, and
hide the books away each time he left.

He opened one window a little to be sure he heard any
SA raid before it reached his door, and settled into his armchair with Mommsen's notebook and a glass of warm beer.
Two hours later he was none the wiser. He'd never been
any good at chess or cryptic crosswords, and it seemed as if
eschewing cryptography had been one of his better career
choices.

He needed help. Discreet help. Tomorrow he would ask Matthias if any of his old army buddies were dab hands at code breaking.

It had been another sub-zero night, but the sun was slowly warming things up as Russell walked the three miles to work, pausing only to imbibe his usual coffee at Café Kranzler. That day the Reichstag was due to vote on the Enabling Act, which, as a British jokester might have said, was akin to turkeys voting on Christmas. The turkeys might have the sense to say no, but no such forethought was expected from the Reichstag deputies. Hitler was due to address them that afternoon, a treat that Berlin would doubtless be forced to share via Goebbels's loudspeakers.

The other interesting item in the papers concerned the opening of a concentration camp outside the Bavarian village of Dachau, where communists and others misfits would be brought back in tune with the new Germany. In the accompanying photograph the camp looked like something a deranged Baden-Powell might have built, barracks and drilling grounds as far as the eye could see, all shipshape and spotless.

Was this good news, Russell wondered, suggesting as it did a level of state oversight that the SA's makeshift detention centres so deplorably lacked? Time would tell, but there was definitely something chilling about the picture.

At the office there was no new story requiring his urgent attention, but the man whose fist had allegedly caused the heart attack in the Neukölln bar was appearing in court that morning. Russell could cover the hearing and mount another vigil in the café.

First he rang the house on Wilhelmsaue. As he expected, Matthias was out, but Ilse said he'd been in after six that evening. When she asked why Russell wanted to see him, he said he'd explain when he got there.

The court hearing was well-attended—the defendant clearly had friends—but Russell was the only journalist present. While the victim's wife claimed that a punch had been landed, every other witness swore that it hadn't. The pathologist testified that he'd found no cut or bruise on the chin, and the victim's doctor admitted that the man had come to him recently complaining of chest pains. Unsurprisingly, the defendant was found not guilty. He and his friends swarmed out, presumably intending to toast their triumph, leaving the victim's wife weeping in her seat.

Russell arrived at his café just as a couple vacated their window table. After ordering and eating his lunch, he spent the next two hours nursing his coffee and avoiding the waiter's eye. The streets outside were busy, probably because people were eager to get their shopping done before Hitler's speech filled the air, but he saw no face he recognised.

The loudspeakers sprung to life around a quarter to two, first emitting music, then commentary from the Reichstag's temporary home at the Kroll Opera House. Hitler was cheered to the rostrum almost immediately, and his all-too-familiar voice started echoing down the street outside. And when, at irregular intervals, it was muffled by a passing tram or a train on the S-Bahn overbridge, the wretched voice seemed to leap back out like a jack-in-a-box.

The message was more inclusive than usual. If granted his four years of untrammelled rule the new Chancellor promised a moral renewal in education, the arts and the media. He praised both the Catholic and Protestant churches, and swore that their rights would always be respected. The same went for the judicial system, though judges would have to be flexible, and sometimes put the national interest above narrow legal considerations. The peasantry would prosper, and industrial unemployment shrink, as the economy was put back on track. The armed forces were Germany's glory, not that he wanted anything but peace.

And no one need worry that the powers that the new Enabling Act bestowed on his humble self would ever infringe
on the rights of the Reichstag or the nation's beloved President.

A lie for everyone, Russell thought, as he sought escape
down the U-Bahn steps. Hitler was still talking when he re-
emerged at Kochstrasse, but seemed to be winding up. By
the time Russell reached the newsroom the commentator
on the wireless was explaining that the actual vote would
follow in a couple of hours.

At the house on Wilhelmsaue, Paul was putting himself to
bed. Going up to say goodnight, Russell was inveigled into
reading *Die Häschenschule*, Paul silently mouthing the verses
he knew off by heart.

Back downstairs, Ilse told him that Matthias was waiting
in his study. Hearing the wireless on in the kitchen, he asked
her if the vote had been taken. "Not yet," she told him. "But
it won't be long."

In the study he told Matthias about the coded notebook,
and his need for help in decrypting it. "Someone who won't
feel obliged to tell the police if he discovers anything unto-
ward."

"One of my crooked friends, you mean?" Matthias said
with a smile. "No, I know what you mean—someone who'll
see it as a puzzle to solve and none of his business otherwise."

"I couldn't have put it better."

"Well as it happens, I do. I haven't seen him for a while,
but I know someone who worked in the Navy's cryptography section during the war. His name's Lossow, Kurt Lossow.
He works at the Borse, or did. He must be near retirement.
I should have his telephone number." Matthias opened a
leather-bound diary and scanned through the pages at the
back. "Here it is. Do you want me to call him and ask if he'll
see you?"

"That would be wonderful."

Lossow was at home, and the two friends spent a couple of minutes bringing each other up to date before Matthias got round to the reason for his call. "How does tomorrow evening at eight suit you?" he eventually asked Russell.

"Fine."

"He lives in Mitte," Matthias said after ending the call. "An apartment on Holzmarkt overlooking the river—I've been there a couple of times. Number forty-two," he added, after checking the diary. "I'm sure he'll be able to help."

"Thank you," Russell said.

"It's nothing. But one other thing—Zollitsch rang me yesterday. He said he hadn't heard from you for several days. He wasn't complaining, but he did sound worried. I take it you haven't made any progress."

"No. And I'll call him tomorrow. There was a development but I can't make up my mind whether or not to tell him about it. You know about the reward I offered the SA Standartenführer?"

"Ilse told me."

"Well, his minion came to my office the other day." He described the trip to Pankow, and the battered blonde who wasn't Lili. "Telling Zollitsch about her might convince him that I'm not just sitting on my arse, but at what cost to any peace of mind he has left? It seems kinder to keep quiet."

Matthias sighed. "You're probably right."

The two of them walked back through to the kitchen, where the leader's voice was again spilling out of the wireless. "Otto Vels spoke well," Ilse said, "and Hitler couldn't bear the thought of being upstaged by a Social Democrat. So he decided to have the last word."

The smooth lies of the early afternoon were gone, replaced by a poisonous harangue. "I do not want your votes," he was screaming at the Social Democrats, and Russell could picture the phlegm spraying out of the twisted mouth. "Germany will be free, but not through you! Do not mistake us for bourgeois! The star of Germany is in the ascendant, yours is about to disappear! Your death-knell has sounded!"

Around the kitchen table the three of them looked at one another.

"This man will kill us all," Matthias said.

After another late supper at the café beneath Wedding Station—by this time he knew the chalked-up menu by heart—Russell took the short walk home and wearily climbed the stairs to his rooms. He felt exhausted, but there were too many thoughts spinning round in his brain for sleep to be a viable option.

There were two inches left in the bottle of Scotch that Thomas had bought him for Christmas, and after carefully pouring one of them into a glass he lifted the loose floorboard in the bedroom and took out Fredo Ratzel's journal. Reading it through was the least he owed Timo and Jet, and might have the added benefit of putting him to sleep.

He resumed where he'd left off, with the journal two weeks old, and Fredo still much concerned with the family he'd left in Stettin. It was the autumn of 1930, and the boy was slowly becoming acquainted with life in Berlin as a young and penniless homosexual. There were many descriptions of trysts, both with other boys of the same inclination and a wide range of paying adults, all of which Russell read with a heterosexual's blend of curiosity and distaste. In clubs and bars, back rooms and back yards, Fredo found himself playing sex games in duos, trios and packs with males of all social classes. Orgies were common and enormously varied.

Fredo rarely had anything good to say about his many brownshirt clients. He noted that the ones who talked toughest were the ones who made sure to bring vaseline, and that they also steered clear of the well-built working class *Bubes*, opting instead for the less threatening perfume-doused *Androgynes* who styled themselves after Valentino.

The journal wasn't all about the boy's sex life. He had a lot to say about the books he was reading and the clothes he was hoping to buy. He also enjoyed movies, and was a fount of information when it came to illicit ways of entering the city's many cinemas.

The clients mentioned in the early part of the journal were only given first names, and it came as a shock when Fredo abandoned what had seemed a deliberate policy and started using an occasional surname. As 1931 went by there were more and more of these; in the early months of 1932, as Fredo's fame as a "Breslauer" apparently spread, Russell began to recognise some of them, albeit in most cases only vaguely. The three he definitely knew from seeing their names in the papers were all prominent SA men: local leaders from Berlin and Köln, and most damning of all, one of the organisation's national leaders. Having been buggered by the latter, Fredo had been surprised to see the man he knew as "Karl" standing at Ernst Röhm's shoulder on the front page of a Nazi newspaper. His real name was Richard Ohst.

Russell took down the names as he read, with a view to checking each one in the *Morgenspiegel* archives.

And then, in the summer of 1932, Fredo's tiny writing told a chilling story. A young Sturmführer, whom everyone thought was besotted with Fredo's friend Benno, took the boy to Rugen Island for the weekend. The Sturmführer came back but Benno didn't, and the former's story, that the boy had simply disappeared, seemed less than convincing to Fredo, particularly once it emerged that others had witnessed the man's violent temper.

Fredo lamented that nothing could be done—even if they had proof, who could Benno's friends take it to?—and clearly took the loss to heart. He was still agonising in the journal two weeks later when something similar happened. This time four young men he knew were involved. After refusing an invitation to visit an estate in the country—one that the absentee owner had loaned the SA for social occasions—this foursome were forcibly abducted from their usual *Diele* and driven off in a truck. Three came back two days later, all wearing bruises and visibly shaken. Save to say they'd been told that their friend had "run away," the three returnees were tight-lipped about their experience, at least in public places. Amongst themselves it was sometimes a different matter—in his journal Fredo reported a convincingly detailed rumour that the missing boy had been killed and buried on the estate. And that the man in whose company he had last been seen was Röhm's friend Richard Ohst.

Though Fredo never said so explicitly, he set about trying to diminish the more obvious risks in his own professional life. He was still in demand in the Schöneberg clubs he knew best, but started refusing invitations to accompany clients elsewhere or spend whole nights away from home. He even invented a sick mother who couldn't do without him for more than a few hours. And more and more as the months went by he eschewed notorious West End haunts like the Eldorado and DeDe Bar in favour of smaller clubs north of the river, where his mostly older clients were either pathetically grateful or incapable of beating him up.

Maybe one of them had killed him, Russell thought, sipping his whiskey. Or perhaps it had been a brownshirt named Hamann whose much smaller cock had caused Fredo to giggle. The man had needed restraining at the time, and certainly sounded violent enough, but the incident had occurred almost three months before. There were no other obvious suspects—the last few pages that

Russell hadn't read were all about Timo and Jet, whom Fredo had introduced, and whose love affair he seemed to unconsciously envy, while obviously wishing the two of them well.

Russell imagined what Glassl would do if the journal ended up on his desk. Once he saw Richard Ohst's name he wouldn't be able to burn it quickly enough. Sodomy might still be illegal, and murder certainly was, but not when committed by Hitler's SA.

What could he do with the journal himself? Burning it probably *was* the safest option, but he felt reluctant to do so, and not just because he'd be letting Fredo and the others down. He had no idea how or when, but the knowledge contained in its pages might be useful to someone. One day it might serve justice, laughable though that seemed at the moment.

As things stood, the journal was far too explicit for publication in any country on earth. For all Fredo's faults as a writer, he had produced a remarkably vivid exposé of that violent *Demi-monde* that many of Hitler's legalised thugs had shared with the city's other *warme Brüder* over the last few years. A piece of writing that the Nazis would find more than embarrassing, should it ever reach the public.

Which might not be likely, but what the hell. Russell poured out the last half-inch of the whiskey and listened to a night freight rumble by on the Ringbahn. As the noise began to fade a dog began barking nearby, and he walked to the window to check that it wasn't wearing brown. The street below was blissfully empty.

Resuming his seat, he realised that one of the journal's more remarkable features was the almost complete absence of women. Fredo's mother and sisters apart, they might as well not have existed. This obviously hadn't worried Fredo, but it did Russell, not least because these days the women in his own life could be counted on the fingers of one hand.

He put the journal back in its hiding place, visited the toilet on the floor below, and took himself to bed. Lying there in the dark, the phrase "love is less likely in times of rape" popped into his mind.

Which was no consolation at all. A lover would be nice, he thought. Love even better.

A Clouded Crystal Ball

The temperature had fallen well below freezing overnight, and when Russell woke up on Friday Wedding's roofs were coated in glistening frost. The blanket of low cloud offered little prospect of an improvement, and according to Frau Löffner snow was possible later. Paul would enjoy that, he thought, remembering the vision of wonder which a first sight of drifting snowflakes had brought to his baby son's face.

On his tram ride into town Russell considered the day ahead. That evening he was seeing Matthias's cryptographer friend, who he hoped would have something useful to say about Konrad Mommsen's notebook. When it came to the search for Lili Zollitsch he was getting nowhere. The lack of any word from Gert Höschle seemed to confirm what Russell already suspected, that the girl was not officially under arrest. The similar absence of any further contact from the Standartenführer might be proof positive that she wasn't in an SA detention centre either, or could simply mean that Wipperman's circle of sadistic friends wasn't as complete as he thought it was.

As for Russell himself, all he had so far achieved was to narrow the search to one of the city's more crowded districts.

And then there was Fredo's journal, ticking away under

his floorboards. If it looked like a slack day on the crime desk, he would start searching the archives for the names the boy had mentioned.

Hiedler's face and frantic beckoning soon put an end to that idea. "Harri Haum's gone missing," he announced when Russell was halfway across the room. "You do know who he is?"

"And good morning to you," Russell said, drawing up a seat. "The fortune teller, right?"

"*The* fortune teller. His client list is a who's who of Berlin celebrities—military and business leaders, film stars, racing car drivers. And Nazi politicians. He does stage shows, he owns magazines, he even knows Hitler. A couple of years ago it was reported that Haum gave our new Chancellor lessons in stagecraft—you know, how to use pregnant pauses and hand gestures, that sort of thing. And the man's just moved into a huge apartment off the Ku'damm after designing all the decor himself. It looks like something a Buddhist gangster would live in, all mandalas and huge leather couches."

Russell laughed. "How do you know all this?"

"My daughter sometimes brings Haum's magazine home—the damn thing has a bigger circulation than we do. It has astrology and romantic advice and celebrity gossip, all very self-congratulatory and pro-Nazi. The man's a nasty piece of work. But an important one."

"I get that. So how do we know he's disappeared?"

"The usual source at the Alex. Which is where you should be."

Russell got up to go.

"One more thing about Haum," Hiedler said. "He's a Jew."

If Russell had doubted his editor's reckoning of Harri Haum's prominence, the number of reporters besieging Kriminalinspektor Kuzorra's office provided a swift rebuttal. However, as soon became clear, the significance of the man's disappearance was highly open to doubt.

As Kuzorra explained, a female client of Haum's had contacted the police that morning after arriving for her appointment. Surprised that her personal seer was not at home and standing there wondering whether to wait, she'd been approached by a man she assumed to be a neighbour—"I must have looked distressed," she said. When she mentioned Haum, this man had told her that he'd seen the clairvoyant being bundled into a car late the previous evening. He'd been too frightened to report the matter—these days, he'd confided in a whisper, one kept as far away from the authorities as one could—but she had proved of sterner stuff.

Or so it seemed. When the local police arrived to investigate, they found no trace of the apparent neighbour, and the woman's description—"middle-aged, medium build, with no distinguishing features," Kuzorra quoted—was worse than useless. After knocking on Haum's door they found that two members of the fortune teller's staff were inside, and had been all morning. Herr Haum, they said, had gone away on holiday, though they couldn't say where or whether he was travelling alone. A woman who arrived while the police were there had no such doubts on the second count. Haum was "off with that bitch Erna."

"You would think," Kuzorra concluded with a smile, "that a fortune teller would anticipate how much fuss his unexplained departure would cause and take the appropriate steps."

Hiedler would be disappointed, Russell thought, as the journalists slowly dispersed. But Eglhofer, who caught up with him on the stairs, was less convinced that nothing was amiss. "The woman might be a fruitcake," he conceded, as they crossed Alexanderplatz in search of a coffee, "but the two most salient facts in all this are that Haum is gone and that no one will tell us where he is. There have been rumours for weeks that he's been asking for trouble. Half the Nazi leaders in Berlin owe him money, and one sure-fire way to cancel a debt is by killing the creditor."

So maybe a story after all, Russell thought as the two of them joined the queue at Herman's mobile coffee bar. Unless and until Harri Haum popped out of the woodwork, there was more than enough to sustain a mystery, and why would anyone object to his ferreting around in the fortune teller's life? The Nazis wouldn't want to be seen obstructing an investigation into their famous supporter's disappearance, especially if the fruitcake's missing witness had truly observed an abduction. Unless, of course, they'd been the abductors.

Russell returned to the office intent on a spell in the archives, both digging up further details on Haum and putting faces and ranks to the names in Fredo's journal. But the Queen of Hearts thief had struck again after a three-week hiatus, and he only had time to give Hiedler the bad news about Haum before heading back to the Alex.

Bellevue was the location of this latest burglary, the victim a well-known conservative politician whom Russell had loathed for years. A pair of antique duelling pistols had been taken along with sundry other valuables. The mode of entry had been the same, the usual playing card left behind.

Much more newsworthy was the thief's announcement—in a letter to Kriminalinspektor Handschuh postmarked the previous day—that this fourth robbery would be the last. It had been fun, the thief wrote, and while he seriously doubted the police would ever catch him, it seemed sensible not to risk some unexpected twist of fate.

When asked if there were any fresh clues, Handschuh admitted there were none. When asked whether it was

worth devoting precious police time to the pursuit of a
retired criminal, his affirmative answer was more than a little devalued by the accompanying shrug and smile.

Returning again to the *Morgenspiegel*, Russell wrote his
copy and then went down to the archives. A political correspondent whom he barely knew was already *in situ*, and
since leafing through pictures of prominent brownshirts
might invite questions he had no desire to answer, Russell
restricted his research to Haum and his circle. The man
didn't shy away from publicity, but most of the articles on
file read like re-written adverts for Haum's professional
endeavours, and added little of substance to what Russell
already knew.

The man was a mystical jack-of-all trades. He read minds
and palms, stared into crystals ball and scanned astrological
charts. He told fortunes on stage, in newspaper columns
and in the privacy of the consultation room, often it seemed
with some success. On one occasion he had tried in vain
to dissuade a well-known driver from entering a particular race at the Nürburg-Ring, only for the man to die in a
fatal crash, and the audiences at his stage shows were always
packed with people whose minds he could readily read. The
man clearly had talent, if only for bamboozling customers.

Some of these were Nazis, despite Haum's rarely mentioned, but openly acknowledged, Jewish ancestry. And the
clairvoyant seemed keen to keep up the relationship, if his
effusive and open letter of congratulation to Hitler on January 30th was anything to go by. The man was protecting
himself and his business, Russell assumed. Why else would a
Jew offer support to anti-Semites?

There was a piece on Haum's new house in the society
pages. The writer describing it managed to sound both con-
descending and awestruck, which Russell considered no
mean feat. Looking at the pictured front door, he felt an
unreasonable urge to see the place for himself, if only from

the outside. And given that his colleague in the next seat was still inhibiting any research into riskier matters, there seemed no reason not to. He would even have time for a decent meal on the Ku'damm before heading back across town to visit Kurt Lossow.

Outside a light sleet was melting on contact with the sidewalk, and the stairs heading down to the U-Bahn platforms were full of people rubbing their cold hands together. A train appeared almost instantly, and there wasn't much longer to wait at Hallesches Tor. Ten minutes later he was out on the Ku'damm, a few minutes' walk from the lengthy Kantstrasse. The number of Harri Haum's building suggested it was close to Savignyplatz, and when Russell noticed a rifle-toting brownshirt less than a hundred yards ahead he put two and two together. Passing slowly by on the other side, he saw lights and movement behind the curtained windows, and what looked like the end of a vehicle parked round the back. He obviously stared too long and hard, because the SA sentry caught his eye and abruptly waved him on with the rifle.

Russell walked on to the next crossroads, wondering why, if no crime had been committed, the SA were treating the place like a crime scene. If there was a reasonable explanation, he couldn't think what it might be. It seemed more likely that Eglhofer was right, that Haum had not disappeared voluntarily. He needed to talk to neighbours, and to the staff. Kuzorra's men had interviewed two of the latter, but a house and business like Haum's would have employed a lot more than that.

Not today, though. The SA wouldn't be taking up permanent residence, and he could afford to wait. In the meantime, dinner called. A large dish of Sauerbraten at Hellwig's would delight his taste buds, fill his stomach and drive out the cold. He quickened his step back towards the Ku'damm.

• • •

Two hours later, the light was rapidly fading as Russell left the Jannowitzbrücke U-Bahn station and walked up Holzmarktstrasse. No.42 was a five-storey block on the southern side, Kurt Lossow's apartment on the top floor. The lift was old, beautiful and somewhat rickety, but he managed to survive the ascent.

After answering the door Lossow introduced himself and his wife, Marthe, an attractive grey-haired woman in her fifties. The former code breaker was probably several years older, but looked in decent health. His hair was white, but the eyebrows and moustache were still holding onto a darker shade. He invited Russell into the living room, which as Matthias had promised, boasted a magnificent view of the river. The lights of the Tempelhof aerodrome were visible a couple of miles to the south, and away to his right the piercing red light on the Funkturm shone out of a fading sunset.

"Marthe is making coffee," Lossow told him. "While we wait could I see the coded material?"

Russell passed him the notebook, and sat down in the proffered armchair. He didn't have long to wait.

"Child's play," Lossow announced before a minute had passed. "It's a simple book code. You know what that is?"

Russell thought he did, but an explanation wouldn't hurt. "I wouldn't claim to be certain."

"There are variations. In its simplest form a number—say 11187, for example—represents a location—either a word or a letter—in the book. So 11187 would be either the seventh word on the eighth line of page 111 or the seventh word on the eighteenth line of page eleven—those are the only two possibilities, given how many words there can be in a line, how many lines on a page, or pages in a book. You see?"

"There are no gaps in the numbers."

"Which makes it slightly harder. You have to make assumptions and check them as you proceed. In this case you know these five numbers go together, because the zero makes it impossible to create a location with only four, and the seven on the end makes it impossible to create one with six, because that would require seventy-plus words in a line. Clear?"

"I think so."

"It's always clear to him," his wife told Russell with a smile as she brought in a tray of coffees. "He has a different kind of brain to the rest of us."

Lossow didn't look unhappy with that thought. "Of course, this code is usually used for communication between two or more people with identical editions of the same book."

"Not in this case," Russell said, after taking a sip of his coffee. "The writer just wanted concealment, as far as I can tell."

"Strange."

"I think he just enjoyed the process."

"That I can understand," Lossow said, looking for a moment like a guilty schoolboy. "Do you have any idea what book he might have used?"

"None."

"You should ask the wife," Frau Lossow said.

"I intend to," Russell told her.

The rain and clouds were gone when he woke on Saturday morning, the sun already reducing the chill in the air. Russell lay there for a while, remembering the sleepless night of seven days before, and the dreadful hours that had preceded it. And he'd got out unscathed. He doubted the others had been so lucky.

He planned to see Donna Mommsen that morning, and ask what her husband's favourite book had been. He could then walk by the Haum house and see if the SA were gone. An hour or more in the archives after that, and it would soon be time to pick up Paul. A busy day, which he would start with coffee and strudel at the Romanisches Café. After a necessary bath across the road.

It was almost ten when he knocked on Donna Mommsen's door. She answered it to say she was on her way out. "The lawyer wants to see me," she said, "and I told him that this time I'd come to his office. I'm so sick of being stuck in these rooms."

"This'll only take five minutes."

"Oh. All right. You'd better come in then."

"It's a book code," Russell said without preamble. "Do you know what that is?"

"Do I need to?"

"Not really. You just need to tell me if your husband had a favourite book." He walked across to the room's only bookcase, a walnut one with glass doors and three sparsely filled shelves. "Are these the only ones in the house?"

"Yes, I think so. He got rid of the books by Jews several weeks ago. All except the one they made into *Grand Hotel*. I can't remember the German name."

He found Vicki Baum's *Menschen im Hotel* on the bottom shelf. Timo's namesake. If Russell remembered correctly the author was an Austrian Jewess.

"Konrad said he was keeping it for sentimental reasons," Donna said. "We saw the movie when it came out last April. When we were on our honeymoon. He said I was his Greta Garbo." She shook her head. "It sounded romantic at the time."

Russell was working his way through the other titles. The only one that grabbed his attention was *Mein Kampf*—which would be too ironic for words, not to mention Konrad Mommsen. "He didn't have a favourite book, one he liked to read over and over?"

"Not that I know of. His funeral was yesterday, by the

way. It was miles away, and they only gave me a few hours warning, so I didn't go."

"I'm sorry."

She shrugged. "It's not as if going would have helped him or me."

"True," Russell said, sliding *Menschen im Hotel* into his coat pocket. He and Mommsen owned the same edition of *Mein Kampf*, so there was no point in taking that.

On Kantstrasse there was no sign of yesterday's SA vigil, and with the building entrance open, and the *Portierfrau*'s door firmly closed, there was nothing to stop Russell from knocking loudly on the astrologically decorated door to Haum's huge apartment.

No one answered, but thinking he might have heard movement within, Russell tried even louder. When this failed to produce a response, he headed up the stairs, intent on interviewing Haum's fellow tenants. All who came to their doors answered his opening question by insisting in one way or another that they didn't know anything pertinent. On the evening in question they'd either been miles away or in with the curtains drawn and the wireless on.

He widened his net, banging on doors in the buildings next door and across the street, but all to no avail. If the fruitcake's witness had given a true account, then no one was going to confirm it.

He was just coming out of the building opposite when a man emerged from Haum's apartment block. There was no way of knowing if he'd come from Haum's apartment, but something in the way he stopped and glanced up and down the street before setting off made Russell think he had. That and the fact that he was carrying a suitcase. If Haum had indeed been abducted by one or other of the authorities, then all the live-in staff would be looking for new accommodation.

Russell tailed the man across Savignyplatz and down Grolmanstrasse to the Ku'damm. After buying a newspaper from a street vendor his quarry ducked into the first café he passed, sat himself down at a table, and started leafing through his purchase. Russell, having followed him in, took a seat at an adjacent table and opened up Konrad Mommsen's *Menschen im Hotel*. When the waitress came round, they both ordered coffee.

The man was about forty, a touch overweight with a few strands of grey in his hair. His clothing was not expensive, which suggested to Russell that if the man was employed by Haum it wasn't as a frontline assistant. An accountant perhaps, but he didn't look that bright. A caretaker, more likely. A chef or a chauffeur, perhaps.

First he needed to know if the man was indeed in Haum's employ, and there seemed only one way to do that. Russell checked his wallet to make sure he had enough for a decent bribe, and brazenly laid claim to the other seat at his target's table.

The man looked up, more annoyed than alarmed at the sudden intrusion.

"I saw you come out of Haum's apartment," Russell told him with a woeful lack of honesty. "I presume you work for him."

"What business is that of yours?" the man asked, rather less angrily than Russell had expected.

"I'm a journalist," Russell told him, noticing as he did so that the paper was open at the accommodation listings page. "And I'm willing to pay for information. Uncredited, of course. I expect you already know that a journalist is not permitted to reveal his sources."

"Yes, of course." The man looked round, presumably to check that no one was listening. "How do I know you're a journalist?"

Russell felt an instinctive reluctance to produce his press

card, but could see no alternative. And once money had changed hands, the man in front of him wouldn't risk telling tales to the authorities.

"How much?" the man asked, returning the card.

"That depends on the information. Can you tell me exactly when your employer went away on holiday?"

The man hesitated.

"He didn't go on holiday, did he?"

"Oh yes, yes he did. I was just trying to remember. It was Thursday, Thursday morning. Around ten–thirty, I'd say. I can't be more precise than that."

"Is he coming back?"

"Of course."

"So why are you leaving with a suitcase?"

A moment's hesitation. "I'm visiting my sister for the weekend. While the boss is away," he added, as if the thought had just occurred to him.

Russell let that go. "How did he—they—go?"

"What do you mean?"

"Haum's car is still in the garage," Russell guessed, realising that was something he ought to check. "So how did they travel?"

"Oh. In a taxi. To Tempelhof."

"An afternoon flight?"

"Exactly."

"To where?"

"Somewhere in Italy, I don't remember where. Somewhere warm." He tried an ingratiating smile. "It's all right for some, isn't it?"

Russell didn't believe a word of it, but neither did he think the man was making it up as he went along. Someone else had authored this particular story. He passed across a ten-mark note, along with one of his cards. "If you want to earn ten times as much, then come and tell me the truth. I promise no one will ever find out." He got to his feet.

"In the meantime"—he gestured towards the open newspaper—"good luck with finding somewhere to live."

At the office there were two copies of Haum's newspaper lying on his desk, along with a note from Hiedler: "found these in my daughter's bedroom." One was from the previous September, the other from the month just past. The front pages were strikingly similar, both featuring portraits of Hitler and circular astrological charts. The earlier edition saw proof in the stars that the leader's rise was unstoppable, and the later paper's "Victory!" headline joyously welcomed the fulfilment of this prediction.

So why, Russell wondered, would the SA have come for him? Haum was a Nazi cheerleader, and an effective one at that, with 200,000 readers ready to lap up his every word. Jewish or not, he'd proved himself more than useful, so why would the Nazis cast him aside? Just having such a prominent Jewish supporter should be worth something, if only as a way of disarming their foreign critics.

Maybe he and Eglhofer were barking up the wrong tree. Maybe the man really had flown off to sunnier climes.

The Tempelhof restaurant had no Coca-Cola, but given the time of year a cup of hot chocolate seemed much more appropriate, particularly out on the chilly observation deck. Paul had acquired a book of aeroplanes since their last visit, one complete with pictures, diagrams and all the facts a six-year-old might need. He had obviously studied it, because a Junker 52 and a De Havilland Dragon were quickly identified. Russell enjoyed his son's excitement, and loved the way he bothered to learn about things. Ilse and he might have been unlucky with each other, but they'd won the prize with their child.

An Italian aeroplane was coming in to land, and as Paul searched his book for its identity, Russell wondered what approach he should use with the staff in the booking hall below. The information he wanted was unlikely to be freely offered, to a journalist or anyone else. A fake police badge might work, but only a man with a death-wish would carry one. His boyish charm would have to suffice. If he could only remember where he'd left it.

Paul wasn't sated after two hours, but Ilse expected him back. "I need to ask a few questions downstairs," he told his son, who reluctantly acquiesced.

After plunking Paul in a chair, Russell approached the ticket desk, where a middle-aged man and pretty young woman were attending to customers. Luckily for him, the woman became available first. "I wonder if you could help me," he began with his best smile. "A friend of mine, a quite famous friend . . . Harri Haum . . . I don't suppose you've heard of him?"

"The astrologer! Of course I have. Some of his predictions . . ."

"Well I'm a journalist, and I'm writing a piece on him for my newspaper. Well, to be honest, we're writing it together. As a team." He gave his best impression of a decent man at the end of a rapidly fraying tether. "Only I've lost my notes. We were almost finished when he left—I just had to fill in a few details—but then I left my notes on the U-Bahn. He took off from here on Friday, and he was flying to Italy, but I've forgotten exactly where. If I name the wrong city I'll look like a fool."

"Oh," she said.

Russell gave her an imploring look and held his breath.

"Well, I don't suppose it could do any harm," she said.

"If it was going to, Harri would have known in advance," Russell offered.

She giggled and reached across the counter for a book. "He would, wouldn't he?"

Leafing through it, her smile slowly faded. "There was

only one flight to Italy on Friday. To Turin. And he's not on the passenger list."

Russell feigned surprise. "Could he have used another name?"

"That would be illegal," she said, but then her eyes lit up. "Unless Harri Haum is his stage name, and one of these is his real one."

"That sounds likely," Russell concurred. "At least I know where he went." Thanks to the *Morgenspiegel* archives, he also knew that Harri Haum was the soothsayer's real name.

"What were you talking to that woman about?" Paul asked, as they exited the terminal.

"I asked her if a man I'm writing about flew out of here last Thursday."

"And did he?"

"No, he didn't."

Paul looked disappointed on Haum's behalf. "I wish I could go up in an aeroplane."

It was dark by the time Russell got back to Wedding. As he walked up Müllerstrasse in search of something to eat, the atmosphere felt more subdued than in days gone by, but there was still no forgetting it was Saturday night. The bars and restaurants were doing good business, the sidewalks full of arm-in-arm couples sharing conversation and laughter. Take away the flags, hanging like blood-soaked sheets above the crowded stage, and you could almost believe the Nazis were just a bad dream.

Finding a restaurant with an available table, Russell ordered a schnitzel and wine. Opening the book he'd been carting around for most of the day, he decided it looked well-thumbed for a single reading, and hoped that was significant. He remembered seeing the Garbo film with one of Olga's colleagues, and the way she had waited in vain the following morning for words he couldn't honestly say.

The wine was good, the food less so, but it filled him up. Back at Gerichtstrasse, Frau Löffner was enjoying a cigarette out on the stoop, some concerto or other blaring away on her wireless within. "Herr Habicht is not coming back," she said, slurring her words ever so slightly. "Herr Dickel came round to tell me that I could re-let his room—someone will be round to clear out his belongings."

"Did Dickel say why Habicht isn't coming back?" Russell asked.

"No, he didn't," Frau Löffner said. "I should have asked, shouldn't I? Herr Habicht could be dead, for all I know."

He probably was, Russell thought.

"Herr Dickel has a friend he thinks might want the room," Frau Löffner continued, looking none too pleased at the prospect. "So we'll all have to be on our best behaviour."

Climbing the stairs, Russell wondered what he could do to deter Dickel's friend from moving in. Nothing occurred to him.

His own room felt less like a sanctuary than it had a few minutes before, and it hadn't felt much like one then. The sense of living on borrowed time edged back into his mind, and sat there like an unwelcome guest. He knew he should get out of Wedding sooner rather than later.

He turned on all of the lights, opened a window to let in some air, and extracted Mommsen's notebook from its hiding place under the floorboard. After making himself some tea he took up residence in the armchair, an exercise book in his lap, *Mein Kampf* and *Menschen im Hotel* on either arm.

The notebook seemed to have seventeen discreet entries, each with five to seven lines of numbers. After what Lossow had told him, Russell was not expecting complexity, and if the entries were indeed client cases, then the first thing he'd come to should be a name.

The first line of the first entry had something between

a hundred and a hundred and fifty numbers, punctuated in groups of one, two and three. The first three groups, which presumably stood for page, line and letter, were 110.14.63. Looking these up in *Menschen im Hotel* and *Mein Kampf* respectively, Russell came up with an *h* and an *f*. The second group produced an *e* and an *r*, the third an *I* and *g*, which seemed to rule out *Mein Kampf*. Twenty minutes later, *Menschen im Hotel* had given him a name—Heinrich Himmelman.

The rest looked straightforward, if somewhat laborious. As the streets outside grew quiet and one in the morning drew near, he completed the first entry:

> Heinrich Himmelman
> Sturmbannführer Charlottenburg SA
> 43/5 Danckelmann
> Frau Mutter jüdisch
> 1M
> Wizleben
> 100

Which, with the exception of the final two lines, seemed clear enough. Sturmbannführer Himmelman of the Charlottenburg SA lived in apartment 5 at 43 Danckelmann Strasse. He was married to a woman with a Jewish mother, and the two of them had a son. If memory served Russell correctly, Jewishness derived from the mother, which meant that Himmelman's wife and son were also Jewish, at least according to Jewish law. Where the Nazis would draw the line still seemed up in the air.

Wizleben was another street in Charlottenburg, and was probably the site of the office that held the relevant records. As there was no other money-suitable figure, the 100 might be marks already paid, or perhaps the amount expected at regular intervals.

Feeling tired but still wide awake, he decoded another five entries. He recognised none of the names, which didn't surprise him—he hardly expected Göring or Goebbels to turn up, and neither he nor anyone he cherished socialised with Nazis. The pattern though was clear: all six men were ranking National Socialists with a guilty secret—they each had relatives or current partners with some strain of Jewish ancestry. If they were the tip of an iceberg, Hitler's racial paradise seemed likely to prove flawed.

It was now past two in the morning, and way past time for bed, but sleep still proved elusive. He felt pleased that he'd solved the puzzle, but still at a loss as to what might follow. Mommsen had presumably threatened these seventeen men with exposure, and as far as Russell knew none had told him to do his worst. Indeed, it seemed more than possible that all of these erring Nazis had chosen to simply pay up rather than lose the wives and children their Party considered tainted.

Which was annoyingly honourable of them.

With Ilse and Matthias visiting the latter's parents, Sunday lunch at Thomas and Hanna's was a cosy three adult, three child, affair. With political worries left at the door, the talk was of issues that still felt theirs to decide. Hanna had looked at two houses in Grunewald, neither of which had a big enough garden; Thomas had been to Essen during the week to see a new printing press in action. The family was split on where they should go for their summer holiday, with Hanna and Joachim favouring the sea, Thomas and Charlotte holding out for a week in the mountains. As far as Paul was concerned, the only future event that mattered was his first game at the Plumpe, now only two weeks away.

The occasion felt like a welcome respite to Russell, but outside the world was still turning. As he and Thomas washed up, he asked if the two of them could meet for a drink once he'd taken Paul home. "I need to talk something through," he said. "Something work-related," he added, in case Thomas thought it concerned his sister. "Half an hour should do it."

The bar in nearby Meranerstrasse that Thomas had chosen was quiet and softly lit, an unnecessary but pretty log fire burning in the huge stone grate. Given the area, many of the patrons were probably Jewish professionals, and the place itself was as unlike a *Sturm* bar as one could imagine. Russell ordered their usual dark beers and whiskey chasers, which had the barman muttering about strange English drinking habits. "So what's the problem?" Thomas asked, once they'd settled themselves far enough away from the heat of the fire.

"About a month ago," Russell began, after checking that no one was near enough to listen, "a few days after the Fire, I was called out to a murder at one of the homosexual clubs on Linienstrasse. One of the rent boys had been killed, a young man named Fredo Ratzel. The police thought—or wanted to think—that his roommate Timo had done it, but they couldn't find him. And they really tried. The SA were right behind them, as if they were frightened the police would dig up something that was better left buried. Which made me wonder what the hell was going on. I talked to several of Fredo's work-mates, and promised that if Timo came to me I'd do my best to help him. He didn't, but his boy-friend Jet did, and the two of us spent two evenings at Luna Park looking for Timo. Without success. After the second night Jet said he'd carry on looking on his own, and as I had no other leads I more or less gave up on the story. Until last Tuesday, when Jet suddenly turned up outside my building in Wedding, told me he's found Timo, that the two of them were leaving Berlin that night, and that Timo wanted me to have Fredo's journal. Which, believe it or not"—Russell lowered his voice still further—"features the names of half the brownshirt leaders in Berlin. Who are not just sodomising boys. They're also killing them."

Thomas shook his head. "Why am I not surprised? I suppose you're wondering what to do with the journal."

"In one."

Thomas gestured towards the fire. "That would seem the obvious answer."

"I know, and this may sound daft, but I can't help thinking I'd be letting Fredo down. I never met the boy—not alive anyway—but after reading his journal, I feel like I did. Him and Timo. Destroying the damn thing would feel like a betrayal." He shook his head. "And if keeping it is obviously asking for trouble, then all that's left is handing the journal over to someone brave or powerful enough to get it out there in the public domain. But who would that be? No publisher would touch it, and if I put it in the post to the police, it'll just end up in one of the Alex's boilers." He smiled. "I suppose I could send it to Hitler."

Thomas scoffed. "I don't imagine our Chancellor's unaware of what Röhm and his acolytes get up to. But you *could* send it to Himmler. Or one of his praetorians."

Russell raised his eyebrows.

"A few days ago I ran into an old business acquaintance, a decent enough fellow I think, though I wouldn't say I know him that well. Anyway, we had a drink together, and he told me his son, who's just turned twenty, had recently joined Hitler's *Schutzstaffel.*"

"The blackshirts."

"Yes. Hitler's personal guard, which used to fill a few taxis, but now has more than a hundred thousand men. Joining it might seem like a good career move, but my friend was obviously far from sure that his son had made a good choice. He had no qualms about the politics—all that guff about breeding Aryan supermen—what worried him was whether or not the SS have a future. Because lots of people who matter have told him that the SS and SA are on a collision course. Both would like to become the national army, both would like to run the police and have their own intelligence services. But they can't both be Hitler's best friend—at some point in the future he'll have to choose between them."

"So Himmler would welcome some dirt on Röhm."

"I doubt he'd throw it in the bin."

"No, but I can't see the SS caring about what happened to the boys in Fredo's journals."

"They will if it's in their interests. And I can't think of anyone else who could or would take on the SA."

"Maybe."

"I still think burning it is the safest option," Thomas added, staring at the fire. "I don't suppose you have it with you?"

"God no."

"A pity." Thomas raised his empty glasses. "Another round?"

While Thomas was getting the drinks in, Russell decided his friend's suggestion had much to recommend it. If nothing else it would sow a little discord among the bastards. And giving some prominent brownshirts a few sleepless nights was better than nothing.

Thomas returned with the drinks and a change of subject, or so it appeared at first. "Did you read about Wilhelm Hansmann?" he asked.

"Wasn't he the guy who said the only way the Army got young men over the top in the war was by filling them full of rum?"

"That's the one. He used to be a Socialist Landtag deputy in Dortmund. Last Friday he was badly beaten and dumped in a ditch."

"Dead?"

"Not quite, but the prognosis isn't good. You don't have to step very far out of line these days. One off-the-cuff remark can kill you."

"I do know that."

"I just don't want *you* turning up in the Panke."

Russell raised his hands. "Point taken. And I appreciate the concern." He considered telling Thomas about Mommsen's notebook and the names he'd discovered inside, but decided that could wait for another day. Involving himself in more than one life-threatening situation at a time might strike his best friend as a trifle reckless.

"How are things at the *Morgenspiegel?*" Thomas asked.

"I don't know," Russell told him. "I think the owners and editor are . . . how shall I put it?—I think they've been made very aware that the government is not going to tolerate any real criticism. Of course a lot of our competitors are Jewish-owned, and they know the Nazis are just waiting for the slightest excuse to pounce. So everyone's self-censoring like mad. The braver editors are sticking their necks out a little bit, but two have already been sacked for their trouble, and I don't expect they'll be the last. Most of the political reporters I talk to think they'll be out of their jobs by the summer. And everyone thinks the number of papers will shrink."

"Until the *Volkischer Beobachter* becomes our *Pravda,*" Thomas said. "Where will all the journalists go?"

"Oh that's the easy bit. They'll just drink themselves to death."

Pass-Apparat

Monday morning found Russell back at the Alex, where his paper's informants had come across three newsworthy crimes. The first however turned out to be unreportable. A gang of students at the Economics School on Spandauer Strasse had badly beaten one of their professors, and been duly brought in to the Alex "before all the relevant circumstances had come to light." The young men had since been released. The "circumstances," almost needless to say, were the Professor's Jewish blood cells. A full investigation would be carried out, and no more information would be released until that was complete.

"Sometime in the next century," Eglhofer muttered in Russell's ear.

The second crime had no obvious political connotations. The body of a young woman, since identified as Ida Falter, had been found in Viktoria Park, and the first indications were that she'd been both raped and strangled. Several lines of enquiry had been established, and there would be a further briefing at five that evening. In the meantime the journalists were invited to visit the crime scene.

Third and least, someone had stolen two Reichspost delivery vans from the yard of the district office in Neukölln. As usual the communists were assumed to be responsible;

equally predictably, no evidence was offered in support of this supposition. As the vans had been empty no mail had been lost, and the vehicle numbers had been circulated to all the city's cop shops.

The briefing over, Russell went to see if Kuzorra was in his office. He was, and willing to give Russell a few minutes of his precious time.

"Are you convinced that Harri Haum took off on his own volition?" Russell asked, seeing no reason to beat around the bush.

Kuzorra didn't duck the question. "Not completely," he said after a moment. "But if he was abducted, the only witness has disappeared. We couldn't find anyone to corroborate this phantom neighbour's story, or even confirm that he exists."

"Neither could I," Russell conceded. "But I managed to speak to one of Haum's staff, and he claimed his boss flew to Italy on Thursday afternoon. The people on the desk at Tempelhof say he didn't."

"Interesting, but . . ."

"I can see there's nothing more the police can do," Russell said. "Except maybe help a poor hack like myself do a little extra digging. A look at Haum's appointment book would help a great deal. So would a list of the people who worked for him."

Kuzorra laughed. "Well it's not as though anyone here bothers with rules anymore." He got up and searched through the files on the shelves behind him. "Help yourself," he said, after pulling one out, and dumping it down in front of Russell. "I have a meeting upstairs," he added. "Close the door when you leave."

The file had everything Russell wanted. He copied out the list of Haum's seven employees, noting that four had lived on the premises, three at their own apartments, all of which were nearby. After writing their addresses down, he turned to the appointments book. This wasn't as full as Russell expected, until he remembered that Haum had been rehearsing his upcoming show on the Ku'damm in the weeks before his vanishing act. Over the last month he'd seen eleven private clients, three of whom had only been once. The other eight, whose names, addresses and telephone numbers Russell also took down, had all seen their personal seer on a weekly basis.

He had a way forward, Russell thought, as he emerged onto Alexanderstrasse. He also had a job to do. Having spent twenty minutes in Kuzorra's office, he was lagging behind his fellow reporters when it came to the murder story. Back at the *Morgenspiegel*, he got Hiedler's permission to requisition one of the photographers, and hurried south to Viktoria Park.

It was a mostly wasted journey. Ida Falter's corpse had already been taken away, and the crime scene consisted of several uniformed Kripo searching through bushes while their plainclothes superiors chatted and smoked. The detective in charge and most of Russell's press colleagues had already departed, but one was still there, and willing to share what he knew. Another Alex briefing was scheduled for five-thirty, by which time it might be possible to talk to the victim's family.

To ask them what, Russell thought. How they felt about losing a child or a sibling? The only newsworthy answer would be saying they didn't care.

Did everyone deserve the chance to show their grief when something like this happened? Maybe they did. And maybe it was part of his job to give them the opportunity, but it didn't feel right. As if those enduring a tragedy were obliged to follow a script that reassured those who weren't.

On his way back to the office he decided that the stolen Reichspost vans were excuse enough for another vigil in Neukölln that afternoon. It was almost three weeks since

Zollitsch had hired him to look for Lili, and he was no nearer finding her. There'd been no word from Höschle or Wipperman, so they had presumably done no better. Which had to mean that Lili was either dead or still at large. If the former, Russell doubted she would ever be found. If the latter, she'd be doing her best to stay hidden. Either way, his chances of tracking her down were minimal, and it was probably time he admitted as much to Zollitsch.

He had planned to set the murder story aside until after the second briefing, but Hiedler had remembered a similar event in Viktoria Park the previous year and told him to check the archives. Hurrying downstairs, Russell admonished himself for not being thorough; he was so involved with Lili, Haum and Mommsen—none of whose stories would ever get into print—that he was falling down on his job.

Hiedler had remembered correctly, and trawling back through the records Russell discovered that Ida Falter's was the fourth female corpse to turn up in Viktoria Park since 1930. Which, like it or not, made the story more interesting to the paper's readers.

Since he was down there on his own, Russell took the opportunity to look up two men—Berthold Kruger and Karl Muhlberg—who had often appeared in Fredo's journal. As he expected, both were high-ranking members of the Berlin SA, close to the leader Ernst Röhm and his sidekick Richard Ohst. There were plenty of pictures of Kruger and Muhlberg, including one with their wives at the Blau-Weiss Tennis Club. The women looked as if they'd been sedated.

After sketching out a provisional piece on the murder, Russell took himself down to the Neukölln Reichspost offices, where no one had anything new to impart about the stolen vans. One minute they'd been there, waiting for the night shift to sort the day's mail, the next they were gone. No one had seen them driven away, or noticed anyone suspicious in the yard.

It was around four by the time Russell reached Berg-strasse, and after picking up an early evening paper, he colonised a window seat in the usual café. Having missed lunch, he ordered an early supper of sausage and spätzle, and over the next fifteen minutes somehow contrived to eat and read the paper while still keeping one eye on the street. The food was good, the newspaper full of a new campaign against Jewish professionals, whose numbers were soon to be restricted in line with the Jewish propor-tion of the general population. A lot of doctors, lawyers and professors would soon be out of a job.

Russell folded up the paper and kept his gaze on the side-walks outside, which were quickly filling up as the workday drew to a close. He had planned to visit Donna Mommsen that day, but what with the second Alex briefing he doubted he'd have time. Which was fine with him, because their next encounter might prove problematic. He hoped she would be sensible enough to settle for the cash and whatever was in the safety deposit box and forget about the notebook, but one never knew.

More and more strangers went by on the sidewalk. The yellow streetlights came on, darkening the sky and adding worry to the faces. It was almost five, and time he left if he wanted to get to the briefing on time. As he reluctantly rose to his feet, Bruno Aretin strode past.

By the time he had paid his bill and got out onto the busy sidewalk, his old Party acquaintance was nowhere to be seen. Hurrying in the same direction, he was starting to despair of spotting his quarry when Aretin suddenly came into view, crossing the street fifty yards ahead at one of the city's new traffic lights.

Russell quickened his pace, and just about managed to get across on the same red light. Aretin was about thirty yards in front of him now, heading east at a decent pace down a road running parallel to the elevated Ringbahn tracks.

Imagining such a sighting, Russell's thoughts had gone no further than a chat in the street, but the look on Aretin's face had already given him second thoughts. "Hunted" was the word Ulrich Beyschlag had used, and Russell could see why. With little idea how the man would react to a sudden approach, it seemed, for the moment at least, more sensible to just keep following. At this time of day the man was probably going home, and a conversation in private would be safer for them both.

An eastbound train rattled by above. At the next junction Aretin took a right turn under the railway, glancing back as he did so. But there were two men between him and Russell, and he showed no sign of seeing anything that worried him. Russell slowed his stride, and reached the junction in time to see Aretin turn left on the far side of the bridge. The streets were now lined with industrial premises, and many walls bore large white squares where slogans had been painted out. Russell only knew this area as one of the grimier parts of his Ringbahn rides with Paul.

The dusk was deepening, the sky to the east a patchwork of dark blue spaces and cream-tinged clouds. An out of sight moon was on the rise, Russell deduced; it was, he remembered from the night before, a couple of days from being full.

Aretin turned right down another street lined with workshops and warehouses, some still lit for an evening or night shift. After a few hundred yards the road crossed a waterway—the Neuköllner Schiffahrtskanal, Russell guessed—before burrowing in between factory walls. A well-lit bar was visible just beyond the next crossroads, and when Aretin turned right again onto a mostly empty road Russell decided to wait awhile and widen the gap between them. But Aretin also stopped, and as Russell loitered in a convenient patch of shadow, he noticed that his quarry was

standing next to some factory gates, looking this way and
that like a man awaiting his chance.

It took a couple of minutes, but the moment the coast
was clear, Aretin slipped from view.

Russell walked down the sidewalk until he was opposite
the gates. These were padlocked, a faded sign announcing
that the factory had once been home to Troeltsch Engineering. The site was seemingly derelict, but a pedestrian gate
beside the main entrance was clearly unlocked, and had,
Russell guessed, been Aretin's means of entry. There was
no sign of him now—the buildings surrounding the yard
and canal dock were dark, silent and apparently empty. If
Russell hadn't watched a known communist make such a
furtive entrance, he wouldn't have given the place a second
thought.

He wondered what he should do. Whatever this was, it
wasn't Aretin's home, so unless he wanted to wait who knew
how many hours for the man to re-emerge, any hopes of a
private chat seemed doomed. Russell's instinct told him that
this was a Party hideout of one sort or another, so another
furtive knock on the gate might conceivably gain him an
audience with people who knew who and where Lili Zollitsch was. But would they tell him if they did? Why would
they trust him—a turncoat, a foreigner, a journalist, a man
who had tailed one of their own to a clandestine base?

Being tossed, dead or alive, into the nearby canal seemed
more likely than a friendly exchange of information.

But just standing there staring was probably the worst
thing he could do, so he forced himself back into motion.
Beyond the factory another railway line crossed the road,
and he stopped in the darkness under the bridge to consider what his next move should be.

Taking another look was the best he could come up
with, which seemed depressingly Micawberish. He crossed
the street and slowly walked towards the gates, all the while

trying to persuade himself that Lili's father deserved some bravery for his money.

He needn't have bothered. As he approached the pedestrian gate it suddenly swung open, and two men lunged out in his direction. Before Russell knew what was happening, each had grabbed one of his arms, and he was being bundled through the open gateway. A glimpse of a third, much older face was followed by the sound of a bolt ramming home behind him as his two abductors frog-marched him diagonally across the cobbled yard. He had a fleeting glimpse of the rising moon before they pushed him up some steps, through a door and into a spacious loading bay, where a couple of men were carrying boxes and crates to two waiting vans. The vehicles' shape was familiar, their paintwork decidedly new; the Reichspost's loss had clearly been the Party's gain.

One crime solved, Russell thought in passing.

He found himself wondering how many of the city's industrial sites were now playing host to triumphant brownshirts or desperate Reds. And how many of them he was destined to visit.

He didn't recognise the men who had seized him, or the ones loading the vans, but all four looked younger than twenty, and would have still been at school when Russell left the Party. The comrade pacing to and fro in the dispatch office was a different matter. Russell remembered the face and the name from a meeting seven or eight years before—Jonni Ohr had been the Neukölln District Party rep at several city-wide conferences to coordinate political strategy. Which was reassuring. Russell doubted he had anything serious to fear from the communists, but it had to be better dealing with one he knew than a perfect stranger.

Since they'd last met the other man's hair had turned grey, an already gaunt face had become even leaner, and the fire in the eyes that Russell remembered had lost a few shades of brightness. All of which was hardly surprising. Men like Ohr had spent the last few years desperately building defences, only to see their whole world collapse in a few horrendous weeks. Now each and every day would feel like it might be the last.

The younger comrades were still holding Russell's arms, but not quite so tightly. And if Ohr had recognised him, he wasn't letting on. "Okay, I don't have time to waste, so you will me tell now—who you are, and what were you doing hanging around outside."

The "or" was unspoken, but loud enough. At least there wasn't a bullwhip on the table. "John Russell," he said. "I saw Bruno Aretin on Berg Strasse, and I followed him here. We used to be in the same district party, and I hoped he could help me find another comrade."

Ohr's face hardened. "Used to be?"

"I left in 1927."

A twitch of the lips. "Which comrade are you looking for?"

"Her name's Lili Zollitsch. Her father's a friend of a friend, and he thought my knowing people in the Party might prove useful in finding her."

"He wants you to bring her home?"

"He just wants to know she's alive. And after the last few weeks he has reason to fear the worst, wouldn't you say?"

Ohr blew out his cheeks. "I'll check your story when I have the time. In the meantime"—he gestured to the young men who had brought Russell in—"put our fallen comrade somewhere safe."

They obliged, escorting Russell farther into the building, until they found a suitable room with a key. The light fitting had no bulb, but despite the filthy windowpanes the moon outside was bright enough to cast the room in a pale glow. The contents were no more interesting than those in his SA cell had been. If his situation, at least for the moment, seemed remarkably *déjà vu*, he hoped it would end as well.

Or at least as well as anything did in his benighted adoptive country.

He was fearful, he realised, but nowhere near as terrified as he had been during the previous incarceration. The communists wouldn't hesitate to kill him if they thought he'd betrayed them, but they wouldn't enjoy it or torture him first. Which was surely some consolation.

And besides, he hadn't betrayed them.

Not leaving anythin g to chance, he checked out the window as a possible means of escape. The canal beneath it looked most uninviting, and it was almost a relief to discover that the frame was rusted shut.

Using his coat as a pillow made lying on the concrete floor a little less uncomfortable, but without it around him he soon grew cold, and had to put it back on. Time went by, the silence only interrupted by the occasional freight train crossing the iron bridge behind the building.

He had probably been there three or four hours when the key turned in the lock and someone came in, shutting the door behind him. It was Ohr.

"I brought you some water," he said, handing over a bottle.

"Thank you."

Ohr leaned against the door jamb. "Aretin confirms that you are who you say. But he wasn't very complimentary."

"We ended up on opposite sides," Russell said. "Not that we liked each other much when we were on the same one."

"You supported the Trotskyist line," Ohr stated flatly.

Russell shrugged in the dark. "To be frank, I had problems with that as well."

"Perhaps you're too fussy," the other man suggested without sounding flippant.

"Perhaps," Russell reflected. He remembered Ohr as someone who had sought consensus when many had not, and strangely, given the circumstances, he felt an obligation to explain his own position. "We had a newborn son, and if the Party was to be my first loyalty, I needed to believe that it was heading in the right direction. And I wasn't sure that it was."

Ohr sighed. "History will judge. Here and now, we are where we are. You can tell your friend his daughter is alive and doing what she wants to do. But not for twenty-four hours."

"Why the wait, for heaven's sake? I won't say a word about this place."

"Not willingly, perhaps, but I can't take the risk. You must know what the Pass-Apparat is?"

"I do." The Pass-Apparat was the Berlin-based Comintern organisation responsible for producing false documentation, mostly passports, but also birth certificates, work records and social security papers. In Russell's communist days it had held over two thousand passports from various countries, and more than thirty thousand rubber stamps to assist in their creation. The Pass-Apparat had made Europe's clandestine communist network possible.

"Well, for obvious reasons it's no longer safe in Berlin," Ohr said, "and I'm responsible for moving part of the inventory. You saw the vans being loaded when they brought you in. By morning we'll have it all on a train, and by evening onto a ship. Once I hear the ship's at sea you can go."

Russell sighed. "Fair enough," he said. In the other man's position he wouldn't have acted any differently.

"Until then, consider yourself a guest of the Party," Ohr said drily.

The door shut behind him, the key turned again in the lock, and Russell was left in his moonlit cell. Again the minutes stretched into hours, the night freights continuing their spasmodic assaults on Berlin's more sensitive sleepers. Around three o'clock he thought he heard motors start, and assumed it must be the vans setting off for one of the yards. Stettin or Lehrter most likely, if the stuff was Baltic-bound.

Not long after he had more visitors. Lili Zollitsch was instantly recognisable from her photograph, but looked a lot more beautiful in the half-light of Russell's cell. A grim-faced young man was with her—the boyfriend, Russell assumed—and he let her do the talking.

"Just so you know I'm alive," she explained her presence. Russell asked if she had any message for her father.

She thought about that for a moment. "Tell him I love him. Which I do. But that I've made my choice. We all have to, don't we, sooner or later? And it's one that I'm happy with. Even if it kills me," she added, managing to sound both younger and older than her years. "And tell him this is not about Ewald. We were committed communists before we met—I would hate my father to think I fell in love like some silly girl and then let Ewald shape my opinions."

"I'll tell him," Russell said. "He does miss you."

She smiled at that. "I wonder. In his heart, perhaps. In his life—I doubt it. But then . . ."

The sound of revving motors cut across the conversation. Shouts and gunfire followed.

"Brownshirts," Ewald said, rather unnecessarily. "Lili, let's go," he said over his shoulder, and seconds later both were gone, the sound of their running footsteps swiftly engulfed by the growing tumult outside.

Russell looked at the open door, wishing they'd locked him back in. As a prisoner of the communists, the SA might have let him go; as a man on the loose they would just round him up with the rest. He supposed he could lock the door from the inside, and hide the key somewhere in the room, but that seemed like tempting fate, like offering himself on a platter. Better to seek escape while he could.

Ewald and Lili had run back towards the loading bay, so Russell went in the other direction, down a passage with offices on either side, across a large high-windowed work-space, and into an echoing stairwell. Down to the cellar or up a floor? Both seemed a bad idea, the cellar slightly worse, so he raced up the metal steps. The sounds of murderous battle were unmistakable, but still seemed far away. If he could find a safe way out of the building, the darkness would hide him as he searched for a way off the sprawling site.

Two floors up a flight of narrow steps led him out onto a wide expanse of flat roof, where cries of pain and revving motors became depressingly audible. The clouds now covering the moon made it unlikely he would be seen, but he still kept his head down approaching the parapet, and carefully raised his eyes above the rim.

The scene in the street below was all too clear—the flaming torches and headlights had created the usual hellish stage for an SA production. Men were being dragged to the lorries, kicked or battered with rifle butts in the process, whether or not they still seemed conscious. Occasional shots were still being fired in the factory complex, but Russell doubted that executions were taking place. The SA liked their foes alive.

And there she was, being dragged mute and bloodied by her long blond hair. Was she alive or dead? When the brownshirt bundled her into the back of a lorry with living captives, Russell felt a smidgen of hope. If he could get word to her father, the colonel might find a way to save her.

To send such a message he first had to save himself. As he shuffled across the roof to explore his options, he heard the tell-tale stamp of boots on metal stairs. They were the searching the building beneath him, and that way out was gone.

Right on cue, another presented itself. As he reached the inner parapet two curved handrails came into view, either side of an iron ladder. Russell reminded himself he wasn't afraid of heights—a trifle wary, perhaps—and that his choices were limited, this latter reality given sharper definition by a fresh burst of pounding on the stairs inside. The bastards were on their way up to the floor beneath, and would doubtless explore the roof.

He studied the geography below, searching for some way out of the yard that didn't involve the canal. There was none he could see from where he was, but maybe there would be once he was on the ground.

Russell took a deep breath, grasped one of the handrails, and sought the top rung of the ladder with a questing foot. It shook rather more than he'd hoped, but didn't collapse beneath him, and as puffs of dark smoke from a passing train billowed above the far parapet he nervously started down.

The gloom was almost total, and he doubted whether anyone could see him. Hearing was another matter, as the ancient ladder occasionally creaked its distress at such unexpected use. The descent, though no more than forty feet, seemed to take forever, and when one foot finally touched the ground in a welcoming pool of shadow the sense of relief was enormous.

There hadn't been any gunfire for a while, but voices were still being raised in the distance, and figures were moving on the farther side of the yard. Looking for better concealment, Russell edged his way round the corner of the building and into the shelter of a convenient doorway, wondering what to do next. He was strongly tempted to stay where he was and hope the search would pass him by, not least because venturing out across the yard seemed like dicing with death.

To his left the gap between the two buildings ended in a high brick wall, and there was nothing on the ground that would help him reach the top. All he could see was a pile of rusty rings that had probably once been attached to mooring bollards. He walked across and picked one up, thinking he might need a weapon, but once in his hands it proved awkward to wield. Perhaps he could challenge the brown-shirts to a game of quoits.

He was still enjoying the thought when he heard movement on the other side of the door. And whoever they were, they were headed his way. Noticing the door opened outwards, he stood where he thought he'd be hidden from view, only to realise too late that the men coming out might close it behind them.

There was nothing for it but to wait and hope that idleness triumphed.

What he got was a surprise. As the door swung open a man leapt out, violently pushing it back as he did so, and raced off towards the wall without even noticing Russell. A cursing brownshirt erupted out of the doorway, and was bringing his up rifle to fire when Russell bounced the ring off his head and dropped him like a stone.

He stood over his victim for several seconds, watching blood course from the wound, thinking that someone would surely have heard the door slam.

"Thank you," a voice said quietly behind him. It was Jonni Ohr, who gazed at the fallen brownshirt for several seconds before picking up the rifle and repeatedly ramming its butt into the open wound. "He saw my face," the communist explained, seeing the look on Russell's.

If he had any real objection, there was no point in making it now. "Do you know a way out?"

"That wall down there's a couple of feet too high," Ohr said. "So I'd say the canal's our best bet."

Russell was staring at the distant wall. "Not if we help each other up. If one of us makes a stirrup . . ."

"Yes," Ohr said, leading the way. "So who's it to be? I'm a bit taller, so I'll find it easier to reach down."

Russell didn't like it, but trusting Ohr was his only option. Once the communist had placed one foot in

Russell's interlinked fingers and been hoisted up within reach of the top, he still had to scrabble his body upwards until he had one leg over. This was the point at which he could have waved his helper goodbye, and before Ohr lowered an outstretched hand to Russell's a momentary hardening in the communist's eyes suggested the thought had crossed his mind.

On the other side, they clambered up the embankment until their eyes were level with the gleaming rails. Going left the tracks crossed the road with the SA vehicles and lights, and the chances of their being seen seemed high. The canal bridge to the right looked a much better bet, or did so until they noticed a posse of men on the road bridge downstream, brownshirts who could hardly fail to spot them if they went that way.

Unless they crossed behind a train, Ohr suggested as the two of them crouch in the grass. He pointed out the narrow walkway between girders and tracks.

It wasn't the best idea Russell had ever heard, but he couldn't think of a better one. And before he had time to try harder, an approaching train made itself heard.

"Let's get across," Ohr said, and without further ado began wriggling up the shoulder of ballast and across the first rail.

Russell followed suit, noticing as he squirmed across the final rail that it was vibrating like a tuning fork.

Hunkered down ten metres from the start of the bridge, they watched the train loom into view, route lights shining, smoke pouring skywards. It was a big engine, which hopefully meant a long train, because the SA would surely be watching and they didn't want to be still on the bridge when the brake van trundled by.

As the locomotive thundered past, they had a quick glimpse of the crew on their fiery footplate before the line of box vans started rolling past. And then they were up on their feet and onto the bridge, picking a path no wider than a door between the girders and the swaying train. The noise was deafening, and their minute on the bridge felt like several more, but they were across and down the far embankment before the train was past them.

A gap in the railings at the bottom offered access to the towpath. The men on the road bridge close to the factory were still there, but as far as Russell could tell in the gloom there were no men stationed on the nearest bridge in the other direction.

"My place is about a kilometre away," Ohr said quietly. "We shouldn't spend any more time on the street than we have to," he added before setting off.

Walking through Neukölln at four in the morning with a prominent communist didn't feel like the wisest of choices, but in lieu of a safer alternative Russell accepted the invitation. As they walked down the towpath Ohr asked him how he'd come to be behind the door, and once that question was answered, what'd he seen from up on the roof.

At the next bridge they climbed a flight of steps to the street, and started wending their way through a grid of run-down housing blocks, pausing at each corner to check out the street beyond. They didn't run into a Kripo patrol—Russell suspected this was an area they would only enter in force—but the sound of an approaching lorry had them scurrying for the shadows of the nearest doorway. The vehicle turned out to be a furniture van, though heaven knew what it and its youthful driver were moving in the hour before dawn.

"The *Portierfrau*'s new, and her husband is a Nazi," Ohr revealed as they approached the entrance to his block. "But I've never seen them up before seven."

There was no sign of either as they crept down the hall and started up the unlit stairs. The smell of damp and rotting garbage made Russell feel almost nostalgic for Wedding.

Ohr's rooms were on the fourth floor. "I have a wife and child," he said before opening the door. "They should be asleep."

The wife wasn't. Ohr and Russell had only been inside for a few seconds when an attractive woman in a nightgown slipped out of the other room and gently closed the door behind her. "Gert's asleep," she said. "How did it go?"

"Badly. Though I suppose it could have been worse. The brownshirts turned up, but only after the shipment had left. There were comrades killed, comrades arrested. But I got out, and I hope I wasn't the only one."

She glanced at Russell.

"He isn't a comrade. An innocent bystander, if such people still exist. But we did help each other escape."

"I should be going," Russell said. "I have to let Zollitsch know that his daughter's been taken before . . . before whatever happens to her happens."

"Of course," Ohr said. "But they'll have found the body by now, and guessed that someone escaped. The patrols will be out, stopping everyone they come across. So wait for daylight, then walk straight to the U-Bahn—it's only ten minutes away, and by that time there'll be too many people out on the streets for the SA to check them all."

Russell told himself that getting arrested would scotch any chance of warning Zollitsch, and allowed himself to be persuaded.

"I'll make some tea," Ohr's wife announced. Her name hadn't been mentioned, and he doubted it would be.

"Do you think you'll get the stuff out?" Russell asked, not at all sure he'd get an answer.

But Ohr must have known that simply by bringing him home, he had passed the point where discretion was relevant. "They should be on the train by now, but who knows? If someone betrayed us, the SA may know all our plans. And they'll be questioning those they arrested. Some will break and talk, but only two other comrades knew which yard the vans were going to."

"Will you be safe?"

"For the moment. We all moved house in January or February, and none of us know where the others live."

"Neukölln's not that big."

Ohr shrugged and looked across at his wife. "How could I leave?"

Here was the man who had just staved a fellow human's head in, Russell thought, and here in these rooms was the reason why.

When he left an hour or so later the sun was squinting over the rooftops and the pavements were sprinkled with people on their way to work. Most were heading the same way he was, and after ten minutes he reached the Rathaus Neukölln U-Bahn station without needing one of the various stories he'd rehearsed on the walk. Six stops later he alighted at Kochstrasse, and hurried down to the almost empty *Morgenspiegel* office.

Colonel Zollitsch was obviously an early riser, because he answered on the second ring.

"Your daughter's been arrested," Russell told him without preamble. "She was picked up in Neukölln, during an SA raid on the disused factory that used to belong to Troeltsch Engineering. I don't know the street, but I doubt that matters, because she isn't there now. The crucial point is the Neukölln SA have her. If you have any way . . ."

"I'll get on it," Zollitsch said, cold fury in his voice.

"One more thing," Russell said. "Last week I came across an SA Standartenführer named Wipperman, and offered the man a reward if he could find Lili in one of their private prisons. He couldn't, but if nothing else works he might be worth trying again, now that you know who has her. I have a number you could ring."

"Give it to me," Zollitsch said. He managed a curt word of thanks once Russell had done so and abruptly cut the connection.

Poor bastard, Russell thought, replacing the earpiece. He blearily scanned the newsroom, empty save for a woman cleaner. There was nothing he could do for Lili that her father couldn't do better, and a nap upstairs might bring him back to life.

It turned out there was a bunk going spare, albeit one with a snorer below. Russell climbed wearily into it, not much caring if he woke the man up, but only succeeding in increasing his bunkmate's volume. He lay there on his back, feeling more awake than he had at his desk, wondering at Zollitsch's response. The man was right to be in a hurry, but he hadn't even asked whether Russell had seen her, or how she was.

The next thing he knew someone was shaking him awake, and telling him it was nine o'clock. The beds needed changing and he had to be out. After putting his shoes and coat back on, he decided work could wait until he'd had breakfast. Once the Jädickes Konditorei had served up rolls with butter and four-fruit jam and the coffee to wash them down with, he made his way back to the newsroom.

"You look dreadful," was Hiedler's greeting.

"I spent half the night in a communist hideout," Russell offered in explanation. "And the other half escaping the SA who raided it."

Hiedler leaned back in his chair and twirled a pencil between his fingers. "That first line sounds like a trashy novel," he observed. "I don't suppose any of it is printable."

"Not if you want me back tomorrow."

Hiedler took his time weighing up the implicit bargain. "So what else do you have on the go?"

"I missed the Viktoria Park murder briefing last night, so I'll follow up on that. Other than that, Harri Haum." He

explained what Kuzorra had allowed him to see the previous day. "I'd like to talk to more of the staff and a few of his
clients. Even I recognised some of their names, so if all else
fails, we should get some decent gossip."

"How the mighty," Hiedler muttered. He scratched
his head and looked at Russell. "Are you okay?" he asked
bluntly.

"As well as anyone can be who's watched the bastards in
action, and knows he daren't lift a finger to help."

Haum's principal secretary and theatre agent both lived in
the West End, so Russell reckoned he might as well get the
meeting with Donna Mommsen over with first.

"Was it the right book?" she asked him the moment he
was inside the door.

"It was."

"And?"

Russell walked through to the living room and took a
seat. "The first time we ever talked you told me your husband wasn't an honest man."

"Did I?" She sat down opposite him. "Well, I don't suppose you're going to tell me I was wrong."

"As far as I can tell, he was blackmailing around twenty
of his clients. They came to him for family trees, and when
he found Jews in one or more of the branches, he asked for
money to destroy the evidence. His own research for a start,
and I think he had people in record offices who he paid to
smuggle out the original documents."

"So if there's any money, that's where it came from."

"I think we can be certain there's money," Russell reassured her. He had already decided that if anyone deserved
it then she did.

"But it's hot," she argued, reverting to her native idiom.

"Assuming it's cash, that'd be hard to prove."

"Not if he wrote it all down." She ground out her

cigarette. "And where the hell is the notebook?" she asked, having suddenly realised that it wasn't on show.

"I didn't fancy carrying it around, so I left it somewhere safe. Can you imagine explaining a notebook in code to an inquisitive brownshirt?"

She looked slightly mollified, but only slightly.

"Look, the only way to make money out of the notebook is by carrying on with the blackmail, and I'm assuming you don't want to do that."

"No, of course not," she said, sounding almost convinced.

"Well then, if you let me keep the book, I promise not to let the police get hold of it. No one but us and your husband's victims will know what has happened, so you'll get to keep all the money."

She was still suspicious. "And what about you? Are you planning to carry on with the blackmail?"

"Nope. I'm going to let the victims know that the records have been destroyed."

"Out of the goodness of your heart?"

"Something like that." And while part of him, most of him, thought it was the right and prudent thing to do, a small voice in his head was suggesting that the notebook, like Fredo's journal, might be a gift from the gods. A dangerous one no doubt, one he still had no clue what to do with, but a gift he shouldn't rush to squander. Keeping it might be worth a little risk.

She gave him a look, but seemed to accept it. And once she thought it through, Russell was fairly confident that she would realise that settling for the money was by far her best option. "Call me if you need any help with the bank or the lawyer," he offered on his way out, and the smile he received in return, though not exactly grateful, was more rueful than bitter.

Outside the sun had appeared, and a warm spring breeze was wafting in from the west. Three of Haum's employees

lived less than half a mile either side of the Ku'damm and
he planned to visit each one in turn. But first he needed to
find out what had been in the briefing he'd missed the previous evening, and after buying copies of three rival papers
he sat down with a second coffee to see what the police had
come up with.

Nothing, was the short answer. When all three reporters
filled their columns with details of previous corpses found
in the park, there was clearly no new information on the
latest.

The first of Haum's helpers on his list was Martin Fobke,
who lived only a few blocks away on Kantstrasse. As he
walked in that direction, Russell couldn't help noticing that
the distance between the West End and Neukölln was more
than a matter of miles: you could see it in the state of the
buildings, the number of cars, the stuff in the shop windows. You could read it in people's faces, and in the clothes
they wore. On the BBC he had heard Germans asked what
living in Hitler's new world was like, as if it was the same for
everybody. It wasn't. What it was like depended on where
and what you came from.

Fobke was—or had been—the clairvoyant's private secretary, which could mean just about anything, but probably
didn't involve much shorthand or typing. The woman who
answered the door didn't ask Russell in, and when Fobke
himself appeared it was only to repeat the claim that Haum
had flown south for a holiday. When Russell told him that
the people at Tempelhof had categorically denied that Haum
had boarded a flight that day, Fobke at first seemed taken
aback, but after visibly thinking on his feet, suggested that
Haum might have disliked the omens that day, and either
postponed his trip or taken a train. And yes, of course he
was coming back. Why would anyone think otherwise?

Alwin Vordung was Russell's next port of call, south
of the Ku'damm on Paulsborner Strasse. Again a woman

answered a door, this time to say her husband was at work. Vordung had been on the list as one of Haum's personal assistants, and now, according to his talkative wife, was advising his new clients on home furnishings at one of the larger stores on the Ku'damm. Russell eventually found him sitting on the edge of a loading bay, smoking a contemplative cigarette. When asked why he'd taken another job if his boss was coming back, he nervously said that this one was only temporary, and refused to say anything more.

Discouraged but not surprised, Russell walked a few blocks east to the third address. Berta Pozl, another of the fortune teller's personal assistants, was probably in her late forties. She was brown-haired and thin, with one of those faces leached of all softness by some enduring bitterness, and Russell introduced himself with little expectation of a positive response.

"Please come in," she said, surprising him.

"Who is it?" a querulous voice shouted from somewhere inside the apartment as she offered him a seat in the living room. "My mother," she explained. "I'll only be a moment."

As Russell sat there, he could hear the women talking somewhere out of sight. He caught the word "journalist" from Fraulein Pozl, and a "you be careful, my girl" from her mother. Looking around the room he was in, Russell took note of the faded carpet and curtains, the paucity of possessions. Whatever Haum had paid her, it hadn't been enough.

"My mother is bed-ridden," Berta Pozl told him as she returned. "And her doctor costs a fortune," she added. Maybe reading minds was catching for Haum employees. "He's Jewish, of course, so she'll probably have to find another before too long. But I'm sure the new one will be just as expensive." She paused for a second. "Mr. Russell, am I right in thinking that you're here to ask me about Herr Haum's disappearance?"

"You are."

She sat herself down in an opposite chair, arms folded across her chests. "Well, I'm willing to answer your questions, and to do so honestly, under certain conditions."

She'd been expecting him or someone like him, Russell thought. "Which are?" he asked.

"Two hundred marks in cash. And a guarantee of complete anonymity."

"I don't have that sort of money on me. And I would expect some real inside information for a sum like that."

"You'll get it. And I will trust you to bring me the money."

Russell was willing to believe that her second sight had seen Hiedler sanctioning such a payment. "All right," he said, "what do you know about Haum's disappearance?"

"I wasn't there at the time, so I didn't see him go. But one of the other . . . I don't have to say who, do I?"

"Another member of staff?"

"Yes."

"That'll do for the moment. This person saw what happened?"

"He saw two men take Herr Haum away. Three if you count the driver."

"He didn't go voluntarily."

"My . . . friend said it was clear that Herr Haum was reluctant to go with them, but that he let himself be persuaded."

"Were they in uniform?"

"No."

"So it wasn't the Kripo or the SA?"

"No."

Russell thought for a moment. What he was hearing confirmed the original story, but were two unnamed witnesses any real advance on one?

But Fraulein Pozl wasn't finished. "I *was* there next day when the men came back. They gathered the staff together and told us they were there on behalf of Herr Haum's new agent, a man named Henning whom none of us had heard of. They said Herr Haum had decided to take a break, that he'd flown to Italy and didn't know when or if he'd be back. If he did return we would get our jobs back, but in the meantime we would all have to seek employment elsewhere. And those who lived in the house would have to move out before Monday."

She offered a thin smile. "As you can imagine, we were dumbstruck. Not just by how sudden it all was, but how unconvincing. We all had questions, but when P . . . when one man threatened to go to the press, they took him into another room, and when they brought him back out we could see how shaken he was. No one argued after that."

That was the Nazis, Russell thought. They knew they should come up with some sort of story, but when violence was there for the threatening, why go through all the trouble of creating something convincing?

"After that it felt like they'd stopped pretending," she went on, holding herself even tighter. "Whoever questioned us—the police or the press—we should stick to the story they'd told us. That and nothing more."

"And none of you had any idea who these people worked for?"

"Well, the government, I suppose. Who else? But they didn't feel like police. Or the SA."

"Communists?"

She considered the idea. "They do have it in for Herr Haum. But why would he have gone with them?"

Why indeed, Russell thought. He thanked Fraulein Pozl, and promised the money within a few days.

"We need it," she said shortly. "But in cash, remember. And don't forget my other stipulation. I won't admit to telling you any of this—I will say you made it up."

"Understood," Russell said in parting.

On the sidewalk outside he stopped to consider his next move. Was it worth pursuing Haum's clients, now that he knew what had happened? None had been there at the time, so even if they wanted to they couldn't serve as witnesses.

But that wasn't the point, he realised—missing a night's sleep had made him slow on the uptake. He now knew what had happened, but he still didn't know why. The regular clients might have something to say in that regard, and as far as he knew they hadn't been threatened.

One woman lived only five minutes away from the U-Bahn stop he planned on using, so he took a small detour and knocked on her affluent-looking door. A maid and poodle came to answer it—their mistress was at a dress-fitting, before lunching with some Count or other.

Russell said he'd be back, and took the U-Bahn to Kochstrasse, rehearsing his pitch to Hiedler as the half-empty train rumbled its way through the tunnels. Because he knew what his editor would say. Unless he had cast-iron evidence that some enemy of the current regime was behind Haum's disappearance the story was dead in the water, and all he was doing on his employers' time was indulging his own curiosity and costing them money in bribes. His actual job, as Hiedler would doubtless point out, was filling column inches.

In the event, Hiedler did just that, but only after admitting that his own curiosity was piqued. It might not prove a printable story, but it was certainly a big one, and he wasn't quite ready to pull the plug. "Not until the man or his corpse turns up, anyway. But no more pay-outs," he warned Russell, after sanctioning Berta Pozl's. "I can't imagine any of Harri Haum's clients are short of cash."

In the meantime there was another police briefing on the Viktoria Park murder at two. Russell reached Alexanderplatz in time to buy a bratwurst from his favourite street vendor, and was on his last mouthful as he entered the Alex. The briefing had two things to offer the reporter with space to fill, the first a statement by the family that offered some details of Ida's life and said what a wonderful daughter she'd been. And maybe she had been, Russell thought, admonishing himself for his cynicism. Though, as one old hack had warned him—it was either that or drink.

The police's second gift was a portrait of a possible suspect, drawn up with the aid of two independent witnesses who had seen him close to the murder site at around the time in question. The face looked Jewish, which might mean that Ida's murderer had been a Jew. Or that these days that was the way a murder suspect was likely to be drawn.

Whoever and whatever he was, the police seemed no nearer finding him. Russell went back to the office, where he wrote and submitted his copy. By then it was gone four, and Hiedler told him to go home and get some sleep. First, though, after some hesitation, he picked up the telephone and asked the switchboard to call Colonel Zollitsch.

He let it ring until the operator pointedly asked if he was still on the line, but no one answered. Which might be good or bad news. Zollitsch and his daughter might be out celebrating her release and homecoming, or both could be down at the mortuary. Or the colonel might still be frantically trying to find out where she'd been taken.

Russell stopped for a drink on his way back to Wedding, thinking he probably needed one after all that had happened in the last twenty-four hours. He had planned to decode a few of Mommsen's entries each evening, but closing his eyes and mind seemed a much nicer proposition, so once he reached home he just went to bed, where his dreams put him back on the streets. He was in Neukölln, walking between towering factories, and then beside a canal when a body erupted up from its oily depths. A second followed, and then a third, and he was the fourth, waking to the sounds of dogs barking outside. A trip to the window showed him an empty Gerichtstrasse—somebody else, on some other street, was on the receiving end.

He was safe. Safe but ashamed.

He remembered the trenches, the guilt that went with surviving each day.

Beautiful Yes, Aryan No

He was up before dawn, and first through the doors when the public baths opened. Coming out, he noted with some satisfaction that Herr Dickel was at the back of a very long queue.

A dry warm day was predicted by Frau Löffner, and for reasons best known to herself the *Portierfrau* was rarely mistaken when it came to the weather. As Russell walked the two miles to the Unter den Linden, he tried to get his tasks in order. Lili was no longer his worry, at least in the practical sense. He was still seeking a suitable recipient for Fredo's journal, and an hour in the archives might provide one. The rest of Mommsen's notebook needed decoding, but he still had no idea what, if anything, he would do with it. Ida Falter's murder would probably take up some of his time, and there was no knowing what new horrors Berlin had witnessed overnight, but if his day didn't prove too crammed he would try to see some of Haum's clients. He and his fellow hacks might, as Hiedler put it, be employed to sell Dante's *Inferno* as *Paradise Lost*, but at least they were having an interesting time.

More grim news accompanied his breakfast at Kranzler's. The government had issued an order that committees should be set up across the country to enforce a boycott of Jewish shops and professionals. Violence was strictly forbidden— "Not a hair of any Jew shall be touched!"—but, as every

German knew, no one who did so would suffer as a result. The loudest complainers in town were the insurance company owners, who feared that they and not the Jews would end up paying for all the broken windows.

The boycott was scheduled to start on Saturday morning—April Fool's Day, Russell wryly noted—but in many places outraged citizens had refused to wait, and were already picketing Jewish shops and other businesses. There were also dire warnings aimed at the press. New committees had been set up to monitor the reporting of the boycott in local and national newspapers, and to "remove from every home" any publication whose support seemed less than total.

A few more nails in the coffin, Russell thought. And not a crowbar in sight.

The police briefing was early that morning, so he walked through the old city to the Alex, struck by how normal everything seemed after all he'd been reading. There were no new developments in the Ida Falter case, unless you counted the several hundred mostly anonymous tip-offs that the drawing had solicited. It was impossible to know for sure, but Russell was not alone in assuming that most came from so-called Aryans wanting rid of a Jewish neighbour.

Nothing new and newsworthy had happened overnight. There had been no spectacular or impudent robberies, and if anyone had been murdered the body was yet to be found. The only event of interest, half hidden away as a casual postscript, was the apprehension of several young pickpockets who'd been working the big Berlin stations. The police's reluctance to take any credit for this seemed strange, but not once it transpired that the young men involved all had brownshirt fathers. The boys' youth was stressed, their remorse much welcomed, and Russell doubted they'd ever see a courtroom. If fathers and sons shared a lawless streak, they also shared impunity.

Once the briefing was over, he dropped by Kuzorra's office

to ask if anything new had come to light regarding Haum's disappearance. No was the answer, and Russell decided against providing some of his own. Before he took his conclusions to the detective, he needed to know two things: why Haum had fallen foul of the Nazis, and whether the reason was safer kept to himself.

At the *Morgenspiegel* an hour later, he asked Hiedler who the paper's expert on Himmler's SS was. "Try Oertel or Wulle," the editor suggested after a moment's thought. "And I won't ask," he added.

Oertel was out but Rudi Wulle was polishing up some copy, and agreed to a chat on the roof in twenty minutes. Russell went up straightaway, and stood at the parapet smoking a cigarette, remembering his descent in the dark two nights before. Today's weather had exceeded Frau Löffner's expectations, the sun blazing down from a clear blue sky, the temperature more summery than spring-like. Nice day for a Jewish boycott, Hitler would probably say.

The tall blond Wulle eventually appeared. Russell didn't know the man well, but was aware that Hiedler valued him highly.

"So what do you want to know?" Wulle asked, joining Russell at the parapet.

"Who the men around Himmler are, and where I can find out about them." He remembered something Thomas had said. "And whether the blackshirts have their own intelligence section."

"They do," Wulle said, his blue eyes fixed on the city before them. "And it's run by a man named Reinhard Heydrich. Heard of him?"

"I've heard the name."

"He'd only been in the SS for a few months when Himmler put him in charge of his new intelligence section. The *Sicherheitsdienst*, or SD for short. Heydrich's young, not even thirty. From a good family—his father founded the Halle

Conservatory, and they say that Heydrich himself plays the violin to that sort of standard." Wulle's laugh lacked any humour. "Next thing you know, we'll be told that Hitler's a virtuoso on the bassoon. But getting back to Heydrich—he was in the Navy for several years, but was asked to leave after committing some social indiscretion—reneging on an engagement, I think. He must be clever—Himmler would want a good organiser—but heaven knows where his heart is. Somewhere dark would be my guess, but it's not an informed one. As for the other men around Himmler . . ." Wulle reeled off several names for Russell to note down, none of which he recognised.

"Where do the SS and SD have their headquarters?" Russell asked.

"In Munich, but I expect they have plans to move to the capital now that their man's in charge. Their current Berlin office is on the corner of Potsdamer and Lützow, right opposite the SA HQ. I imagine they exchange hostile looks across the street."

Russell laughed. "Thanks."

Wulle was still gazing out at Berlin. "Looks so normal, doesn't it?" he said, echoing Russell's earlier thoughts.

With nothing new requiring his attention, Russell went down to the archive room and looked up the names in the picture library index. Reinhard Heydrich certainly wasn't camera-shy—there were pictures of the young blond SD chief stretching back almost a decade, including several with his wife of two years, the former Lina van Osten. In one photograph from early 1931 she was wearing a large swastika brooch, which suggested that her Party allegiance had predated his. The marriage, and the doomed engagement to another woman that preceded it, suggested the man would not come to Fredo's journal as a fellow homosexual, and was unlikely to have any qualms about using tales of stormtrooper sodomy against the rival SA.

So far so good, Russell thought. Searching through the

more recent pictures of Himmler, he eventually came across everyone Wulle had named, either alongside the prim-looking leader or at some event or other. Next time he was here he needed to seek them all out in the newspaper archive, and hope to find one who seemed like a good recipient, because the idea of sending the journal straight to Himmler or Heydrich felt perilously presumptuous.

Upstairs there was a note on his desk asking him to call Ilse. Doing so, he discovered that Paul had been sent home from school with a stomach upset, and shouldn't go out again that day. "He'd still like to see you," Ilse said. "But he seems quite weak and I think he should have an early night, so . . ."

"I'll be there by four," Russell said. "And I won't stay long." After hanging up the receiver he sat there for a moment marvelling at how much better he and Ilse were getting on. At least something in his life was moving in the right direction.

His canteen lunch was followed by an utterly pointless Alex briefing, at which the spokesman's moving plea to "allow the young sons of Germany their right to make amends" produced laughter and retching mimes from many of the assembled hacks. All the captured pickpockets, the officer sternly continued, had been released into the care of "patriotic fathers," who could and would guide them down the road of national and personal renewal.

"Hallelujah," Russell heard himself murmur. When it came to shameless invention, National Socialism could give any religion a run for its money.

By the time he got back to the office it was almost time to leave, but he still had a few minutes to try and reach Zollitsch. On this occasion the phone was answered, but not by the colonel. Remembering the middle-aged housekeeper who had let him in on his only visit, Russell assumed it must be her.

"The colonel's still at the hospital," she told him, once he'd explained who he was.

Russell's heart sank. "How is Lili?" he asked.

"I don't know. It was touch and go the last I heard, but that was yesterday. So I don't know," she repeated, sounding close to tears.

"Which hospital is she in?" Russell asked. "I'd like to send flowers."

"The Elisabeth. A private room, of course."

Russell thanked her and hung up. Zollitsch had succeeded in getting his daughter released, which had to be better than not. And whatever the SA had broken, she was now in a place where she might be able to mend. Though with her comrades still in custody she might not feel that grateful. As for those still held . . .

Russell grabbed his coat and hat and set off to see his stricken son. Paul had had stomach trouble as a baby, but not, as far as he knew, in the last few years. He hoped it was something the boy had eaten.

When he reached the house on Wilhelmsaue shortly after four the news was good. "He looks better," Ilse said. "And he seems to have finally stopped being sick and you-know-what."

Paul jerked up in bed when his father appeared, but instantly seemed to regret it, and gingerly lowered his head back onto the pillow. "I'm all right now," he insisted, this judgement somewhat undermined by the green shade of his cheeks.

"You will be," Russell told him, "but it takes a while to get over something like this. The more rest you get the quicker you'll be back to normal."

"I know, but . . ."

They talked about what was happening at school. Paul had a new friend named Gerhard Reheusser, who was good at football and clever as well—"when Herr Frump drew a map of Germany on the wall and asked us to fill in the places, Gerhard knew more than I did."

"Well he must know a lot then," Russell retorted,

reminding himself that one of these days he should tell his son that being clever and knowing a lot were not the same thing. A misapprehension that in his experience was shared by most adults.

"But he's never been round the Ringbahn," Paul added.

"Well, next time we should take him with us," Russell said. "What does his father do?" he asked, hoping it was something politically neutral.

"Gerhard told me he's a draughtsman, but I'm not sure what that is."

"Someone who's paid to draw things really precisely. Like a plan for a house that's someone's going to build. And probably lots of other things. I'm not that sure myself."

"It sounds like a good job."

"It does," Russell concurred, especially in times like these. "Now I think you need to sleep," he said, noticing how much effort Paul was expending just to keep his eyes from closing.

"No, I don't."

"You need to get better—the Hertha game's only ten days away."

"I'll be better tomorrow."

"You will if you get some sleep."

Paul rolled his eyes at that, but then allowed them to close. "Goodnight," he murmured.

Downstairs Russell found Ilse in the kitchen, and told her Paul was falling asleep. "Is Matthias in?" he asked.

"He's just got back from work. Why?"

"Has he heard from the colonel in the last two days?"

"I don't think so."

"Well if he hasn't I have some news of the daughter."

"Bad news," Ilse assumed from his tone.

"Not completely," was the best Russell could offer.

"I'll get him."

Matthias appeared a minute later, his face full of concern. Russell gave him and Ilse a potted history of what had

happened over the last forty-eight hours: his finding and losing of Lili, his telling the colonel that the SA had her, what
he'd heard from the housekeeper. "I thought you should
know," he told Matthias, "because Zollitsch is going to need
all the support he can get." He reached for his hat. "I'm going to
the Elisabeth now," he said, having just decided to do so. He
needed to know how the girl was.

"I'll come with you," Matthias said. "We can take the car."

Outside the rush hour it would have been a fifteen-minute
drive to the hospital, but the traffic was particularly bad that
evening, and it took them twice as long.

"What was she doing in that factory?" Matthias asked as
they queued to get across Potsdamer Strasse.

"The KPD are moving stuff abroad," Russell told him,
keeping it vague. He instinctively trusted Ilse's new partner, but over the last few weeks he'd begun to realise that
openness—even between friends—was becoming a luxury.
Explaining the Pass-Apparat to Matthias might be an enjoyable way of passing the time, but it wouldn't be a wise one.
The days of blurting out whatever one happened to know
were gone.

Visiting hours were over when they eventually reached
the hospital reception desk, so he left the talking to Matthias, trusting in the other man's natural air of authority to
get them where they wanted to go. It didn't take long. Lili
Zollitsch was on the fourth floor in room 23, and they should
talk to the nurse in charge of that section.

Once the lift had carried them up they soon found the
woman in question, but she wouldn't countenance access to
room 23. "Colonel Zollitsch is asleep," she told them. "He's
been sitting at her bedside for twenty-four hours, and I won't
let you wake the poor man."

"We're more concerned about his daughter," Russell said.
"Is she going to live?"

"Oh yes. The physical injuries are certainly serious, but

they'll heal. There's nothing life-threatening. The mental . . ." She stopped herself. "I shouldn't say anymore. It's for the colonel to decide what he wants you to know. And his daughter."

"Of course," Matthias said. "If you could tell him we came by?"

After she'd written their names on a scrap of paper, the two men headed back to the lift.

"Thank God she lived through it," Matthias said while they waited, and Russell found himself hoping that Lili would feel the same.

Out in the twilight, Matthias offered to drive him to Wedding.

"The Potsdamer Platz will do," Russell told him. "I'll take the U-Bahn home from there." He didn't want to put the other man out, and he did want to be alone.

They agreed to let each other know if they heard from Zollitsch, and Russell said to tell Ilse he would call the next day to see how Paul was. From God knew what brutalities to a six-year-old's stomach upset, he thought as he walked down the stairs at Flughafen. A normal day in Hitler's Germany.

He didn't have long to wait for the train, and once aboard he shut his eyes and tried to let his mind go blank. It didn't work. The broken young woman in Pankow slipped under his guard and refused to leave. As far as he knew—as far as he *could* know—she was still there, still being abused, unless her will to live had finally fallen away. How could ordinary men behave that way? There had always been violence between males, always been men who beat women, and anyone who'd served in the war knew how appallingly normal the maiming and killing of other human beings could come to seem. But this was different. The cruelty of the trenches had been in the orders, the only sadism in the twisted minds of a few martinets. Here in Nazi Germany these had become the norm for half a generation.

Walking up the steps at Wedding he told himself that nothing lasted forever. Nothing except hope.

After supper at the usual café he headed home. It was Wednesday, so Frau Löffner was out playing cards with her friends. After checking the table and board for any post and telephone messages he climbed the stairs to his rooms. It was only just gone seven, and though he felt tired there were too many things going round in his mind for sleep to be an option.

The notebook, he thought, after making himself a cup of tea. The decoding needed doing, and was just the sort of job to take his mind off everything else. He went through to the bedroom and extracted Mommsen's record from its hiding place.

Three hours later he was starting work on the final client, and rubbing his eyes to keep awake. Once decoded, the name rang a definite bell. Thinking back over his day, Russell was fairly certain that Heinz Treue had turned up in his search through the archives for SS and SD officials on Wulle's list. Decoding the second line offered what looked like corroboration—Treue was an SD Obersturmbannführer. According to the third and fourth, he lived in swanky Schmargendorf at 160 Forckenbeck Strasse. With a Jewish wife and their two Jewish sons.

A possible recipient for Fredo's journal, Russell thought as he placed the notebook back in its cache. He had just rolled the carpet back over the boards when someone rapped softly on his living room door.

Who the hell? he thought. On those rare occasions when she tackled the stairs Frau Löffner had a distinctive rat-a-tat knock. The SA, of course, would use a rifle butt.

Russell went to open the door.

He recognised her at once, despite the years that had passed and the strange expression on her face. Almost the lack of one. Her eyes, which had always seemed to sparkle, seemed dulled and deep in their sockets. "Can I come in?" she asked in an overly matter-of-fact voice.

"Of course," Russell said, standing aside and closing the door behind her. She was carrying a suitcase, which didn't bode well.

"I . . ." she began, standing in the middle of the living room, still holding the suitcase. "I don't know where to begin."

"Why don't you sit down," Russell suggested. "I'll make some tea?" he added.

"I . . . yes, that would be good. Thank you."

There was enough water in the kettle, so he put it back on the electric ring.

She was sitting on the edge of the armchair, back ramrod straight and hands tightly clasped, looking for all the world like she was only just holding herself together. "You do remember me, don't you?"

"Of course." Eight years ago he and Evchen Keller had been in the same KPD local. As had Ilse and Evchen's boyfriend, Karsten Sattler. When he and Ilse had left the Party, Evchen and Karsten had stayed, he out of conviction, she because leaving the Party would have meant also ending their relationship. Her communism had always struck Russell as more instinctive than ideological, and following Sattler's sectarian zigzags was easier for her than it might have been for others. They were both artists, he a fairly successful painter of abstracts, she a disciple of the photographer Alfred Stieglitz.

She was Jewish, Sattler wasn't.

"I'm sorry," she said abruptly, as he turned to bring her the tea. "I couldn't think of anywhere else to go."

"How did you know I lived here?" he asked, when the obvious question was why had she come. She had taken her beret off, revealing the lustrous dark brown hair he remembered. It was shorter now, not much more than shoulder length. There were dry tracks of tears down both of her cheeks.

She held the cup between her palms, as if they needed warming. "I knew you lived round here—I've seen you on the street and on the station. A few weeks ago I was heading for the Baths and I saw you come out with your towel and walk across here."

"Why did you never say hello?" Russell asked, though he knew the answer.

"You left," she said simply. "You and Ilse. I haven't run into her, and I didn't know whether I would find you both here. Are you still married?"

"Only legally."

"I'm sorry." She took a sip of tea. "John, I know it's a lot to ask, but could I stay here tonight? I'll sleep in this chair."

Russell didn't like the idea, mostly because it was only a lot to ask if she was keeping something important back. But he couldn't put her out on the street at this hour of the night. "You can sleep in the bedroom," he said. "I have a sleeping roll for when my son comes to stay. I'll bring it out here."

"You have a son."

"Paul. He's six."

She smiled, but only with her lips; the eyes still seemed far away. Life in the KPD had always been fraught with danger, but he had never seen her like this. Something terrible must have happened. Something, he thought with a pang of shame, that she had now brought to his door.

"You and Karsten?" he asked, hoping against hope that it wasn't as bad as it looked.

She raised her lifeless eyes. "He's dead. The bastards shot him."

It didn't take an Einstein to know who the bastards were. "When?" he asked as gently as he could.

"This evening," she said, her eyes suddenly awash with tears.

"Why?"

She shook her head, shaking off tears. "John," she said,

her voice suddenly hard as nails, "I can't go through it again. Not now. Please, please, can we talk in the morning? I'll tell you everything then."

He couldn't say no. "Okay, but you have to answer one question—does anyone know you're here?

"No," she said. "No, how could they?"

"How did you get in downstairs?"

"The door was open."

Thank God for Wednesday's card game, Russell thought. "And you didn't meet anyone on the stairs."

"No."

"Good. Okay. There's a washroom one floor up and one floor down, and I imagine everyone's asleep by now."

Ten minutes later they were sequestered in their separate rooms. Laid out on Paul's surprisingly comfortable bedding, Russell found himself nervously listening for sounds from the street below. Thinking back on what she had said, he realised that all he actually knew was that Karsten Sattler had been shot. He didn't know whether she had actually witnessed the shooting, or simply heard that it had happened. If the former, how the hell had she—a Jewish communist—got away? And if the latter, why had she needed sanctuary? The urge to demand some answers grew stronger as his sleeplessness persisted, but died away when the sobbing started on the other side of the wall.

Russell woke up on Thursday wondering what he would say if she asked to stay, and decided the answer would have to depend on what she told him. He got himself up, and put on the kettle. If she didn't make an appearance soon, he would have to wake her up. He couldn't just leave and go to work without knowing what had happened or whether she'd be there when he got back.

Sounds of movement in the bedroom set his mind at rest, as did hearing the men from the rooms above traipsing downstairs on their way to work. The washroom above would be safe, as he told her when she appeared. Evchen looked like she'd hardly slept, but the deadness in her eyes was gone, replaced by an almost luminous sadness.

Returning from upstairs, she wasted no time. "I'm sorry I wouldn't tell you everything last night," she said, perching on the side of the armchair. "I was afraid you'd throw me out if you knew what had happened."

"I doubt that," Russell said, hoping it was true.

"But I didn't lie to you. There was no way they could know I'd come to you."

Which was something. "So what did happen? How did Karsten get shot?"

Evchen closed her eyes, as if to block out the memory. "They came to the flat. I was in the bedroom getting dressed. We had just made love," she said. "For the last time, as it turned out," she added, sadness and bitterness intertwined. "There was a knock on the door. Not the hammering they enjoy so much, so we weren't alarmed. Karsten just went to answer it in his dressing gown, and suddenly there was shouting. Our bedroom door always closes itself, so I couldn't see what was going on, and they didn't know I was in there."

She shut her eyes again, and let a breath escape. "I could hear things being broken, Karsten shouting. I didn't know whether to go out or not. Whether it would help or make things worse. Whether I was being sensible or acting like a coward. And then I remembered our gun, which we kept in the drawer by the bed just in case. And I took it out and stood there wondering if threatening to use it was the best thing I could do or the worst thing. And I was still wondering when there was a shot on the other side of the door, and Karsten stopped yelling.

"I couldn't help myself. I went through the door, and there they were, two fat brownshirts, standing over him, and leering at me in my underwear. And by the time they noticed the gun in my hand it was too late. I shot them both. One in the chest, one in the face. I couldn't believe it—I'd never fired a gun in my life, and I'd killed them both."

Oh my God, Russell thought.

"And Karsten was dead. They'd shot him in the head. There was . . . you were in the war, you can imagine. I just cradled his head and sat there for I don't know how long."

"And nobody came?"

"Nobody. I was beyond caring, but when I eventually . . . I don't know—when I came back to the world, I realised that everyone in the house had seen or heard the SA arrive, and weren't about to butt their noses in. When I eventually left, all the tenants' doors were closed, and the *Portierfrau* looked like she'd seen a ghost.

"But I'd already taken the time to gather up everything that could help them find me, and I didn't think the *Portierfrau* would tell them she'd seen me leave."

"They'll be looking for you now," Russell said. "I don't suppose you tried to make it look like Karsten shot them and died in the process?"

"It didn't occur to me."

"So where's the gun?"

"In my coat."

"You should get rid of it."

Evchen shook her head. "They won't take me alive. You've heard what they do to women in their camps. Ten men for a communist, twenty if she's also a Jew."

There was no answer to that.

"You don't have to worry," she said. "I'll be leaving soon."

This was the moment to agree that that would be best. In time he might even manage to persuade himself he'd done the right thing. "Do you have somewhere to go?" he asked.

"No, but . . ."

"Then stay. At least until this evening. Look, I work for a newspaper, the *Morgenspiegel*. And I'm on the crime desk, so

if the police were called in last night it shouldn't be hard to
find out whether they're looking for you. It'll be harder if the
SA are dealing with things on their own, but in cases like this
they usually get the police to conduct any search."

"But . . ."

"It's better you know what you're up against before you go
out there."

"All right," she said, looking relieved. "Thank you."

"You're welcome. Now, there's no reason anyone should
knock on the door, but try not to make any noise. The washroom upstairs should be safe until people come home from
work, but only use it when you have to, and listen for people
on the stairs before you go up. There's some food in the cupboard . . . not much, I'm afraid . . ."

"I'm not hungry. And I'll be fine."

"As long as there isn't a story I need to pursue, I'll be back
around six," Russell said. He was running late, and had to go.
"I didn't say it last night," he said, one hand on the door, "but
I'm sorry about Karsten."

She just nodded. "I'll see you tonight."

Russell walked down to the U-Bahn on Müllerstrasse, wondering how stupid it was to feel relief at getting out of the flat.
Not being there when the SA turned up was hardly going to
save him. And if she used her gun again they'd probably both
get the axe.

What in God's name was he doing?

What he had to, he supposed. What he could live with.
Hopefully.

He needed to get her to safety, for his own sake as much
as hers. But how? Could he borrow Thomas's car and drive
her out of Berlin? Not without putting Thomas at risk. Could
he go to the comrades for help? Perhaps. He remembered
the name of the SD officer whose name he'd recognised just
before Evchen had rapped on his door. Could he blackmail

a man like that into helping her get out? Now that *would* be playing with fire.

With ten minutes to spare when he reached Alexanderplatz, he bolted down a roll and a coffee before heading across to the Alex, where the name of the woman concealed in his flat was chalked on the briefing room blackboard. Kriminalinspektor Glassl was in charge, which was the best news Russell had heard that morning. If anyone could fail to find Evchen, he could.

Glassl opened the proceedings. The communist Jewess Evchen Heller was wanted for the shooting of two SA officers, Truppführer Franz Dornacher and Scharführer Ulz Czichon, in the apartment on Hochstadt Strasse that she had shared with her communist lover, Karsten Sattler. Czichon had been killed at the scene, but Dornacher was now fighting for his life in Wedding's Rudolf Virchow hospital. The two men had been there to arrest the two Reds, both of whom were strongly suspected of involvement in the burning of the Reichstag. When confronted, the cowardly villains had opened fire on the unsuspecting SA men, and while Sattler had died in the subsequent exchange of bullets, the woman Heller had fled the scene, and had as yet eluded capture. But with all the police's resources now being brought to bear, her arrest could only be a matter of time.

After minimal coaxing Glassl succumbed to questions, and Russell had time to take in what he'd heard. The bad news was that one of Evchen's victims had survived, at least for the moment. The good news was the lack of a photograph beside her name. If the police went back far enough they might be able to find one—in the mid-1920s Evchen's photos had caused quite a stir in artistic circles—but she looked a lot different eight years on. Russell doubted there were any more-recent pictures—the Party had always warned its rank and file to steer clear of the bourgeois press. And without a picture, the police would badly need a detailed description from Dornacher.

Though if Evchen had been in her underwear the Truppführer might not have studied her face.

Meanwhile Glassl was still answering questions, albeit with some difficulty. If one SA man was dead and the other had not regained consciousness, how was the Kriminalinspektor so sure what had happened?

"Deduction" was his answer, which begged every question going, but seemed to satisfy some of Russell's colleagues. After another briefing had been scheduled for five o'clock, the gathering dispersed, and Russell caught a tram to the office. *En route*, it occurred to him that arranging an escape for Evchen was going to take days, and that his first priority should be a plan to safely keep her where she was.

How long could she stay hidden in his rooms? He supposed he could buy a commode, and obviate the need for her to ever leave them, but how would he get such a thing up the stairs without being seen? Not to mention the food he'd have to bring in or the laundry he'd eventually have to take out. Sooner or later someone was bound to suspect.

No, if she was going to stay, it would have to be openly. Which ruled out her staying as his girlfriend. The rules of the house were clear—he could have a woman up to his rooms, and fuck her to his heart's content, but staying the night was *verboten*. And claiming the woman was "only a friend" was too obvious a ruse to pass muster. Evchen would need to be a relative, a rather thin possibility given that Russell was English and that she, as far as he knew, spoke not a word of his mother tongue.

He was no nearer finding an answer when the tram deposited him at the end of Kochstrasse. Up in the newsroom he recounted what he'd heard at the briefing, careful not to confuse what Glassl had said with what he already knew. When

Hiedler advised him to look for local witnesses, he refrained from admitting that he already had the best one under wraps. Writing this story was going to be surreal.

Back on the street he decided there was no point in pestering Evchen's former neighbours. No one had actually witnessed the confrontation, so what could anyone tell him he didn't already know? That she'd always seemed such a nice young woman? That she and the young man had always kept themselves to themselves?

And not seeing Wedding for the next few hours didn't feel like a hardship. Reckoning there was nothing else he could do for Evchen, and that he already had Hiedler's permission to interview Harri Haum's clients, he decided to just get on with his job and revisit the poodle-owner's house on Uhland-strasse.

She was out again, this time with the dog at a grooming parlour, so he took the tram out to Grunewald, where two other clients lived close to each other. Johana Matschmann lived in a spacious villa not far from the forest, and was more than willing to talk about Haum. She took Russell through to a lounge at the rear, where large windows looked out across an English-style patchwork of trellises, rose beds and lawn.

She was about fifty, trim and healthy-looking, but her face had seen too much of the sun. "My husband was in the colonial service," she announced, which explained the wrinkles and the African relics spread around the room. Her hairstyle was too young for her, he thought, but there was something beguiling in the way she walked, as if she's taken lessons from the local lions.

"What do you want to know?" she asked when they'd sat down. "He hasn't come back, has he?"

"No, I'm afraid not."

"I didn't think so. I was so disappointed when he went away. He never even hinted he was going, and he's always been so good about that in the past—he knows that it upsets us. If you know someone's not going to be there you can make adjustments, can't you? Emotional adjustments, I mean."

Russell supposed you could. "How long have you been seeing him?" he asked.

"Oh, years. He's been so helpful, so perceptive. And so many of his predictions have come true. Not all of them, of course; he never claimed to be infallible. But everything he's ever said about my husband's investments has turned out to be true, which has saved us a fortune. And my sister's marriage—well, he saw the cracks before they did."

"I've often wondered," Russell interjected when she paused for breath, "does knowing what the future holds make unwelcome events easier to deal with? I think I might just get depressed."

"Well that would be silly. You have to make the most of forewarnings. You have to adjust."

"Emotionally?"

"In every way."

"I suppose so. When did you last see Herr Haum?"

"He always insists on my calling him Harri. But it was on February twenty-fourth—I know because it was the day before my birthday. And because he predicted the Fire."

"The Reichstag Fire?"

"Yes. He looked in the big crystal ball he sometimes uses, and he saw the flames. A big fire, he said, and then he recognised the building. He said it was the Reichstag."

And there was the why, Russell thought.

He thanked Frau Matschmann for her time, and made his way down a succession of affluent leafy streets to an even larger villa, albeit one with a smaller garden that hosted three separate garages. Elfriede Kahl was probably still in her twenties, small and slim with a blond bob and a face more pretty than beautiful. Her husband was apparently a famous motor racer, which might explain all the garages.

Russell had never heard of him, but Paul would probably have the cigarette card.

She'd been seeing Haum for less than a year, but had become "quite addicted." "It's not just that he sees into the future," she said; "he sees right into your soul." She'd been "so sad" when he went away, but had since found a new young astrologer, who was just as insightful but more—she didn't know quite how to put it—"more in tune with the new Germany."

"Less Jewish" would have been more pithy, Russell thought.

Frau Kahl's last meeting with Haum had been on the 25th, the day after Frau Matschmann's, and the imminent Fire had still been on the soothsayer's mind. She hadn't thought much of his prediction at the time, but had been "completely bowled over when the communists burnt the place down."

Few people were blessed with such gifts, she said, as she showed Russell out, "and I guess those of us who aren't have to make sure we listen to those who are."

Haum would have agreed, Russell thought as he walked away. So would Hitler.

In his stage shows Haum reportedly picked out members of the audience whom his staff had already researched, and so was able to make it appear as if he had read their minds. In this case he must have learned about the intended arson from his Nazi friends, and then been stupid enough to use that knowledge as proof of his future-telling skills. In doing so, he had signed his own death warrant. If he hadn't realised that people would put his prescience down to his Nazi connections, those connections most certainly would have.

"Dead to rights," Russell murmured to himself. In more ways than one, most likely. A pity the story would only see the light the day if someone set fire to Hitler and all his cronies. A tunnel packed with explosives under the Nuremberg Ehrenhalle might do the trick.

Walking back towards Kronprinzen Allee he wondered whether he should even tell Hiedler. This was the sort of story that could actually get you shot, but then his editor knew that as well as he did. And actually knowing that the bastards had set the Fire was the sort of thing you had to share with *someone*.

If he did tell Hiedler, he wouldn't do it yet. Since the story was unprintable there wasn't any hurry, and he needed to focus on Evchen's escape, where haste most certainly was an issue. As long as she was hiding in his flat, there was always the danger of the SA turning up, and if the men in brown conducted a thorough search they'd find more than his resident fugitive. It was high time he disposed of Fredo's journal and Mommsen's notebook.

In that it compromised several Nazi leaders, getting rid of the journal seemed the most pressing priority. Hiedler was at lunch when he got back to his desk, and no urgent messages demanding his attention, Russell went down to the archives and revisited every reference he had to the SD Obersturmbannführer in Mommsen's notebook. Heinz Treue had been born in Königsberg in 1901, the first and only son of Dietrich and Anna. He had two older sisters, and his father had been killed at Tannenberg in 1914. He had joined Hitler's Party in 1926, and the SS a year later; he had been a high-ranking member of Heydrich's SS intelligence service since its formation in 1931. Russell could find no definition of the man's actual role in this organisation, but supposed that such details were rarely divulged to the press. One surprising fact was that Treue had married his Jewess in 1928, a year after joining the racially pure SS. Which suggested—as did his hiring of Konrad Mommsen—that he hadn't been aware of his wife's ancestry, either at the time of their wedding, or when she gave birth to his twin sons eighteen months later. Jewish sons, given that blood was passed on through the female line.

After going through all he could find on Treue, Russell had not found a home address, but meeting the man on official ground was probably more appropriate. The news-room copy of the latest government listings confirmed the SD address that Wulle had given him, and also provided a telephone number. He noted the latter down, but decided against an immediate call. He didn't feel ready to talk to these people.

After taking a late lunch in the canteen, Russell headed over to the Alex, where Glassl would soon be holding court. He was hoping and praying that the detective had nothing new to report, unless of course it was Truppführer Dornacher breathing his last.

Reaching the police HQ, he found Glassl already in full flow. The Kriminalinspektor was, as usual, unshakably optimistic, but any actual progress in apprehending the newspapers' "Red She-Devil" was hard to detect. According-ing to Eglhofer the police had found several people who had overheard the confrontation, but those who admitted to knowing the missing woman had offered such radically different descriptions of her appearance that the police artist had been unable to produce a drawing. "Wedding's way of taking the piss," as Eglhofer put it.

On the minus side, Truppführer Franz Dornacher was said to be out of danger, albeit still dead to the world. Russell thought of asking Glassl if he'd sent his artist to wait at the bedside but didn't want to give him ideas.

Back at his desk he took great care with the story, making sure he didn't slip anything in that only Evchen or her victims could have known. It was a strange experience, spinning a tale from what he'd been told officially, when he knew for a fact that most of it was untrue. Maybe one day he and Evchen would get to laugh about it. Maybe they wouldn't. For all he knew the stormtroopers were dragging her out of his door at that very moment.

As he left the building the idea of catching a train to some-where far away briefly crossed his mind, but what would he do when he got there? The odds were on her still being safe, at least until the man in the Rudolf Virchow Hospital woke up and described his assailant.

And she deserved his support. He had liked and admired Evchen when they were comrades, and the last twenty-four hours had done nothing to change that. Like Ilse, she'd always been an adventurous spirit, but whereas his wife had needed to conquer her own natural caution to be so, Evchen had sim-ply given herself free rein. Which was something you could no longer do with a face like hers. Beautiful, yes. Aryan, no.

She would be hungry, Russell thought. After leaving the U-Bahn, he went to the grocer he usually used, and bought a selection of cold cuts and breads, along with some choco-late and fruit. Enough, he hoped, to see her through another twenty-four hours, but not so much that Frau Löffner would be suspicious.

Walking slowly down Gerichtstrasse towards his build-ing he couldn't see anything out of the ordinary. There were no men loitering on the sidewalks, their faces buried in newspapers, no nondescript cars suspiciously parked. A lorry full of brownshirts could be waiting round the corner, but why would they bother when a couple of men with pistols would do? Reaching his steps without trigger-ing any alarm, his relief made him take them in twos, and he was halfway past Frau Löffner's open door when she leaned out her head out asked how long his cousin would be staying.

"Ah," he said, his brain suddenly racing through all the possibilities. "You've met her," he conceded, playing for time.

"On the stairs," she replied, venturing out into the hall. "It was quite a surprise."

"I'm sorry. I meant to tell you this morning, but I was in such a rush I simply forgot. I'm sorry," he said again, floundering somewhat. Having no idea what Evchen had told her he didn't know what else he could safely say.

Frau Löffner didn't seem unduly concerned. "I just need to know how long she'll be staying," the *Portierfrau* repeated. "Herr Dickel will want to know."

"Of course," Russell agreed. Of course the bastard would. "I'm not sure of her plans," he said, "but a few days at most. I'll let you know in the morning," he added, inching towards the stairs.

Mercifully, she took the hint. "I would appreciate that," she said, stepping back across her own threshold.

Russell's sense of relief was more acute than long-lasting. He hadn't detected anything sinister in the exchange, but Frau Löffner was no fool. And then there was Dickel, who'd see any stranger as a chance to prove his vigilance.

As he closed the apartment door behind him, Evchen emerged from the bedroom. "You met Frau Löffner," he said.

"Yes. On the stairs. I was . . ."

"I just ran into her and I had no idea what you'd told her," he added almost accusingly.

"I'm sorry. But there was no way of letting you know. I just had to hope she'd miss you. Or you'd be quick on your feet. I take it you were."

"I think so," Russell said, realising he was being unfair. He let a long breath out. "So what did you tell her?"

"I was lucky. It was early this afternoon when I ran into her, and I'd spent most of the morning wondering how I would explain my presence if somebody saw me. And I'd decided we could be family. If one of two brothers in a German family emigrated to England in the middle of the last century then you could be his grandchild. And I could be a grandchild of the one who stayed, which would make us cousins. And your German ancestry would help explain your wanting to be here and how well you speak the language."

"You told Frau Löffner all that?"

"No. Just that we're cousins, and that our two sides of the family had no contact for almost fifty years, that we two only met when you came to Germany and looked up your long-lost relations in Hannover."

"Ingenious," Russell said. And not unbelievable. Using his fluency to bolster the story was a nice touch. "So what's your name?" he asked.

"Clara Janssen. It was the first that came into my head."

"And what are you doing in Berlin? When did you say you came?"

"I said I arrived on Tuesday evening. I wanted her to think I was already here when it happened, and I couldn't see how she could know any different."

"That was probably a good idea," Russell said. He doubted Frau Löffner had been out that evening, but surely she hadn't spent every last minute standing in her doorway.

"I was making that part up as I went along," Evchen admitted. "It's astonishing how many different ideas you can have and discard in a few seconds. When she asked why I'd come to Berlin the first thing that came to mind was that I'd come to study, but of course it's the wrong time of year to start doing that. Then I thought of coming here to be a photographer—that my English cousin had offered to help me look for a job with one of the Berlin newspapers. But that would mean going out, when I needed a reason to skulk at home. So I went with a broken heart—not such a hard part to play at the moment. I told her my fiancé had just broken off our engagement, that I had to get away from Dresden and my family, who were all suffocating me with their sympathy. That staying with a cousin who was out at work all day I could just mope and cry and feel sorry for myself. I laid it on with a spade, I think."

Russell was impressed. "I haven't known Frau Löffner long but she seems to have a good heart. That said, she's a stickler for the rules, and one of those is letting the *Blockleiter* know when a tenant has a guest staying over. So we're going to get a visit from him." He sighed. "And there's another problem. One of the brownshirts you thought you'd killed—you didn't. He's in hospital, still unconscious, but they do expect him to wake up at some point. Your neighbours, by the way, have been doing you proud, describing your appearance in a hundred different ways, so until the brownshirt comes round no one has any idea what you look like."

She took it all calmly. "Well, something inside me is glad I didn't kill him. Even if it means I'm more likely to be caught."

"We have to get you out," Russell said. "Out of Berlin at least, and preferably out of Germany."

"Yes, but how?"

"Do you know a comrade named Jonni Ohr?"

"He was in the Neukölln Party. I met him a few times, several years ago. Why?"

"Can you think of any reason he'd refuse to help you?"

"I doubt he'd even remember me."

"Well, I only met him a few days ago." Russell told her about his search for Lili Zollitsch, and how he'd found her in the Neukölln factory only hours before it was raided. "Ohr was in charge of getting a part of the Pass-Apparat's stocks out of the country, and purely by chance we probably saved each other's lives that night. If he feels as grateful as I do, and he can still lay his hands on some ready-made false papers, he might be willing to help."

"Would they need a photograph? They could use the one in my passport."

"Maybe." Being caught with Evchen's passport on his way across Berlin was not an appealing prospect. "I'll go and see Ohr tomorrow," he promised. "But even if he agrees to help, it'll probably take several days, and waiting has its own perils. If the brownshirt wakes up and everyone in Germany gets to know what you look like, the best false papers may not be enough."

"You want me to go now?"

"I'm just examining the options. If you did leave now you might get out of Berlin, but you'll need a passport to get out of their reach. Either way it's a gamble."

She gave him a long look. "I know it's selfish of me, but if it's all right with you, I'll wait until we know whether Ohr can help. I don't think your *Portierfrau* suspected anything, and I'll make sure I have my story well-rehearsed for your *Blockleiter*. Is he flirtable with?"

"God knows. If he flirts with anyone, it's probably himself."

The smile transformed her face, but only for a moment. "It's good to see you again," she said. "Even in circumstances like these."

Russell reached for his shopping. "You must be hungry."

"I should be, but I can't say I am. I remember hearing that fear destroys the appetite, and I have to admit I'm petrified."

"You hide it well."

"I can't let anything out. Not the fear, not the grief. Not till this is over."

After eating they sat and talked, mostly about people they'd known in the past, and the partners the two of them had chosen. After trying to explain what had happened to his marriage, he was surprised to hear that hers had also been in trouble. "I did love him," she said, tears in her eyes, "but he seemed so hell-bent on chipping away at who I was. Chip chip away, a little bit more each year. It feels cruel to say it now, but sometimes I felt it was only the Nazis who were keeping us together."

Which was doubtless no compensation, Russell thought, once they'd retired to their separate beds. Was he being a fool letting her stay? If he was, it was too late to change his mind.

If she was caught then only a careless torturer would prevent her from eventually giving him up. His future safety was now dependant on hers, and until she was out of the country every barking dog and revving motor would be arrowing chills down his spine.

Columbia-haus

Russell woke the next morning feeling more than a little conflicted, and lay there wondering what sort of world it was when trying to do the right thing also came gift-wrapped in a lingering sense of dread. That thought, and the fact that he was already late, got him up and dressed. Evchen had been sobbing her heart out in the middle of the night, so he decided to let her sleep. When he got back that evening he hoped he'd be a bearer of good news.

In addition to seeking out Jonni Ohr, he had decided to approach Heinz Treue without any further delay. The SD might prove grateful for his gift, and if so there was no point in waiting to bank the gratitude. The means of approach were more problematic. Should he just turn up at the SD office on Potsdamer Strasse, or should he call for an appointment? The latter seemed to offer the better chance of seeing the man himself.

All of which had to be put aside the moment he reached the office, where events were already awaiting his attention. A young man had hanged himself in a Kreuzberg cellar, but only after penning a confession to the Viktoria Park stranglings. This sounded straightforward enough, but grew less so as the day unfolded. First it was revealed that over the last few years the victim had been in and out of the Herzberge Asylum, then that his confession lacked any corroborative details. The police seemed torn between wanting to claim a much-needed success and the fear of looking like fools when the real killer struck again.

The other story, which had Russell and his colleagues trekking out to distant Ruhleben, concerned a robbery at a disabled veterans' charity. Like all his fellow citizens, Russell could remember days when a man lacking some limb or other could be seen on almost every corner, and burglarising one of the few institutions that helped these men felt, to both him and Hiedler, like a moral outrage. It was, moreover, a chance to publicise the issue, and that was how Russell eventually wrote it, ignoring the local authorities' usual attempt to blame the communists.

By the time he'd written both stories up, it was almost time to clock off, and he was sorely tempted to put off calling Herr Treue until Monday. As before, the conversation in prospect made him nervous, but he told himself he was overreacting—he was, after all, trying to do these people a favour.

He took a deep breath and dialled out the number.

With no prior experience of calling up intelligence organisations, Russell was curious as to the likely reception. There would, he suspected, be some sort of screening process before he could make his enquiry. But all the woman who answered wanted to know was his name, and rather than display his ignorance of whether or not Treue worked there, Russell simply asked to speak to the man. A few seconds later he was doing just that.

The Obersturmbannführer sounded unsurprised at receiving a call from a total stranger. "And how can I help you?" he asked politely after Russell had introduced himself.

Russell said that he was not calling as an employee of the *Morgenspiegel*, but as a friend of the new Germany. "In the course of my work, a private journal has come into my possession," he explained. "It contains information pertaining to a certain mass organisation. One which most people associate with the new Germany," he went on, assuming Treue would realise the organisation in question could only be the SA. "In this journal the degenerate activities of certain well-known figures are described in detail, and should these ever become public knowledge then the whole movement's reputation will, however unjustly, be seriously tarnished."

There was a pause while the Obersturmbannführer digested Russell's announcement. "And you wish to sell this information?" he eventually asked in an icy tone.

"No, no, you misunderstand me. I wish to pass it on to a responsible authority, and I regret to say that in the circumstances I cannot see either the police or the SA in that light. Someone suggested the *Sicherheitsdienst* as an appropriate recipient, and your name came up as someone to whom I could send it. But things get lost in the post, so I was hoping to make an appointment, hand you the journal in person, and explain how it came into my possession."

The pause was shorter this time. Expecting to be asked where he'd heard Treue's name, Russell had already invented a well-informed Nazi colleague, but in the event there was no need to bring him forth. The Obersturmbannführer asked if Monday at nine would be convenient, and simply hung up when assured that it would be. Russell was left staring at the telephone, marvelling at how one person's life-and-death issue could become another's diary entry. He could only hope the appointment would go off as smoothly.

One down, one to go, he thought, as he descended the stairs to the street. It was still light outside, and thinking it better to visit Ohr under cover of darkness, he decided on an early dinner before taking the U-Bahn out to Rathaus Neukölln. The paper he perused while waiting to be served was full of the next day's anti-Jewish action, and strikingly unconcerned by the drastic fall on the Borse that had

followed the boycott's announcement. Russell had always
believed that economics trumped everything else, but in
Hitler's Germany bullying the Jews was clearly more important.

Fed and wined, he took the U-Bahn south. Retracing his
morning walk from Ohr's apartment block in the opposite
direction proved easier than he expected, but once in sight
of the entrance he thought better of walking straight in.
Ohr was a wanted man, who for all Russell knew had already
been caught. If so, there'd be men waiting inside to arrest
any visiting comrades. Even if Ohr was still free, Russell
would be needlessly advertising himself to Ohr's *Portierfrau*
and neighbours.

He took up position in a shuttered doorway on the opposite side of the street, intent on watching the building for
any sign of the enemy. If anyone came to question him he
would say he was a reporter, waiting to meet an anonymous
caller who'd promised him information about the burglary
in Ruhleben.

After a while it began to rain, not heavily, but enough
to blur his view of the entrance, and when a man emerged
with his collar turned up and hat pulled down it was only
the watchful glances and long-striding walk that provided
recognition. Russell started off down his side of the street,
and was just about to cross when Ohr beat him to it. He
finally caught the other man up at a busy intersection, and
for want of something better asked if Ohr could tell him
the time.

"No," Ohr said automatically, in the time it took him to
register Russell's voice. "What . . ."

"Have you got time for a drink?" Russell asked, having
noticed the bars on both sides of the street.

"Not really."

"Please. Not for me, for a comrade."

That seemed to pique Ohr's curiosity. "A quick one

perhaps. At Gansser's," he added, nodding towards a bar on the opposite corner.

It was more than half-empty, but most of those present seemed to know Ohr, judging by the number of slight nods and raised eyebrows he received. The communist headed for the table farthest from the street, alongside a door that presumably offered another way out.

Russell bought them beers, and got down to business. "Did you read about the shooting of the brownshirts in Wedding?"

"Yes."

"The woman they're looking for . . ."

"Evchen Keller."

"Yes. She's hiding in my apartment."

Ohr smiled and shook his head in wonderment. "Well well."

"I knew her a long time ago. She just turned up at my door, and I couldn't turn her away."

Ohr gave him a quizzical look.

"I need your help to get her out."

Ohr wasn't slow on the uptake. "She needs papers."

"And a new passport. Can you help?"

"I don't know. I'll try. After . . . you know, things are disorganised. Those of us still at liberty have gone to ground. But I will try. I do remember her," he said. "And I'd hate to think of them getting their hands on her."

"I have her old passport with me if that's any help."

"Probably not. Most of the artists and forgers have already left by now, so one from stock is more likely. Hopefully we have one with similar details and a good enough picture, but I'll take the old one in case."

Passing Evchen's passport under the table, Russell felt relieved to be rid of it. "Thank you," he said. "If you can get hold of the papers she needs, I think it would be safer to post them to me at the *Morgenspiegel*. The address is Kochstrasse

42-53. If you can't, then just a note saying no, so we can try something else."

"It may take me a few days to find out. But if you haven't heard from me by the end of next week then assume I can't help."

That seemed an awful long time to Russell. "Did you hear what happened to Lili Zollitsch?" he asked, knowing he was being unfair.

"Her father got her out," Ohr replied tartly.

"A day too late. And Evchen doesn't have a daddy on the General Staff." Looking round the bar, Russell guessed that most of its patrons were or had been in the Party, and that now they were living like bears in hibernation, waiting for the Nazi winter to pass.

"Look, I can't promise anything. I'll do what I can, as fast as I can. And now I should go," Ohr added, standing up. "Good luck. To both of you."

"And you," Russell said, trusting that the man would try. He sat with his drink, creating an interval between their departures, thinking that now it was just the waiting. Something he'd never been good at, especially since the war.

The walk back to the U-Bahn was rainy but uneventful, the train warm enough to generate steam from all the wet clothes. Back at home, he found Evchen reading *Mein Kampf.* "You know the phrase 'if you didn't laugh, you'd cry'? Well whoever thought that up must have been reading this."

As she wolfed down the food he'd brought home he told her what Jonni Ohr had said.

"Did he sound optimistic?" she asked.

"Better than fifty-fifty," was Russell's reassuring guess.

After eating she went through his evening paper, starting with her own story on page two, and continuing with the Jewish boycott pieces, which spread across most of the others. "It's just so *ridiculous*," she concluded. "Who would have thought people would go along with this nonsense, when they know in their hearts it's wrong? But so many of them do."

It was a Saturday work-day, which Russell didn't mind at all. It got him out of the house, and gave him something else to think about other than who was coming up the stairs. The notion might not bear much scrutiny, but he always felt safer moving than standing still.

It was also the day of the Jewish boycott, and as his tram crossed a mostly empty Leipziger Strasse he could see small knots of brownshirts already in place outside the big Jewish stores. "*Erster April,*" he murmured to himself. April Fools Day.

There were no new crime stories awaiting his attention, and no fresh developments in any of those still running, so Kempka added him to the team that was covering the boycott. "Can you use a camera?" the deputy-editor asked him.

"More or less."

"Then sign one out and get over to the Ku'damm. But don't waste film taking pictures we can't print. The only ones they're allowing are of actions—and I quote—'within the limits of the legal boycott.'"

"So a brownshirt and his anti-Semitic placard are okay, as long as he doesn't use it as a weapon."

"Correct. Smashed windows are okay, because the boycott committee has already announced that the communists are planning to do just that."

"Why are we bothering?" Russell asked.

"Because that's what we're paid for. Some pictures of ordinary people defying the boycott would seem to be permissible, but only from the back. The Nazis have promised to film and photograph transgressors, and show the film in cinemas. We don't want to help them identify opponents."

"Let's hope there are some," Russell muttered.

There were, although on the Ku'damm at least, many of those willing to defy the boycott seemed to be foreigners out to make a point. But some were Germans, and for the moment at least the stormtroopers guarding the Jewish establishments were only putting words in their way.

There were lots of people on the wide boulevard, and it seemed to Russell that most were there to satisfy their curiosity rather than support either side. Walking along the southern sidewalk he overheard several good-natured arguments about the rights and wrongs of the boycott, and one man's cheerful comment that it was all too silly to take seriously seemed to sum up the general mood.

As Evchen had said, it was ridiculous, but Russell doubted the Jews saw it in that light. They were no longer welcome in Germany—that was the message of the bright yellow posters with the thick-lipped mouth and large hooked nose, of the placards braying "Germans awake: the Jews are our disaster." And this wasn't some crackpot group touting outlandish opinions, this was the State laying down the law, absurdity backed up by carbines, and all the more sinister for it.

Germans awake, Russell thought, the Nazis are your disaster. He stayed another couple of hours, walking slowly up and down the street's two miles, taking the occasional picture and trying to ignore the scripted hatred pumping out of the many loudspeakers.

By two he'd had more than enough. The boycott, on the Ku'damm at least, hadn't been the roaring success a Nazi would have yearned for, but the fact that it had taken place at all would be depressing enough for its targets. More Jews would decide to leave, Russell guessed, which one might think would make the Nazis happy, if they weren't also planning to confiscate Jewish passports. He was beginning to think that causing others distress was not so much a consequence of Nazi policy as the policy itself.

As far as Russell could see, the communists hadn't succeeded in smashing any windows.

Back at the office he handed in the camera, wrote out his impressions and eavesdroppings, and passed them on to the reporter in charge of pulling the story together. He was halfway to Wilmersdorf when a light rain started to fall, and by the time he got off the tram the mass of dark grey cloud stretched as far as the eye could see. He and his son would not be taking a ball to the park.

There were two stormtroopers stationed outside a Jewish doctor's at the end of Paul's street, but no sign of any patients demanding treatment. The same yellow sign was on display but, for reasons Russell found hard to fathom, what had been obnoxious on the Ku'damm seemed merely pathetic on an empty suburban avenue.

He walked on to Paul's house, wondering how he was going to explain the brownshirt sentries, but in the end he didn't have to. His son had his heart set on seeing a new Mickey Mouse at the cartoon cinema, and Ilse would only let Paul go out in the rain if Matthias went too and gave them a lift. Russell felt a pang of annoyance that his time with his son was being invaded, but knew he was being foolish, and half an hour later Paul was sat between his two fathers laughing his way through a series of American cartoons. *Building a Building*, which had Mickey creating mayhem on a construction site, was the last on the programme. Russell was particularly impressed by Minnie Mouse's hat, which boasted a single long-stemmed flower that swayed as she moved her head.

Pastries and hot chocolates followed at the cinema café, and Matthias seemed determined only to speak when spoken to. Russell suspected Ilse had told him to act like a chauffeur.

On the way home they did drive past the stormtroopers outside the doctor's, and Paul brought up the subject

himself. "They're there to stop people seeing the Jewish doctor," he explained, as if the two adults might not
know.

"Yes, but why?" Russell asked from the back seat.

"Because he's Jewish," Paul said, sounding surprised that
his father had to be told.

Once the boy had raced off to tell his mother about
Mickey, Russell had the chance to ask Matthias if he'd
heard from Zollitsch.

"Just to tell me Lili's still in hospital," Matthias told him.
"If she's told him what happened to her, he hasn't told me."

It was dark when Russell got back to Wedding, and he
approached the house with his now-habitual trepidation.
Herr Dickel might have been round, might have seen
through Evchen's story and realised who she really was. If
so, he had probably pretended not to—everyone in Berlin
knew the missing she-devil had a gun, and Herr Dickel was
not the sort to risk getting shot when a call to the local SA
would do.

Still, according to Frau Löffner, Sunday was his usual day
for annoying tenants, so they probably still had that treat in
store. Whenever he came he came. Russell and Evchen had
thought about going out for the day, but Dickel would only
come back on Monday if he didn't find them at home, and
there was always the chance they would run into someone
who knew her out on the street. Better to take their chances
with the *Blockleiter*.

Frau Löffner was at her usual post, giving no indication that anything bad had happened. "Five days of rain,"
was her greeting. "That's what they're saying. Welcome to
spring. Every bone I have is aching, and we're only in the
second day!"

Russell expressed his sympathies, and asked if Herr
Dickel had been round.

He hadn't. "Something to look forward to," she said with a wintry smile.

With the *Blockleiter* expected sometime that day, Russell and his fugitive guest spent Sunday morning and afternoon in a state of nervous anticipation. They had spent much of the previous evening discussing tactics, and had decided on an approach that would require some acting skill on Evchen's part. Her stories of theatrical success at school were encouraging, but also seemed somewhat beside the point when death rather than disappointment would be the cost of failure.

After Russell had gone over his only previous meeting with Dickel in exhaustive detail, he and Evchen had agreed that the *Blockleiter* would not appreciate a woman who was sexually provocative or had strong ideas of her own. Or indeed a woman who challenged him in any way whatsoever. Docility was the key, that and what Evchen dubbed a "subtle fawning." When it came to German politics, a naive enthusiasm for the new regime seemed to fit the bill, with a special mention for Hitler. The Nazi leader's penchant for making women swoon seemed utterly bizarre to them both, but was widely believed, and presumably fostered hope in the great man's followers that they would inherit some of his sexual magnetism.

This particular acolyte rapped on their door soon after five that evening, and Russell ushered him in with all the bonhomie he could muster. "This is my German cousin Clara Janssen," he said, "and this is Herr Dickel, our *Blockleiter*," he told Evchen.

She put the bookmarked *Mein Kampf* to one side and rose to offer her hand with a smile. When Dickel couldn't resist clicking his heels together, her eyes widened slightly, conjuring up a shy but starstruck provincial. The school drama teacher would have been proud of her, Russell thought.

"I hope I'm not disturbing you," Dickel said, "but my role obliges me to check all guests."

"Of course not," Evchen told him.

"So how long will you be staying?"

"I'm going back at the end of the week," she replied. Ohr had said not to expect any papers after that, so one way or another she'd be on her way.

"And where are you going back to?"

"Oh, Hannover. All my family live there. Do you know it?" she asked. Russell prayed he didn't.

"A lovely city," was all he said. "Now, I need to see your papers."

This was the moment they'd dreaded. Evchen gifted Dickel a rueful smile. "I'm awfully sorry, but I don't have them with me. You see, I came away quite suddenly, because I'd just had a terrible shock and . . ."

"Frau Löffner told me about your circumstances," Dickel interjected. "And of course I'm . . ."

"We could ask her parents to post the papers," Russell suggested. "They might not get here before my cousin leaves, but you could always send them back to Hannover."

"Or I could stay a few more days," Evchen said before Dickel could get a word in. "I'm so excited to be in Berlin. So much is happening. I so love the torchlight parades. They're so romantic."

Russell wondered if she was overdoing it, but one look at Dickel's face put his mind at ease—the *Block-leiter* was lapping it up. Any man acting like this would have instantly raised his suspicions, but an attractive woman . . .

"Are there any special events over the next few days?" Evchen was asking. "I would love to hear Herr Hitler speak. In person, I mean. His wireless broadcasts are so . . . so *inspirational.*"

Dickel was beaming. "I'm afraid I can't help you there.

Our government is new, and I'm sure all the leaders are working every hour God sends. There is so much to do."

"Of course, of course. And maybe he will come to Hannover."

"I'm sure he will. They say that addressing rallies is his favourite occupation. They bring him so close to the people." Dickel sighed, probably with pleasure. "But I've taken up too much of your reading time," he said, with a knowing glance at *Mein Kampf*. He had either forgotten the papers, or decided that causing Fraulein Janssen inconvenience was more than he could bear. "It has been a pleasure," he told her, clicking his heels once more before moving towards the door.

Russell was given a single curt nod. After closing the door behind Dickel, he leaned his back against it. Evchen was sunk back into the armchair, her eyes shut.

"You were brilliant," he said.

"Oh my God," was the heartfelt response.

Another day, another Nazi, Russell thought as he left the café on Potsdamer Strasse in which he'd spent the last hour. Determined not to be late for his appointment with Obersturmbannführer Treue, he had arrived at his destination far too early. Now, approaching the corner where the SS offices were situated, he wondered for the tenth time that morning whether inserting his head between the jaws of this particular lion was such a good idea.

The office décor was encouraging, all clean lines and light colours, enlivened by a vivid swastika carpet and spotlit portrait of Adolf Hitler. As he waited for the blond receptionist to get off her phone, Russell imagined the SA headquarters opposite: a brown rug pockmarked with black cigarette burns, a painting of Röhm splattered with beer. The Nazi class struggle.

He was eventually escorted up to Obersturmbannführer

Treue's fifth floor office by a young SS Rottenführer, who tapped on his superior's door and ushered Russell through it when the man inside called "enter."

It was quite a large room, and less deliberately spartan than the reception area downstairs. Through the window Russell could see the roof of the Elisabeth Hospital, where Lili Zollitsch was presumably still recovering. Rather to his surprise Obersturmbannführer Treue came out from behind his desk to shake hands, before gesturing Russell into the elegantly carved upright chair that faced it. He was as tall and blond as an SS man should be, but with a face that seemed soft and almost kindly to Russell. He was not in uniform, but the suit was decidedly crisp, the shoes shiny as mirrors.

The desk, neatly organised and sparsely populated, put Russell's own at the *Morgenspiegel* to shame. The woman and two infants he could just make out in the framed photograph were presumably the wife and twins.

He took Fredo's journal out of his inside coat pocket and laid it on the desk. Rather than reach out for it, Treue just gave him an enquiring look.

"It's the journal of a young male prostitute named Fredo Ratzel," Russell began his carefully rehearsed explanation. "As you would expect, a lot of what's in it would disgust most normal people, so it is not a read for the faint-hearted. But in my opinion most of it also rings true. It's no secret that this sort of degenerate behaviour became rampant among certain groups during the years of the Republic."

"Indeed."

"Fredo Ratzel was killed and mutilated a month ago in one of the upstairs rooms of a homosexual bar on Gormannstrasse, and I was one of the reporters who attended the scene and followed the investigation." Russell described how the police had quickly settled on Ratzel's roommate Timo Baur as the likely culprit, and had abandoned all other lines of enquiry. And that once they had failed to find Baur, they had simply given up on the case.

"But you did not."

"No. I thought the police had got it wrong."

"Why?"

Russell marshalled his thoughts, and decided against mentioning the high-ranking SA officer who'd been looking for Timo. "Because I got to know some of Ratzel's friends in the course of my investigation," he told Treue, "and none of them believed that Baur had killed him. There was no motive." He paused. "But I never found any evidence connecting anyone else to the murder either."

"There is nothing in the journal?"

"Nothing specific. What he does in his journal is describe a series of crimes, up to and including murder, which he claims were committed by SA clients of young prostitutes like himself. And while I realise it can't be assumed that Ratzel is telling the truth, the level of detail is very convincing and I can't see why he would fill a private journal with made-up stories featuring real people."

"There are names?"

"Many. Some of them very well known."

The look on Treue's face was hard for Russell to read, but one thing was clear—the SD officer was a very serious young man. He might pursue political goals that Russell found despicable, but he didn't seem cynical about the means. In earlier times he might have been a thoughtful priest.

"You haven't told me how the journal came into your possession," Treue said. It was his longest sentence by some distance.

"It came in the post," Russell lied. "There was no accompanying letter, but I assume it was sent by one of Ratzel's friends who knew I was still investigating his murder."

"When was this?"

"Ten days ago? When it arrived I just glanced through

the first and last few pages, which as you will see could only be of interest to Ratzel himself. It was only last Thursday that I idly looked through the rest, and found myself truly shocked."

"The SS and SA are on the same side," Treue reminded Russell matter-of-factly, as if that was something that needed stating before they could move on.

"Of course," Russell agreed. "But—how shall I put this? War on the streets is a dirty business, and defeating the Reds was not a task for a legion of angels. But the SS, as I understand it, is supposed to represent the best ideals of the new Germany: noble, incorruptible. And this," he added, tapping the journal with an index finger, "is corruption."

"I shall read it," Treue told him. His voice was flat as ever, but was there a hint of excitement in the Obersturmbannführer's eyes? "And thank you for bringing it to us," Treue added, getting to his feet. The audience was apparently at an end.

Should he go for it? Russell wondered. He decided he had nothing to lose. "If I could just have one more minute of your time."

Treue looked surprised, but sat back down.

"A few weeks ago," Russell began, "I was asked to attend an appointment at the Resident Foreign Nationals section of the Prussian Interior Ministry. With a man named Mechnig, who wanted to see me about my residence status. I want to stay in Germany for several reasons—I'm settled here, I have a good job, and I'm excited about the direction the country is taking. But the main reason is having a German son. My wife and I are separated, and while we may get back together, I wouldn't want to count on that, so Herr Mechnig may decide that I am no longer welcome here. And if he does, I was wondering if you could put in a word for me."

Treue looked neither overjoyed nor outraged at the suggestion. "A favour for a favour—is that your idea?"

"I would just like Herr Mechnig to know that I am a foreign visitor who takes his civic duties seriously."

"I understand," Treue said, which Russell supposed was better than saying no. As they both got up he stole another glance at the family photograph, and was interested to see that the wife fulfilled none of the usual Nazi criteria when it came to looking Jewish.

The meeting had gone better than expected, he thought, on his way down in the shiny elevator. The Obersturmbannführer hadn't said yes, but the idea of a *quid pro quo* had not been dismissed. It wasn't much but it was something. If nothing more, he had a name to drop.

And who knew what damage he might have wilfully caused to SS-SA relations? There was no doubting the Nazis had a split personality. The brownshirts were rude, hot-blooded and anarchic, the blackshirts polite, cold-blooded and calculating. They might be two sides of the same disgusting coin, but deep down they had to loathe each other. And anything Fredo could posthumously do to set them at each other's throats had to be worth a shot.

As for Obersturmbannführer Treue, well, the man's sangfroid had surprised him. Russell had looked in vain for any underlying anxiety. But if Treue was unconcerned about having a Jewish family, then why had he gone to Mommsen in the first place? Had the SS man somehow bought himself immunity? Or was panic welling up behind the impassive mask? Russell hoped he never had to find out.

He felt relieved to be rid of the journal. If Fredo was to get any justice, the SS looked his best bet, but if anyone was convicted and punished it would be away from the public spotlight. Which, if it ever happened, would have to be enough. Russell didn't see what more he could have done without putting himself at serious risk.

• • •

The story that awaited him at the office, and which ate up most of his day, was one to make any honest journalist throw up his hands and scream. Several days of rain had washed four fairly fresh corpses out of a shallow grave in woodland near suburban Köpenick, and the local authorities had proved somewhat remiss when it came to agreeing on their explanations. The police had put out a statement claiming the dead men were gypsies, probably killed while feuding with "others of their kind," while the local SA had definitely identified them as Polish migrants killed by communists fleeing to the Soviet Union. Unfortunately for both, one of the ambulance men charged with taking the bodies to the nearest morgue had not only misheard that instruction and brought them all the way in to the Alex, but had also recognised two of the dead men as prominent local communists, and had then been foolish enough to pass this on to an equally naïve local reporter. All of which had given rise to a hasty rewriting of history on the part of the newly united authorities, who were now claiming, with no supporting evidence whatsoever, that the victims had died in a vicious dispute between rival Reds.

What was a journalist to do with such rubbish? Anything but a proper job, Russell thought, as he left the latest briefing at the Alex. Every single person in the room behind him knew that the SA was responsible, but none would say so in print.

Outside the building he decided he needed a drink. Vaguely recalling a decent bar on Grunerstrasse, he found it just beyond the Stadtbahn bridge. The polished oak interior was dimly lit and sparsely populated, but contained a familiar face.

"May I join you?" he asked Kuzorra.

"If you buy me another beer," was the less than ecstatic response.

"An early evening?" Russell enquired as he put the stein down.

"The night shift," Kuzorra replied. "Is this a professional visit?"

"Just two ships passing," Russell replied. "I've just been force-fed the latest misinformation."

"The Köpenick murders?"

Russell nodded. "For now. They may be suicides by morning."

Kuzorra laughed and lifted his glass. "Thanks for the drink."

"You're welcome," Russell said, lifting his own. "Can we have an off-the-record talk?"

"I don't have anything to tell you."

"It's more a matter of me having something to tell you. About Harri Haum."

"Ah."

Russell recounted his conversation with the lady clients, and their both saying Haum had predicted the Reichstag Fire. "The man was a fool," Russell said. "He thought he could use his inside knowledge to boost his reputation, but all he did was make it clear that the Nazis started the fire. If he thought about it at all, he probably assumed that being their friend would protect him, but the opposite was true. Being their friend made him a credible witness, so they had to get rid of him."

A wry smile appeared on Kuzorra's well-worn face. "Sounds about right, but I'd be interested to know how you plan to get that story *on* the record? Will your paper dare to print it?

"I shouldn't think so. Is there anyone at the Alex I could take it to?"

"Not and hope to see it investigated. And I would warn against it. If they were willing to kill Haum to keep the matter quiet, then I don't suppose they'd baulk at killing you."

Russell looked at him. "So why are you still working there?"

"The same reason you're still working at the *Morgenspiegel*—because I need the money. The moment I find an alternative source I'm out."

Russell couldn't say he was surprised—Kuzorra had always seemed unusually principled for a Berlin policeman. "Are there many others who feel the way you do?" he asked.

"A few. The older ones will be looking to retire early, if they can afford it. Most of the younger men will tell themselves it can only get better. That they can do more good inside the force than outside. The usual shit. When it's in their own interests I find that people can convince themselves of almost anything."

"Maybe it's the almost keeps us human," Russell mused.

"Keeps us from being a completely lost cause, perhaps."

Russell had to laugh. "I shall miss you when you go."

"I suspect you will find yourself in much the same bind."

"I already am. But given my somewhat precarious situation, I suspect I'll be holding my nose for quite a while. As for Harri Haum, I think I'll save any martyrdom for someone more worthy. He doesn't feel like much of a loss in the grand scheme of things."

"Maybe not. But . . ."

"Yes. But."

Kuzorra drained his glass and looked at his watch. "I owe you one, but it's time I clocked in."

Their conversation was still running through Russell's head when he got back to his desk, and watching Hiedler across the room he wondered how closely his editor's thoughts would chime with Kuzorra's. The paper wouldn't be the same without him, but Russell couldn't see Hiedler staying for many more months. The bitter choices had been piling up, and there were more to come. The paper still employed Jews, still printed stories that questioned government policies, albeit in an increasingly obsequious tone. It wasn't yet a Nazi *Pravda*, but this government wouldn't rest until it was.

Two months after their ascension, Hitler and his cronies were still rampaging through the German house, knocking things flying, throwing people out of its windows, both metaphorically and actually. But surely at some point they would need to take a breather, do a bit of tidying up, come to terms with the undisputed fact that half the country had never cast a vote in their favour. They couldn't just carry on breaking things and people.

Or could they?

On the tram out to Wedding Russell stared out at the rain and wondered what sort of world Paul would grow up in. The papers were already full of Nazi plans to enrol the nation's children in organisations set up to vie with parents for control of their hearts and minds.

When he got home Evchen was reading a volume of Heine's verse that Ilse had given him years before, and after eating they both settled down with books. Like an old married couple, Russell thought at one point, albeit one being sought by a sizable chunk of the city's police.

Bodies in woods was this week's theme, according to Hiedler next morning. Another shallow grave had been discovered a short distance from the first in the Köpenick forest, and the prime suspect in the Viktoria Park murders had been released by the police for reasons as yet unknown. Briefings on both cases were scheduled for later that morning, and Russell was just getting ready to leave when two men who looked like policeman walked across the newsroom and spoke to Hiedler. The finger then pointed in his direction had his stomach in free-fall.

They were polite at least, and even seemed vaguely bored. "You must come with us," the older of the two said.

"Where to?" Russell asked with equal insouciance, as he reached for his coat and hat.

"The Alex."

"I was heading there anyway."

"Then you've got a free lift."

Russell accompanied them down to the street, where their car was blocking a sidewalk. It was raining too hard for the windscreen wiper, and the driver had to drive with his nose against the glass. "Nice day," Russell commented to no one in particular. It had been raining on and off since Friday, but never as heavily as this. A dramatic finale, perhaps. He hoped it wasn't his own.

"What's this about?" he asked his escorts, not really expecting an answer.

"No idea," the older one said cheerfully. "We're just the taxi service."

Crossing the Fischerbrücke, the Spree was hidden behind a dense curtain of rain. Russell told himself that the Alex was a much better destination than an SA detention centre.

Once there, he was led into a section of the enormous building with which he was unfamiliar. Though disoriented by the many twists and turns, he guessed they were somewhere close to the morgue, which he had visited a few weeks before. It felt chillier in this part of the building, but maybe that was just his imagination.

Or maybe not. After knocking at an unmarked door, his escorts ushered him into a much warmer room, where a man in a uniform Russell didn't recognise was seated behind a large metal table. He was probably in his forties, light-brown haired, weasel-faced and wearing rimless glasses.

"John Russell," his inquisitor enunciated carefully, as if determined to pronounce the name correctly.

"And who am I talking to?" Russell asked as meekly as he could.

"The Prussian Political Police. I am Kriminaldirektor Sasse."

One of Göring's men, Russell realised. Which wasn't a comforting thought.

The first few minutes of the "interview" were devoted to gathering Russell's personal details and history, a process that was becoming depressingly familiar. Ex-communist foreigners living alone weren't that popular with Nazis.

But what he had done was more likely to be the issue than what he was, and he waited for Sasse to get to the point.

He duly obliged. "I understand you have been investigating the disappearance of the Jewish charlatan Harri Haum," Sasse said, confirming Russell's suspicions.

"I think every crime reporter in Berlin was shocked by Haum's disappearance."

"They were. I have all the articles here," he added, lifting a folder cover to reveal a sheaf of cuttings. "And all but you eventually realised that there was nothing suspicious about the circumstances, that Haum had simply travelled abroad for a holiday."

"I have not written anything that suggests otherwise," Russell said defensively.

Sasse snorted his disbelief. "Come, Mister Russell. Your hints have hardly been subtle, and you haven't abandoned your investigation. Only last Thursday you interviewed one of his clients, Frau Elfriede Kahl."

So she was to thank for landing him here, Russell thought. "I thought there might be more to the story," he said. "So I kept asking questions. It's what a journalist does."

"It's also what trouble-makers do. Which are you?"

This was not going well. "The former, I hope," Russell said. He decided he might as well go for broke. "And in this case a good one, because I have discovered the truth about Haum's disappearance."

Sasse sat back in his chair, giving his victim all the space he needed to dig his own grave.

"He was abducted by the Reds," Russell said simply, wiping the incipient smirk off his inquisitor's face. "And no doubt killed," he added.

"And how have you reached that conclusion?" Sasse asked after a few moments' pause.

"It's obvious, really. Haum was predicting the Reichstag Fire days before it happened, so someone must have tipped him off. And since we know that the communists set the place alight, it must have been them who told him."

"But if that's true, why would they kill him? Assuming they have."

"To silence a witness. The Reds who fled abroad are mounting this big propaganda campaign, claiming that your people started the Fire, and they couldn't risk Haum telling the world that wasn't so."

Sasse took a while to ponder this. "Your explanation does have a ring of truth about it. Why have you not spelt it out in your paper?"

"I'm hoping to very soon," Russell prevaricated, desperately seeking a credible reason for why he hadn't yet done so. He stumbled across one. "The problem I have is that the police refused to see the truth when it was staring them in the face. I suspect it was individual incompetence, but I'm reluctant to make specific accusations without being sure of my ground. As I'm sure you understand," he continued, trying not to sound too obsequious, "a crime reporter has to stay on good terms with the police. And there's always the wider issue of the public needing to trust those in authority. If the powers-that-be were to tell us that publishing this story was not in the public interest I'm sure my editor would be happy to pull it."

"I can't imagine that would be the case," Sasse told him. "On the contrary, by exposing these villains you would be doing the country a service."

He would certainly be doing the Nazis a service, Russell thought. If the *Morgenspiegel* cleared the Nazis of involvement in the Fire, many doubters would be convinced. Getting Hiedler to print such rubbish might prove a mountainous task, but as of that moment he seemed to have talked his way out of a rather deep hole.

Or so he thought for a few blissful seconds.

"So I shall expect to see your story in the next few days," Sasse told him. "And if not, we shall have to renew this discussion. You do understand me?"

"I do." And Russell did. His ludicrous story was a fiction that served them both. He would be allowed to go home, and the Nazis would get their false account of the Reichstag Fire rubber-stamped by one of Berlin's most respected newspapers. Sasse had the win, but at least Russell hadn't lost.

On his way back to the street, he thought about what he could say to Hiedler. If he told his editor the truth, and made him choose between hanging a journalist out to dry and driving a horse and cart through the paper's integrity, he would be putting the man in an impossible position. So much as Russell disliked the idea, he would have to lie to Hiedler, he would have to insist he believed his own ridiculous story. But how would he explain the volte-face? After thinking about it for several moments, he came up with something that might be believed. What if the people who'd come to take him away that morning had noted his continuing interest in Haum's disappearance, and decided in the interests of the state to share some sensitive information that they held? Information that had surprised him, but that he'd been able to confirm from another source. One he couldn't reveal.

It might work. It also felt bad, but Russell suspected such bargains with the Nazi devil were going to be par for the course over the next few years. The communists had bigger things to worry about than an adverse headline in a liberal Berlin newspaper, and a shortage of Nazi crimes to condemn looked an unlikely prospect. A self-serving thought, Russell realised, but staying alive seemed like it should be his first priority.

Outside it was raining even harder, but he needed to get away from the Alex's cold embrace, if only for a few minutes. The dash to the square was rather like running through a waterfall, but the hot coffee and bratwurst roll he consumed under the dripping shelter of Herman's canteen more than made up for the drenching. While he waited for the rain to ease he thought about the files with his name on the front, which seemed to be proliferating at such an alarming rate. The police, the SA, the SD and Mechnig's department, whatever that was called. And now the Prussian political police. Germans being Germans, they would doubtless pull them all together into one great bulging file, probably with "Enemy of the People" heavily stamped on the cover.

Back at the Alex he ran into Eglhofer, who had just attended the latest Viktoria Park murder briefing. "One of the junior detectives stumbled across an alibi for the prime main suspect," the other man reported. "His superiors are furious. They thought they had everything sorted out, and now they're back to square one."

"Did they ever believe in the boy's confession?" Russell wondered.

"I don't think they cared one way or the other."

At the Köpenick briefing that followed, the new official version proved as unconvincing as the old one. It was now the contention that all seven victims had been communists, members of two separate groups heading eastward through the forest that had collided in the dark and stupidly opened fire. To bolster their story, the police had found a new witness, who remembered hearing many guns firing from roughly the right direction and around the right time. Some of the Reds had survived, and before heading on towards Russia must have taken the time to bury the bodies. Not out of any respect for the dead, Glassl added gratuitously, but to increase their chances of getting away.

Russell found himself remembering Marx's line about history repeating itself once as tragedy, the second time as farce. Anyone wanting to know what the third and fourth time would look like should keep their eye on the Berlin police.

The rest of the day passed slowly. His success with Kriminaldirektor Sasse, such as it was, had not completely erased the original shock of the summons, but unfocused fear was something he was learning to live with, and perhaps things might soon begin to look up. He had disposed of Fredo's journal, done all he could for Lili, and washed his hands of Harri Haum. All he had left to do was take a decision on Mommsen's notebook and get Evchen Keller on a train.

During his last hour at work, the latter ambition suffered two setbacks. The final post arrived with nothing from Ohr, and news came in from the Rudolf Virchow Hospital. Truppführer Dornacher had recovered consciousness, and was talking to the police. In the morning the papers would probably show a new artist's impression, but Russell decided not to tell Evchen until that happened. He felt frightened enough for both of them, and she would function better after a good night's sleep.

When Russell studied Evchen's picture in Kranzler's on Wednesday morning it was not as bad as he'd feared. It looked more like her than any of the previous drawings, but the artist had made her look so angry and serious that even a hint of cheeriness might prove disguise enough. Might, though, was the operative word. Even if Ohr came up with the goods that day, could they risk an attempted escape from the city with this image fresh in so many minds? Giving people twenty-four hours to forget would probably make more sense.

He ordered a second coffee from a passing waiter and thought about Evchen. Either she'd stopped crying at night or he was just sleeping through it. She was certainly putting on a brave face by day, but the excitement of outwitting Herr Dickel had long since faded, and the frustration of confinement was clearly beginning to tell. She was no longer in shock, but that seemed almost a mixed blessing, in that she now seemed more aware of how much she'd lost. Karsten would have been hard enough, but every picture she'd taken in the last ten years had fallen into Nazi hands, and had probably already been turned to ashes.

She had told him the previous evening that Hamburg was where she intended heading first, partly because she knew people there—"or used to at least"—and partly because it was close to both Denmark and Holland. England was her ultimate destination, that or the United States. "Whichever will let me in."

Russell went back to the newspapers, more out of duty than any desire. There had been a rash of Jewish suicides over the last few days, and the tone of their treatment in the various papers ranged from formal sadness to unforgivable glee. The recordings of the classical conductor Toscanini were no longer to be played on German National Radio because the US-based Italian had recently signed a letter deploring the persecution of Jews and Marxists by Hitler's government. Proving his point, the Mosse publishing house had announced the firing of 118 Jewish employees, only to be outbid by the huge AEG electrical concern, which had fired every one of theirs. And in Chemnitz, Dusseldorf and Bonn, another three communists had been shot "while attempting to escape."

Why were the Nazis so eager to build more camps and

prisons, Russell wondered, when taking people alive seemed beyond them?

Old-fashioned crimes were in shorter supply, as he found when he reached the office. No more bodies had been dug up in woods over the last sixteen hours, and run-of-the-mill burglaries were either dying out or considered too trivial to report, so Russell spent most of his day in the archives researching the *Ringvereine* gangs of the early 1920s for the "crimes of old Berlin" series and wondering how he was going to sell his fictional account of Harri Haum's disappearance to Hiedler. Sasse had wanted it published in the "next few days," so he still had some time to play with.

Several trips upstairs to check for mail were unavailing, which worried him less now that Evchen's picture was all over the morning papers, but still felt somewhat ominous.

He was halfway to the newsroom door, *en route* to see Paul, when the telephone on his desk called him back.

"It's in the post," the familiar voice told him. "Should be there first thing tomorrow."

"Thank you."

"Wish her luck."

"I will," Russell said, but the connection had already been cut. One more night and then she could leave. He felt a mixture of relief and trepidation. Now she could go, now she would be out in the open.

With the sun shining for what felt like the first time in weeks Russell expected his son to want to play football, and was somewhat relieved to be told that a trip to Siggi's was what was required. Though consuming the obligatory pastries put a temporary brake on conversation Paul was clearly in a talkative mood, and once every last crumb had been put away he barely paused for breath. His new friend Gerhard had just started a stamp collection; he already had a collection of footballing cigarette cards that rivalled Paul's, and both had benefitted from the swapping of doubles. Having seen Paul's train set Gerhard now wanted one of his own, and in craft class at school the two of them had built a papier-mâché tunnel.

There was also a new boy named Stepan, whose family had just moved to Berlin from Essen, and whose father worked at Tempelhof, and might be willing to show them around. Stepan was short, and some of the others had tried to bully him, but he and Gerhard had persuaded them not to. Other boys were frightened of Gerhard because he was not afraid of anything. And after school on Monday Gerhard's mother had taken them to Volk's Park and told them lots of stuff. "She knows the names of all the trees and all the birds. She grew up in the country," Paul added, as if that explained it. "She knows so much."

Russell had rarely enjoyed his son so much. The boy had always been curious, but what shone through on this particular day was what a nice boy he was, how kind and empathetic. If it hadn't felt like he was taking some of the credit, Russell would have said he was proud of the boy. As it was, he just liked him so much. And that was a wonderful thing.

Their time was over too quickly, and when they got back to the house a grim-faced Matthias was waiting. "I've some news of Lili," he said, before leading Russell into his study and firmly shutting the door.

"I had a drink with Willi Zollitsch," he said, once they were both sitting down. "At a bar near his house, because he didn't want to be away for too long." Matthias ran a hand through his hair. "He brought Lili home on Monday, and he says she's physically all right—no one who knew her before would know that anything had happened until they looked into her eyes.

"She may well be with-child, but apparently it's too soon to tell. There were a lot of them. She doesn't know how many."

There were no words, Russell thought. No wonder Evchen refused to give up her gun.

"There's more," Matthias said quietly. "The boy she was in love with. They made her watch while they tortured and mutilated him. First they poured acid into his penis, then they gouged his eyes out."

Russell closed his own. "Is he still alive?"

"Willi hasn't been able to find out for certain, but the fact that the SA are denying all knowledge of the boy suggests not."

Russell had seen men blinded in the war, seen their genitals blown away, but from a distance, or in the heat of hand-to-hand fighting. Wrongly, cruelly, but not deliberately. Not for sport or out of spite. Not for entertainment or enjoyment.

"I thought you should know," Matthias was saying.

"Yes," Russell said, "I should." Though what one could do with such knowledge was another matter.

The conversation with Paul seemed a long time ago.

Evchen's face mirrored Russell's blend of hope and fear on receiving the news that her papers were in the post. "I'll go in early tomorrow morning," he told her, "and just wait for them to arrive. When they do, I'll come straight back here. Then we'll go the way we agreed."

"You don't have to come with me," she said. "I know where I'm going."

It was a tempting offer, but not one that bore much scrutiny. "We already talked this through," he said. "They're looking for a single woman, not a happy couple."

"But . . ."

"And you getting safely away is in both of our interests."

She gave him a wan smile. "I know. But I will be taking the gun," she added, as if expecting an objection.

Before his talk with Matthias he might have raised one. Not anymore.

Russell was at work before his boss on Thursday morning, and eventually received a pair of raised eyebrows for his trouble. "I shall probably need a couple of hours off this morning," he told the editor.

"Fine, if there's nothing urgent," Hiedler said without looking up. His hair looked wilder than usual, as if straining to escape from his scalp.

"Whether or not," Russell said firmly.

Hiedler allowed himself a quizzical glance. "Fine," he repeated when Russell offered no further explanation.

Ohr's envelope arrived mid-morning. Examining the contents in a toilet cubicle, Russell found a passport and internal papers in the name of Ute Schellert. The photograph in the former was not the one of Evchen he had given to Ohr, but of a woman—perhaps the real Ute Schellert—who looked enough like her to pass any casual inspection. Which was better, Russell thought. The picture Evchen had given him had looked stern as the latest artist's impression.

He took the U-bahn home, told the lurking Frau Löffner that he was taking his cousin to the station, and headed on upstairs to find Evchen sitting beside her suitcase. She had her dark hair tightly wound in a bun, and was wearing a dark red coat over a deep blue dress that he hadn't seen before. "I've had to leave things behind," she told him apologetically.

"I'll get rid of them."

They had thought long and hard about the suitcase. Taking it would draw attention to her here in Berlin, but not having any luggage would have the same effect once she was travelling. With the balance of risks seeming more or less equal, the need for a change of clothing had tipped it in the suitcase's favour.

They had considered adding *Mein Kampf* to the wardrobe items, but decided that might be egging the pudding, even where the men in brown were concerned.

Russell had consulted the office railway timetables before heading home, and written down the times that the slow and semi-fast Hamburg trains called at Spandau. Just taking the tram down to Lehrter would have been much simpler, but police armed with her picture were bound to be watching at all the main termini, so they'd decided on taking local trains to Spandau, and picking up the main line train there.

It was eleven o'clock, and the next Hamburg train from Spandau was at ten past twelve. If they wanted to be sure of catching it, there was no time to waste.

"Are you ready?" Russell asked.

"As I'll ever be."

They headed downstairs, Russell carrying the suitcase, she with a shoulder bag that he guessed contained the gun.

"Heading back to Hannover then?" Frau Löffner said cheerfully as they reached the hall.

"And late for the train," Russell added, hoping to deter further conversation.

"It was lovely to meet you," Evchen told the *Portierfrau*, kissing her on both cheeks.

"And you too," Frau Löffner said, looking slightly taken aback.

Russell opened the door and led the way down the steps to the sidewalk. Evchen had just joined him when he noticed the figure walking towards them.

It was Dickel.

Evchen had seen him too. "I'm so pleased to see you," she gushed as he strode up. "I was afraid I'd be leaving without saying goodbye."

"Well, that would . . ."

"Wouldn't it? Next time I'm here I'm hoping you'll show me some of the city."

"I would be honoured, Fraulein Janssen. But when will that be?"

"In June or July, I hope. I've never seen Berlin in summer . . ."

Russell was beginning to wonder if they'd ever get away when Frau Löffner suddenly spoke from the top of the steps. "You'll be late for your train," she admonished them. "Herr Dickel," she added teasingly, "you must let the Fraulein go."

"Of course," he said, blushing. "I'm sorry."

"Until the summer," Evchen told him, with a wave of the hand.

Russell picked up the suitcase, glanced gratefully up at Frau Löffner, and received a knowing look in return that truly shocked him. She knew who Evchen was. Had probably known all along.

Dickel was smiling, waving goodbye to the woman his Party was scouring the city for. And Evchen was smiling back, looking, Russell thought with relief, nothing like her picture in the papers.

The walk to Wedding Station felt like a long identity parade, in which any passing stranger might suddenly shout "it's her!" But none of them did, and within a few minutes they were climbing the tunnel-like staircase up to the Ringbahn platform. There were few people waiting, which suggested they'd just missed a train, but one arrived only a few minutes later. Their carriage was mostly empty, and blissfully devoid of uniforms.

They got off again at Jungfernheide, and waited for the local train to Spandau. Here the platform was more populated, and the minutes seemed to pass with agonising slowness. Evchen somehow kept the smile on her face, every now and then gazing at Russell like a starstruck lover. He hoped that only he could see the terror lurking behind the over-bright eyes.

They'd been there for what seemed an age when Russell noticed two brownshirts on the other side of the tracks staring at Evchen. Just men eyeing an attractive woman, he hoped against hope, but when they exchanged words without shifting their gaze he could all too vividly imagine what they were saying: "I tell you, that's the woman on the posters!"

At this moment the local for Spandau pulled in, cutting off his view, and once inside the carriage Russell was relieved to see that the two men were still standing in the same spot, not rushing to sound an alarm.

During the ten minute ride to Spandau he could feel the beat of his heart gradually slow to its normal rate.

At the much larger Spandau Station a sizable crowd was waiting for the Hamburg service, and Evchen retreated to the relative calm of the waiting room while Russell went down to buy her ticket. He'd only been back on the platform five minutes when the train appeared in the distance and Evchen emerged with a man in an unfamiliar uniform. Russell's stomach was still in free-fall when he realised that the officer was actually smiling. After a few more words and an almost courtly salute of farewell her new companion strode off down the platform.

"Reichsbahn police," she tersely explained on rejoining Russell. "He was very keen to be helpful."

Russell handed over her ticket.

"'And thank you," she said as the locomotive steamed and clanked its way into the platform. "You've probably saved my life," she added, moistness in her eyes.

He pulled her into a parting embrace. "When you're safe, send me a postcard," he whispered in one ear. There was still fear in her eyes, but perhaps a little less than before.

The train squealed to a halt beside, and she was one of

the first aboard. When the train pulled out a few minutes later he saw her ensconced in a corridor seat, already talking to one of her fellow passengers. She had the air of a born survivor, but would still need all the luck she could get. Safety was a long way away. For both of them.

After watching her train recede into the distance, Russell took the tunnel to the opposite platform. The quickest way to the office was by Stadtbahn to the city centre, but leaving Evchen's belongings where they were for the rest of the day felt risky, so he went straight back to Wedding. When he arrived Frau Löffner was nowhere to be seen, which was probably for the best, because Russell was still coming to terms with the look she had given him.

Up in his rooms, he found that although Evchen hadn't left much behind, it was probably enough to have him shot. The clothes were neither here nor there, but the photographs and letters could belong to no one else. Destroying them seemed the logical step, but flushing everything down the toilet would probably block it, and burning things piece by piece might raise a smell that someone felt obliged to investigate. Better to get the stuff out of the flat, Russell decided, and then find somewhere to dump it. Or, he suddenly thought, stash it at a station left luggage. It would have hurt to leave such mementoes behind, and perhaps one day he'd be able to send them on.

He bundled everything into an old carpetbag and walked to the U-Bahn, keeping a nervous lookout for uniforms. Fifteen minutes later he was depositing the bag at the appropriate counter in the Friedrichstrasse Station booking hall. As the ticket he was handed would also link him to Evchen, he memorised the number and dropped it in a convenient bin, reasoning that if ever he wanted to reclaim the bag, he could simply say he'd lost it.

But that, he realised too late, wouldn't work. If he didn't have the ticket, one, they would ask him to describe what was in the bag, two, they would open it up to check his description, and three, they would find Evchen's now notorious name and face all over the contents. There was no way he could ever go back to collect it.

At least it was gone.

He walked the mile to the office, and stopped off at Hiedler's open door. "Sorry it took so long," he told the editor. "A friend needed seeing off."

"You didn't miss anything important. A bookshop's been torched in Neukölln, and I've sent Ernst down to take a picture. You'll have to get the details at the Alex."

"Do we know what sort of bookshop?"

"It used to be a Party shop, but the SA closed it down after the Fire, and someone else took it on."

"Sounds like retaliation."

"Uh-huh."

"So just this once the communists really are responsible."

"Even a broken clock's right twice a day," Hiedler noted wryly.

"Which reminds me," Russell said casually. "It looks like the comrades were also responsible for Harri Haum's abduction."

Hiedler's eyes widened. "You're joking."

"An employee I talked to was once in the Party, and he recognised one of the men who came to collect Haum as a former comrade."

"But why in God's name would the Reds want to kidnap him?"

"Haum was forecasting the Reichstag Fire a week before it happened, and my source was told by another member of staff that the tip-off had come from another communist, one who needed money quickly to get his family out of the country. And with the Party leaders in exile waging a huge propaganda campaign to blame the Fire on the Nazis, they didn't want Haum around to queer their pitch."

Hiedler shook his head, but more in surprise than denial. "Wonders never cease."

"Indeed," Russell said, feeling decidedly guilty about the deception, but glad that he'd come up with something at least halfway convincing.

His trip to the Alex proved unenlightening in more ways than one. There might be general agreement that a Red had torched the bookshop, but the police had no idea which one, and with all the comrades already fair game, little incentive to try and find out. Truppführer Dornacher was apparently on the road to recovery, and had given the fullest account yet of the shooting in Wedding. It seemed that the fugitive Evchen Keller had not only shot him and Scharführer Czichon in cold blood. In order to cover her tracks the Red she-devil had also finished off her wounded lover.

No more bodies had been found in the Köpenick woods, and no one as yet had suggested the involvement of men from outer space.

There was an hour or so left of the shift when Russell got back to his desk, and writing the updates took half that time. After deciding that writing up his inventive account of Haum's disappearance was something he would rather put off, he spent twenty minutes pulling together his notes on the *Ringvereine* gangs before calling it a day.

The thought of going home to his empty flat was much less appealing than a meal at the Green Dragon. That and a movie, preferably one set in some other world. As the tram carried him westward he wondered whether Frau Löffner would ever admit to knowing who Evchen was. He suspected not, that they'd just go on as if nothing had happened.

The food came up to his high expectations, and *Liebelei* at the Union-Palast was a movie he'd been meaning to see for a couple of weeks, if only because its well-known Jewish director had recently been forced to flee the country. Imperial Vienna wasn't as distant in time or space as Russell would have liked, but the tragic story was engaging enough and Magda Schneider was easy to look at.

That said, he felt less than contented as he walked back out to the street. When all was said and done, there was something depressing about going to the cinema alone, and over a couple of drinks at the Romanisches Café he decided that now he was more or less free of embroilments it was time to stop living like a refugee from his marriage. There were plenty of old friends he'd been neglecting, and a world full of people who might become new ones. Life went on, even under the Nazis.

Suitably encouraged he took the tram home to Wedding, and only noticed the car outside the baths when the two men leapt out of it. As he hurried towards his door neither shouted for him to stop, and for one blissful second he allowed himself to hope that their appearance was coincidental. But then the door ahead swung open and another two brownshirts came rushing out with grins on their faces and pistols prodding him back down the steps. Hands grabbed his arms and pinned him up against the nearest wall, where his pockets and waistband were searched, presumably for a gun. Satisfied he had none, they dragged him across the asphalt and bundled him into the back seat of their car, banging his head in the process. Two men got in on either side of him, the other two in front, and the waiting driver let out the clutch and pulled away down Gerichtstrasse. Not a word had been spoken, but the last thing Russell needed was an explanation. Frau Löffner or Evchen had given him up, and either way he was done for.

The car turned right towards Chausseestrasse, so they weren't on their way to Wipperman's factory. Which was something. One of the men in the front seat had the three leaves of an SA Sturmführer on his collar; the rest of Russell's assailants, as far as he could make out in the dark interior, were no more than ordinary privates. Which might mean anything, but probably meant nothing.

Reaching an almost deserted Chausseestrasse the driver headed south towards the city centre, across the wide and equally empty Invaliden, past the dark block of the Kaiser Wilhelm Veterinary College. Now on Friedrichstrasse, they drove over the Spree and under the railway, drawing curious stares from a few late night revellers. It occurred to Russell that they might be going to his office—to search his locker perhaps—but the car swept on past Kochstrasse and round Belle-Alliance-Platz before heading under the elevated tracks at Hallesches Tor and continuing on towards Tempelhof.

With a shiver of fear Russell suddenly remembered that the SA's most notorious detention centre was near the airfield, a place of horrors from which few had returned unbroken in body and mind. Columbia-Haus, it was called. An abandoned military police station, which the Nazis had given a new lease of life. Or death.

Sure enough, the driver turned left just before the airfield, and left again a few minutes later into a forecourt crowded with lorries and other cars. The large square building beyond had more lights still burning than any they'd passed on the ride from Wedding.

"Why have you brought me here?" Russell asked as they went inside, because not asking seemed like an admission of guilt. The Sturmführer ignored him, merely pausing at a desk to check the number of Russell's cell before sending him off in the right direction. The privates who formed his escort, and took away his coat, belt and shoes, clearly had orders to make him feel at home. After one had doubled him over with a punch in the gut, the other brought him crashing to the floor by pistol-whipping the nape of his neck.

And then they starting kicking. After the first boot had caught him in the crotch, he tried to roll himself into a ball, but the kicks kept coming until the rhythmic peaks and troughs of pain began to feel almost hypnotic, and he could feel his mind and body shutting down.

That, of course, was when they chose to stop. "Welcome to Columbia-Haus," one said, before slamming the cell door behind him.

Russell just lay there. The pain in his genitals was intense, but no worse than he'd known on a football pitch. Some tentative movement suggested nothing was broken, but his body ached in every conceivable place. And this, he knew, was just the warm-up. The serious stuff was yet to come.

Looking around for the first time, he could see that his cell had been built as one, with a heavy steel door and bars on the windows. The bare bed looked like standard prison issue; the light in the ceiling was behind a protective grille. Anyone contemplating suicide would find it a challenge, and in a place like this, who wouldn't be?

Getting his back up against a wall took several painful minutes, but once he had done so he suddenly realised that none of the kicks had landed on his face. Which given the number delivered must have been the intention. Could it possibly be that they weren't yet sure of his guilt? And that given his foreign status, they needed to be? If so, the reprieve was unlikely to last for long. If they were bringing Evchen back from Hamburg surely she'd be here soon. Or maybe they were waiting for morning. He hoped she wasn't suffering too much, and knew that she probably was. He batted away the shameful thought that her dying under torture might be his only chance.

The whole place was deathly quiet, and had been since his arrival. No shouts, no screams, he was thinking, just as the first cry of pain scythed through the silence. A woman but not Evchen, he thought, as if that scarcely human sound could be tied to an individual. Whoever she was, she was somewhere below. A basement, most likely.

It went on for about ten minutes, and when it ended the silence seemed thick with grief. Russell—and, he imagined, hundreds of others elsewhere in the building—sat there for what seemed like ages expecting the screams to return, before eventually daring to hope that the torturers' work was done for the night. Even men like that needed sleep.

There was no chance he was going to. For one thing he hurt too much, for another he couldn't stop thinking the worst. What had happened to Lili's boyfriend might have happened in this place—it wasn't that far from Neukölln. He shuddered at the thought, and at the prospect.

He'd been an idiot to take the risks he had. This was his third arrest in less than three weeks, and it looked like third time lucky as far as the Nazis were concerned. Wippermann, Sasse and whoever was waiting for him now. At the very very least, he was looking at instant deportation. An end to his life in Germany, an end to being a real parent, and he'd be returning to a country he'd not set foot in for almost six years, one in which he'd never felt wholly at home.

And that was the good outcome.

One that Evchen couldn't even hope for.

Well, none of them could say they hadn't seen it coming. They just hadn't thought it would come for them.

Look on the bright side, he told himself. Like everyone else who'd survived the trenches he'd always felt he was living on borrowed time, and nothing more noble than luck had given him fifteen years more than many of those he'd served with. Fifteen years he didn't think he'd wasted. Those years in the Party, the early ones so full of righteous purpose, the later ones full of equally principled doubts. Raising a child with Ilse, and such a fine child at that. He'd always scoffed when people said your whole life passed in front of your eyes, and here he was living the cliché.

The sky between the bars was beginning to brighten, and he tried to brace himself for whatever the morning had in store. With the daylight almost full the first aeroplane took off from the nearby airfield, reminding him of Paul. It was Saturday, and tomorrow he was supposed to be taking his son to his first football match.

Not long after that, he was fed and watered, along with all the other inmates. The bowl of slop masquerading as food made him glad he wasn't hungry, but the cup of rank-tasting water was more than welcome—Russell couldn't remember his mouth ever feeling as dry as it had that night. After taking a crap in the bucket provided he settled down to wait, half of him dreading the sound of footsteps, half of him wanting the wait to be over.

It was around mid-morning when they came for him, and just the sound of the key in the lock made him glad he'd emptied his bowels. As the two escorts marched him down corridors lined with cells he was struck by the lack of noise, as if every single captive was desperately intent on not attracting his captors' attention.

After the cells came a series of empty rooms, many with freshly washed floors, but all of them mercifully free of terrifying instruments. Those were in the basement, Russell guessed, remembering the screams in the night. A few seconds later the three of them walked past a well-lit flight of steps leading in that direction.

Which was certainly better than heading down them. Were they going to give him a chance to confess before applying the thumbscrews?

The room he was finally parked in boasted a desk, several chairs and not much else. It looked a lot like Wipperman's—there was probably an SA protocol on creating the perfect setting for interrogations. This one,

according to the swastika-embossed nameplate on the
desk, belonged to Standartenführer Alard Spilker, but he
was nowhere to be seen.

Russell was told to stand in front of the desk while his
escorts stood either side of the door.

The Standartenführer appeared about five minutes later. He was probably no more than thirty, young
enough to have missed the war. With his short dark hair
swept back and flattened with oil, his deep brown eyes,
aquiline noise and thinnish lips, Spilker looked like
someone on his way to a Hollywood audition. Even the
outfit impressed, every crease crisp, every shiny surface
like a mirror.

But, as his first look at Russell made obvious, the man
wasn't stupid. Which was probably a good thing. Clever
could go either way, but stupid was always a problem. Think
before you speak, Russell reminded himself. Saying the
wrong thing could cost him his life.

"So where is it?" Spilker asked. His voice had a faint rasp
to it, but there was nothing menacing in the tone.

"I'm sorry," Russell said, genuinely bewildered. "Where
is what?"

"The pervert's diary."

As far as he could remember, Russell had never told
Evchen about Fredo or his journal, so how . . .

And then he knew. He had got it all wrong. This had
nothing to do with Evchen. She was still free. It was Timo
and Jet the bastards had caught.

"We know the boy gave it to you," Spilker was saying in a
level voice. "So what have you done with it? You will tell us
eventually, so why not now?"

"I will," Russell said, his mind racing through possible
ways of doing so. If he said he'd destroyed the journal, there
was no way he could prove it, and the chances of Spilker
just taking his word seemed remote. "I have done nothing

wrong," he insisted, playing for time. "But you are correct. The boy gave it to me, told me it was Fredo Ratzel's journal, and ran off before I could ask him anything more. I'm afraid I just put it to one side." He paused, and gave Spilker an apologetic shrug. Telling the truth was all he had left, and there was no time to work out what perils that course might involve. "The police were confident they knew who Ratzel's killer was," he went on, "and confident of catching him. So the story was dead, and I didn't look at the journal until a week or so later. Once I did, and once I realised what it was, I handed it over to the authorities."

He might have just made the biggest mistake of his life, Russell thought, but if only for a moment he had utterly nonplussed the man in front of him.

"Which authorities?" Spilker asked. The tone was still casual, but anxiety showed in the eyes.

"The *Sicherheitsdienst*," Russell blithely informed him. "I only read the first quarter, and to tell you the truth I was afraid to read any more. If the whole thing wasn't a forgery, then it certainly didn't belong in the public domain, and . . ."

"When did you hand it over?" Spilker asked.

"Monday morning."

"And what made you choose the *Sicherheitsdienst*?" Spilker asked. The undertone of menace was faint but unmistakable.

Russell had anticipated the question, but his answer was still a work in progress. Since sending a journal jam-packed with SA crimes to their SD rivals was clearly a hostile act, his motive for doing so had to be something else. He had to be sending it to someone he knew and trusted. He would, he realised, have to claim a prior friendship with Treue, and pray that Treue went along with the fiction. It felt like leaping off a cliff, but what other choice did he have?

"I didn't even know I was sending it to them," he

admitted. "I met Heinz Treue at a social event, and I liked him. I knew he worked for some sort of Party intelligence outfit, and when it came to sending the pervert's journal to someone he seemed my best bet. Do you know him by any chance?"

Spilker's silence felt like a no, and Russell resisted the nervous need to keep on explaining himself. What, he wondered, was the Standartenführer thinking?

Spilker got up and left the room, and Russell, with his back to the men on the door, was able to breathe a surreptitious sigh of relief. If nothing else, he had given Spilker something to think about. But what was the Standartenführer doing now? Calling the SD, calling Treue himself? Spilker hadn't seen the journal, and could only have a vague idea of what was in it, so surely he'd check with his own superiors first.

When he returned ten minutes later he didn't look any happier. "Are there names?" he asked Russell bluntly. "Official names, I mean."

"Not in the part I read," Russell answered. "But as I told you, I only read the first quarter, and the people accused of crimes were sometimes described but never named."

"Described how?"

"The size of their . . . you know. Physical attributes."

Spilker stroked his chin and stared at his desktop.

Think it through, Russell silently urged him. You're talking to a foreigner who seems to have friends in high places. One who behaved responsibly by handing this journal over to the authorities, and who says he didn't read enough of the contents to learn anything truly damaging. If, indeed, there were any such things to learn. And even if there were, and the man is lying through his teeth, having memorised every last sordid detail, how could he ever put them in print without losing that right of residence he so badly wants to keep? So why not let him go?

Spilker smiled for the first time, giving Russell cause to fear that logic was no match for malevolence. But this time he'd misread the enemy. "I think this has all been a foolish misunderstanding," the Standartenführer said, as if they'd both been the victims of a prankster. "And I apologise for any overzealous behaviour on the part of my men."

"As you said, a misunderstanding," Russell graciously replied.

"Then you are free to go. Can my men give you a lift to the U-Bahn station?"

"Thank you, but no. Though I would like my coat and shoes."

Five minutes later Russell was walking as fast as his battered body allowed towards the Flughafen U-Bahn station. An almost giddy relief at being free was tempered by Jet and Timo's probable fate, and the knowledge that Evchen might still be caught. Not that he was out of the woods himself. He needed to telephone Treue and convince the man to back up his story. And he had to do something about Mommsen's notebook, before that also came back to bite him.

As the train rumbled northward through the tunnels he thought about what he would say to Treue, and how best to get the response he needed. The first part was easy: tell him the truth. The second was not: if Treue refused to back him up he was left with only one means of persuasion, one he didn't want to use.

Hiedler was out when he reached the newsroom, which saved him the minutes an explanation would take. Dialling the SD's number, he reached the same helpful woman as last time, and wondered again how she stayed so cheerful in such surroundings. As before, she only asked for his name before putting him through to the Obersturmbannführer.

"Herr Russell," Treue said with a distinct lack of enthusiasm.

"I'm sorry to interrupt you," Russell said diplomatically, "but there's something you should know." He described his arrest and incarceration, and how he'd been questioned about Fredo Ratzel's journal. "They demanded to know what I'd done with it, and of course I had to tell them."

"You said you brought it to us?"

"I said I brought it to you. And because I didn't want them to think that I was deliberately handing it over to a rival organisation, I said I had sent it to you because we already knew each other socially."

Treue said nothing for what seemed a long time. "How did they know you had it?" he eventually asked.

"I assume they caught the young male prostitutes who sent it to me."

"How much do the SA know about the contents?"

"Not much as far as I could tell. The man who questioned me—Standartenführer Spilker—he asked me if any names were mentioned. I told him not in the parts I'd read."

As the second pause grew longer, Russell found himself holding his breath. If Treue tried to cast him loose, he would have no choice but to threaten the man with Mommsen's findings. To save himself from the Nazis he would have to become one.

"How did we meet socially?" Treue asked, sparing him that fate, at least for the moment.

"Have you ever played tennis at the Blau-Weiss Club?" Russell asked.

"I have. So that's where we met." There was the slightest hint of amusement in the Obersturmbannführer's voice.

"It's been a pleasure dealing with you," Russell said, resisting the temptation to ask Treue what he'd made of Fredo's journal.

"Goodbye, Herr Russell."

Russell hung up his earpiece with another sigh of relief, and after writing Hiedler a brief explanatory note—"spent the night at Columbia-Haus and in need of a day off"—set off for home. Considering he hadn't slept for a highly stressful thirty-six hours, he felt remarkably alive. Which, as he learned from the paper he found on the train, was more than could be said for Harri Haum. "Fortune Teller Found Dead in Wood," was the headline, bearing out Hiedler's theme for the week. According to the accompanying text, the corpse was "riddled" with Russian bullets.

"The communists must have done it," Russell murmured to himself, drawing several strange looks from his fellow passengers.

The brownshirts were not noted for leaving rooms as they found them, and the second expression he saw on Frau Löffner's face confirmed his worst fears. The first had been one of surprise that she was seeing him at all. "A misunderstanding," he told her. "It was nothing to do with my cousin," he explained, and received a smile in return.

His rooms were a wreck. The armchair looked like it had suffered a bayonet charge, and most of his few possessions were scattered in pieces across the floor. In the bedroom his clothes were hanging in ribbons as if they'd been literally put to the sword, and someone had pissed on the bed. Above the fray, stood up like an icon on the living room mantelpiece, Herr Hitler stared sternly out from the cover of his dreadful book.

Spilker not having Mommsen's notebook had seemed a sure indication it hadn't been found, and here it was, still nestling under his floorboard. The SA's incompetence would be its undoing, Russell thought, as he painfully reached down to pick it up. Brute force untrammelled by conscience might be a sure way to power, but brains were needed to keep and wield it.

After opening the window, he took the notebook across to his washstand, and started shredding it into the basin. He wasn't sure whether or not he'd have threatened Treue and his secret Jewish family, but he hated the thought that he might have. Some things were wrong. Some lines had to be drawn and kept to.

He struck a match, held the bright flame to a corner, and watched the first page darken and curl.

Compensations

By Sunday Russell's badly bruised body was a Swedish-themed patchwork of yellow and blues, but he was moving more or less normally. The day was chilly but sunny, and the swastikas hanging above the Hertha stands that afternoon looked remarkably vivid against the clear blue sky. For Paul they were doubtless all part of the drama—he spent his first game pressed up against the pitch-side wall, wide-eyed and open-mouthed, silently willing his heroes on. And when they salvaged a tie in the final moments no one in the stadium could have looked more ecstatic.

For Russell, these few happy hours offered a welcome break from anxiety. Until he heard from Evchen there was no relief from the constant fear that some Nazi nemesis would rear up in front of his office desk or hammer away at his apartment door. The SA, the SD, Sasse's political police—it wouldn't really matter which one, because all had their torturers ready and waiting.

There was little comfort to be had at work, and none at all in the actual news. The Nazis, being experts on cruelty, placed a ban on performing bears, and the Quaker Oats firm issued a statement refuting any connection to the actual Quakers and their deplorable pacifist creed. A wooden statue of a woman gazing eastward at the "lost territories" was erected on the Polish frontier, complete with a list of towns awaiting "liberation." As a likely harbinger of things to come, two small gangs of Nazis crossed into Liechtenstein and Austria to murder exiled opponents of the regime. Such patriotic verve was applauded by Göring, who gave a speech complaining how cramped things were in the new Third Reich with so many people sharing so little space.

The postcard came on Saturday. The picture was of Copenhagen's famous mermaid, the text on the back short and sweet: "Arrived today, Cousin Clara." Russell was still walking on air when he took Paul back that evening, and Ilse asked to see him alone. As he'd suspected weeks before, she and Matthias were having a baby.

Russell was pleased for the two of them, and after telling her so, expected the other shoe to drop. It didn't. She and Matthias had talked it through, and decided that Paul needed his father more than their child-to-be needed its parents' names on a wedding certificate. "I hope we'll be married by the time this child grows up," Ilse said, "but if we're not we'll just have to explain the reasons."

He couldn't remember a better gift.

The spring that fully arrived in mid-April wasn't like any he'd known. The flowers in the parks were opening up, but it felt as if everything else was closing down. Within a month the socialists and the unions had followed the communists into oblivion, and any centrists or conservatives who stepped out of line were reminded that *Gleichschaltung*—social coordination—was now the name of the game. The art cinemas and *avant-garde* galleries were going or gone; so were the myriad clubs that had celebrated human diversity in all its weird and wonderful forms. The Berlin that some unknown wit had dubbed "Prussia by day and Babylon by night" was no more. As Eglhofer lamented, it was "nothing but fucking Prussia now."

• • •

Donna Mommsen went home with a sizable chunk of her husband's ill-gotten gains. She had plans, she told Russell, to open a hair salon somewhere on the Upper East Side.

Lili Zollitsch went to another place, hanging herself in her father's house when he finally thought it was safe to leave her. Russell went to the funeral and found himself doubting the colonel would ever get over it.

The city was another matter. As spring turned to summer it felt like it was slowly adjusting to all those losses incurred since the Fire: of people and places, of a way of life. The new normality was still replete with flags, uniforms and endless torchlit parades, but safer and more predictable. The SA's unofficial detention centres were mostly closed, and their lorries no longer roamed the streets like marauding sharks. Police were back in charge, in the form of the new *Geheimes Staatspolizei*, or Gestapo for short. This was Sasse's old bunch expanded nationwide; unlike the SA, it was there to enforce the nation's laws, albeit in their newly Nazified form.

The country was more or less at peace, and years of running around in circles had given way to movement in one coherent direction. The wrong one perhaps, but for those who longed to believe, there were some signs it might be the right one. The beggars were gone from the sidewalks; the economy seemed to be waking up. Some of the Jews who had left in March were actually coming back.

The new status quo was not so good for the press, implying, as it did, levels of censorship and self-censorship that any journalist worth his salt found irksome at best and immoral at worst. At the *Morgenspiegel* Hiedler took early retirement in August, passing the poison chalice on to Kempka. Russell stayed on, knowing his time was limited, but eager to get some marks in the bank before throwing himself at the dubious mercy of a freelancer's world. Over the summer he'd started frequenting the West End bar where Berlin's foreign correspondents liked to gather, and had met a couple who proved as useful as they were good company. The American Dick Slaney and the Brit Andy Hollis put him in touch with editors eager for pieces on Europe's travails, and soon he had more work than he could easily handle. In September he took on his first two English pupils, both of them daughters of Nazi diplomats.

That month he also moved out of Wedding. The district now felt like an empty husk of its previous self, full of people who were locked in some limbo they couldn't admit to, still in thrall to the barely visible slogans that clung to so many walls. Haldesches Tor, where he finally found affordable rooms, was closer to work and closer to Paul.

A new start, but not a slate wiped clean. He hadn't been prone to so many nightmares since the year right after the war, and on some days it was hard to forget the camps still springing up, or what had happened to Lili and so many others. The image of the woman in Pankow never seemed to lose its sharpness, or its power to bring forth shame.

What did a political person do when political hope was gone? You tried your best to keep your values alive, in your work, in your dealings, in how you explained the world to your son. You shared your despair and whatever new hope you could muster, with colleagues, friends and family. You nursed a resistance of the heart, one that might someday find expression on the streets.

And when your like-minded brother-in-law took you to see the house and garden in Grunewald that he and his wife had decided to buy, you shared his joy in a piece of the future that had nothing to do with Nazis, and might bring so much happiness.

• • •

One day in October, Kempka asked him to fill in for a sick colleague at a press reception. It was at the Adlon, and in honour of some visiting American actress he'd never heard of. The hotel was known for its sumptuous snacks, but once he'd had all he could eat Russell saw no further reason to linger. He was heading for the exit when he saw her again—the dark-haired young actress who'd returned his gaze out at Babelsberg. The serving wench costume was now a gorgeous crimson frock.

"We almost met once," was his opening line. "My name's John Russell."

Her smile was a heart-stopper. "I remember," she said, raising his hopes. "I'm Effi. Effi Koenen."

Other Titles in the Soho Crime Series

SEICHŌ MATSUMOTO
(Japan)
Inspector Imanishi Investigates

MAGDALEN NABB
(Italy)
Death of an Englishman
Death of a Dutchman
Death in Springtime
Death in Autumn
The Marshal and the Murderer
The Marshal and the Madwoman
The Marshal's Own Case
The Marshal Makes His Report
The Marshal at the Villa Torrini
Property of Blood
Some Bitter Taste
The Innocent
Vita Nuova
The Monster of Florence

FUMINORI NAKAMURA
(Japan)
The Thief
Evil and the Mask
Last Winter, We Parted
The Kingdom
The Boy in the Earth
Cult X
My Annihilation

STUART NEVILLE
(Northern Ireland)
The Ghosts of Belfast
Collusion
Stolen Souls
The Final Silence
Those We Left Behind
So Say the Fallen
The Traveller & Other Stories
House of Ashes

(Dublin)
Ratlines

KWEI QUARTEY
(Ghana)
Murder at Cape Three Points
Gold of Our Fathers
Death by His Grace

KWEI QUARTEY CONT.
The Missing American
Sleep Well, My Lady

QIU XIAOLONG
(China)
Death of a Red Heroine
A Loyal Character Dancer
When Red Is Black

MARCIE R. RENDON
(Minnesota's Red River Valley)
Murder on the Red River
Girl Gone Missing

JAMES SALLIS
(New Orleans)
The Long-Legged Fly
Moth
Black Hornet
Eye of the Cricket
Bluebottle
Ghost of a Flea

Sarah Jane

JOHN STRALEY
(Sitka, Alaska)
The Woman Who Married a Bear
The Curious Eat Themselves
The Music of What Happens
Death and the Language
   of Happiness
The Angels Will Not Care
Cold Water Burning
Baby's First Felony
So Far and Good

(Cold Storage, Alaska)
The Big Both Ways
Cold Storage, Alaska
What Is Time to a Pig?

AKIMITSU TAKAGI
(Japan)
The Tattoo Murder Case
Honeymoon to Nowhere
The Informer

CAMILLA TRINCHIERI
(Tuscany)
Murder in Chianti
The Bitter Taste of Murder

HELENE TURSTEN
(Sweden)
Detective Inspector Huss
The Torso
The Glass Devil
Night Rounds
The Golden Calf
The Fire Dance
The Beige Man
The Treacherous Net
Who Watcheth
Protected by the Shadows

Hunting Game
Winter Grave
Snowdrift

An Elderly Lady Is Up
   to No Good
An Elderly Lady Must Not
   Be Crossed

ILARIA TUTI
(Italy)
Flowers over the Inferno
The Sleeping Nymph

JANWILLEM VAN DE WETERING
(Holland)
Outsider in Amsterdam
Tumbleweed
The Corpse on the Dike
Death of a Hawker
The Japanese Corpse
The Blond Baboon
The Maine Massacre
The Mind-Murders
The Streetbird
The Rattle-Rat
Hard Rain
Just a Corpse at Twilight
Hollow-Eyed Angel
The Perfidious Parrot
The Sergeant's Cat:
   Collected Stories

JACQUELINE WINSPEAR
(1920s England)
Maisie Dobbs
Birds of a Feather